The
Jericho
Trumpet

OLIVE ETCHELLS

WARNER BOOKS

A Warner Book

First published in Great Britain
by Warner Books 1996
Reprinted 2000

Copyright © Olive Etchells 1995

The moral right of the author has been asserted.

A CIP catalogue record for this book
is available from the British Library.

ISBN 0 7515 1032 7

Typeset by Solidus (Bristol) Limited
Printed and bound in Great Britain by
Clays Ltd, St Ives plc

Warner Books
A Division of
Little, Brown and Company (UK)
Brettenham House
Lancaster Place
London WC2E 7EN

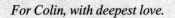

For Colin, with deepest love.

A good name is rather to be chosen than great riches, and loving favour rather than silver and gold.

Quotation inscribed inside the great dome of the Royal Exchange, Manchester

CHAPTER ONE

1876: Secret Friends

Rosanna Raike was hiding. Bales of straw and sacks of oats gave ideal cover for games of hide-and-seek in the stable loft.

She liked playing with Charles. He was ten, a year older than her; a large, gentle, slow-moving boy with the bright blue eyes and blond hair of the Schofield family. And she was sure he liked playing with her – he must do, because he'd told her that she was more like a boy than a girl – praise indeed. What was more, he sometimes used her given name when everybody else called her Rosie. 'Rosanna's a pretty name,' he said, 'and it's different. That's why it suits you – you're pretty *and* you're different.'

She was glad he thought her pretty but not sure why he found her different; he'd blushed when he said it, just as he'd done when he said she was like a boy, though perhaps that remark had been wishful thinking because there was no boy for him to play with at Meadowbank House. He sought her out whenever he came to visit, though for the last few weeks they'd had to play in secret because of his mother. She was a strange lady, a bit like a bird – a pretty, pecking little bird with claws and a sharp beak.

All Saltley knew that Esther Schofield had made High Lee Court into a grand mansion, living there with her husband and son as if they belonged to the aristocracy. One day she'd come down to Meadowbank House in her carriage and settled herself in the big sitting room; then she'd sent for Rosie's mother and made it very clear that Charles was on no account to play with a gardener's daughter.

Rosie had known as soon as she came in from school that her mother was upset, because her soft little mouth was in a straight line with the corners tucked in. When her mam did that you realised that she wasn't even nice looking; it was only when she was happy that she looked almost pretty.

'Mrs James Schofield has been here, Rosie,' she'd told her. 'She says you're not to play with Master Charles when he comes to see his grandfather an' his uncle. He's not allowed to mix with the labourin' classes.'

Puzzled, Rosie had stared up at her mother. 'But he doesn't mix with the labourin' classes, Mam, he plays with me. He chases me round the yard an' we play whip an' top an' have games of hide-and-seek in the stables.'

Her mother had given her a squeeze. 'He's a nice young lad,' she'd conceded, 'but his mother's made a rulin' that you're not to play with him, so that's that. She says he's been told, but if ever he should forget an' seek you out you're to tell him it's forbidden. Is that clear?'

Rosie pouted and narrowed her eyes. 'Me dad's not a labourer, so how can I be one of the labourin' classes?'

Pride and devotion had illuminated her mother's small face. 'Your father's no labourer,' she'd agreed. 'He's Mr Schofield's head gardener – that's his proper title – and he's groundsman at his Working Men's Institute. What's more he has folk queuein' up to buy his woodcarvin'. But you see, love, we're well set here at Meadowbank. We mustn't do anythin' to upset the applecart and risk losin' our lovely little house, now must we?'

Rosie had been silent, inwardly appalled. Lose the house? She'd seen the houses of some of the girls in her class at day school – those who went part-time and didn't have to pay. She'd nearly been sick once, when Becky

Cropper had taken her home to look at their new baby. The house was in a yard below the level of the street and inside it was all browny-black – walls, floors, ceilings, everything – with wooden boxes to sit on instead of chairs. Becky's mother had been lying on sacks filled with wood shavings, and the baby had been in an old shopping basket. It had been awful, horrible, but it had been the smell that had turned her stomach.

When she'd got home her mother had told her sharply that a smell like that came from bugs. She'd made her take off all her clothes and she'd shaken them outside and then put them in soak ready for the wash, declaring that she didn't want wick things brought in.

Rosie's brown eyes had swivelled thoughtfully from side to side, observing the bright little room with its view of the leafy stable yard. She didn't see how Charles's mother could make them lose their house, not when her dad was in the pay of Mr Joshua Schofield himself. Still, grown-ups could do bad things, spiteful things; the girls at school said so. Sighing, she bobbed her head in agreement that they mustn't upset the applecart. It wasn't so very hard agreeing to that because she was a bit frightened of Mrs Schofield. Charles didn't like her either, she could tell; he didn't like his own mother, but he never said so. He never even mentioned her if he could help it . . .

Now Rosie crouched in the dim silence of the loft, her restless body still. She'd been shocked but deeply admiring when Charles had followed her to the buttercup field one day and announced that they would still play together. 'It will be in secret, that's all,' he'd said calmly. 'I've thought it all out. I won't be able to chase you round the yard but we can meet in secret out here under the hedge and we'll have to be very quiet when we play hide-and-seek. You'll see – it'll be more exciting.'

It was. He might be big for his age but he wasn't clumsy; he could move in silence, with a kind of slow, painstaking grace, while for her part she was quick and light and sure-footed. They both tried never to raise their voices, but once she forgot and let out a squeal when she found him hiding under the manger in the end stall. Scared that her mother had heard and would know she'd been disobeyed, Rosie burst into tears and had to tell Charles why she was frightened.

He expanded his chest with a burst of bravado. 'I'll tell her I made you play with me,' he promised, but there was no need for that: her mother had been in the back kitchen and had heard nothing.

The floorboards of the loft creaked under her, and Rosie knew he was coming. She breathed so quietly she could hear the beat of her own heart and the hum of bees in the climbing rose outside the hoist. It was late afternoon and very warm, the empty yard slumbering through the peaceful hour before the mills shut down and workers clattered through the streets. Then a warm hand touched her shoulder. 'Boo!' laughed Charles in her ear.

She knelt up, eyes bright with admiration. 'Ooh, you're that good at bein' quiet!' she whispered. A sunbeam pierced the gloom and shone down on his hair; she could see specks of stable dust in the shaft of golden light above his head. Joy flooded through her, sudden and over-powering; it was a special moment, a shared moment, tinged with the magic of their silent game. 'I do *like* playin' with you, Charles,' she told him earnestly, 'oh, I *do*!'

He leaned towards her and all at once took hold of her hand. His hair still glittered in the sunlight, but his eyes seemed very dark. 'Rosanna,' he said hoarsely, 'will you marry me? When we're old enough, I mean.'

Her jaw fell open, so she closed it with a snap of her teeth and chewed her bottom lip, considering. 'Your mam won't let you,' she pointed out flatly.

'She won't be able to stop me when I'm twenty-one. I'll be earning my own living long before then and I'll buy us a house of our own. That's – that's if you want?'

'Oh, I want,' she assured him, then gave a wriggle and sat on the floor instead of kneeling. It occurred to her that it should be the man who knelt for a proposal of marriage, yet Charles was just sort of squatting, his smart knick-erbockers covered in straw.

'That's settled then,' he said in relief. 'Uh, kissing and stuff, that'll come later, will it?'

Rosie rather liked kissing, even when her dad's chin was all bristly. She looked at Charles's smooth young face and crushing her disappointment, spoke with authority. 'Yes, much later. We'll just be friends for now, shall we? Secret friends, though.'

'Oh, very secret.' He stood up, smiling. 'It's my turn to hide, so close your eyes.'

Obediently she put her fingers over her eyes and her thumbs in her ears, telling herself that by the time they got married they'd be too old to play hide and seek . . .

Her dad worked late in the summer months, even on Saturdays, so it was Sunday dinner time before they all three sat down together and she could be sure of her parents' full attention when she asked about getting married. She would deal with it in a roundabout way, of course; there must be no mention of Charles.

She liked Sunday meal times; they used an embroidered tablecloth instead of the everyday hemmed calico, and she always wore her best dress because of Sunday school. Her mother would be wearing her blue pinny with the frills and, in his good shirt and waistcoat, her dad looked more handsome than ever, especially when he was suntanned, like now.

She made herself wait until they'd finished their roast lamb and vegetables, then as her mother cut into a strawberry pie asked, 'Mam, Dad, how old will I have to be before you let me get married?'

Matthew Raike exchanged an amused glance with Martha, who shook her head in amazement. He swallowed a grin and said seriously, 'Well, it'd depend on who wanted to marry you. Have you met Mr Right already?'

Rosie willed her cheeks not to turn red. 'No,' she lied. 'I'm just wonderin', that's all.'

Martha eyed their daughter carefully. Chatterbox she might be, but she never 'just wondered'; there was always a reason for her questions, especially the more startling ones. 'It's the law of the land that you can't marry without your father's permission until you're of age,' she said weightily. 'That's when you're twenty-one – twelve years off – so there's no need to get worked up about it just yet.'

Rosie shot her mother a look from under her lashes and concentrated on her father. 'If somebody suitable asks me before I'm twenty-one, will you give your permission, Dad?'

Matthew reached across the table and touched her cheek. She was so like his sister Dorcas who had died as a child; they might have known how she would develop when they had her christened Rosanna Dorcas. Three names they'd chosen: Rose for the deep-red bloom he gave to Martha the first time he kissed her; Anna for Martha's mother, who had died within a week of their wedding; and Dorcas – pretty little dark-haired Dorcas, laughing and skipping and good at her lettering ... Yes, Rosie had eased the ache inside him, the nightmare ache for Dorcas that had dogged his teens and early twenties. She'd eased something else as well – the grief that he and Martha had known when their baby died; the bitter, bitter grief of losing Luke, their first-born son ...

'We'll have to see, my liddle maid,' he said gently. 'If some fine young fella with good prospects asks for your hand, we might let you leave us a year or so before your twenty-first. He'd have to be able to support you, mind.'

Rosie thought about that. Charles would be twenty-one before he could defy his mother, and by then she would be twenty. It was going to be all right.

Suspicion was tugging at Martha's mind, instinct telling her to issue a gentle warning. 'Look, love, as you grow up you must always remember that though you might be friends with somebody above your station, they'll always stick to their own class when it comes to gettin' wed. Don't ever get set on somebody above you.'

Matthew directed a steely glare at his wife but kept silent. They didn't argue in front of Rosie. In any case, what was there to argue about? An innocent question from a child? He knew what lay behind Martha's remark, of course – the ban on Rosie playing with young Charles. It was just like the lad's mother to shame Martha, who needed no telling that working class and moneyed class must never mix. Their children must never play together, not even in a household as liberal as Joshua Schofield's; certainly not when the mother of the moneyed class child was the vengeful little shrew who had married the eldest Schofield son ...

While Martha and Rosie cleared away and washed up, Matthew sat in his wicker chair by the open back door, looking out on his small garden. It backed onto the great curving meadow that lay behind the Schofield house, a view that normally satisfied him in the way a good meal satisfies a hungry man. Now, though, he was restless and on edge because of Rosie's question; or, more accurately, because of her mother's warning.

Life had taught him that it never paid to cross those who were better off than yourself, but oh, it had galled him to hear Martha preaching at their daughter about keeping to her class, especially when the one 'above' her was Joshua Schofield's grandson. It might be bigheaded of him, but Matthew often felt that there was a bond between him and the master of Jericho Mills; there was certainly respect – mutual respect, at that. Years back, when Martha had worked in the weaving shed at Jericho, Matthew had laughed at her because of the way she doted on her employer. Now he had to admit that his own feelings equalled hers, maybe even surpassed them. He shrugged. There might be a certain closeness between him and Mr Schofield but it would be criminal of him to give Rosie false ideas about who she might end up with. He stared out at the sunlit afternoon and chided himself. There was no call for bad humour because his wife had used her customary good sense and looked to the future ...

The washing up finished, Rosie was putting on her best bonnet ready for Sunday school when Matthew got to his feet and looked at Martha. 'Do 'ee fancy takin' a walk through Soar Park?' he asked.

She avoided his eye. At that moment there was nothing she fancied more than a stroll with her husband, both of them dressed in their best, seeing and being seen by half the population of Saltley in the town's splendid park. But she was acutely perceptive where Matthew was concerned – she could read the merest flicker of his eyelids or the set of his mouth as clearly as if they were words spelled out on a slate. At this moment he was restless in his mind, and when that was the case there were only two courses of action that brought him comfort: a spell with his wood-carving or a long, solitary walk in the hills that climbed and folded away into the distance beyond the meadow.

Placidly she said, 'I'm sorry, Matthew, but I think I could do with puttin' me feet up for an hour.' She pretended not to see the glint of relief in his eyes. 'Why don't you go off on your own for a good walk, or have an hour or two at your bench?'

'Well, if you're sure ...' It wasn't easy to sound disappointed, so he bowed to his daughter, who giggled in delight. 'I'll accompany Miss Rosie Raike to Sunday school,' he said, 'and then perhaps stroll up towards Holdwell.'

Savouring solitude, Matthew climbed the track that led to the hill side overlooking Saltley. His good boots trod the rough ground in comfort; his best suit, though, was too warm for the day, so he slung the jacket over his shoulder. That morning it had occurred to him that it was almost exactly twelve years since he had arrived in the town, so it was not by accident that he was now treading the very same path as on the evening of that first exciting day in Saltley. Twenty-two, he had been: a man of Devon come all the way to Lancashire because a one-legged old sailor had told him tales of his home town ...

Always ready to indulge in fancy, Matthew let himself imagine that his earlier, younger self walked by his side: lean, eager, adventurous; boots falling apart, a bundle holding all he possessed over his shoulder, a faded red kerchief round his neck and an old, wide-brimmed felt hat on his head. Ah, that hat ... powerful fond of it, he'd been.

Now Matthew touched his newly acquired bowler and smiled. That young fella had yearned for a proper home, for respectability. And now he had it; oh, indeed he had. He was verging on the prosperous, with a clean, loving little wife and a pretty, bright-eyed daughter ... His thoughts went back to Rosie, causing the adventurous young man to fade from his side unnoticed and return to the fringes of his memory.

Joshua Schofield walked through Jericho Mills, exchanging greetings with his managers and overlookers and nodding amiably at the respectful murmurs of his workforce. He kept to no set times for such inspections; he wanted no special shows put on for his benefit, no preparations for his visits. It took him half a day to do a good walk through, as he called it; twelve floors in all – six in West Side, six in East – then the weaving shed, the yards, the engine house and boilers, the coal tip where his waggons came straight from the pit...

Hair snow white, face deeply lined, his body taut because flesh was now spare on the broad frame, he deliberately slowed his stride, reluctant to finish what gave him such pleasure – the contemplation of his mills, his workers, his products. As always he observed the smallest detail and from time to time made notes in a little cloth-bound book that he kept in his coat pocket.

The need for the book irritated him, but it was a fact that in the last year things had sometimes slipped his mind. He could hardly credit it – his memory had always been one of his main assets in business. He told himself that he was sixty-nine, not some old dodderer in his eighties, but since he couldn't abide anything to be missed or neglected he wrote down whatever merited action or discussion with his son.

'I shouldn't worry about it if I were you', Sam had laughed when, somewhat shamefaced, he had first produced the book. 'You still see more on a walk through than all your overlookers put together *and* take action on ninety-five per cent of what you query.'

Joshua was far from reassured by that. Ninety-five per cent was no good to him. He'd always aimed for a hundred per cent efficiency and had encouraged Sam and James to do the same. He kept back a scornful retort because he was always careful of Sam's feelings; he was like his right arm, was Sam, pure gold, but under that confident front he was sensitive – aye, and maybe easily hurt. Seeing the rueful grin on his face, Joshua knew that his son had read his thoughts about the ninety-five per cent. It was a strange, unspoken bond between them, the linking of their minds, but it was Sam who had the real gift for it – a gift he shared with his sister, Sarah . . .

On impulse Joshua turned and reclimbed the last flight of stairs, then went up through the trap door to the roof of Jericho's tower. Above him the company flag flapped against the post, its emblem of the trumpet and the rose visible one moment and obscured the next. It was almost peaceful up there with the hills rising silently behind the great mills, but as always Joshua looked to the town, his hands flat on the parapet. He could hear the clop of hooves from a grocer's cart climbing the road that led past Jericho, the shouts of a ganger as his men unloaded raw cotton down in the yard, the clatter of the hoist, the rumble of the colliery waggons behind the boiler house. And under his feet he could feel a steady thrumming – the endless vibration of machinery that was the heartbeat of Jericho.

He felt an easing of tension inside him, putting him in mind of engine oil on hot, dry metal. He sighed. Folk might think him a bit soft if they knew, but he always felt close to Rachel up here on the tower. She'd been gone eleven years, and God only knew he missed her every hour of his life, but he'd managed – aye, he'd managed to live without her. Up here under the flag he felt her very near. In the terrible weeks after she'd gone he'd sometimes found himself talking to her out loud, not just in private but in the street or on the train. Now, though, he could just let everything flow to her unspoken.

Maybe he felt her presence because from such a vantage point he could view what he'd achieved over the years with her, and that gave him strength: the mills beneath him, the pit over there in the distance, Meadowbank House, the Working Men's Institute with its velvety bowling green and gardens, the glass roof of the swimming baths for his cotton operatives and his colliers. Rachel had always listened to his schemes, always encouraged him . . .

Then, blue eyes glinting, he smiled. Sam was down there in the yard examining the consignment of cotton, and – yes – there was young Charlie running along the road towards the mill gates. Since he'd been coming into Saltley for his schooling his grandson liked to meet him and Sam and walk home with them before being taken back to High Lee. Joshua stared down, intrigued. The lad was touching the embossed trumpet on the gates, running his hand over the brass in the way some folk stroked a horse or a dog that they loved . . . Then he glanced up to the flag and saw his grandfather outlined against the sky. He smiled – even at this distance Joshua could see the glint of his teeth, and at the sight he laughed aloud, taking off his hat and waving it before heading back to the stairs.

Laughter gave way to serious thought as he made for the ground floor. He had always imagined that grandchildren would bring undiluted joy – all the pleasure of children with none of the responsibility. But that wasn't the case with Charlie; he loved his only grandchild, but the joy was well diluted. He needed protecting, guarding against being damaged by his mother; Joshua had to give him the backing he should get from a strong father, because James wasn't strong at all – he wasn't a fighter. His eldest son was good, truly good, but in common with many a man he liked peace on his own hearth. And in order to keep that peace he gave way to Esther in the ordering of their lives and the upbringing of their child.

The three of them walked home with Charles in the middle. In fine weather Joshua always walked the half mile between home and mill, using the carriage or horseback for longer journeys. He was well aware that the other mill-owning families thought him mad to walk the same pavements as his operatives, but that didn't worry him. If Eli Walton and Ezra Boulton and the rest of 'em chose to race around in their carriages with footmen bowing and scraping then let 'em get on with it. He himself had never found that walking diminished his authority with the workers. And in any case, he liked it.

Charles was trying to match his stride to theirs, taking several overlong steps and then a scuttle of short ones. Over his head the men exchanged amused glances, and unobtrusively shortened their stride.

'How are you getting on at Mr Wild's place, Charlie?' asked Joshua. 'Do you do much figuring, or is it all Latin and Greek and such?'

'We do everything,' Charles informed him dolefully. 'They keep on telling us it's an all-embracing education for the sons of gentlemen. Arithmetic, English, history, geography, French, Latin – oh, lots of stuff. They don't teach technical engineering, though, and there's no music except in assembly.'

Joshua refrained from pointing out that at his grandson's age he himself had had three years' technical experience behind him from working in the mill. 'You can afford to wait another year or two before you study engineering,' he comforted, 'and as for music, you get that at home, don't you?'

'Pianoforte, yes; it's easy, and it – it pleases Mama. But when I'm older I might change to some other instrument.'

Joshua thought of him at the mill gates only minutes earlier. 'Any instrument in particular?' he asked with interest.

Charles looked up with his wide, eager smile but didn't
reveal a preference. 'I haven't decided yet, Grandfather. It
might – it might have to be something pretty quiet.'

Sam gave his father a look. They both knew why that
should be. 'You could practice in my room at home,' he
offered. 'We could all plug our ears, couldn't we, Father?'

In shared good humour they reached Meadowbank, but
Joshua had noticed the intent tightening of his grandson's
mouth; he didn't know whether to be pleased or sorry at
what it might herald for the boy's future. A flair for
engineering in the mill or the pit would be grand; an
interest in the business side of cotton, such as went on at
his Manchester rooms, even better. Maybe a fondness for
estate management and country life, like his father ... but
what would they do with a musician in the family? He
watched the boy leap ahead of them up the front steps and
knew that he would back him in almost anything. He
smiled somewhat grimly at his mental reservations.
'Almost' anything. As he moved into old age it sometimes
seemed that nothing was certain, nothing was absolute.
Life was a sequence of 'all being well' or 'when cotton
picks up a bit' or 'if the markets are stable'. The days were
gone when he sailed through life with never a doubt or
misgiving.

It was his habit on reaching home to turn for a last look
at Saltley before going indoors. The town was getting more
and more grimy, but it did him good to see the forest of mill
chimneys, especially the tallest of them all – that of Jericho
Mills. Jericho – his own model community, the fruit of a
lifetime's work. He couldn't help but be proud of it.

He turned to go indoors and saw a small figure standing
by the hedge that separated the front garden from the stable
yard. It was Matthew's girl, young Rosie. She dipped her
knee respectfully, and when he smiled and waved his stick
she blew him a kiss, clapping a startled hand to her mouth
when she realised what she'd done. Pink cheeked, she ran
off with her skirts bouncing and the ribbons fluttering in
her dark hair.

She was a lively one, he told himself. Maybe one day he would have a granddaughter, and happen she'd be as lively as young Rosie, though of course she wouldn't be dark haired. It stood to reason that a Schofield would be blonde, like the rest of the family . . .

Ridings' pawnshop was neat and well scrubbed, its windows shining in the glow of a setting sun and its three gold balls swinging gently in the breeze. Albert Lomas was about to lock up for the night when he saw that the flagstones outside needed sweeping. He sighed. It had been a long day so he'd tell the lad to do it first thing in the morning . . . No – he'd better get the brush and do it now; Miss Ridings was fussy about such things.

Too fussy, some said, to run a business that dealt with impoverished folk and their paltry belongings. Fussy or not, she'd told him that they had the highest turnover of any mill-town pawnshop in Lancashire, and it was Albert's belief that they took in more trade than some of those in Manchester. As he finished his sweeping a cab drew up at the kerb, so he hurried indoors to call up the stairs. 'Mr Jellicoe! Your cab's here!'

Barney Jellicoe came down, dressed in his good business clothes, his hat brushed to a sheen and set square on his pelt of curly grey hair. The top of the tall hat just reached Albert's upper arm, but the younger man had long since ceased to notice that the pawnshop manager was a dwarf. 'Is it all right if I get off as soon as I've locked up, Mr Jellicoe?'

The dwarf looked round to check that everything was in order, then picked up the leather case that held the pawnshop books. 'Aye, get off home, Albert. I've got me keys.' He swung himself up into the cab with the odd sideways lurch that helped lift his short legs, then directed the driver to Farthing Lane, an area of the town that belied its name: there was money there of far higher denomination than farthings. At the bottom of the lane were high-class shops – jewellers, shoemakers, tailors; but higher up were four-bedroomed detached houses with gardens and views of open fields. It was said in the town that those who lived on Farthing Lane were either comfortably off or going up in the world. Tizzie Ridings was both.

Three years earlier she had caused a sensation when she'd bought a house at the age of twenty-eight. She'd been running her own business since she was twenty and had lived all her life over the pawnshop, they said; now she was buying a house, and on Farthing Lane at that! Respect battled with amazed envy whenever her name was mentioned. It was accepted that she stayed unmarried by choice, because many a young man of business had tried his hand with her and been given short shrift ...

Now Tizzie waited for the visit of her second in command. She allowed nothing to interfere with the weekly meeting when she and Barney went through the books, analysed the week's profits and discussed new ventures – ventures that would have led to more amazement if the rest of Saltley had known about them.

Like her father before her she possessed business acumen to a marked degree, but whereas he had hidden prosperity behind a dingy shop, Tizzie shouted it out loud, the only pawnbroker in southeast Lancashire to do so. Her clean, bright shop had brought changes. Where once the needy had sidled through a network of ginnels and entries to pawn their goods, they now carried their bundles openly through the streets, if not relishing the task, at least performing it without shame.

Wearing a dark-green poplin dress that emphasised her pale, unfreckled skin and with her springy red hair anchored on top of her head with combs, she was already at her desk when her housekeeper brought in Barney. Over the years she had taught herself to remain seated when dealing with him. She didn't know whether it pleased him, but she felt easier facing him eye to eye, rather than looking down on him.

'Come in, Barney.'

'Good evening, Miss Tizzie.' As always, he was polite

without being subservient. She saw his dark eyes taking in her new hairstyle, but he made no comment. They would both have considered a personal remark to be overfamiliar. She saw a faint smile touch his mouth, though, and recognised approval. Unexpectedly her spirits plummeted. Was she so bereft of friends that she must hanker for Barney's unspoken praise? If that was indeed the case it was her own fault – she scorned the friendship of those she couldn't respect.

Tizzie had no lack of respect for Barney Jellicoe, however. Sometimes it unnerved her, the regard she had for him – a stunted, flat-faced dwarf – but she knew she could trust him with her life. He was her equal in intelligence, no doubt about it, but more important, he had regard for her feelings. He cared about her, not as a man cares for a woman, nor yet as a faithful employee cares for his employer, but as a friend – a friend who watched over her welfare. Nobody knew of the closeness between them; it was, in a way, their secret, but he had shown his concern for her in a hundred little ways over the years, and she hoped that in some small measure she had repaid him.

When she had bought her house he had moved in over the pawnshop rent-free, turning the rooms that had been her family home into a bachelor apartment, with a daily woman to look after him. Invitations to go there were rare, for Barney was a man of contradictions: he had low self-esteem and a reluctance to put himself forward alongside a dogged independence and a horror of evoking pity – almost a perverse kind of pride.

He stood at Tizzie's side as they discussed the week's business, his dark, unreadable eyes meeting her bright emerald gaze whenever she turned to him with a question.

'I see the dolly shop has been busy again,' she said keenly, referring to the pawnshop basement where the very poor took their pots and pans and bundles. 'Is it because of the state of cotton?'

'Aye, there's laying off at some of the mills. They're saying the markets are down again.'

Tizzie nodded. All Saltley knew the basic facts of the cotton trade. 'You can't blame India for getting their own back,' she said thoughtfully. 'Didn't we encourage them to increase production when we couldn't get cotton from America?'

'Aye, and dropped them flat without so much as a thank you when it started to come across the Atlantic again. That's why they started manufacturing on their own account. They say the Bombay mills are working round the clock, supplying markets that have always been ours.'

'Sometimes I think English cotton masters are a bit stupid,' declared Tizzie. 'Look at the way they over-produced after the cotton famine just so they could use all their expensive machinery. They flooded the markets, didn't they?'

'Aye, and lived to regret it. By the way, Braithwaite's mill is closing and the family fighting bankruptcy. They brought jewellery in today and asked if we'd make a firm offer for it if they can't manage to redeem.'

'What did you say?'

'It's good stuff, Miss Tizzie, I've brought it to show you. I said we'd make a fair offer if and when the need arises.'

Tizzie nodded. Jewellery was one of her interests, gemstones in particular. After her father's death she had paid good money for a course of instruction with the best working jeweller in Manchester; then she'd done the same for Barney, so that between them they could evaluate whatever came over the counter. Now she did business with other pawnshops and second-hand jewellers, buying and selling and acting as go-between. There had been prejudice against her at first because of her age and sex, but it had diminished over the years – business was business, after all. Tizzie Ridings was keen, they said, but she was honest; if she was full of herself, well, she had good cause. The men of Manchester and Oldham and Rochdale knew business sense when they saw it; they traded with her and had no complaints.

The affairs of the pawnshop dealt with, Tizzie brought out a linen folder which held details of her assets: the pawnshop, half a dozen shops in the town, a couple of terraces of well-built dwelling houses and five plots of land. In her case, ownership of land was always short-term; since her first purchase of a plot ten years earlier she had often bought land and sold it at a profit. She laid a slim hand on the folder and gave an impatient shake of the head. 'It's a long haul, realising my ambition, Barney.'

He knew exactly what she meant. At the age of twenty she had promised herself that by the time she was forty she would own half of Saltley; then in an unguarded moment she had told him of it and could still recall his reaction. He hadn't laughed, he hadn't preached caution; he had just given her his rare smile and said simply, 'I'll help you in any way I can, Miss Tizzie.'

Nobody except Barney knew exactly what she owned, not even her sister, Mary. She dealt with more than one agent, more than one lawyer, had money in more than one bank. Complex financial arrangements were meat and drink to her – she thrived on them.

Still at her side, Barney turned an enquiring hand palm upwards. 'A long haul, aye, but have you put in an offer?'

'Yes – through channels, of course.'

He looked at her with the air of a proud parent observing a talented child, because the offer he referred to was for Bennison's jewellers at the foot of the lane. 'You'll trade there under Ridings?' he asked intently.

'I want your views before I decide on that, Barney. I'd like to own it openly, but I haven't the time to be there in person. And something keeps telling me not to make too much of my properties. What do you think?'

'There's envy of you in the town, Miss Tizzie – you know that. It's your first jewellers, and I wouldn't like folk to say you're using it as an outlet for your unredeemed pledges.'

'But you know I would never sell Saltley stuff this side of Openshaw – or this side of Oldham, come to that.' He wriggled his broad shoulders and she eyed him irritably. 'Come on, Barney. Tell me what you think. I want an opinion not an instruction.'

His reply held a touch of irony. 'Ee, I'm not brave enough to give you instruction, Miss Tizzie, but since you ask, it's my opinion you'd be better to keep it under the Bennison name or happen some sort of trade name. There's a bit of resentment here and there about how you've got on, and the master of Bluebell Mill doesn't exactly love you, nor do some of his cronies. I'd say keep it dark that it's your shop, and make sure your staff do the same. Time enough to reveal who owns it when it's gained a fine reputation. You've got somebody reliable dealing with it?'

Tizzie nodded, still deep in thought. 'Kenworthy – he's discretion itself. Right, I'll give heed to what you say and decide by breakfast time tomorrow. There, that's business finished with. You'll stay for a bite to eat, Barney?'

It was a ritual – she always asked, he always accepted. She rang for Rebecca and they moved to two comfortable chairs. She had never told him that she'd had them made specially, and she didn't know if he'd guessed. They were low seated and low armed so that he could sit down with ease and yet feel he was the same as her. Similarly, a cold supper was laid out on a low table which he could reach in comfort.

The housekeeper brought in coffee on a tray and they had a leisurely meal, chatting of what was happening in Manchester and the progress of the magnificent new town hall there. Tizzie waited until they were having a last coffee before asking him, 'Barney, are you by any chance free a week on Sunday?'

Wariness settled on him like a cloak. 'I'm not sure, Miss Tizzie. Might I ask why?'

'My sister is having an afternoon tea party for the family and a few friends – just an informal affair. She wondered if you would be free to go.'

She saw Barney relax a little. He knew Mary from the days when he had worked for their father. He'd been to tea at her house once before – the usual substantial Sunday meal with Mary's husband, William, and their four children.

'It will be the same as last time,' she told him, 'except the food will be handed round and there'll be some of William's relations from up Holdwell way.'

She didn't press him to accept; he made his own decisions about his social life. Nor did she tell him that it was at her suggestion he was invited. She had thought it would be a change for him because he seldom mixed, apart from a weekly visit to the Salters' Arms and tea at Dolly Redfern's place on his afternoon off. Sometimes he accompanied Tizzie to Manchester on business, but if she suggested that they took a meal together in public his discomfort was so extreme that she always wondered why on earth she'd bothered. If she didn't mind being seen out with him, why should he mind being seen out with her?

Barney sat there considering the invitation at length, perhaps battling with his strange, inverted pride. At last he said, 'Thank you, I'll be pleased to go. It's very kind of Mrs Hartley,' and Tizzie was content.

At ten o'clock Rebecca came in to say that Barney's cab had arrived, handing him his hat and giving her customary dip of the knee. Grave and polite, he said goodnight to Tizzie.

'Goodnight, Barney.' For no particular reason she added, 'Sleep well.'

He gave a small, mirthless smile. 'That'll be the day, Miss Tizzie.' He touched his hat and stumped to the door, then walked down the path to the cab.

CHAPTER TWO

Families

'Tizz! You look lovely – just like a fashion plate!' Mary greeted her sister with a delighted gabble. 'Your hair's gorgeous, and that dress! You do the princess line justice if anybody does, and who would even think of a redhead wearing lilac?'

'I would,' replied Tizzie drily, 'because I'm sick to death of green and cream and brown.' She disentangled herself from Mary's hug and offered a cheek for her brother-in-law's kiss. 'Hello, William. How's business?'

William Hartley smiled. 'Pretty good, thanks. Since my father retired I've inherited some of his best customers. Has Mary told you I'm thinking of extending the shop? I'll show you what I have in mind later on, if you like.'

Dimples flashing, lace cap sliding back on her silky brown hair, Mary clucked her tongue. 'Come on, you two, no talk of business – this is a tea party.' She drew Tizzie aside and whispered, 'You'll take your hat off, won't you? If you keep it on some of the others might feel a bit awkward.'

Tizzie rolled her eyes in resignation and felt for her hat pins. No doubt she should be pleased that the Hartleys saw her as a leader of fashion. Mary turned to her eldest. 'Billy, take your Aunt Tizzie's hat and lay it carefully on my bed, will you? Are your hands clean?'

Billy sighed and held them out for inspection, then took Tizzie's elegant silk hat. 'It's purple, not lilac,' he pointed out, 'and so's the dress.'

'Call it what you like,' said his aunt, eyeing him in amusement. 'Though there is such a thing as purple lilac, you know. Where are the others?'

'Abel and Elizabeth are singing hymns to everybody, and Johnny's having a rest so he can stay up late.' Billy flashed her a grin and went upstairs, carrying the hat on outstretched palms like an offering.

Tizzie took her sister's arm. 'Is Barney here yet?'

'No. Why?'

'I thought you might offer him a low chair – perhaps that sewing chair of mother's?'

Mary shot a triumphant look at her husband. 'Didn't I say she'd ask that?' The bright brown eyes were guarded, though, when she turned back to Tizzie. 'Don't worry – we'll look after Barney. If he *needs* looking after, which I very much doubt.'

Was there censure in her tone? Again? Tizzie decided to think about it later. Mary was a love, not to mention a relaxed, light-hearted hostess who cooked like an angel, but with a tribe of in-laws to feed and four lively children under her feet it wouldn't have been surprising if she'd overlooked a detail such as Barney's comfort.

Tizzie entered the crowded parlour and put herself out to be pleasant. The Hartleys were a robust, good-looking family, with a capacity for noisy banter that was almost overpowering when they were all together. Over the years she had found that she liked them. They were real people, she thought; honest and hard working, not pretentious status seekers like many of the families in trade. Whether they liked her in return she had no way of knowing; they might respect her as a woman of business, but then so did half of Saltley.

Young Abel was playing the piano with more enthusiasm than skill when Barney arrived. The dwarf nodded pleasantly at the company and sat in the chair produced by

William and placed next to hers. 'Miss Tizzie,' he said with composure.

'Barney,' she replied, equally calm. Why had she been concerned? He seemed quite at ease. Then she noticed his hand, clenching and unclenching as it lay in his lap. So she'd been right in thinking it would be an ordeal for him. The Hartley men were all big and well set up, which made his stature seem more grotesque than ever.

And yet as the tea party proceeded he seemed to enjoy himself. At one stage young Johnny climbed on his lap with the confidence of a well-loved toddler who is always welcomed. For an instant Barney seemed transfixed, his eyes seeking Tizzie's over the child's head, then he took out his pocket watch and let Johnny listen to it until the child slid down and wandered away.

As always at Mary's, the food was excellent. Billy and Abel circled the room with trays of plump little sand-wiches, chicken patties and tiny jellied pies, while Elizabeth offered a selection of cheeses and what was acknowledged to be the best celery in Lancashire – that grown on Saltley Bog. She was a striking little girl: leggy, impatient, very bright, the only one of the four with red hair. Tizzie watched her with interest and remembered Mary displaying her like a battle trophy when she was three hours old, saying, 'We're calling her Elizabeth after you, Tizzie. When we saw this fuzz of red hair there was never any doubt what her name should be.'

There would be no pawnshop stigma to spoil childhood for the young Elizabeth, reflected Tizzie. Butchering was hardly a high-class trade but at least William dealt in good, wholesome produce. There would be no smell of camphor and flea powder as she ate her meals, no trying to ignore the very poor making for the dolly shop with their pitiful little bundles. And with William and Mary as parents, no hours, weeks, *years* of stultifying boredom, either. Maybe the child would be like her aunt in more than name and the colour of her hair. Would she too be restless, unsatisfied, yearning for the unattainable, or would she have her mother's sunny, undemanding nature?

Mary poured tea in her best china cups, offered a variety of home-made cakes, kept an eye on her children, chatted to the Hartley aunts and uncles and cousins, and never stopped smiling. Watching her, Tizzie experienced a familiar little ache beneath her ribs. Her sister was so happy, so well loved. Plump, giggling little Mary had been brought to bloom by domesticity. Marriage and mother-hood suited her.

When the meal was over two cousins descended on the piano and everyone joined in a singsong. The Hartleys were great ones for singing. Tizzie exchanged glances with Barney and was relieved to see him smile. For half an hour she joined in singing the gospel hymns of Mr Moody and Mr Sankey, surprised to find how much she enjoyed it. Then it was time for the country dwellers to set off for home. In the flurry of departures William brought in a tall, dark man who had just arrived. 'This is Richard Barnes,' he told those who hadn't yet left. 'I expect you've heard of Barnes Brothers, the builders from Droylsden. He's called to give me an opinion on the extensions to the shop.'

If Tizzie hadn't turned to bid farewell to Barney just as the man stepped indoors she would have missed the swift, conspiratorial look that passed between Mary and her husband. Here we go again, she thought wearily.

William introduced her. 'Tizzie, I don't know if you've met Mr Richard Barnes? Perhaps you'd like to join us when we go down to the shop?' And to the builder, 'Meet my sister-in-law, Miss Tizzie Ridings, Richard. She has a flair for business, as you'll see for yourself.'

Tizzie gritted her splendid teeth. Very clever. Bring in yet another possible husband, but this time on a business rather than a social footing. She smiled, shook hands and weighed him up. Presentable enough, she decided, but basically nondescript. Still, it would be interesting to see if he had ability. Mary would expect her to stay until about ten, so discussing the alterations would help to pass the time.

Down in the clean-scrubbed shop it was something of an eye-opener when William announced that he had bought the greengrocer's premises next door. Well, well! There were times when her brother-in-law showed signs. And so did Richard Barnes – signs of knowing the retail trade in addition to how to knock down a wall without the whole building collapsing. Tizzie quite enjoyed the next half hour. She suggested lengthening the counter and changing its position, selling the cooked meats and pies from a table at the other side of the shop and, recalling establishments in Manchester, she recommended the building of a partitioned off cash desk where customers could settle their bills and where orders and invoices could be stored and referred to. It was almost laughable the way they both listened as if she was speaking the wisdom of Solomon.

Richard Barnes eyed her when he thought she wasn't looking and tried unsuccessfully to conceal his astonishment at being treated as a business equal by a female who couldn't be more than thirty. When he promised to put in an estimate within three days it was clear that he couldn't wait to get away. Tizzie smiled to herself as they saw him off and went back upstairs.

Mary was waiting to hear what had happened. 'He seems to know what he's doing, love,' William assured her. 'And Tizzie's given me plenty of food for thought, as well.'

'What did you think of him, Tizz?' asked Mary.

'As a builder – pretty good. As a prospective husband – not my type.'

'Tizzie!' Mary was mortified. 'How did you guess? And how can you say that when you've only just met him?'

'I guessed because I have eyes in my head. I'm not some little dimwit who needs help in finding a husband,' Tizzie told her shortly. 'And I can say it quite easily – he doesn't appeal to me in the least.'

'But Tizz, you'll end up an old maid!' Mary was on the verge of tears and William was shuffling his feet in embarrassment.

Tizzie shrugged. 'That seems to worry you more than it does me.'

Her sister glared at her. 'But you can't go through life doting on that – that dwarf!'

Tizzie became very still. 'What exactly do you mean?'

Mary plucked at the ribbons of her lace cap. 'Well, Barney's nice enough, of course. I like him, but—'

'But what?'

'I'm sorry, Tizzie, but I thought you'd have realised by now that there's talk in the town.'

'About what?' asked Tizzie blankly.

Mary's cheeks were bright pink. 'You and Barney,' she said.

Amazement robbed Tizzie of speech. For a full half minute she gaped at her sister, who stared back defiantly. Tizzie clutched at a chair and sat down. She hadn't felt so humiliated since Eli Walton had suggested she became his kept woman eleven years ago. 'Do you mean to say that people think that I'm – uh – involved with Barney? As – as a man and woman?'

'Nobody actually says that,' admitted Mary. 'It's more a "Tizzie Ridings and her tame dwarf" sort of thing. Or, "He spends his time lying down so she can wipe her feet on him." You know.'

'No, I don't.' Tizzie felt sick. 'Surely nobody says such things to you?'

'Of course they don't! It comes back to me in roundabout ways through my friends. They want me to warn you, that's all.'

Tizzie still sat there, stunned into silence. This was the reason for the touch of censure when Mary spoke of Barney. She felt her pride sinking like some damaged old barge on the canal. People couldn't seriously imagine that she was interested in Barney in a – a romantic way? In a – she gripped the back of the chair – in a sexual way?

Mary and William hovered anxiously in front of her chair. 'Tizzie, are you all right?' asked William.

'Let me think,' she said shortly. Once before Mary had

warned her about her relationship with a man and it had turned out to be the most important warning of her entire life. Minutes passed and then she stood up. 'Barney is my best and dearest friend,' she said quietly. 'I respect him, he respects me. That's all there is to it. If I wanted a romantic involvement with somebody I think I might possibly manage to find myself a full-grown man – if I tried very, very hard, of course. Now, would you mind getting my hat?'

Mary hurried upstairs, and William muttered awkwardly, 'Tizzie, she'd die rather than hurt you, she would honestly, but we've been that worried . . .'

She was fighting nausea, sickened by her own horror at people thinking she might be romantically involved with a dwarf; bile stung her throat because of what she'd just said about a full-grown man. Barney deserved better of her than that. She looked down at the carpet under her feet and searched for the right words. When Mary brought her hat she anchored it firmly to her wayward hair and looked at her sister. 'You were right to tell me,' she said quietly. 'I'll give the matter some serious thought.'

She waved aside William's offer to take her home in the trap and set off on foot for Farthing Lane. Mary and William had never guessed that there was only one man who could tempt her to a romantic involvement. And he had made it clear years ago that he wasn't interested in her. Tizzie walked home slowly through the glow of the setting sun, an elegant, colourful figure against the sombre black grime of the mills.

The six o'clock blower sounded through Jericho Mills. It was Friday tea time, the start of Saltley Wakes; the great twin engines whined to a halt and a last drift of smoke issued from the chimney as the boilers were banked down until Tuesday morning.

In spite of their weariness, those who had saved money in the wakes clubs were in high spirits as they streamed out through the gates; any who had been less prudent grumbled

among themselves that they had nothing to spend on the
wakes fair and would be a day and a half short in their next
week's wages.

News was passed through the throng that the fair would
arrive during the night and be set up by the next morning.
With the fine weather still holding it promised to be a good
weekend: there would be the fair and the opening of the
new indoor market on Saturday, chapel or church on
Sunday, followed by a walk out to the well dressing at Low
Holden, then on Monday the Morris Men's display followed by public dancing round the Old Cross. It was said
that the Morris dancers encouraged drinking and bad
behaviour, but so far nobody had attempted to ban them.

Along the road from Jericho, Matthew was making a
final inspection of the grounds of the Workers' Institute. A
fortnight of fine weather meant that his flowerbeds were in
prime condition, though constant watering had been needed. The bowling green was a picture – his pride and joy –
and the shrubbery that he'd planned with such care five
years earlier positively gleamed in the evening sun. No
grimy, half-dead foliage for him – constant spraying kept
it clean; with two men under him he was able to protect
plants from the increasing amount of Saltley grime.

Sometimes he wondered whether there was any future
in growing flowers and shrubs in the mill towns. Ups and
downs there might be in the cotton trade, but in the main
the mills kept busy and created their own fallout of soot.
And in Saltley the pits that fed the mills produced spoil
heaps that grew ever wider and higher beyond the smelly,
tumbling waters of West Brook.

Because of the holiday Matthew was due to finish early,
at seven o'clock, but he had no intention of leaving until
Mr Schofield had been. His employer always called for a
look round on Friday evenings, and those eyes of his were
like a hawk's. It was a rare day, though, when he found
cause for complaint. Matthew smiled to himself and tipped
his hat to a more jaunty angle. Rare? It was practically
unheard of!

From the clatter of clogs in the street he knew that workers were heading for the Jericho Baths. Mortal busy they'd be tonight, he told himself, with everybody wanting to be nice as ninepence for the holiday. He'd been there once with his men, after a muddy session laying a land drain. The place had impressed him: rows of little cubicles, each with a chair for a man's belongings and a bath tub with hot and cold running water. The three of them had had a good laugh, shouting to each other over the partitions, then he'd sneaked out and moved Jonas's trousers. The little fella hadn't know whether to laugh or cry as he scuttled around in his singlet and long drawers trying to find them, but the attendant had soon put a stop to such fooling around ... Not that he needed to go there, nor to Saltley's new public baths for that matter. Martha had the kettles and pans on for baths at home every Saturday night, and on Wednesdays as well for Rosie. She was one for organising, was his little Martha. Happy as a lark when everything was in order ...

'All ready for the wakes then, Matthew?' Joshua Schofield had arrived, accompanied by his son Sam.

'Mr Schofield.' Matthew raised his hat. 'Yes, everything's in order for the weekend. Would you be wanting me to walk round with you?'

Joshua was already weighing up the flowerbeds and shrubs, nudging his son to admire the velvety surface of the bowling green. 'No, we'll look round on our own,' he said amiably. 'Oh – remind me some time this weekend to have a word with you about the big front border at home, will you? Come on, Sam, I want to see the rose beds and the greenhouse, then we'll go in and have a look at the library.'

Minutes later they disappeared indoors, but Matthew still lingered. He could trust the caretaker to lock up as usual, but he could hardly set off for Meadowbank ahead of the two Schofields. And what if they should want to ask him something about his work?

It was half an hour before they came out of the institute,

arguing good-humouredly. 'Ah, Matthew, I'm glad you're still here,' said Joshua, 'I might have forgotten in the morning. You'll be taking young Rosie to the wakes fair, I expect?'

'Why, yes, Mr Schofield. In the afternoon.'

'I thought so.' Joshua felt in his pocket and handed over a sixpence. 'Give her that from me, then, to spend on whatever she likes.' With a wave of his stick he dismissed Matthew's thanks and set off down the road with his son.

The small act of generosity had the odd effect of lowering Matthew's spirits. His little girl had no grandfather to give her such treats. His own father had died when he was nine years old but he had shed no tears about that; his young life had been taken up with looking after his sisters and dodging his stepmother's strap.

Looking back, Matthew knew that if he could have chosen a grandfather for Rosie it wouldn't have been Joshua Schofield, no matter how he might respect the man; it would have been Luke Fawcett, the one-legged old sailor who had been born and bred in Saltley before ending his days in Devon. Peggy-oh Luke had been more of a father to him than his own had ever been, sharing the squalor of the stables behind the run-down inn that had been their home in Plymouth. Luke had breathed his last before Rosie was born, long years before, but his influence lay on her father like a woollen cloak on a frost-bound day.

Matthew put the sixpence in his waistcoat pocket and told himself to count his blessings instead of standing there moping. It wasn't in his nature to be downcast for long, but of late he'd seen it in himself time and again. What ailed him? He had a job he loved, a compelling hobby, a comfortable home, a loving wife and an adorable child. What more could he want from life?

The wakes fair was bigger than ever before, filling the market ground and banishing the produce stalls to the pavements and gutters. It seemed as if all Saltley must be there, paying to see the sideshows, trying for prizes on the

catchpennies and jostling for a view of the platform where
Lord and Lady Soar and the mayor were to sit for the
opening of the new indoor market. Lines of bunting were
crisscrossed between tall poles, and a huge Union Jack was
pinned up behind the platform, while in front of it was a
roped off area with seats for leading citizens; everybody
else would have to watch as best they could.

Wearing a cotton sunbonnet and her second-best pinafore over her pink dress, Rosie Raike held her father's hand
very tightly. She wasn't sure if she liked it when there were
so many people crushed together. They were all shouting
to make themselves heard above the band and it was very
hot. She peeped behind the travelling caravans and wondered what it must feel like to run around in skimpy rags
as the fairground children did.

The Saltley people seemed to be wearing more clothes
rather than less, in spite of the heat. Many of the men were
in their best broadcloth coats and their womenfolk in
Sunday dresses with shoulder shawls, while Mrs Eli
Walton was clad in layers of yellow lace over a tight brown
satin dress, looking square as a box because of her bustle
and poking people in the face with the edge of her parasol.
Rosie thought that the only one who looked cool should
really have looked hot because of her flaming hair – Miss
Ridings, the lady who was boss to a dwarf. She was sitting
in the special seats, though without her dwarf, looking cool
and unruffled in palest green poplin with a hat to match.
She was the only one on her own, the only one not talking
or listening. Everybody else was excited.

Rosie couldn't understand why the grown-ups were
making such a to-do about the new market hall when the
wakes was there right under their noses. The new building
was very grand; built of smooth red brick and pale creamy
stone. Anybody could see it was going to be there for ever
and ever but the wakes fair came only once a year.

Hannah and Ellie and Lilah at Meadowbank had talked
about the indoor market for weeks, but Rosie's mam
wouldn't see the opening because she'd been asked to help

get ready for Mr Schofield's wakes party. It was a family do, they said, the same as every year, so Charles was sure to be there. She didn't think he'd be allowed to talk to her but she was almost sure they could exchange looks. She liked exchanging looks. She liked reading the messages that people wore on their faces, though sometimes you got a shock, like when she read Charles's mother's face.

There'd been a lot of messages on her mam's face when she'd seen them setting off for the wakes fair. She'd been crossing the yard with a bowl of cream from the cold room, smiling because she was helping with the party. Rosie had come out of the house, and her mam had looked her up and down the way she always did, saying, 'You'll do, love. See you keep clean, now.' And then her eyes had opened wide as her dad came out as well. 'Where'd you get that hat?' she'd asked. It was new: a wide-awake made of soft black felt with a low crown and a wide brim. Her dad looked ever so handsome in it, but a bit – a bit like a gypsy.

'I bought it,' he had replied, tipping it forward over his eyes, 'out o' my woodwork money. It do remind me somethin' powerful o' that old hat I were so fond of in the early days.'

Devon talk, Rosie noticed. Most of the time he didn't sound much different from Saltley people, but now and again, when he was annoyed or excited, he talked as if he'd never left home.

Her mam had noticed as well. She noticed everything about her dad. Messages were written on her mam's face as clearly as if they'd been written on a blackboard with chalk. The first one was, 'I love you.' The second was, 'You look like somebody else – somebody I'm not easy with,' and the third, 'Don't change – stay the same. Don't go away!' It was silly, really. As if he *would* go away.

Rosie had looked from her mam to her dad, twisting one leg around the other in the way that helped her to fathom things out. He did look different. A bit like a gypsy, yes, but younger, as if he didn't have a care in the world ... less of a family man, somehow. And nobody wore hats like that any more. It was flat caps for working men, bowlers and billycocks for the ones who were more important. Her dad had just started wearing a bowler. Her mam had liked it.

Her dad had just laughed. 'Don' 'ee worry, Martha. At least I bain't wearin' a red neckcloth!' He had dropped a kiss on her cheek, then taken hold of his daughter's hand and set off for the wakes fair.

The reserved seats were all occupied. In fact, Sam had offered his to Joe Chadwick because the mine owner had arrived late. Irritated at Sam leaving his side, Joshua had been mollified when he'd realised it was his old friend sitting next to him.

Sam stood near the ropes with the crowd behind him; he always preferred to have a good overall view of what was happening. The mill-owning families were all seated, dressed in their best, waiting for the arrival of the man who owned the greater part of their town and the huge swathe of land that ran from either side of Saltley far up into the Pennines. Over there was brother James with his wife and son, looking as if he'd lost a sovereign and found a sixpence, though for once Esther was almost cheerful, perhaps because she would be seen by everybody as being close to the aristocracy … As for young Charles, he was sitting there in a dream, his Schofield-blue eyes wide and unfocused, listening to the band.

The music came to an end, and for half a moment everything was quiet apart from the shouting of the barkers on the fair, the wheeze of a distant hurdy-gurdy and the smack of the hammer on the try-your-strength machine. Then from the band came a drum roll and a flourish of trumpets to herald the arrival of the Soars. Behind him Sam heard a sound like a vast expelling of breath; with a tightening of his heart he realised that it was the crowd sighing with pleasure, because even the down-to-earth people of Saltley liked a touch of romance. What could be more romantic than a commoner marrying into the aristocracy, a commoner close to their hearts, at that?

Sam joined in the applause when Lord and Lady Soar were led to the platform with the mayor, John Fairbrother: the young earl tall and confident and maybe a little overweight, his countess slender, silver blonde and quite beautiful. His sister Sarah, his little Funny Face, married to an adoring Francis Soar ... For the people of the town it was the stuff of fairy tales, even though the marriage was nearing six years old. Who cared now that she'd been a widow when he'd married her? A widow who had left her first husband four months after the wedding. Not Francis, that was for sure. He helped her up the steps of the platform, and Sam was touched by his brother-in-law's expression; it revealed love for his wife – a selfless love and a deep, measureless devotion. Sarah had transformed her husband. These days Francis was a man of energy and purpose, a different being from the plump, amiable, uncertain young man who had carried his family name like a burden until he married the woman he loved.

Sam smiled and gave a little nod when his sister saw him. She wrinkled her nose very slightly – a grimace that she had saved solely for him since their childhood. He looked down at his father's white head and saw that he too was watching her with well-concealed pride. Running a finger round the inside of his sweat-damp collar, Sam told himself that if only old James had been happy in his marriage he himself would be fairly content.

The ceremony was over. The Earl of Soar had made an excellent speech, praising the townspeople, the borough council and the occupants of the new market hall. The mayor had replied and handed a great iron key to his Lordship, who solemnly unlocked the main door of the market. The band struck up with the Grand March from *Aida*, and the special guests were ushered to the town hall for refreshments while everyone else was free to go inside the market and inspect the stalls.

This swallowing up of the crowd left the wakes ground almost deserted. Dismayed at the drop in custom, the fairground people bellowed their wares and tempted people to pay for a full viewing of the sideshows by giving tantalising glimpses of the freaks.

Matthew and Rosie were in front of a sideshow called 'The Fattest Child on Earth' when a curtain was twitched, half revealing an enormously fat female seated on a stool, nursing a rag doll. She was wearing a child's frilly white dress, with her hair in ringlets tied with blue bows. Rosie gasped in amazement at the size of her, while Matthew saw at once that she was no child but a young woman, perhaps in her late teens or even her twenties. Pity seared him when he looked into the immense red face that topped the mountain of flesh; the eyes were resigned, hopeless, humiliated. The old woman in charge lifted the hem of the frilly dress to display a massive shiny red calf and in shame the young woman bowed her head, her chins cascading. The old crone would be stripping her next, thought Matthew in disgust, and urged Rosie on.

But tears were glinting on his daughter's dark lashes. What a soft-hearted liddle soul, he thought tenderly. With a delicacy of feeling that made Matthew want to swing her up in his arms and kiss her, Rosie gave the fat woman a small, friendly smile and wiggled her fingers in a wave. Then, releasing Matthew's hand for an instant, she dropped her a perfect curtsey. The sad eyes in their cushions of fat brightened for an instant, but seeing that she couldn't tempt them to pay for a full viewing, the old woman flicked the curtain across and they heard the sound of a slap.

Rosie at once burst into tears. Matthew gathered her to him and carried her to the low wall that bordered the edge of the marketplace, sitting there with her on his knee. 'It's not kind!' she sniffled against his neck. 'She's not a child – she's a lady! Why does the old woman dress her up and show her off like that?'

'For the money, my love,' he said honestly. 'Folk do bad things for money, Rosie – always have and probably always will. The fat lady has to be fed and clothed and looked after. I doubt she'd be able to work, so they put her on show for money rather than go out and leave her on her own. Come on now, dry those eyes and we'll find something for you to spend your sixpence on ...'

They walked along, free of the crowds at last, and soon Rosie let go of his hand and skipped ahead with three ha'pennies in her hand, looking for the roll-ha'penny stall.

It was then he saw the girl.

She was working on the hoopla, watched by a sombre old man smoking a clay pipe on the steps of a caravan. Her long dark hair was free of pins, tumbling around her head as she darted to retrieve the hoops that a broad-chested farmer was tossing. Her face was tanned to a pale gold, her eyes were light coloured; grey, he thought, or green, and they seemed to have been set in her head by fingers dipped in soot. She had a very red mouth, the lower lip full and moist as if it was often caught between her teeth.

She whirled back and forth along the boards that covered the cobblestones, her ragged green skirts flapping round bare ankles. At last the farmer departed, disgruntled that he had won nothing. Catching Matthew's eyes on her the girl turned hurriedly away, putting him in mind of a startled young fawn that he'd seen long ago on a rare outing to Exmoor.

A sudden ache in his chest told him that he was neglecting to breathe. He took in air and still he stared at her – he couldn't seem to help it. He told himself it would be impossible to find anyone less like the mill women of Saltley, less like – he gathered his wits and breathed out again – less like his little Martha.

He looked around for Rosie. She was no more than a furlong away, rolling her ha'pennies, so he felt in his pocket for a coin to try his luck with the hoops. The girl was ready to take his money, her eyes wide and wary. Seen so close she seemed half wild, like a creature from the depths of some enchanted wood. He found himself watching her upper arm as the tattered green sleeve revealed it, and was filled with a rush of desire so intense he had to grip the wooden bar in front of him so as not to reach out for her.

He didn't know if the girl sensed it, but perhaps the old man did, because he shifted on the caravan steps, leaning forward and eyeing him intently. Staggered and somewhat ashamed of his feelings, Matthew told himself he must get away. He shook his head slightly to indicate that he didn't choose to play hoopla, then touched his hat in farewell, his dark eyes absorbing every detail of how she looked. He clamped his teeth together in a spasm of astonished pain; it was as if his chest was being torn open and his heart wrenched from his body.

Disturbed by the intensity of his gaze, the girl put up a hand and clutched at her wild mop of hair, as if regretting that it wasn't neatly brushed and combed. Matthew sighed just once, then without a backward look he walked away to join his daughter.

Joshua's wakes party was well underway. Fourteen had been round the table for what he called 'a good knife and fork tea', a meal that had proved Lilah's worth in the kitchen. When Alice had retired he had never expected to find another cook to equal her, but he had to admit that Lilah came close. She'd have suited Rachel.

He watched them all as they drifted out through the conservatory to the sunlit garden: James and Esther and young Charles; Sam in high spirits, laughing and joking with his sister, Sarah, and her Francis ... It pleased Joshua to entertain his son-in-law. Earl he might be, with dwellings here, there and everywhere, but it was quite clear that he enjoyed being in a proper family home. He'd been good to Rachel when she was ill, had Francis. And she'd liked him. They'd all liked him, but Joshua hadn't realised the way the wind was blowing with Francis and Sarah. It had taken Sam, perceptive as always, to see that ...

As for his other guests, there was Luther and Janey Dobbs; the Fairbrothers, John having completed his mayoral duties; his old pal Joe Chadwick; and the faithful John Wagstaff from Mosley Street, now well into his seventies and a widower like himself. Oh, and Tizzie of course, always invited to family do's because of her friendship with Sarah. She was a girl of ability, was Tizzie, he thought admiringly. Girl? She was a woman, not much younger than Sam, and destined to be an old maid by the looks of it.

At this sort of do natural pairing off should have meant that Sam and Tizzie at least exchanged the odd word, but somehow they both made it seem quite natural never to be alone together, even for a minute. Years back he'd thought that there was something brewing between them but he'd been wrong. There was no love lost there.

It annoyed him at times – nay, it upset him – that Sam was still unmarried. He was thirty-two, and at the rate he was going he would be as confirmed a bachelor as his uncle Charlie had been before him.

The door opened and the maid, Ellie, came in. 'Hannah says will it be in order to have our tea when we've cleared away, Mr Schofield?'

He stared vaguely at the cluttered table. Domestic matters baffled him. 'Whatever Hannah thinks best,' he agreed, but Ellie still hovered.

'We've put a trestle up in the stable yard for our tea, Mr Schofield. Will that be in order?'

Joshua looked at her, intrigued. It was almost unheard of in Saltley for anyone to eat a sit-down meal out of doors. 'Why didn't I think of that for us?' he asked her.

She chewed her lips. 'I don't know, Mr Schofield.'

'Well, if we have weather like this next year, I'll have to consider it, won't I? For now, though, have your tea, all of you. We'll see to ourselves. Oh – ask Lilah to come here for a minute, will you?'

With a tap on the door the cook entered; she'd put on a clean apron and it crackled as she moved. Joshua rocked back and forth on his heels and toes as she stood in front of him. He thought he knew why she didn't use her full name: she was as straight up and down as a stair rod, with dull mouse-brown hair and a long, disastrously plain face ... nobody's idea of a Delilah.

'Lilah, I want to congratulate you on the tea,' he said, fixing her with his intent gaze. 'It was an excellent meal. You've done well, all of you – you can tell the others I said so.' He pulled at his side whiskers and nodded his head at her. 'My wife would have been well pleased.'

Lilah coloured slightly and smiled, revealing her only redeeming feature, excellent white teeth. The staff had warned her that when Mr Schofield mentioned his wife, you took notice. She herself had thought it must be put on, affected, prating about a woman who'd been dead for eleven years. But when Mr Schofield spoke her name it was so natural, so warm, you felt as if she might walk through the door at any minute. 'Thank you, Mr Schofield,' she said. At that moment, like many a one before her, she was drawn to him. She almost felt herself to be his equal. Lilah worked for her money, she gave of her best; he respected her for it. They *were* equal, in a way.

'Off you go then,' he said with a smile. 'Go and enjoy your tea.'

Sarah came back indoors, halting in the dimness of the room after the glare outside. 'Papa, come on! Matthew and Zacky are putting up an awning so we can all sit in the shade. It's too hot for croquet so we'll just have to talk, won't we?'

Joshua smiled. 'That'll be no hardship for some of us, will it?' He opened the sideboard and took out a brown paper parcel.

Sarah kissed his cheek. 'Now's a good time,' she whispered, and they went outside.

Seeing him with a large parcel, silence fell on the others. Sam eyed his father with interest, knowing he liked a touch of drama and that he had a talent for timing his moves to the best effect.

Esther gave her tinkling little laugh. 'This looks interesting, Grandfather Schofield. Has somebody bought you a present?'

'No,' said Joshua good-humouredly. 'No, it's me who's bought a present for somebody else. Francis here has advised me on it. It's for you, Charlie.'

Charles blushed at being the focus of attention. His mother was looking on, concealing her annoyance at him being called Charlie but pleased that he'd been given a present and highly gratified that the Earl of Soar had advised on it. Sam looked across at his father and could have sworn that his eyelid flickered in the suggestion of a wink.

There were two layers of wrapping, no doubt to build up the tension. Removing the second one, Charles revealed a black leather instrument case. His mouth opened wide with delight, then he lifted the lid and let out a squeal of pure joy. 'A trumpet! Oh, Grandpa, thank you, thank you, thank you!' Eyes blazing with delight he ran to Joshua and kissed him. 'How did you know? How did you guess?'

Joshua looked down at him and nodded benignly. 'You're pleased? Then let's just say I made an inspired guess, shall we? I've paid for your first ten lessons, as well, with a man who knows what he's about.'

The boy lifted the trumpet and stroked it. 'Brass to begin with,' said Joshua, 'then if you take to it we'll see about a silver-plated one. That's the thing these days, so they tell me.'

At last James spoke. 'That's a very fine present, Father. Charles seems to have a gift for music, so we'll see what he makes of it, won't we, Esther?'

Esther gave them all her delightful smile; it almost concealed the steely glint in her eyes as she shot a sideways look at her father-in-law. 'How kind of your grandfather, Charles. We'll have to see about getting you a special practice room, won't we?'

Joshua laughed heartily. 'I've heard tell that a brass instrument is less trying on the ear than an untrained violin, so you shouldn't suffer all that much, Esther. A gift for music must be nurtured. Talent must have its chance, and so forth.'

Francis Soar broke in. 'You'll be able to give us all a recital when you're proficient, Charles. And we'll all come and watch when you march with the town band.'

Esther's eyes almost shot out of her head, but she managed to smile sweetly at Francis. 'Saltley Brass Band? Ah, who knows? One day he might be the star turn at your musical evenings up at Alsing, Francis.'

He turned his candid gaze on her, slightly puzzled at the undertone. 'There's nothing that would please us more. Is there, Sarah?'

Lady Soar agreed with a smile but told herself that there was one thing that would please her very much more, one thing in particular. Nearly six years married and there was still no sign of a baby ... Her eyes met Sam's and she saw that he knew her thoughts. They were still so close, a closeness that came from a childhood during which they spent every free moment together and had a twin-like linking of minds. Francis knew of it – he'd always known. He approved of it. For the thousandth time Sarah marvelled at the unselfishness of the man she'd married.

She saw Tizzie watching her with something of the same understanding as Sam. Her dear, dear Tizzie – so strong and clear headed, so staunch a friend ... It was Tizzie who had set her on the road to recovery after the travesty of her marriage to Edward; Tizzie who had helped her to rebuild her self-esteem ...

Charles was fingering the trumpet and scuffling his feet on the grass, so Sam asked him quietly, 'Do you want to try out your first notes in private? You can go up to my room and experiment, if you like.'

The dazzling eyes opened wide. 'Thanks, Uncle Sam!' The boy made to go and then, remembering himself, turned and gave Esther a stilted little bow. 'Excuse me, Mama ... everybody.' Then he ran indoors.

Pleased with the outcome of his plan, Joshua leaned back in his chair and watched them all as the light of the sun deepened to a darker gold. From the stable yard came the sound of laughter as his servants and the visiting coachmen had their tea. Then, above and beyond the talk, he heard the first hesitant notes of a trumpet, muffled and muted behind closed windows.

In her place at the long table, Rosie heard it too and gave a small, triumphant smile. She knew at once that it was Charles who was playing, because in their secret place under the hedge he had confided that he longed for a trumpet. Could it possibly be that his mam had bought him one?

Rosie was glad that something good was happening because she wasn't enjoying the wakes tea as much as she'd expected; she kept remembering the fat lady looking so ashamed in her little girl's dress. It made her chest hurt when she thought of her.

The others were all listening to the coachman from Alsing tell a funny story, except – yes – except for her dad, who seemed to be thinking of something else and putting no messages on his face. He'd been quiet ever since they came away from the wakes fair, so perhaps, like her, he was sad about the fat lady.

Rosie leaned forward to look at her mother, who was laughing with the others, her pretty little mouth stretched wide. Behind the laughing, though, lay a message, plain as plain, directed at her dad: 'What is it, love? What's wrong?'

CHAPTER THREE

Enchantment

All of Saltley seemed to be at the wakes, laughing and shouting as they pushed their way between stalls and sideshows. Children squealed on the swingboats and merry-go-rounds, excited by the annual treat and thrilled to be staying out late. A few drunkards reeled among the crowd, but as yet there was no fighting apart from that in the boxing booths. It was almost dark, the hanging lamps hissing and spluttering above a scene that seethed, inferno-like, beneath the remote calm of an indigo sky.

In his shirtsleeves and waistcoat, Matthew stood silently in the shadows beside the hoopla, his wide-brimmed hat pulled low. Disappointment screamed inside him because the girl wasn't there. The old man who had been on the caravan steps was handing out hoops and taking the money, while an elderly woman in a faded apron trudged back and forth along the boards, collecting the hoops and now and then handing over a prize.

He had wrestled with his conscience for hours before telling Martha that he thought he might go and see if he could meet up with Billy or Jonas to spend an hour or two watching the prizefighting. So unaccustomed was he to lying to her that he feared she might guess his intentions, but she had been resting in the wicker chair that had been her mother's, her small face glistening with the heat.

'Aye, you do that, love,' she said. 'I'll have a quiet hour an' happen a cool wash down. I'm that sweaty. You can bring our Rosie some toffee if you want, but make sure the stall's nice an' clean. Take your key, in case I'm asleep when you come in . . .'

Gratitude had fought with guilt as he had kissed her, though to be sure all he had wanted was to come and look at the girl again, just for the pleasure of it; to give himself another picture of her to store away in his mind. And now she was nowhere to be seen, so it served him right for telling lies, unless . . . unless she was in the caravan? Keeping to the shadows of shrubs and trees, he moved along the grass that bordered the market ground until he was close to the side of the caravan. It was darker there, a single street lamp throwing its pale yellow beam against the harsh red and gold of the fair.

He caught his breath. There was a dimly lit window covered by faded curtains that held the shadow of someone standing inside. It was the girl, washing herself. Her hair was bundled on top of her head, her arms outstretched as she washed herself down to the waist. He stepped backwards, conscious that he was viewing what was private and personal, seeing the graceful curve of her neck and bare shoulders, the swell of high round breasts. He watched and knew that he wanted her. The force of his desire was like a pile-driver in his entrails.

He closed his eyes to the sight of her but didn't move; instead he stood there and argued with himself. How often in his youth had he witnessed the coupling of a man and a woman and been disgusted at their greedy easing of the flesh? How often had he seen his stepmother, Fat Annie, with her sailors in the stables of the Mizzen Mast, or the serving maids obliging lustful guests? A couple of dozen times or more, and he'd hated it – always he'd hated it. 'Twas amazing strange that when temptation came to him it should seem so very different . . .

He found himself watching again as the girl dried herself. The light flickered and he knew it came from candles, wavering as they met the draught of her towel. Would she go to her bed? Would she come out for a breath of air? The wakes fair blared only yards away and he stood in the gloom, incapable of movement.

Then the back door of the caravan opened and the girl appeared, clad in the same dress as before, carrying a pail of water. She stepped down to empty it on the grass and, turning to go back, saw Matthew in the shadows. Her teeth gleamed as she smiled, and his heart gave a single heavy stroke as if on an anvil, then fell to a fast, regular beat. She seemed unafraid at the sight of him, so he stepped forward and touched his hat. 'Good evenin',' he said quietly, marvelling that he should speak such ordinary words.

She stared at him. 'What do you want?' she whispered, looking over her shoulder at the old couple in charge of the hoopla.

Matthew shifted his feet. What did he want? Ah, if only he could tell her.

She walked towards him and said simply, 'I thought you might come.' It could have sounded flirtatious, but it didn't. It was as if she was pleased and maybe a trifle nervous, but not in the least surprised. She was waiting for him to answer, her head on one side, her eyes shining in the light of the streetlamp. He saw that they were grey, putting him in mind of rain-washed sky above the Pennines.

'What be your name?' he asked hoarsely.

She flicked a hand as if names weren't important. 'Jess,' she said. 'It's for Jessamine.'

Perfect. He thought of jessamine, as some folk called the jasmine bush: white flowers tinged with pink, scenting the air from among climbing dark-green foliage. As a name it suited her awful well. He said, 'You bain't on the hoopla this evenin'?' Fool! More ordinary talk, when he yearned to speak the language of the gods, to have poetry fall from his lips like honey ... magical words to enchant this most enchanting of creatures.

'Not when it's dark,' she replied. 'My granny and grandpa won't let me work on any of the fairgrounds at night because—' She stopped short, and he wondered if she'd been about to say, 'because the men would be after me'. She bit her lip and marked a circle on the grass with a slippered foot.

He kept absolutely still, knowing that if he touched her nothing could ever be the same again – not for him. Maybe she felt it too, because though she seemed poised for flight, she stretched out a hand towards him and then drew it back. 'We could talk for a bit,' she said simply. 'Get to know each other.'

From deep within him came words uttered so low they were almost a groan: 'I have a wife and child.' It didn't occur to him to keep it from her.

'Ah.' The tone of that one syllable revealed that she was resigned to the good things of life being beyond her reach; that she accepted the sanctity of marriage vows and believed that though married men might be tempted to stray, they must never yield to that temptation. She gave a sad little nod of the head and held out her hand to shake his in farewell.

Matthew took it. Her skin was still cool from her wash, but her touch burned him as though it were red-hot. At once he leaned forward and pressed his lips to her palm then, still keeping his distance, kissed her outstretched arm on the inside of her elbow. 'Can 'ee take a liddle walk?' he muttered desperately.

Silently she stared at the palm of her hand, as if seeing the imprint of his lips; then she clasped the inside of her arm. He could hear her breathing, shallow and very rapid. She was shocked, he could tell, but undecided. A foreign instinct was goading him, the instinct of the hunter, out to tempt and then capture his prey. He took her hand again and coaxed, 'You did say we could talk for a bit.'

She bit her lip, that full, moist lower lip. His heart lurched. 'I s'pose it wouldn't hurt your wife,' she said doubtfully, 'not if we just talked . . . and not if nobody sees us.'

In the end they did far more than talk. Separately they

slipped through the wagons and caravans that bordered the fair-ground, then hurried along the side of the new market hall and behind the crowded Salters' Arms into the dark rising streets on the outskirts of the town. No sooner were they alone beneath a hedge than he took her in his arms and kissed her, smothering her protest with his lips.

Her mouth tasted of fresh raspberries and she smelled of some woodland herb that he couldn't have named. He stroked the wild tresses of hair away from her sweat-damp neck and twined his fingers in it, triumph filling him because after her first guilty protest she was as eager as him. Instinct told him that she wasn't used to being kissed; she was slightly clumsy, her mouth sweet and eager but far from practised. He dragged his lips from hers and looked around them. It was very hot, very dark; there was no moon, but above them was the limitless sky, spangled with stars. In the distance he could hear the sound of the wakes and nearer at hand the barking of a dog. They were on the road to Jericho Mills, so he took hold of her hand and led her to a path behind the Working Men's Institute. He knew that along that path was a grove of birches on land belonging to the Schofields.

Jess was beside him, swift and sure-footed in the long grass. Trees circled them like sentinels as he folded her in his arms again. Martha and Rosie never so much as touched the fringes of his mind; it was Jess, Jess, Jess, with her sweet untried lips and her warm slender body.

The silver birches stood guard, their leaves motionless in the heavy air; the stars looked down, distant and unconcerned; the grass was soft and dry. One voice came to him through the enchantment, a voice from his youth: Peggy-oh Luke speaking of a girl he had loved. 'Matthew,' he had said long years before, 'it was a glimpse of heaven when we lay together.'

A glimpse of heaven? Amazed laughter rose in Matthew's throat. This was no glimpse, this was heaven itself – very heaven, here on earth. Nothing else mattered as Jess gave herself to him – not that she was fully clothed, with her skirts rucked up around her thighs and her ragged bodice unfastened, nor that the long dry grasses somehow came between his hands and her soft, untouched flesh. Against her lips he gasped words that sprang from the depths of his being. 'I love you, I love you, I love you!'

The hot weather broke with a thunderstorm in the early hours. Lying awake, Matthew heard it approaching and found that it eased him to have the turmoil of the weather echoing what was inside him. He had expected that with Martha asleep next to him his time with Jess would appear unreal, dream-like, but it wasn't so. It was Martha who seemed out of place, lying on her back with the covers thrown aside and the long plait of her hair falling over the edge of the bed. He knew it was wrong of him, but he wanted her out of that bed and Jess there instead.

Sleep wasn't possible because it would rob him of the opportunity to recall their lovemaking: every kiss, every caress, the deep satisfaction of their union. Thunder rolled nearer while he searched his mind and delved into his heart, until at last he recognised what had been ailing him, making him so restless for the past year. It was simple: there had been something missing from his life. His virtuous little Martha, so clean, so loving, so surprisingly passionate, had never in eleven years of marriage given him what Jess had bestowed in one brief hour. That was how long it had been from seeing her shadow on the curtain to leaving her at the caravan steps.

He had taken her back to the wakes, longing to do so openly with his arm around her but of necessity disclaiming her and following from a distance. The underhand nature of their return shamed him, but Jess just walked ahead of him in the starlight, her feet seeming to skim the cobblestones.

In his arms, amid the grasses of the birch grove, she had told him that if her grandparents had missed her she would say that she'd taken a walk because it was too hot to stay in the caravan. He hoped they would believe her. After the silence of their time together the clamour of the fair seemed deafening. Matthew followed Jess through the maze of carts and caravans and saw the old couple clearing away the hoopla boards, apparently unaware of her absence. The crowd was thinning and two drunkards were being dragged home by their wives.

Jess had turned to face him as she'd reached the steps of the caravan, the lights behind her making a red-gold nimbus around her head. For a moment she'd stood there just looking at him, then she'd kissed her fingers in farewell and her lips had framed a silent 'goodbye'.

Matthew had left at once, stumbling across the grass like an injured man, past a straggle of folk waiting to scavenge when the wakes was closed. Seeing their curious stares, he had pulled himself erect so as not to draw attention, until he realised that they would only imagine him to be another drunkard.

Thunder cracked directly overhead and next to him Martha stirred and mumbled in her sleep. Drunkard? Not from alcohol, that was certain, for he'd made a vow never to touch it again, but drunk with kisses? With love? Yes, indeed he was. A married man drunk with the memory of adultery.

Restless with the noise of the storm but not yet awake, Martha felt for his hand. Turning on his side he waited for the next flash of lightning to illuminate her face. When it came he was cut to the heart to see her so plain, so very plain compared to Jess with her apricots-and-cream skin and her great, dark-lashed eyes. He had told Jess that he loved her within thirty minutes of first speaking to her, but he recalled that he hadn't told Martha he loved her in the whole of their wedding night. He'd never so much as thought of it.

No, he had only told Martha he loved her when he had thought he was going to lose her, in the terrible days following the death of their baby. If ever a woman had shown her love for a man, Martha had shown her love for him then. She had shown it even though she'd been riven with grief for the child who had fed at her breast. With his fingertip Matthew traced her soft, pretty mouth – her one good feature – remembering the countless times he'd been glad to take kisses from those lips. There was no enchantment, though, with his virtuous little wife, no magic . . .

All at once her eyes opened in the darkness; his touch on her lips had wakened her. Her hand was still over his. 'You got back before the storm, love?' she asked sleepily.

'Yes, long before.'

'An' did you see the prizefightin'?'

'No. No – I just walked round a bit and then came home. Go to sleep, now . . .'

Martha closed her eyes, but not to sleep. Unease had stabbed her at the tea party and now it was back again, worse than before. She had slept from weariness and from the heat, but suddenly she was wide awake. She didn't say anything, though. What could she say? 'Something tells me things aren't right with you, love,' or 'What's the matter? Why aren't you easy in your mind?'

They lay side by side, each silent and wrapped in their thoughts. Matthew was still caught by magic, but underneath it guilt was stirring, brought to reluctant life by thoughts of their wedding night. Martha had been a virgin, of course she had – he'd been so thankful that his first lovemaking was with a virtuous woman. She'd been twenty-six, with his gold band on her finger, but how old was Jess? Seventeen, she'd told him. A fairground girl but closely guarded, watched over, untouched. Oh, yes, untouched until she met Matthew Raike.

Already he knew that he must relinquish her. The thought of it cut at him like pruning shears. One day she would marry some upright young man – the grandparents would encourage it. And the upright young man would find his bride to be no virgin . . . an adulterer in some far-away cotton town had seen to that. Shame and guilt lay like a weight inside him, but oh, he loved her.

Outside the rain poured down. He told himself it was like tears for a love that was lost – lost to duty and marriage vows and the deep devotion of his wife.

Rosie was put out to find it pouring with rain on a wakes
weekend. It would be Sunday school as usual, but after
dinner they'd hoped to walk to the well dressing at Low
Holden, along with half the population of Saltley. 'Mam,'
she wheedled, 'shall we go this afternoon if it's still
rainin'?'

Martha was cleaning vegetables for their dinner. 'What,
an' get our best clothes wet through? No, love, we'll have
to stay in, but don't get in a stew, there's time for it to clear
up. Now, you've got your pinny on? Come here an' wash
this cauliflower.'

Rosie managed not to sigh. She'd found that things like
washing vegetables weren't so bad when you had something good to think about, like she had now. After the
wakes tea she had arranged to be crossing the yard when
the High Lee coachman harnessed his horses, knowing that
Charles was always on hand to watch. There'd been
nobody else about, so he had run across to her and pulled
her inside the stable. She goggled at his daring but he was
too excited to notice.

'Rosanna!' he whispered, 'I've got a trumpet! A real
B-flat trumpet with valves – it's from Joseph Higham of
Strangeways in Manchester! Grandpa Schofield's given it
to me – I'm to have lessons twice a week!'

She didn't tell him that she'd guessed as much – it
would have spoiled his pleasure in surprising her. 'What
does your mam say?' she asked curiously.

For once he didn't lose his good humour at the mention
of his mother. He'd just shrugged his shoulders and
grinned. 'She was furious. She thinks brass instruments are
common. But my grandfather arranged it, so she couldn't
object. I say, Rosanna ...' He scuffed his foot through the
wisps of straw on the floor.

'Yes?' she prompted.

'One day I'll play something on my trumpet just for
you. Not when I'm learning – when I'm really good.'

He believed he was offering her the highest possible tribute. For an instant she felt old and very wise – older than Charles, wiser than anybody in the world. She almost patted his cheek, like a loving mother does with a child. Collecting herself, she asked practically, 'What will you play for me, then?'

His eyes had gleamed in anticipation. 'Purcell's Air and Tune in D,' he said promptly.

She'd never heard of it, but she nodded as if well pleased by his choice . . .

'Come on, love, stop dreamin'.' Her mother had a pan ready for the cauliflower, so Rosie dragged her mind to the present: the grey skies over the meadow, the steady drumming of rain in the yard outside and her dad's home-grown vegetables.

When it was time to set off for Sunday school her mother brought out the old waterproof cape with the hood. Rosie squirmed. 'You put it on,' said Martha firmly. 'I'm not havin' your best dress wet through. Your dad says he'll walk you there under the big umbrella.'

It was the perfect excuse for Matthew to leave the house when it was pouring with rain. With Rosie deposited at Sunday school, he hurried through the downpour to the wakes fairground. At dawn he had wondered if the cold light of day would show up his time with Jess as madness, some sort of brainstorm, but it seemed to him that the previous evening was more real than the wet empty streets, more full of meaning than all the hymns that would be sung in Saltley that morning.

He had to see her once more – just once, to wipe out any suspicion she might be harbouring that he'd used her like some men used loose women. He would tell her that he loved her; he had to be sure that she knew it. Then he would have to convince her that he must stay with his wife and child. He couldn't bear her to wait in vain for him to come again or even to join the straggle of casual hands who followed the fair waggons.

Matthew turned the corner then stopped in his tracks. The

wakes ground was empty but for a great pile of wet rubbish. Not a stall, not a merry-go-round, not a caravan remained. Dazed, he turned in a circle, rain spinning horizontally from the edge of his umbrella. A man was passing, soberly dressed as if on his way to chapel. Matthew barred his way and whirled an arm towards the empty square. 'Where be 'ey to?' he asked, lapsing into Devon talk. He knew the answer but needed to hear it out loud.

The man eyed him curiously. 'I reckon they've gone like the sons of Eliab.'

Uncomprehending, Matthew stared at him, and the man tutted. 'You don't know your Bible, then? Deuteronomy – where the earth opened and swallowed folk up with all their tents and belongin's. I don't say the earth opened up, but they'll have packed up in the night and gone on to the next place, won't they? Happen they thought they'd have no trade tomorrow if the rain keeps up.'

'But they've *all* gone,' insisted Matthew.

'Aye. They travel together, do most of 'em.' The man nodded and hurried away, seeing no point in discussing the obvious when it was tippling down.

Matthew walked across the cobbles to the stretch of grass where Jess's caravan had been. He peered at the ground as if expecting to find some message, but there was only the grass – brown from the drought but now waterlogged and trampled. Nothing was left to show that she'd ever been there.

Behind him two women hurried out of Rope Street, dragging a weeping child. Seeing him standing in the downpour they passed a remark to each other and guffawed, ignoring the child who snivelled and hiccupped between them. Aware that they were laughing at him he turned away and headed for home, deep in sombre, fatalistic thought. The heavens were weeping; he had been prevented from seeing Jess again; he didn't know where she was heading. There was a finality about it that he knew to be right and proper. He must accept that she'd gone and not try to trace her.

That man had been right in saying he didn't know his Bible. The reason he had kept his copy all these years was that his mother had written his name in it in her own hand – not that he set any store by religion. His father had been a churchgoer and that was quite enough to put him off it for life. But he had a suspicion that if he'd been a believer he might have felt that some power far stronger than himself had taken a hand in things.

When he reached home he went round to the back as usual. He could smell meat cooking but for the first time in his married life it didn't tempt him. He felt sick and quite without appetite. If only he had something, anything at all of hers to keep and look at when he was alone . . .

Then through the open door of the outhouse he saw his workbench, his gouges, his knives. Perhaps he *could* have something to remind him of her, and through his own efforts, at that.

CHAPTER FOUR

None So Blind

Tizzie walked beneath the three gold balls of the pawnshop and felt her customary relief that she didn't live there any more.

She often thought that, though the smell of camphor and flea powder was less overpowering than in her youth, the place still held the whiff of a prison. Once she'd referred to it as the Saltley Strangeways, causing Barney to shake his head gravely. 'There's many a one who'd jump at a stretch in Strangeways if it was like this place, Miss Tizzie.' It was gently said, but a rebuke lay behind his words rather than a compliment to the shop. One of the things she liked about Barney was the way that he could pull her up short ever so quietly and disagree with her.

She found him up the big ladder, straining to reach a customer's suit from the ceiling rails, so she went behind the counter and found Albert Lomas in the counting house sorting through ticket stubs. 'Albert,' she said briskly, 'I thought I told you to spare Mr Jellicoe climbing the ladders.'

Albert was wearing a neat striped shirt and a white calico apron, attire that was another of her innovations to combat a seedy atmosphere. Smoothing the apron he said politely, 'Mornin', Miss Ridings.'

'Good morning. Well?'

'I do try,' he protested, 'but if you want to stop him climbin', happen you should tell him yourself, Miss Ridings. He's – well – you know what he's like.'

She knew. Barney wouldn't admit that any physical task was harder for him than for a full-grown man. She sighed impatiently. 'All right, I'll have a word with him. It's just that it worries me to see him do it.'

Albert's eyes wavered before her straight, green stare. Miss Ridings was one on her own, he thought. She was fair, he'd admit that, though in the main she was a keen, hard-headed business woman; yet when it came to Mr Jellicoe she was like a hen with one ailing chick. Why couldn't she accept that the man didn't need mollycoddling?

Tizzie saw his eyes evade hers and wondered if he was one of those who talked about her and Barney. She found herself wondering that about everybody, these days. 'Carry on with what you're doing,' she said abruptly. 'I'll have a look downstairs until he's free.'

Down in the dolly shop she prowled between the racks and shelves while Gideon, the young assistant, eyed her warily. Six weeks had passed since Mary's outburst about her and Barney, she thought, during which time she herself hadn't once felt at ease with him. Something had gone from their relationship and she wasn't sure what it was. All she knew was that there was a void in her life because things weren't right between them. When they talked he seemed much as usual, perhaps a shade tense and more serious, but then he'd never exactly won prizes for light-hearted repartee.

Common sense argued that the change couldn't be in Barney because he didn't know what Mary had said; neither did he know what half Saltley was saying, come to that. It must be her own mental turmoil that was putting a blight on their friendship.

It galled her to admit it but she was unsure of herself, uncertain how to handle the situation. She didn't know whether to carry on as before and let everybody think what they liked, or whether to discourage his Friday night visits to Farthing Lane and go without him on her trips to Manchester. It was so against her nature to be undecided that for six weeks it had affected everything she had done or said.

Barney came down the stairs and stopped on the second step from the bottom. 'Miss Tizzie – I didn't see you come in.' There was colour along his jaw line, a sure indication that he was on edge, making her wonder if Albert had said anything about him being up the ladder. 'I thought you'd be at your infirmary meeting.'

'They've delayed it by an hour to accommodate Lady Soar, who has an earlier engagement.' She fiddled with the straps of her leather folder. 'You always know where I should be at any time of day, don't you, Barney?' There was a touch of sadness in the question, but she was unaware of it.

Their faces were on the same level and he looked carefully into her eyes. Then he smiled and shrugged his thick shoulders. 'Oh, it always pays to know where the boss is! Would you care to take a cup of tea with me, Miss Tizzie? Mrs Siddall is up there this afternoon, cooking.'

It was the first time in months that he'd asked her upstairs; he never invited her unless his part-time cook-housekeeper was present. 'Thanks, Barney,' she said, 'that would be lovely.'

He called to Albert and then led her up the stairs to the big square room, once familiar to her but now unquestionably the room of a man. Some of the furniture was what her mother had left behind when she'd moved out all those years ago; other pieces – the two chairs in deep-red leather, the low dining table, the long bookcase between the windows – were Barney's own additions, as were the plain brown linen curtains.

The housekeeper, plump and middle-aged, dipped her knee and beamed when she saw Tizzie. 'Miss Ridings will take tea, Mrs Siddall,' Barney told her and ushered Tizzie to a chair. Tea in her mother's china pot arrived quickly, along with home-made currant cake. Barney asked her to pour, and they sat and talked business, much as they did in Tizzie's house on Friday evenings.

The urge to get back on the old easy terms with him was almost overpowering, but she didn't know how to do it. The plain speech and down-to-earth manner that served her so well in business were of no use in the sphere of her own personal pride and Barney's fragile self-esteem. The matter of him straining his short legs and arms on the ladder and that of there being gossip about them in the town were whirling through her mind and taking on equal importance.

Calm down, she told herself, but in vain. 'Barney, I was concerned to see you up the big ladder when I came in,' she said bluntly. 'I've asked Albert to spare you any menial jobs that could be done just as well by him or Gideon, but he tells me you'll have none of it.'

The dark eyes were cool and guarded. 'There's no job here that's too menial for me, Miss Tizzie. I was in the dolly shop under a trap door in the floor for many a year in your father's time, as I'm sure you recall.'

'Of course I recall it, but things have changed since then. You're the manager now, in charge of a man and a boy.'

'And you don't think I should tackle any job that comes to hand? I thought you believed that a boss shouldn't expect an employee to do anything he wasn't capable of doing himself?'

Oh – he was quoting her own words at her, was he? 'Albert and Gideon are far younger than you,' she said, 'and therefore less likely to have an accident climbing a ladder. It's common sense, Barney – prudence. Surely you see it?'

'I've never fallen off a ladder in me life,' he said quietly.

'There's always a first time,' she retorted. Her temper was rising and she was too on edge to control it.

Then to her amazement he broke his self-imposed ban

on any mention of his stature. 'I look ridiculous up a ladder because of me size – is that what you're saying'?'

She opened her mouth to snap, 'Yes it is!' but her in-built concern for his feelings kept the words back. Habitual honesty, though, wouldn't be silenced. 'It looks such an effort for you to stretch up for things from the racks,' she said awkwardly. 'You pretend it's easy, but I can see it's not. It worries me, Barney.'

He didn't look her in the eye; instead he stared down at his hands, splayed out on his short thighs. He said nothing at all for fully a minute, his head bowed low. In the end he said simply, 'Your concern does you credit, Miss Tizzie, especially as you've got other things on your mind at present.'

She was hard put to pretend she didn't know what he was talking about. 'What do you mean?' she asked weakly.

'Somethin's been on your mind since that tea party at the Hartleys', an' I can make a guess what it is. He's a steady man, you know, is Mr Barnes. He's in a good way of business and well thought of.'

Tizzie stared. 'Mr Barnes?' she repeated blankly. 'Richard Barnes? The builder?'

'Aye. He arrived that day just as I were leavin', an' I could see what was in the wind. Now, I've found out that he's equal partners with his brother. They have a good reputation an' I reckon they're solid.'

'Thanks, but I'm sure my brother-in-law will have made sure he's safe to do business with.'

'Business?' There was no mistaking the surprise in Barney's tone.

Tizzie glared at him. Why was everybody determined to marry her off? Evidently she'd given Barney credit for more insight than he was capable of. More fool her. 'My sister saw Mr Barnes as a prospective husband for me. I didn't agree. Sorry to disappoint you.'

He writhed in embarrassment. 'Miss Tizzie, what must you think of me? I just took it that you were a bit worried whether he's sound, like, as a future – that is – I presumed—'

'Well, don't!' she snapped. 'Don't presume anything. I haven't been worried about that boring pipsqueak, I've been worried about the goss— I've had other things on my mind, all sorts of things, you know how it is—'

He cut through her gabble to the one essential word – a word only half formed, at that. 'Gossip? What gossip? Who about?'

Suddenly she found it was all right to tell him. Why had she thought otherwise? Limp with relief she leaned forward. 'About us,' she said simply. 'You and me, Barney.'

The colour drained from his face. Naturally pale, he now looked ghastly. Ghastly, she saw, but not surprised. 'How dare they?' he asked himself savagely. 'How *dare* people link you with me?'

She had always expected him to be embarrassed or even humiliated if he found out, but angry? Furious? He looked as if he was on the verge of a seizure. 'Miss Mary told you?' he asked at last.

'Yes, and I'm grateful to her for it. She ... uh ... she didn't think that—' oh, how to put it— 'she didn't think that the talk was about anything personal between us. You're angry, Barney, but I can see you're not surprised, so I take it you've heard something as well?'

He pulled himself together. 'I'm sorry to have to tell you this, Miss Tizzie, an' I know I should have taken action long since, but I couldn't – I just couldn't bring myself—'

'Sorry to tell me what? Take action about what? Out with it, Barney!'

He shot a glance at the kitchen, but the door was firmly closed. 'There's been talk for years – remarks made in my hearin' – specially since I moved in here.' He shook his big head from side to side. 'I never thought it would get back to you, though.'

'What sort of talk? That you lie down so I can wipe my feet on you? That you're my tame d— tame servant?'

She'd said it now, except for the term 'dwarf'. The pain of hurting him staggered her: it was very deep, pulling and wrenching in her chest. Tears ran down her cheeks and dropped from her chin to the bodice of her dress, but she didn't think to wipe them away.

He looked at her wet face and his mouth twisted. 'No,' he said reluctantly, 'far worse than that, I'm afraid. Lewd remarks, shouted comments, obscene at times – I couldn't possibly repeat them.' His short legs jerked as he wriggled in the chair. 'But Miss Tizzie, I thought they were aimed at me – just at me – out of jealousy, like. And so I ignored them.'

'Did . . . did the remarks link us – together?'

His big face flushed dark red. 'I'm afraid so.'

The feelings that had swamped her at Mary's that night returned tenfold. Humiliation came first, followed by disbelief that anybody could imagine that she and this man shared any kind of physical closeness. 'But Barney, we're friends, aren't we?' she asked urgently. 'I might pay your wages, but we're friends, true friends?'

'I told you years back that I'm your friend for life. It was true then, it's true now.' He slid off the chair and stood up. 'Miss Tizzie, will you please accept my notice. Albert's not really up to bein' in charge yet, but I reckon you'll have no trouble replacin' me.' He held his hands palm upwards in front of him, as if he were offering her a gift. 'I apologize for not doing it years ago, an' I'll stay till you're fixed up with somebody else.'

She gaped at him and the tears hung on her lashes like diamonds around emeralds. 'You're not leaving me, Barney! How could you think I'd let you?' All at once her course of action shone clear, like a road that has twisted through forests and ravines emerging to a bright flat plain. 'Listen to me, Barney. We're friends. We respect each other. We have nothing to hide. Is that right?'

'Of course it is.' He sounded infinitely tired.

'Then we carry on as usual. We fight it. We'll be circumspect and very correct, but we carry on. Listen, I'm going to tea at Mary's tomorrow because it's Abel's birthday. I want you to come with me. Albert and Gideon can manage on their own for once. We'll arrive together, as friends and business partners. My sister knows how I feel about all this and I'm sure she'll support us. I'll call and speak to her on my way home.'

He looked at her pityingly. 'Do you seriously think I could let you carry on being linked to a dwarf who's nearly old enough to be your father? In that way? And have your name on the lips of the scum of Saltley? Think again, Miss Tizzie.'

'I won't think again!' She grabbed his hands. 'Say you'll do it, Barney. Please say you'll do it – it's the only way. If we split up it's as good as admitting that what they say is true.'

He stared at her, unmoving.

'Look, I know it's easier for me than it is for you because nobody says anything to my face, but I can't manage without you. Please!'

He sighed as if his breath was as heavy as lead. 'Very well. We'll try it.'

She felt almost sick with relief. 'Thank you, Barney, thank you. I'll pick you up in a cab at four, and we'll arrive together. Agreed?'

He nodded. 'Agreed.'

'And we'll carry on as usual? Be friends as always in front of my sister's family and be seen in public as business colleagues?'

'Aye. And now you'd better be off to your meeting. If I'd had time to gather me wits I'd walk you there and shake your hand on the doorstep where everybody could see, but I need a bit longer to get used to the idea.'

Filled with relief, she said, 'We'll do it now instead,' and they shook their hands as if confirming a business arrangement. Then he led her down to the shop door and showed her out, shaking her hand again for the benefit of anybody who was passing.

*

'Goodbye, Papa. 'Bye, Sammy. It's been lovely seeing everybody in the mill.' Sarah gave Joshua and Sam a kiss and a hug, then took the footman's hand and climbed into her splendid carriage.

Her maid, Polly, smiled when Joshua faced her and said, 'Well, Polly, I hear congratulations are in order?'

'Her Ladyship told you, Mr Schofield?' Five months' pregnant, Polly blushed at Mr Schofield mentioning it, then beamed at her own good fortune: in radiant health, married to the strapping second gardener at Alsing and still in close contact with her beloved mistress. 'I'll still see her every day, Mr Schofield, though we're training a new undermaid to replace me.'

Joshua shot her a keen blue glance. A good young woman – he'd known it since he first set eyes on her. Devoted to Sarah, as well – she'd proved it a thousand times over the years, especially in the days of Sarah's marriage to Edward. 'What do you think of the new sickbay, then?' he asked. 'A bit different from the one you and my daughter set up in the old days, eh?'

'It's excellent, Mr Schofield. Me granny says you should give Mr Walton and Mr Boulton a guided tour. She's heard that all they have at the Bluebell is a tin box with bandages in it on one of the landings.'

'Aye, I've heard the same. Tell your granny that Mr Walton's never set foot inside Jericho yet, and I don't think he's likely to start now. Off you go, Polly, it's good to see you.'

'An' you, Mr Schofield ... Mr Sam.' She bobbed her head to them both.

Father and son stood outside the mill gates and watched the carriage drive away, but Joshua's pleasure in his new sickbay evaporated with each turn of the wheels. He pulled at his side whiskers. It would be hard for Sarah to have Polly in the family way only twelve months after the wedding while she and Francis waited in vain ... That degenerate swine Mayfield couldn't – he couldn't have made her barren? It happened – he'd heard it spoken of at the club or in the coffee rooms around the Exchange. Husbands who couldn't keep away from the stews of Manchester passed disease to their innocent wives. The health of both man and wife was ruined, and if they managed to conceive a child it would likely be stillborn or ailing.

'The doctor gave her a clean bill of health before she married Francis,' said Sam in his ear, as if they were in the midst of discussing the matter. 'And even then she insisted on waiting another year, Father. She's extremely well informed on things medical, so I'm sure she'd know if she'd been infected by Edward.'

Relief eased through Joshua. 'Is that how you see it, Sam?' They rarely spoke of such things, considering it to be disloyal to Sarah.

'Yes, that's my view. It's just as likely to be Francis's fault.'

Joshua rocked back and forth on his heels and toes. He'd read something of the sort, that it could be the man who was barren – sterile, they called it. 'What are your grounds for such a view? Francis was never a womaniser, was he?'

'Of course he wasn't – I'm not meaning that. I've heard that now and again a man can't father children because, well, because his seed is weak. Don't forget Francis is an only child himself, so there might be such a weakness on his father's side.'

'Happen so,' agreed Joshua doubtfully, 'but having seen his mother I can't say I've ever been surprised he's an only child. A cold, hard woman, I always thought.'

'Yes, so did I. But cold or not, the aristocracy know their duty when it comes to keeping the line going. It's just an idea I have, Father. I don't think we should take it for granted that it's Sarah's fault.'

'Sam ...' Joshua put out a hand to delay his son from moving away, oblivious to what anybody might think if they saw the Schofields in close discussion outside their own gates. 'Sam, it isn't – you don't think it's because Edward made her ... uh ... made that side of things unbearable to her? She wouldn't speak to you of that, I suppose?'

'Yes,' said Sam gravely, 'she did speak of it. She told me that when Francis proposed he said he was prepared to have a marriage in name only if she couldn't face a full union.'

Joshua decided that his son-in-law was an extraordinary man. 'What did she say to that?' he asked.

'That it was all or nothing – a full marriage or none at all, and to give her another year to make sure she was in good health and able to put Edward behind her once and for all. Try not to worry, Father. I think Sarah's more concerned than Francis about not having a child. He's just thankful he's got her.'

'And so he should be,' agreed Joshua, straightening his shoulders. 'Come on, let's get inside.'

Crossing the yard to the office Sam said: 'I didn't mention it earlier, what with Sarah being here and a lot going on, but the East-Side spinners have put in a complaint about that last consignment – the one the card room queried. Saul Bracewell says the piecers are run off their feet and the men grumbling that their pay will be down.'

'Has any of the yarn got through to the winders?'

'Yes, they're not having much trouble – mainly due to Saul keeping a close eye on the spinning.'

Joshua walked on thoughtfully. 'This is the third shipment to give us a bad time in, what, ten months? Do you know, Sam, in the old days we had a poor consignment less than once a year. In fact we only had one case in all of last year, didn't we? What do you make of it?'

'It could be just coincidence. Sheer bad luck.'

'But you don't think so?'

'I don't know what to think,' admitted Sam. 'We buy according to sample, so either the samples for these three lots haven't been true to shipment, or the man who examined them doesn't know cotton as well as he thinks he does, or there's something funny going on.'

'But Tetley's as straight as a die!'

'He's a good man.' They both knew they were fortunate in their agent.

'He's got the best eye for cotton in Lancashire,' went on Joshua, 'apart from me and Arthur Lawton, of course.'

Sam hid a smile. 'Of course.' His father had a high opinion of the Rochdale mill owner and an equally high one of himself – both well justified, as it happened. 'Have you heard any rumours from the other manufacturers?'

'Such as what?'

'Such as the general standard of American cotton being poor, or somebody else having three bad lots in less than a year?'

'No, but I'll damn soon find out. You know as well as I do, though, that manufacturers who don't buy high quality staple would expect to have trouble now and again.'

'Yes, but we do buy high quality – and pay high for it.'

Joshua pulled at his whiskers. 'I know. Look, clear Tuesday of any appointments up here. We'll both go to Mosley Street and the Exchange and make a few enquiries for ourselves. It isn't as if we have a string of enemies who want to make things awkward for us. Even Eli Walton wouldn't stoop so low as to interfere with our shipments.'

He beckoned to Sam and veered towards the new brick sickbay that linked the West and East Sides. Two nurses were clearing up after the official opening and getting ready for patients. It was a light and airy place with treatment cubicles, a quiet room with a bed, a small dispensary and a comfortable waiting area. Joshua stood in the middle of the floor, feet apart, staring at a plaque on the wall. 'I just wanted a proper look at it,' he said, 'now things have quietened down a bit.'

He read again the words that he and his sons had decided on:

*The Jericho Welfare Centre
Opened on 29 September 1876
by Lady Sarah, Countess of Soar,
who in 1865 first instituted this service
for the workers of Jericho Mills*

Above the plaque was a glass-fronted case holding an enamelled replica of Florence Nightingale's lamp. Joshua looked at it, memories filling his mind. At twenty years of age Sarah had pestered him to set up a sickbay in the mill and to put her in charge. He'd done it, hiring Polly to help and chaperone her. It had been a success, so much so that a grateful patient had secretly carved the lamp on the sickbay door as a sign of the workers' regard. Sam, who possessed a flair similar to his own for the popular gesture, had had it enamelled as a surprise for her. And now, removed from that original door, here it was, still on view to the patients, a permanent tribute to that beautiful, earnest young daughter who was now the Countess of Soar, continuing her interest in medicine from the board of management of Saltley Infirmary.

Joshua cleared his throat and blinked at the little lamp. 'Aye,' he said, swallowing hard, 'that enamelling was a bright idea of yours, Sam. You use your head for something else besides putting your hat on, you don't part.'

'I'm going down to see William Hartley later on,' announced James over tea at Meadowbank House. 'Sam, Charles, do you fancy a stroll?'

Charles looked up from his plate and shook his head. His mother had stayed at home because of a headache, so he had been able to spend all afternoon playing his trumpet upstairs. 'Thank you, Papa, but I think I'll stay in and practise some more.'

'I'll come,' offered Sam. He liked to walk the Saltley streets at dusk, when it was too dark to see the grime and the folk who went hungry but too early for the Saturday night drunkards. Not only that, it wasn't often these days that he managed to be alone with James. 'Do you want to talk to William about putting the beasts to market?' he asked with interest.

'Partly that, and partly about the workhouse enquiry. You recall that I quoted them for supplying beef? They jibbed at the price, so I suspect our quality is simply too good for them. I don't agree with feeding those poor devils in the house on any old muck, and I know you feel the same, Father, so I thought I'd ask William where they could get less expensive meat that's still fit for human consumption.'

Sam eyed his brother. Henpecked he might be, but his heart was still in the right place. 'Would the workhouse buy where you tell them?' he asked dubiously.

'Only if they think I can save them money. I went on a conducted tour of the place with Esther a couple of weeks back, you know. We were taken round the kitchens and saw the food being prepared.'

Sam and his father exchanged a look. Neither of them could imagine Esther strolling among the paupers at Saltley Workhouse. 'You weren't asked to sample a plateful, then?' asked Joshua.

'No. The sight of it was as much as I could stomach, but I did have a word with the master. I said I would be willing to give him favourable terms for good, wholesome meat. First thing next morning he sent up to High Lee for the quote.'

Joshua nodded, knowing that he could safely leave anything to do with the farm and the High Lee estate in James's hands. He had other things on his mind, such as inferior cotton finding its way to his mills. 'Young Hartley's a good man,' he said absently. 'He'll give you straight answers to straight questions, I don't doubt.'

Later, Sam and James followed the lamplighter along Holden Street, seeing each lamp splutter to life against a darkening sky. Sam never pried into his brother's private affairs; he knew that James's marriage was a disaster, and James knew that he knew. Once he had told Sam that he'd been right in trying to warn him against Esther, but apart from that Sam could count on the fingers of one hand the times his brother had spoken of his domestic life. He knew that Charles had been conceived at a time when James was following his advice and asserting himself, but since that reluctant pregnancy he doubted if his brother had ever enjoyed the privileges of a husband. Still, a man could live without such things – he himself was proof of that. He wanted a woman of his own – oh, how he wanted one – but not just any woman. The daughters of the mill-owning families were all married off by now, their mothers weary of trying to catch a Schofield. The others, the endless stream of young women from surrounding towns, were either too stupid, too mercenary or – he had to admit it – too plain to tempt him.

They walked on, Sam so deep in thought he almost forgot that he'd been looking forward to a spell of his brother's company. Years ago he had decided that he would be a fool to search for a wife who was like his mother and his sister; they were gentle, beautiful women, naturally sweet natured and intelligent. He had told himself that he wouldn't find their equal in the whole of England, so he hadn't tried. Once he'd thought he had found somebody: a woman who was almost beautiful, outwardly strong but with what he had imagined to be a soft, vulnerable heart. Softhearted or not, she was as unlike his mother and Sarah as a lioness is unlike a gazelle. Deluded fool that he was, he had thought she was attracted to him. He had certainly been attracted to her – he had been on the point of proposing marriage ... And then, just in time, he had seen the way the land lay. It wasn't the Schofield son she was after, it was the father! Yes, she had set her cap at his father, the most respected man in Saltley, a man so deep in mourning his wife he had never so much as noticed. Even now, ten years later, the bitterness of that discovery could still take Sam by the throat ...

'You're quiet, Sam,' said James at his side, after they'd covered half a mile without exchanging a word.

Sam gave himself a mental shake; so much for enjoying his brother's company. 'Sorry, Jimmy, I was miles away. Reflecting on past mistakes, past misjudgements. You know how it is.'

'Oh, I know how it is, Sam. I have plenty of those to reflect on.'

They both knew what he meant. Sam sighed, both for his brother's empty marriage and for his own unmarried state. 'Nothing in this life is ever certain, is it, Jimmy?'

'Nothing,' agreed James.

'Except that you have a good lad in Charles. Maybe a gifted lad, who should be given the chance to develop his talents.'

James was silent for a minute, then he said, 'I hear what you say, Sam, and I'll give it some thought. Once before I ignored your warnings, but you can rest assured that I shan't make the same mistake regarding my son.'

They passed beneath a streetlamp and exchanged a long, deep look; two Schofield men, alike in their blond hair and vivid eyes but somewhat different in their strength of character.

The rooms above Hartley's butchers were alive with the noise of the birthday party. William had left his assistants to deal with the Saturday night trade for ten minutes and, still in his apron, was watching a rowdy game of blindman's buff. His parents, two aunts, Tizzie and Barney were sitting in a row against one wall, with a bench from the shop barricading them from the game, while the Hartley children and their cousins played in the middle of the room.

Pink cheeked and dimpling, Mary was in charge of the blindfold. Billy, her eldest, was loving every minute but trying to give the impression that it was all too young for him; Elizabeth, red ringlets whirling, was being bossily impatient with the younger ones. Abel was solemnly smug because he had reached the age of six, and young Johnny was running around and getting under everyone's feet.

Tizzie was watching her niece. Everyone said the child was like her, but of late she found she didn't want to hear it. The physical resemblance was clear, but had she, Tizzie, been quite so self-willed as a child? So impatient of younger children? So determined to be the centre of attention? She leaned over and whispered to Barney, 'Was I really like Elizabeth when I was eight?'

He actually chuckled, a sound rarely heard. 'Like her, only more so, Miss Tizzie. If your mother hadn't kept you in hand I shudder to think how you might have turned out.'

She stared at him. His reply was probably the nearest he had ever come to familiarity, yet he hadn't quite over-stepped their self-set boundary. It was just that he was so light hearted all of a sudden. Well aware that he found socialising a strain, she was baffled by his good humour. After the tensions of their confrontation the previous day she would have expected him to be, at the very least, subdued.

But Elizabeth was stamping her feet and defying her mother. 'They're hopeless,' she said, flipping a scornful hand at the younger ones. 'Let's have some grown-ups joining in – somebody with sense. Aunt Tizzie, you play with us – you'll be good. Oh please . . . come on . . .'

'And what about Aunt Jane, Elizabeth?' It was a gentle reminder from Mary, who always wanted harmony: no friction, no favouritism, not even for her dear Tizzie. But the other grown-ups all declined to join in, Barney shaking his head at once, yet watching with a hint of amusement as Tizzie allowed herself to be pulled into the game.

Dodging outstretched young arms and fumbling hands, she was surprised to find that she was enjoying it, perhaps because her presence lent order and extra excitement to the game. Before long a young cousin touched the folds of her dress and yelled, 'Aunt Tizzie!' which led to Mary fastening the blindfold around her sister's eyes. She turned her round three times and then gently pushed her to the middle of the room.

Hands held out in front of her, Tizzie blundered around,

wondering why she was enjoying such a mad, childish exercise. They were all shouting and laughing, so none of them noticed the young errand boy from the shop usher Sam and James Schofield into the room and then whisper to his employer.

Sam, always ready to enjoy a game, laughed aloud from the doorway at what was going on, until he saw who was wearing the blindfold. Tizzie! His smile disappeared like sun behind cloud. Who would have thought to find her playing with children?

James was apologetic at their intrusion, so William edged sideways to put him at ease. Mary, her lace cap askew, had scooped Johnny up out of harm's way and was calling encouragement to Tizzie, who was whirling recklessly round the room, her hair shedding its pins, her skirts dipping and swirling. James stared at the sisters, his lips clamped tightly together. Sam thought he was comparing the scene with his own home life.

Then Tizzie caught her foot against the leg of a chair just as the tips of her fingers touched Sam's sleeve. A child bumped into her, and she thudded against Sam's chest. His arms went out to steady her and everyone fell silent, the children abashed that the two Mr Schofields were suddenly part of their game.

Tizzie's searching hands felt a man's shoulders, then a broad chest wearing an outdoor coat. This wasn't her brother-in-law in his butcher's apron, nor was it Grandpa Hartley in waistcoat and shirtsleeves. The arms were still around her, but she sensed tension in them and then they released their hold. She caught the smell of him – very clean, a soap and water smell, overlaid by evening damp on a worsted coat and maybe a faint whiff of cotton, a smell familiar to everyone in Saltley. But underneath it all was a warm, wholesome male smell that she remembered very well indeed.

'Oh, poor Tizz!' gasped Mary. 'You'll never guess who this is! Look – we've got visitors!' She whipped off the blindfold, anxious to spare them embarrassment yet so caught up in the game she was still laughing. Tizzie's eyes met Sam's for perhaps twenty seconds, while the blood drained from her face and left two spots of colour high on her cheeks, like daubs from a child's paintbox.

'What a good thing you two know each other,' said Mary in relief. 'It might have been awkward for you both, Mr Schofield, if you'd been strangers.'

Sam turned to her, ignoring the woman he had just released from his arms. 'Your sister is no stranger to the Schofields, Mrs Hartley. In any case, we were at fault for barging into your party. Is it somebody's birthday?'

Telling herself she must be mistaken in thinking that he was deliberately snubbing Tizzie, Mary beckoned Abel to come forward, and to everyone's surprise the boy bowed from the waist. Sam laughed and felt in his pocket. 'A happy birthday, young fella!' He handed over a florin, and Abel beamed and thanked him.

Then William spoke up. 'Happen we'd do better away from all this noise if you want a word,' he suggested and led the way to the door. Sam smiled at Mary and waved to the children, then followed William. James, silent and oddly sombre, bent his head in polite farewell and joined Sam and William at the top of the stairs.

Desperate to wipe out the memory of the last few minutes, Tizzie joined in the game with more energy than before. She didn't notice that Barney's dark eyes were observing her intently; nor did she see the expression that for an instant lay unguarded on his face. It was as if something that had puzzled him for a long, long time had at last been made clear.

CHAPTER FIVE

Memories

'What do you think of it, then?' It was Joshua's habitual question every time they studied progress on Manchester's new town hall. Sam smiled. His father insisted on walking to Mosley Street by way of the vast building site every time they came to Manchester. And when they arrived he always asked the same question, phrased in exactly the same words. This habit of repeating the same remark at widely spaced intervals was one of his few signs of ageing – that, and his use of the little book for jotting down reminders to himself.

'It's impressive,' Sam acknowledged, eyeing the structure.

'I defy anybody to show me better buildings than the Royal Exchange and this place,' declared Joshua, waving his stick. 'I'm looking forward to opening day so we can see if the inside's as good as the outside.' He watched as workmen toiled over the laying of steps at the main entrance. 'Clothier to the world, they call Manchester,' he said with satisfaction, 'and a town hall like this goes to prove it.'

'Waterhouse is a fine architect,' agreed Sam, then shot a quick look at his father. Sarah's first husband had been an architect; capable in his profession, an unprincipled lecher in his private life.

Joshua's only response was to say calmly, 'Shall we be off, then?' They headed up Princess Street side by side, coat tails flapping in the chilly breeze, and a scattering of leaves swirling past their feet. 'We needn't have got all steamed up about those three consignments, need we?' Joshua said ruefully. 'It *was* just bad luck, like you said.'

'It must have been, though I still think it's a good move to insist on opening every bale before we take delivery.'

'Try telling that to Tetley,' laughed his father. 'He's still smarting over what he calls our "investigations" at the Exchange six or seven weeks back – he's always getting a dig in about it. As for examining bales down at the docks, when I told him we planned to do that I thought he'd go down with a seizure.'

Sam shrugged. 'If he can't stand having his expertise questioned now and again he shouldn't be an agent. He's good, but I sometimes wish we could keep that side of things just among ourselves. You know, in the family.' At once he wished the words unsaid. His brother Ralph had worked at Mosley Street. He had been good at the job, brilliant even, but he had lined his own pockets at the expense of the firm's good name.

His father made no reply, but it seemed to Sam that the two grooves that scored his face from nose to jaw were suddenly so deep they looked black against his natural fresh colouring. 'Sorry, Father,' he muttered. 'Slip of the tongue. Didn't mean to open old wounds.'

Joshua's step slowed. 'Open old wounds?' he repeated quietly. 'What makes you think they're healed?'

Sam blinked. 'I don't think any such thing, but you must admit you never mention Ralph.'

Joshua stared emptily ahead. 'I disowned him, Sam. You don't disown your eighteen-year-old son and then keep him at the forefront of your mind by indulging in chitchat about him at every turn. If it comes to that, you and James haven't exactly filled your conversations with his name.'

Sam warned himself to tread warily. He could speak to

his father on any subject under the sun and know that his
views would be treated with respect; in fact, he had often
heard him say, 'Sam's a chip off the old block, you know.
We think alike, we do that.' It was true, but his own
uncanny gift for reading people's thoughts – Sarah's
especially but, sometimes with amazing accuracy, his
father's too – was rendered null and void when it came to
his father's thoughts about Ralph. Maybe that was because
Sam rejected any mental link with a murderer – even if the
link was channelled through a third party. He often
wondered if his own moral code formed a barrier against
memories of his brother, but then they'd never been close;
nobody had been close to Ralph, not even their mother. He
had gone his own way: clever, self-obsessed, secretive and
– it seemed melodramatic even to think it, but it was the
only word that fitted – evil. That was what Ralph had been
– a misfit changeling in their lovely, close-knit family.

Sam regretted bringing him to their minds. And yet just
now his father had hinted that he often thought of him.
Sam's instinct was that to think of Ralph occasionally was
healthier than pretending he'd never existed. But it wasn't
for him to decide what was healthy for his father, a man
who had the keenest mind and strongest will of anybody he
knew. He was more than capable of sorting out how to
handle memories of the son he'd had transported to the
other side of the world.

'Put him out of your mind,' instructed Joshua now.
'He's in the past, is Master Ralph. Let him stay there.' He
walked on in silence. At last he said, 'Look, we both know
why we employ an agent; it's because we haven't a single
employee with the experience to handle the markets, the
shippers, the Liverpool merchants and the Manchester
Exchange. Tetley employs seven men, so an agent with
work enough to keep that lot going can't be short of clients,
nor be an amateur when it comes to judging cotton. And
another thing, Arthur Lawton speaks well of him. Oh, I
don't think we need worry. I'll be surprised if Bill Tetley
isn't his pleasant old self when we see him later today.'

With relief Sam watched the spring return to his father's step. What a man. What a father. Long ago he had dealt with Ralph as though he'd spent months in the planning of his downfall rather than the three anguished days following his wife's death. And he'd accomplished it without besmirching the family name. Love and admiration flooded Sam's heart, and he told himself that being Joshua Schofield's son was like being anchored to a rock. His own working life was so full, so challenging, that he never yearned to branch out on his own, never fretted for more responsibility, because his father treated him as an equal in every aspect of the business. He was happy at his work, no doubt of it. As for his private life ... well, happen that was different.

The Schofield rooms were similar to all the others on Mosley Street except for the emblem of the trumpet and the rose above the main entrance. A keen observer might have noticed that the company name was engraved rather than painted on the windows and that the doors were of solid oak, but to a casual passer-by the place looked merely dignified and well cared for.

Most of the manufacturers had offices on their ground floors, along with salesrooms where they could dazzle customers with the vast selection in their pattern books. Upper floors were sometimes used as living quarters for clerical staff but more often were simply warehouses for both raw cotton and the finished cloth. The narrow street that ran behind was a jumble of loading bays and stables, echoing endlessly with the rattle of hoists.

Sam had often thought it odd that his father, who had a touch of the show man about him, should be happy with such restrained business rooms. Back in the summer he had suggested modernising the place, and his father had promised to think about it. Sam had been satisfied with that. If Joshua Schofield thought about something, he made a thorough job of it and always came up with an opinion, though not always the one that people expected.

Sure enough, after a week or so he had said, 'Answer me this, Sam. If you were about to spend money – big money – on, say, fine cotton zephyr suitable for dyeing, would you go to a place that looked solid and long established or one with elaborate brickwork and a fancy new nameplate?'

'I'd choose one with experience, I suppose,' Sam had admitted, 'or better still, one I'd done business with before and been satisfied with. Or happen a firm that had been well recommended.'

'Exactly. So I've had Nathaniel Lee sorting through a list of folk who've bought from us in the last six months – you know how he likes doing his big pages of analysis. It seems that only one and a half per cent of customers were new to Schofields. And their total spending was less than half a per cent of our invoicing for that period. The rest of 'em were either our regulars or those who buy fine weave from us when they need it and all their coarser stuff elsewhere.

'Now I admit we can't afford to ignore the possibility of a new customer walking in off the street, but I can't see that updating the place will do much for us. Everywhere you look in Manchester these days there's somebody tearing down good buildings to put them up again in a different style. I'd rather spend the money on new machinery. Folk will judge us by what we produce at Jericho rather than what sort of fancy tiling we have outside our rooms or whether they like the carpets when they come through the doors.'

'Point taken,' Sam had agreed. 'I'll say no more.'

'You've set me thinking, though. When you're in a place two or three times a week it's easy to get so accustomed to it you don't really *see* it. I think it's time we went through the ground floor with a fine-toothed comb. And took a look at the staff, as well. Nathaniel's satisfactory as head clerk. Granted, he isn't John Wagstaff and he doesn't even approach your uncle Charlie, but he's not bad on cotton, he's conscientious and he's loyal. The two young ones will improve, I reckon, but I have to admit I'm a bit dubious about the orders.'

'You think we need another man on that? Just for the selling?'

'Aye, I do. Nathaniel's happier doing the books than showing samples, James only gets down once a fortnight and you're only there on Tuesdays with me and maybe Thursday afternoons. You'll recall that once or twice lately we've walked in and found customers cooling their heels, waiting to order. Now that's not service, is it?'

'No, of course it's not. But who do you suggest?' They both knew that there was a shortage of experienced salesmen in Manchester.

'Not a youngster. The customers like to have you and James attending to them, but I doubt if they'd want to do business with a youngster unless he was one of the family. I've been wondering whether we could bring somebody in from Jericho.'

'One of the floor managers? No, it would have to be a cut-looker, wouldn't it?' A cut-looker, whose proper title was inspector of cloth, had the keenest eye and widest knowledge of the finished product of anyone in Jericho, apart from the master and his son . . .

Joshua had nodded. 'What do you reckon to asking Will Grimshaw?'

Sam had considered the name. 'He's bright, is Will. Old enough to inspire confidence but not too old to adapt to a new job. Why not give him a trial?'

Within a week Grimshaw had been working at Mosley Street, wearing an unfamiliar business suit as if to the manner born and getting on well with the customers. Sam had been delighted with the way he settled in, Joshua satisfied but not particularly surprised. He rarely made a mistake in suiting a man to a job.

Now, weeks later, Joshua entered the rooms with his customary cheerful greeting. At other times they would descend unannounced, separately or together, but on Tuesday mornings every file and every book would be laid out ready for inspection: shipping manifests and bills of lading, the sales and purchase ledgers and Joshua's favourite tome, the order book.

Broad and bald headed, Nathaniel Lee was ready and waiting for them, but Sam saw at once that he was nervous. Joshua exchanged a look with his son and marched through to the inner office, removing his coat as he went. 'Everything all right, Nathaniel?' he asked keenly.

The man stretched his neck as if his collar was too tight. Honest brown eyes in a shiny red face swivelled from side to side. 'There's been a bit of trouble, Mr Schofield,' he said awkwardly. 'The order book's gone missing. Will says he brought it in here last thing, the same as always. We didn't miss it until we got the first post from London – Barrington's want a double up of their last order. He went to check on it and couldn't find the book.'

Joshua stared at him and gave a disbelieving snort. 'Get away! One of the youngsters'll have locked it in the safe by mistake or something of the kind.'

'No, Mr Schofield. We – we've searched the place, knowing it was Tuesday, like.'

Joshua was pulling at his whiskers. 'You'll be able to check Barrington's last order from the copy invoice, won't you?'

'Yes, of course we will. That's all in hand. It's just that the order book is our primary record, almost like our right arm. It's – well, it's vital.'

'I do know that,' Joshua agreed drily. 'Now, in confidence, Nathaniel. How's Will doing? Do you reckon he's up to the job?'

'I do, Mr Schofield. He's good. He's made a difference here. He's right upset about this. We all are.'

'I'll have a word with him. In the meantime, look again in the same places, but this time with Mr Sam. Sam – see to it.'

But Sam had other ideas. 'Has anybody checked the doors and windows? Could it have been stolen?'

They all stared at him. One of the young clerks gave a nervous giggle and abruptly silenced himself. Joshua eyed

his son keenly. 'We do have a night watchman,' he
reminded him. 'Still, go and examine all windows and
doors and *then* search the place. It's a big, heavy ledger –
it can't be a mile away.' With a nod to them all he walked
off to the sample room to see Will Grimshaw.

At five o'clock Joshua and Sam sat side by side on the Saltley
train as it puffed out of Victoria. They had been to the
Exchange, but for once neither of them had enjoyed the
lively business activity there. As for the missing order book,
they had left Nathaniel and his assistants writing up a
makeshift copy. Orders not yet fulfilled were of course on
record at Jericho so there was no actual catastrophe, but
unease sat with them in the compartment, real as a fellow
passenger.

Joshua stood his stick upright between his knees and
clasped both hands round the silver knob. 'Listen,' he said
heavily. 'We both know that spying isn't new among cotton
manufacturers, nor in other trades, so they tell me. I'm
naming nobody at this stage, but do you think that one of
our competitors could have paid somebody to hide inside
the premises during one of our busy spells and then walk
out with it later? That would leave no sign of a break-
in.'

'No, the staff would surely have heard or seen a stranger
in the place; so would the night watchman if it was outside
working hours. Let's think. Maybe we'll come up with
something.' He simply could not remind his father of a
break-in at Mosley Street eleven years before. A contrived
break-in that had been a smoke screen for murder. Charlie
Barnes had been murdered – oh, not according to the
coroner, he'd said accidental death, but Uncle Charlie had
been lured down from his rooms on the top floor in the
early hours and pushed out of the hoist; maybe even
finished off as he lay in the street at the back. With an effort
Sam dismissed such memories. 'Are you sure you don't
want to bring the police in?' he asked.

'What? Without a door or window that's been tampered

with? They'd be less use than they were when your uncle Charlie died.'

Sam jerked his head in agreement. He needn't have worried about not reminding him; their minds were on the same track. He looked up, but his father was staring absently out of the window at a ploughman following his horse across a field on the outskirts of Clayton. Sam thought of his uncle Charlie, the tall, ungainly man who had been so close to his father – so close to all of them, except of course Ralph. It was no exaggeration to say they were still feeling his loss. He'd been an expert on the buying of cotton and the selling of cloth and yarn, he'd been respected on the Exchange and the docks; a straight man, honest as the day ... Aye, he was still missed.

Something had happened at home. Everything was different. Rosie couldn't have told anybody what was wrong, not even Charles, because whatever it might be was hidden away behind smiley faces and polite talk. She watched her mam and dad all the time, because even when there were no messages on their faces she could sometimes catch a sudden look from one of them or a tightening of her mam's soft little mouth.

They were too polite, she told herself impatiently. Why didn't they have sharp words like Hannah Bennett's mam and dad, who bellowed at each other no matter who was in the room, then five minutes later roared with laughter and gave each other smacking kisses? Her own mam didn't laugh much these days, neither did her dad; he didn't tell them funny tales about what had happened at work. He was as gentle and kind as ever with her, but he didn't call her Miss Rosie Raike and sweep his hat off and bow low like he used to.

He was gentle with her mam as well, but very serious. Now and again, though, he snapped at her as if he couldn't help it, which would put questions on her mam's face, clear as clear: Who? When? Where?

It had been going on for weeks, and she'd noticed that

even his woodwork brought him no ease. He had always carved and chiselled in front of the fire in winter, with an old sheet over the rug to catch the wood shavings. In summer he would sit by the open back door with his tools laid out on top of the kitchen drawers, but now he marched away to his bench in the outhouse and shut the door behind him, using lamps and candles galore as the evenings became too dark to see unaided.

'It's a difficult piece I'm working on, Rosie,' he said stiffly when she asked him why he shut himself away. 'I have to concentrate very hard, so I need to be quiet.'

'If you let me watch I won't say a word,' she assured him, knowing quite well how difficult that would be, but he just looked away and shook his head.

'It's a sort of secret, liddle love.' He said it in a funny way, as if there wasn't enough room in his mouth to let the words out. 'It's, uh, it's a – a confidential undertaking for – for a customer.'

After that, whenever the latch clicked as he closed the outhouse door behind him, she would say to her mother, 'It's his confidential undertakin' again, Mam. It must be really important, mustn't it?'

The sixth or seventh time Martha heard this same remark, she looked up from her sewing and snapped, 'Aye, more important than sittin' with you an' me. Don't keep *sayin'* that, Rosie!'

Remorse stabbed Martha as her daughter's bottom lip shot out in rebellion. It's not the child's fault, she told herself. Rosie never missed a thing, so she must know that all wasn't well between her and Matthew. 'I'm sorry to be so sharp, love,' she said wearily, 'but your dad's got a lot on his mind, an' so have I.'

Rosie observed her mother intently. 'Do you know what it is, then?'

'Know what what is?'

'What he's carvin'. The confidential undertakin'.'

Martha stared at the earnest, rosy-cheeked face and only just prevented her jaw from dropping. She felt as if her whole being had turned into one huge question. Could she have been wrong all these weeks, imagining that he had taken up with another woman? She'd always dreaded it – half expected it, even – so perhaps she'd convinced herself it was happening when it wasn't. In fact she'd often ridiculed herself for thinking any such thing. How could he have another woman when he never went out without either her or Rosie except to go to his work or for a walk in the hills every second or third Sunday afternoon? He could hardly carry on with another woman if he only had a couple of hours to himself every two or three weeks.

But what about the marriage bed? Their lovemaking used to be the joy of her life – the mainstay of their marriage, she sometimes thought. Oh, they had made love in the last few months – five or six times at the most. And always he'd been swift and forceful, as if he was driven to it, with not a smite of tenderness and none of the sensual leading up to it that had always delighted her.

At first she'd thought he was poorly. Then she wondered if he was in low spirits because she'd never fallen for another child, been disappointed in her. She'd always felt guilty about not giving him another son to love as he'd loved little Luke, but it was simply a decision of nature. Since Rosie there'd never been the slightest sign of another baby, no matter how often they came together ... In any case, she was thirty-seven now, so there was less likelihood than ever that she would manage it.

She stared down at the tiny stitches on Rosie's new petticoat, her mind racing. The child's question just now had suggested explanations for his behaviour other than carrying on with somebody else. Once before he had saved up his woodwork earnings and bought her a new dress as a surprise. When she asked him how he had judged such a perfect fit he had laughed and said he was a good guesser.

Happen he was working on a special carving now with the idea of saving the fee for another surprise. Happen it was more important work than the newel post for Mr Schofield's staircase, more complicated than the overmantle that Lord Soar ordered for his small dining room. She was sick with worry, but her cheeks flushed with pride as she recalled how Lady Sarah had sent her carriage for the three of them to go to Alsing and view the carving when it was in place.

"Fruits of the Vine", Matthew had called it: grapes and leaves and branches all intertwined, because of course they drank wine up at Alsing. His Lordship had said the work was worthy of Grinling Gibbons, which pleased Matthew so much he was lost for words. Lady Sarah had given them afternoon tea on a platform that they called a terrace, overlooking the vast, beautiful fields that were the grounds of the house. A funny tea it had been – tiny sandwiches not much bigger than postage stamps and delicious little cakes in fancy papers.

Then before they had left Lady Sarah had given Rosie a little silk purse with five newly minted shillings in it. Rosie had done them credit by saying thank you like a grown-up and dropping a perfect curtsey. On the way home Matthew had told them about the famous woodcarver Grinling Gibbons, and Martha had understood that Lord Soar had paid him a great compliment. Oh, it had been a lovely afternoon ... back in the summer, of course, before everything had gone wrong.

'Time for bed, Rosie,' she said now.

'Mam, it's Saturday. Can't I have a bit longer?'

'Five minutes more an' that's final.' It wouldn't have hurt to keep her up just for her company, Martha thought, but of late she had found herself resenting the constant regard of those watchful brown eyes. It was almost as if Rosie was the adult and she the child. What with the worry of Matthew and with Rosie watching her like a hawk, she was starting to feel worn out.

Five minutes later Rosie went to wash her hands and face ready for bed, then tapped at the door of the outhouse. 'Dad, I'm goin' to bed. Can I have me kiss?'

Matthew came out and gave her a kiss and a squeeze, which was enough to send her upstairs happy. 'Nearly finished, Martha,' he muttered, returning to his lamp-lit bench. It was almost ten o'clock before he emerged, carrying the lamp and wafting the smell of blown-out candles into the room.

As always, Martha made him a cup of tea and cut him a slab of cake, putting them at his side on the scrubbed table. She looked at him and caught her breath. He was different . . . still cut off from her, still apart, but there was an ease about him that she hadn't seen in months. The rigid look had gone from the sides of his mouth; his work-hardened hands were flopped loosely over the arms of his chair; he was half lying on the seat with his legs stuck out on the hearth rug.

All at once she knew beyond doubt that he *had* been working on something special. What was more, every line of her body told her that he'd finished it. He made no mention of any such thing and neither did she, but in the depths of her heart she said a prayer of thanks, adding an impassioned plea that he might revert to the man she had loved since that morning long ago when the wind had blown her off her feet as she walked to work. She had opened her eyes to find him bending over her, all worried . . . a lean, sun-tanned young man in a wide-brimmed black hat.

She knew she would die if she lost him.

Eleanor Boulton was in good spirits. Eyes glinting with satisfaction, vast bosom heaving with suppressed laughter, she occupied her customary seat at the fortnightly meeting of the management board of Saltley Infirmary.

It was going well, the members in full accord. Lady Sarah was responsible for that, of course, with her ability to create a pleasant atmosphere. Sickly sweet she might be, thought Mrs Boulton, ridiculously informal for a woman in her position, but there was no denying she could put everyone at their ease just by entering the room. And why? Because she was a commoner, married into the aristocracy rather than born with blue blood in her veins.

In spite of such irritations, Mrs Boulton could hardly stop smiling. She and Bessie Walton, wives of the two top manufacturers in Saltley, had – as was only right and proper – got their way in an argument about where the next fund-raising event would be held. Lady Sarah had backed them and what was more had congratulated Eleanor on her work at the recent autumn bazaar in the town hall.

It was all very gratifying, but what pleased Eleanor even more was that her knees were less painful than for weeks past, no doubt due to the fine dry weather, and – she concealed another deep chuckle – Tizzie Ridings had made a mistake! The joy, the absolute bliss of pointing it out to her! Not a big mistake, admittedly, but she had got a date wrong in her minutes of the last meeting.

Unfortunately Lady Sarah had made light of it instead of reprimanding her, but that was only because Tizzie had scraped up a friendship with her. Well, Lady Sarah might have brushed it aside, but it was plain to see that Tizzie was furious with herself. Serve her right, the conceited little madam. She acted as if she owned half Saltley – and in fact rumour had it that she did own more than anybody imagined – but this afternoon they'd all been given proof that she could make a mistake like anybody else.

One of these days she would come a cropper. Either she would make an absolute botch-up of arrangements for some big fund-raising do, or she would overreach herself in the property market and go bankrupt, or – there was no harm in hoping – she would be revealed without question as a woman who kept a dwarf as an adult catamite.

For years Eleanor had listened to talk about Tizzie Ridings and her dwarf. Under cover of being impartial she had even encouraged such talk, because after all she owed Tizzie nothing whatsoever – quite the reverse, in fact. Secretly, though, she had doubted whether a woman with Tizzie's looks and business ability, who was said to have suitors practically slavering over her, could possibly be in the throes of unnatural relations with the dwarf.

Then Bessie, in one of her rare clear-headed spells, had

pointed out that Jellicoe might not be equipped like a real man and so would be unable to father a child. If that were the case, said Bessie, it stood to reason that his employer might see him as a safe partner. Still Eleanor had been dubious. Surely the pawnbroker had too high an opinion of herself to consort with such a disgusting oddity?

Soon after that, she and Ezra had been round at the Waltons for the evening; Eli had been giving the port what for, and it had loosened his tongue. Talk turned to Tizzie Ridings, which wasn't surprising as Eli detested her; he never missed an opportunity to drop acid in people's ears about her. All at once, to Bessie's confusion and dismay, he changed the subject and began to speak of the houses of ill repute in Manchester, using tones of disgust for a subject on which he seemed to be remarkably well informed. 'Not in front of the ladies,' Ezra had protested weakly, but Eli was enjoying himself too much to stop.

Eleanor hadn't joined in trying to silence him. There was a certain fascination in the facts he related, and she saw it as her duty to be informed about such things. She and Ezra were strictly proper in their relations, of course; they'd followed a once-a-week routine all their married life until at the age of fifty he declared himself past it.

Seeing her interest, Eli's little eyes had narrowed intently. 'Oh aye,' he said, with a sad, worldly-wise shake of the head, 'they deal with all sorts in Manchester. In my terms of office as mayor of Saltley I sat on committees where I heard things that staggered me. Like I said, there's always men who'll use young children, but I know for a fact that there's houses in the city where they cater for folk with, shall we say, unnatural desires. They have animals up in the bedrooms and—'

'Eli, steady on,' Ezra groaned.

'But their main trade is in freaks,' went on the master of Bluebell Mill, undeterred. 'Cripples, men and women born deformed, or who've lost a limb. Hunchbacks, dwarfs ...'

Bessie, who veered between vagueness and normality, did her utmost to silence him until she saw his purpose.

'Ee, do you mean to say folk lay out money to go with cripples and suchlike, Eli?'

'Aye. No accounting for taste, is there? I've heard it said that anybody who has problems in that direction themselves feels easier consorting with somebody who's far from perfect ...'

But Eleanor Boulton had latched on to the most telling word of the whole recital. 'Did you say men and women born deformed, or dwarfs? *Men? Does* that mean women can have unnatural preferences?'

Eli beamed in approval. 'That's exactly what it means, Eleanor. Does it remind you of anybody we know?'

This was what she'd been waiting for! Eleanor leaned forward intently. A word here, a delicate, half-embarrassed explanation there and Miss Tizzie Ridings' reputation was in ruins – as it would have been years ago if she, out of the goodness of her heart, hadn't warned her to watch her step. The carriage ride home with Ezra passed in a flash, she had so much to think about.

Now Eleanor looked at Tizzie's bright head bending over her notes. She saw her glance up at Lady Sarah and the two of them exchange a quiet little smile. That smile and the closeness it revealed set the blood thudding in her temples: She let out a long heavy breath, divesting herself of all the suppressed chuckles and good humour. Tizzie Ridings must be brought down a peg. Eli Walton was taking too long about it, so she would give him a helping hand.

Later, with business finished and the tea cups cleared away, the meeting broke up. Lady Sarah sailed out to her beautiful carriage and the ride back to Alsing, while Tizzie, declining all offers of transport home, packed up her papers and put on a heavy velvet coat. She gave Mrs Boulton a straight green stare and wondered why the older woman was eyeing her so oddly.

'Are you quite well, Tizzie?' Eleanor asked her.

'Yes, thank you, Mrs Boulton.' Brief but polite. They each knew how the land lay between them. There was a

familiar glitter in Eleanor's steel-grey eyes; Tizzie had
seen it before, many times – the glitter of raw malice. She
buttoned her coat.

'And what about your Mr Jellicoe? How is he?'

Tizzie dealt in fact and certainty rather than instinct or
intuition. The ill feeling that stared her in the face now was
fact. The suspicion that this woman was one of those who
spread tales about her and Barney became, all at once,
certainty. She managed an amused smile. 'He isn't my Mr
Jellicoe, Mrs Boulton, merely my employee. I might pay
his wages but his life is entirely his own.'

'But you would say that, Tizzie. I quite understand; in
fact, I sympathise.'

Tizzie forced herself not to frown in puzzlement. What
was the venomous old bag getting at? Thank goodness the
semicomatose Bessie wasn't at her side, nodding her head
like a clockwork dog. At the other end of the table the
mayor was watching them both with interest, but Tizzie
stood her ground. Someone she respected had once told her
that she was a fighter. Very well, she would fight. 'I don't
follow you, Mrs Boulton. What exactly do you mean?'

'I'm told that lots of people have urges they can't
contain,' declared the other silkily. 'Abnormal urges. It's
very sad, but in my opinion they're more to be pitied than
blamed.'

Tizzie felt as if the floor had tilted to a dangerous angle,
causing her to press the table with the tips of her fingers to
maintain her balance. Face her out, she told herself;
challenge her. 'Urges?' she repeated. 'What urges?'

'Of the flesh,' replied Mrs Boulton weightily. 'I gave
you warning about that many years ago, as I'm sure you
recall.'

'Oh yes, I recall. And I took note of the warning, as I'm
sure *you* recall. I was young and impressionable in those
days.'

'And of course in that particular case a proper man was
involved, wasn't he? A whole, normal man.'

Tizzie's eyes took on the green of a submerged iceberg,

though beneath the icy calm she was floundering. This repellent mountain of flesh was hinting at – what? That she was involved with Barney, not in spite of his handicap but *because* of it? There was depravity in the idea. She could see it in the other woman's expression, the way she moistened her lips.

Nausea tightened Tizzie's throat but she managed to speak. 'There's a saying that beauty is in the eye of the beholder, Mrs Boulton, but I believe it to be equally true that sin is already in the mind of those who most denounce it. I'm not sure what you're getting at, but I warn you now that if you slander me I'll sue you and see you in court. And I'll win!'

'Ooh, quite the little tigress,' mocked the other. 'Don't be stupid, Tizzie. You must know that such a case would ruin you for life. You'd be hounded out of Saltley as a perverted woman, and your dwarf would be sent after you. Your sister would go down under the shame and your parents would turn in their graves.'

'Let me worry about that,' said Tizzie between her teeth. 'Here's the truth, if you can recognise such a thing. Barney Jellicoe is a good and faithful friend. I respect him, he respects me. He has an excellent brain and he uses it. I'm considering making him my business partner.'

The other woman's eyes widened and Tizzie saw that she was shaken. Considering it? Until this moment such a course had only touched the fringes of her mind, but now she was committed to it and she didn't care. It was something she could give him to make up for all this. She would insist on it. She picked up her papers and called a farewell to the others, then without so much as a glance at Mrs Boulton she walked from the room.

It wasn't far to Mary's but by the time she arrived she was breathless from hurrying. Ignoring William and his assistants in the shop, she pushed past two men erecting scaffolding and ran up the stairs.

'Tizz! How lovely!' Mary was slicing bread for the children's tea, and the young mother's help was laying the table.

Tizzie flopped down unasked in the big kitchen chair. She could hear Elizabeth shouting in the next room while somebody, probably Abel, played simple scales on the piano with heavy-handed accuracy. She eyed Mary's apron and the pile of bread and butter with distaste. Did she ever do anything that was unconnected with the running of her home and the feeding of her family? 'I just called for a talk,' she said shortly. 'When you can spare the time, of course.'

Mary shot her a look, then turned to her young helper. 'Bread and jam and sliced apples,' she said. 'A piece of cheese each and milk as usual. Then they can all have a fairy cake. Will you see to it, Annie? Come on, Tizzie, we'll have a quiet five minutes upstairs.'

Tizzie followed her and refrained from groaning. It would have been easier to talk against the noise of the children than go into a huddle within sight of that big double bed ... but it was too late, Mary was ushering her into the bedroom. She put a light to the fire and offered her sister the upholstered nursing chair that had been her gift to them when Billy was born. Then Mary seated herself on the fender stool, skirts billowing up around her chest. 'I'm listening,' she said quietly.

Because she was listening and because there wasn't another living soul she could possibly speak to about it, Tizzie told her what Mrs Boulton had said and what she had replied.

Mary listened without interruption, eyes wide with disbelief. 'Oh, that horrible old woman! But Tizz, why must you always *confront* people?'

'What do you want me to do? Have a fit of the vapours?'

Mary rolled her eyes. 'No, that's not your way, is it?'

Tizzie leaned forward. She must know. 'Mary, she was hinting at something peculiar. Do you know what she was getting at exactly?'

'Me? No, of course not!'

Tizzie glared at her. A retarded two-year-old would

have seen she was lying. 'Listen to me! There's only you and Barney who will speak to me frankly. I can't very well ask him, so I'm asking you. Do people say that I have some kind of peculiar relationship with him? *Mary! Tell me!*'

'Nobody has even hinted at such a thing to me, but William has often heard talk in the town. Just lately it's, well, it's taken on a new slant.'

Tizzie was on her feet, twisting her lips as if she was about to spit. 'What – do – they – say?' she asked, spacing her words to give them more weight.

Mary burst into tears and wailed, 'I can't tell you, Tizz – don't ask me!'

Tizzie bent and grabbed her by the upper arms, shaking Mary until her lace cap fell into the hearth. At that Mary jumped up from the stool and delivered a stinging slap to Tizzie's right cheek. Tizzie gaped at her in amazement, but the blow brought a glimmer of reason to the black chaos that filled her mind. 'I'm sorry, Mary,' she said limply. 'I'm – I'm a bit worked up.'

'So I see,' retorted Mary tartly. 'Well, I don't want you tackling William about it and upsetting him. He's up to his eyes with the alterations.' She stared resentfully at Tizzie, her brown eyes still full of tears. 'As you're so very curious, here it is. They've been saying that you have relations with Barney because you aren't a normal woman and you don't like proper men – that's why you've never married. They say that – that you use him because he could never father a child. He's – he's safe, sort of. And—'

'And what?' asked Tizzie quietly. There was more?

'William blurted this out to me – he'd almost come to blows with a man in the market . . .'

'Well?'

'People are saying . . . they're saying that you must be one of those who'd rather have cripples and hunchbacks and – and dwarfs than somebody who's normal. That's all, Tizzie: I'm very sorry.'

'That's all, is it?' said Tizzie bitterly. 'Oh dear, what a pity; I expected more.' She sat down and stared blankly at the wall behind Mary's shoulder. 'Well,' she said defiantly, 'I've told Mrs Boulton that I'm going to make Barney my business partner.'

Mary was still sniffling. 'And is that true?'

'Yes. They can go to hell. They can go to purgatory. And stay there.'

'Oh, Tizz, you're so strong!' Mary looked at the kindling in the grate and added coal very precisely, as if under orders not to put a piece wrong. Her mind was on Barney. 'Will it work, him being your partner?'

'Yes. He's that now, in everything but name. I've thought of it once or twice in the past but never pursued it because I didn't think he'd accept.'

'And will he? Will you tell him why you're making the offer?'

'Of course not. He would die of mortification. I'll make him a straight offer as soon as I've thought out the details. What do you think?'

'It might silence the talk,' admitted Mary, 'and if it doesn't, it can't make it much worse.' She planted a soft kiss on Tizzie's cheek. 'Good luck, my Tizz-wizz. Never fear, you'll come out on top, I'm sure of it.'

They sat facing each other in silence, two unalike women bound together by the ties of sisterhood and a deep, abiding love. Then Mary said, 'You never told me there'd been anything between you and Sam Schofield.'

The moment was full of revelation, and Tizzie's guard was lower than it had been in years. 'You saw him push me aside in the game of blind man's buff?'

'Yes, but it wasn't until later, when things were quiet, that I recalled the expression on your face. Did he like you once upon a time?'

Tizzie smiled slightly. 'Yes, he liked me. I liked him as well – more than liked, in fact.' The relief of talking about it was like the severing of a tight rope around her chest. 'The trouble was, I liked his father as well. Not in the same way, of course, not remotely the same. I was fascinated by Mr Schofield. Power appeals to me – it always has. He had

– he still has – power, wealth, brains and principles: everything I admire. I could see in him what Sam would be like when he was older; it was like looking into the future. I just wanted to sort of absorb it.'

Mary was wide-eyed. 'But Tizz, I never noticed any of this.'

'You weren't meant to,' said Tizzie drily. 'You were busy with your first-born at the time, and four months later Mother had her final illness.'

'So what happened about Sam?'

'I didn't think to hide my interest in his father. Sam saw it and withdrew his regard at once. He's very perceptive, so they all say, but not perceptive enough to see that I felt differently about his father than I did about him.'

'Felt?' asked Mary intently. 'Past tense? You don't still like him, then?'

Enough was enough, decided Tizzie. No more confidences; some things were too painful to share. 'No,' she said with finality. 'You can't breathe life into ashes.'

She didn't know that her tone was too emphatic. Mary squeezed her hand in silence and kept her conclusions to herself.

CHAPTER SIX

Partnerships

It had been the driest November in years. No rain, no mists, certainly none of the black fog that shrouded Saltley so often in winter. Instead there had been frost, keen and sparkling, with cold, hard sunshine.

Matthew said goodnight to Jonas and Billy at the back gate of the institute, put up his coat collar and set off for Meadowbank and home. Then he stopped. A breeze was blowing from the hills, freeing the town of the day's smoke; it smelled so good he turned his back on the lights of Saltley and the wide cobbled road that led towards Jericho heading instead for a path that crossed the hill side behind the mills.

At one time it had been his customary short cut home, but the path wound past a little grove of birches that held memories, so since the night of the Wakes he hadn't once gone home that way. From the grounds of the institute he had sometimes looked up and seen the cluster of trees as they changed to their brief autumn colour: pale, dazzling gold above the silver bark, then in the manner of birches the leaves fell almost overnight and all he could see was bare branches.

Now, after months of avoiding the place, he decided to face it. A full moon was rising, but he had never liked that smirking silver face; he preferred the stars, pure and brilliant and remote ... though admittedly the moon had its uses – it would illuminate the place where he'd made love to Jess.

At a turn in the path he confronted the birch grove. Amazingly, it didn't hurt to see it, perhaps because everything looked so very different now. No long soft grasses, just dry stems above drifts of dead leaves. No sheltering foliage whispering in the warm night air; just silver trees with graceful, empty branches. They didn't look like sentinels now, he told himself; they were just ordinary trees, harnessing their strength to face the winter. As he had harnessed his own resources to face the winter of a life without Jess, finding to his own surprise that he could do it. He had the image of her in his heart and in his mind; he had carved the image of her in wood, the best work he had ever done, now swathed in layers of new muslin and hidden away at the back of his cupboard. 'Twas awful strange that once he finished it he should have felt so much better. Almost as if the hours of frenzied concentration had been some sort of penance for betraying Martha; then the work completed, the penance was served. Not that he was free of guilt, nor deserved to be for that matter; it was as though his love for Jess was in its proper place, locked away where it could do no harm.

Martha knew nothing, of course, except that he'd been a bit sharp with her sometimes and hadn't made love as often as before, a state of affairs that might happen with any husband. All that was over now, thank heaven. Things were almost back to normal. Rosie, who had sensed the strain between them and been upset by it, was back to laughing and chattering and skipping around. His heart had smitten him time and again when she had questioned him about his carving. And if he'd heard the words 'confidential undertaking' one more time, he felt sure he would have been a candidate for the madhouse.

With a last sombre look at the grove of birches he continued along the path, arriving at Meadowbank by way of the big meadow that Rosie called the buttercup field. No matter what time of year it might be, even if it was covered in snow, to her it was always the buttercup field. Light was shining out from the kitchen, where Martha would be making his tea and Rosie doing her spelling for school. Thoughts of Jess faded to the back of his mind, and he told himself for the thousandth time that he was a lucky man to have a wife and child who loved him.

Matthew still had money put by in the little tin where he kept his woodworking earnings; not much, but enough to buy them both a bit of something extra for Christmas. Should he ask Martha what he must get, or should he give them both a surprise? He was still smiling about it as he opened the back door.

When the latch clicked Martha moved an iron pan to the red heart of the fire. The three of them ate their dinner at midday, but in winter she always had something hot and tasty for Matthew's tea. Tonight it was lentil broth, one of his favourites. Her face flushed from the fire, she watched as Rosie ran to her father for a kiss. He looked happy again. Oh, life was good, life was lovely! Three weeks back she'd thought that the three of them would never be happy again. He came over and kissed her cheek. Something about the way his lips lingered told her that if Rosie hadn't been there he would have kissed her mouth and her eyes and her throat and then carried her upstairs, because their loving was almost as good as it had been before whatever it was happened.

She put a slice of bread on the toasting fork and knelt in front of the fire with it. Matthew enjoyed buttered toast with his broth ... She could hear him whistling as he went out to the kitchen to wash his hands, the same as he always did. Everything was the same again – or very nearly.

Sometimes she told herself she was imagining that he'd grown older, more serious; that he'd given over laughing and joking. All she knew was that for the first time since they met he seemed to be older than her instead of four years younger. There'd always been a touch of the boy about him; she'd put it down to him making up for his childhood ... Now, though, all trace of the boy had gone. He was a man, her man, and she loved him.

Later, with Rosie long asleep in bed, Matthew said, 'I been thinkin' to buy you an' Rosie a liddle somethin' for Christmas, Martha, so if there's anythin' you're wantin' let me know. I've only got two pound odd, mind, but 'tis enough for a liddle treat.'

'Thanks, love, that'll be nice.' She touched his hand and smiled, but questions clanged in her mind like a badly cracked bell. There'd been three pounds in the little blue tin weeks back – no, months – before he ever started on his confidential undertaking. She knew because she'd looked once, when she first became worried about him after the wakes. She hadn't said anything to Matthew because it was an unspoken agreement between them that she never touched anything to do with his woodwork, not even his earnings. The money came to her in the end, anyway, unless he bought tools or special wood or gave a few shillings to the destitute. He was softhearted, was her husband; she'd had to agree to him giving away money before they got married, and that was in the days when they needed every penny. He didn't go to chapel like her and Rosie, but he certainly believed in helping the poor.

If he only had two pounds odd, he hadn't been earning woodworking money during those awful weeks. He hadn't been carving something special for a great big fee. Not that the money itself mattered, she reminded herself hastily; during the last nine or ten years money *hadn't* mattered – at least not all that much; they'd been better fed and better housed than she'd ever expected to be in her entire life ... Still, if he hadn't put money in the tin as a result of those endless obsessed hours, what had he done with it? Had he been paid for the work at all? Had he actually *done* any work behind that closed door? Of course he had. She'd heard the familiar sounds of gouging and carving, the soft squeak of metal against wood. Every night he'd taken the hand brush and shovel in there to sweep up after himself, something he always did ... In fact, one day he'd burned a huge sack of wood shavings on a bonfire down the garden.

Hastily Martha rearranged her face so it wouldn't show she was worried, then watched as he took the kettle from the hob to the slop stone for his wash. Deep in uneasy thought she started her nightly tasks and was setting the table for breakfast when he came and stood in the doorway, bare chested, with the towel slung round his neck and his dark hair wet and tousled. There was a familiar gleam in his eyes and he was smiling just like he used to.

Her heart sang. What did the contents of the blue tin matter? What did it matter that he was older and more serious? What did anything matter when he looked at her like that?

'I'll be up in a minute, love,' she said.

He slept like a baby afterwards, but he turned away from her in his sleep. Wide awake, Martha stared into the darkness, telling herself that God must be sick of hearing her thanks for being proved wrong about him having another woman. But if she'd been wrong – and she must have been – what had he spent his earnings on?

No sooner was Rosie off to school and the washing-up done than she took the lamp and opened the door of the outhouse. She went in there sometimes to give the little place a good clean, but she was always careful never to disturb anything, never to open his cupboard. He hadn't spelled it out for her, but she just knew that he needed a bit of privacy, something that was his alone.

To her astonishment the cupboard was locked. Surely he had never locked it before? She spotted a shiny new key on a nail right next to the cupboard and would have laughed if she'd been in a laughing mood. Wary of disturbing so much as a speck of sawdust, she unlocked the cupboard door.

As she'd expected, there was wood inside: special wood, dark and heavy, wrapped in an oiled rag. There were two clean neckcloths, old and threadbare from many a wash; one a faded red, the other blue, patterned with little stars. He must have kept those for years – he'd been wearing the red one when she first saw him ... His best tools were on the middle shelf, a full set of gouges still in their box and a variety of smaller ones that must have been too good to keep on the rack behind his bench. There were several bottles of wood oil and three illustrated books about woodcarving – all the things she would have expected. And there was something else, hidden behind a pile of clean rags. A bundle, wrapped in muslin.

She knew at once that this was the confidential under-taking. She stood there, twisting her hands in her apron. It was clear that he didn't want her to see it. Perhaps he'd made a mess of it and the customer had cancelled the order – she'd never thought of that, had she? He was proud of his work; he wouldn't want her to see anything that wasn't up to his usual standard. But even as her mind was questioning whether to look at it, her fingers were moving without instruction: lifting out the bundle, laying it on the bench, unwrapping it.

Before her was the figure of a young woman, hardly more than a girl, carved from pale, close-grained wood. She was very beautiful: slender, with long, unbound hair and an alert, startled expression like a wild creature disturbed in the forest. She wore a dress that hung in tatters around her arms and ankles, and on her feet were little slippers such as nobody would dream of wearing outdoors in Saltley.

Martha stood her up on the heavy base and saw that the slippers were deep in grasses and flowers. She had an arm outstretched, as if her hand was being held by someone who hurried her along. She was half smiling, her lips full and – Martha gave a little groan – and ready to be kissed.

She groped for Matthew's chair and sat down with the figure in front of her on the bench; it looked almost alive in the light of the lamp and with the first rays of morning sun behind the unruly hair. Martha crushed down all emotion and let her mind register facts in brisk rotation.

She had known that Matthew was talented, but this was amazing. The workmanship of the face was unbelievably delicate. The figure was about fifteen inches high and yet every detail was there; she wouldn't have been surprised to see each eyelash shown separately – certainly each finger-nail was clear on that outstretched hand. She was carved out of lime wood; Matthew had used it before and told her it was soft and very close grained, suitable for fine work. She thought it a pale, pale wood for a girl who looked as if she should have been dark haired. Like Matthew she had a touch of the gypsy about her.

Martha stared and stared, absorbing everything about the girl so that she would recognise her if ever they should meet. Then she emptied her mind of facts and let it join her heart in being swept by instinct. She propped her small face on her work-hard palms and found that her calico house cap was level with the thick wild tresses of the girl. The very quality of the work revealed how he felt about her; the skill, the care, the way her lower lip seemed to glisten, her expression – shy but excited – the curve of her breasts against the ragged dress ...

A single tear welled in the corner of Martha's eye and slid down her cheek. This was what she had dreaded all her married life. She had been right all along in thinking that he had another woman, though to be sure this was no Saltley woman, she was more like one who travelled in a caravan ... That was it! She was a woman from the wakes! Bitterness lay on Martha's tongue like acid. A woman from the wakes, trundling from town to town with the sideshows and merry-go-rounds and boxing booths ... How *could* he?

Still she sat with her chin propped on her hands, thinking about everything that had taken place since the wakes had come to Saltley, every word that Matthew had spoken, every expression on his face. She didn't move except to blink, and that only when her eyes became sore. At last she heard the clock indoors strike ten. For the first time in her life she had sat down for an hour and a half in the morning! Quietly she stood up and rewrapped the figure in its layers of muslin. She put it in the cupboard and locked the door, making sure everything was as she had found it. Then she returned to the kitchen, moving carefully, like a woman recovering from a long illness.

Reason and logic insisted that Matthew was in love with the girl; instinct and intuition confirmed it. But he had come back to her, Martha, his wedded wife. She felt so weak with relief she had to clutch at the mangle. In that instant she vowed never to challenge him, never to mention the girl; she would pretend she knew nothing about her. He had chosen to stay with her, his life's partner, and with Rosie. She would have to make do with that.

Still moving with care, she went through to the fireplace. There she sank down on the rug and, taking the cushion from his chair, pressed it to her chest, mumbling prayers mingled with sobs and broken words of endearment. He might have dallied with an unknown girl, he might even have loved her, but he had come back. She could face anything as long as she didn't lose him.

Friday evenings were no longer the same. Tizzie had convinced herself that she was content for it to be so, but no matter how she filled her time after eight thirty, she missed Barney's weekly visits. Their intent business talk, the sharing of a meal, the pleasure of relaxed conversation with an informed, intelligent man ... Above all – though this was something she rarely admitted to herself – she missed the deep reassurance bestowed by his concern for her welfare.

It had been his idea to stop the visits – in fact, he had insisted on it. Having been under the impression that he enjoyed Fridays as much as she did, she'd been surprised at his suggestion, then irritated and finally hurt. Until it became clear that, as always, he was thinking of her.

He raised the issue only minutes after she asked him to become her partner in the pawnshop. Moving at her usual speed, she had taken legal advice and had an agreement roughed out within three days of Mrs Boulton's comments. She'd put it to him as soon as they were settled for the evening. Prepared for arguments and objections, she'd been ready to insist, but he agreed so promptly it was clear that the idea had already occurred to him.

After the first telltale flush of his neck and jaw he had been calm and very polite. 'I'd regard it as a privilege to be in partnership with you, Miss Tizzie. You're thinkin' of a proper legal agreement, I take it, with me payin' in to the business? With conditions an' safeguards for both parties?'

Reassured of it, he said solemnly, 'In that case of course I agree – I'd be a fool not to, wouldn't I? We trust each other, an' that's more than many a one can say about their business partner.' She thought she'd concealed her surprise at such an easy victory, but he knew her too well. 'I've been thinkin' that a more obvious business arrangement between us would be no bad thing,' he informed her gently. 'Seein' as we're tryin' to demonstrate to all an' sundry that we're just business colleagues.'

Such frankness on the subject would have been unthinkable a few months ago, she told herself. What did it cost him to admit, if only by implication, that their names were linked by gossip and innuendo? What in heaven's name would he do if he found out what Mrs Boulton had said? Every muscle of her body turned rigid with horror at the thought of it. Now they could at least speak of the gossip. Barney himself had admitted that obscene remarks had been made in his presence, but he didn't – he couldn't possibly – know of the latest foul slander? She fussed with her papers and handed over a draft agreement.

Barney studied it closely. She watched him, aware that the terms were scrupulously fair, though of course he would benefit enormously in the long term. Any hint of generosity on her part would only embarrass him, so she had asked her lawyer for a simple business agreement, requiring Barney to put in a sum that he could pay in instalments deducted from a quarterly halving of profits.

'Very fair,' he said judiciously, leaning back in his chair.

'But I'd prefer to buy in with cash rather than pay it off quarterly.'

Hastily she looked down at her papers. That was no surprise. He was well paid, he lived rent-free over the shop, he had a simple style of living and no dependants. Perhaps, like her, he dabbled in property? Certainly he would never have amassed money at the expense of the pawnshop. His honesty over her affairs verged on the fanatical. 'Just as you wish,' she agreed mildly.

'So we'll make joint decisions from now on, is that it, Miss Tizzie?'

'Of course. We've been doing it for ages, anyway.'

'I suppose we have. In that case I shan't need to bring the books over here on Friday nights, nor make my report on the week's trade.'

She stared at him. 'Oh, I wouldn't like that to change, Barney. It sort of rounds off the week. We have to discuss pawnbroking some time, don't we?'

'Happen we could have a couple of hours at the shop instead – say on Saturday mornings. It's always quiet then, before folk get paid.'

For once words failed her. She looked round her comfortable, lamp-lit room with its chairs and table specially sized for Barney. From the kitchen she could hear muted sounds of Rebecca loading the trays to bring in their supper. At last she said, 'We can talk here without interruption. It's – it's convenient. Look, I *like* having you round for supper.'

He appeared to be studying his large, well-kept hands. 'I've found that in this life we can't always do what we like, Miss Tizzie.'

'For goodness' sake stop talking in riddles,' she snapped. 'Do you have more pressing things to do on Fridays? Are you making other plans?'

She detected the hint of a smile – only a hint. It annoyed her intensely. 'I have no other plans,' he said quietly.

'Well then? Surely if we're partners we'll have more to talk about, not less?'

'Happen so. I'm just sayin' we can talk in the countin' house, during shop hours.'

Belatedly, it dawned. 'Huh!' she said scornfully. 'I'm not prepared to go through life trying to silence a tribe of foul-mouthed gossips!'

'Give them nothing to gossip about and they'll *have* to fall silent,' he retorted. 'I come here late in the evening week after week, don't I?'

'But Rebecca's here,' she protested. Even as she said it her mind was rejecting the words. Did she really have to flaunt her housekeeper as a chaperone for her and Barney? A man so – she swivelled her eyes away from his – so physically unattractive that no woman in their right mind would touch him if it wasn't strictly necessary. No, that wasn't fair – he was just like any other man except for his arms and his legs and his thick, ungainly body and his great white moon face . . . She didn't know she was chewing her lips almost to the point of making them raw.

'Miss Tizzie, look me in the eye!' he said urgently. 'Weeks back I gave you my notice, didn't I?' You refused it – you said you couldn't manage without me. Did you mean that or did you not?'

'I did,' she admitted sulkily.

'Well then, if I'm to stay on as your partner I insist that we give nobody – not the Waltons, the Boultons, the men at the bar tops nor the women in the markets – the slightest cause for slander. No matter that it's unbelievable – we're both well aware of that. If we're never seen together except in public or openly in the shop, it will eventually be accepted that we're nothing more or less than business partners. Don't see it as pandering to them, see it as playing them at their own game – and winning.'

She gave him a cold green stare. 'You've become very forceful all of a sudden.' For a moment she saw uncertainty in him, then obstinacy tightened his mouth. He was waiting. 'All right,' she said tightly. 'No more Friday evenings.'

'There's one thing that would silence the gossip for ever, of course.'

She knew quite well what he meant. 'I'm content to remain single, thank you.'

'That's all right, then.' He jerked his big head backwards, as if dismissing an argument.

They faced each other in unaccustomed silence, until at last she said, 'You'll stay for a bite to eat, Barney?' It was a return to their long-established pattern; a peace offering.

'I will an' all, Miss Tizzie. For the last time.'

When Rebecca came in with the supper she glanced from one to the other in surprise. She thought they both looked as if they'd lost a guinea and found a sixpence.

'Children!' When Mary used that particular tone her family took notice. At once they fell into line, young Johnny raising his face for Tizzie's kiss; then Abel, owlish and plump, bowing from the waist with a hand against his middle. The child was obsessed with bowing and scraping, decided Tizzie; it would have been laughable if he wasn't so uncommonly smug. Elizabeth was next, red hair subdued beneath her Sunday bonnet, eyes alert and enquiring.

'Good afternoon, Aunt Tizzie,' she said briskly, giving her a cool peck on the cheek. 'Have you got any puzzles for us to do? Really hard ones? The last lot were too easy.'

Tizzie swallowed a sharp retort. Her niece liked to be occupied and made sure that everyone was aware of it. 'Oh, I might find something to tax that amazing brain,' she said lightly, and was given a wary green stare. Elizabeth couldn't bear to be teased; as for being ridiculed – she had once thrown a screaming fit when her grandpa Hartley had good-naturedly made fun of her. Billy, last in line and with his mother right behind him, took his aunt's hand and bent his head over it, then flashed her a half-embarrassed grin.

Smiling, Tizzie looked at the four children, intrigued as always by the differences between them. She'd been surprised to find how interesting it was to see them develop as individuals. Her ideas on children had changed considerably since Billy had been born. Then, she had thought

Mary quite mad to be so besotted by the red-faced little creature who made such demands on her; but within two days he had taken on a strong facial likeness to William and by six months old he was a miniature person in his own right. They were all people in their own right.

If they'd been her children she thought she could have enjoyed helping them develop their minds and personalities; she would have made sure they never experienced the boredom that had blighted her own childhood. She would have felt – yes, she would have felt fulfilled. It was the other side of motherhood that she couldn't stomach: the endless preparing and supervising of their meals, the washing and ironing of their clothes, keeping their hands and faces clean, not to mention putting up with their noisy prattle and the way they were never still for more than five seconds. Her elegant, spacious house always seemed crowded and in a muddle as soon as they came through the door.

'Rebecca will take your hats and coats,' she told them, 'then you can go through to the parlour. I've put out the bagatelle for you.'

Mary was beaming. 'Tizz, you look lovely! Doesn't she, William?'

'She always looks lovely,' he agreed with a laugh.

Tizzie eyed her brother-in-law with affection. He was capable, good-natured and devoted to his wife and children. Somehow he seemed to radiate wellbeing; why, at one time she used to call him Bull-beef – not to his face, of course, but when she thought about him. He was even more beefy now than in those early days, but as her respect for him increased over the years, she had stopped her mental use of that unflattering name.

Mary removed her bonnet to reveal her newest lace cap, secured not only by its ribbons but also by an army of hairpins. She tugged and, finding it immovable, gave it an approving pat. 'We came by way of the pawnshop to look at your new sign, Tizzie,' she said. 'It seemed funny, it being Ridings and Jellicoe.'

'Funny? You mean different? The sign writer finished it last week. It's done, Mary; the partnership's all signed and sealed and legal. Life goes on as before, except that Barney won't be coming round here again. We meet quite often, but only in public or at the shop.'

William shifted his feet and fiddled with his watch chain, obviously uneasy at her speaking so openly about her relationship with Barney. 'Mary told me about Mrs Boulton,' he muttered awkwardly, 'and that she'd had to let you know what's being said in the town. I'm right sorry you've been faced with all that. I can hardly credit folk thinking such things, never mind putting them into words.'

Tizzie looked at him and told herself that far from being unique, her brother-in-law was probably typical of the majority of men in Saltley; decent, chapel-going individuals who would never dream of linking her name with Barney's, certainly not in the realms of perversion and depravity. Most of them wouldn't even know the meaning of such words.

'Forget it if you can,' she said shortly. 'Nobody likes a pawnbroker, William, least of all one who's a woman with a head for business; so count your blessings that you're in butchering, and a man. As I see it somebody starts a rumour and if it's salacious enough there'll always be those who'll repeat it, maybe even embellish it if they can. Well, they've picked on the wrong one with me. I've threatened to sue Mrs Boulton, and I'd willingly face those two bladders of lard, the Waltons, across a courtroom . . . Come on, let's go and sit down. Rebecca's in her element in the kitchen – you know how she loves it when you all come for your tea.'

The afternoon proceeded with the three older ones playing bagatelle and Johnny nodding off to sleep on his father's lap. Then they played word puzzles, the jumbled names of Saltley streets on scraps of paper dotted around the room. Billy let Abel help him, but Elizabeth whirled back and forth on her own, pale cheeks flushed with pleasure because she was winning.

'Tizzie, you're so good at preparing these sorts of

games,' said Mary admiringly. 'They enjoy them and yet all the time they're learning. You should have been a teacher, you know – you have a certain authority. They behave better here than they do at home, or when we take them to William's family.'

Tizzie wasn't sure if she should take that as a compliment, though obviously it was meant as one. 'Don't you remember I once asked Mother if she would let me apply for a position as assistant teacher? She refused – said I hadn't the patience for teaching and in any case she was more interested in us making good marriages.'

Silence descended at that, Mary looking out of the window and tweaking at her cap ribbons. 'Don't say a word,' warned Tizzie, managing a laugh. 'I'm happy as I am – an independent woman of business!' She turned to the children. 'Right, let's check your answers, then I have a competition for you. You can go all over the house and see who can find and write down the most objects beginning with the letter *B*. Abel, that's *B* like in bed and butter and bagatelle. You can come and tell me yours and I'll write them down for you. Off you go, but no getting under Rebecca's feet in the kitchen.'

After a splendid tea Elizabeth, with calculated charm, asked if she could go up to Tizzie's bedroom, where she liked to examine the toilet articles on the washstand and dressing table.

'I'll come up and light the gas for you,' agreed Tizzie good-humouredly. 'No opening cupboards, mind, but you can look in my top drawer and sort through my hair ornaments. You can try on my everyday jewellery as well, if you like.'

In the bedroom Elizabeth stood in front of the washstand, fiddling with bottles and jars and examining the silver-backed hairbrush and the tortoiseshell combs that Tizzie sometimes used in her hair. She sighed heavily. 'It's so much more interesting here than at home, Aunt Tizzie. My bedroom's so boring.'

'So was mine when I was your age,' Tizzie told her. She

had the sensation of speaking to her niece across a gulf –
a chasm that was deep and dark and echoing; calling out
loud to her without knowing whether she could hear. Why
should that be the case when everyone insisted they were
so much alike? Elizabeth was a handful at home, Mary had
said as much; the mutinous set of the child's mouth
confirmed it. Perhaps she should really try to understand
her niece. She would have to give it some thought ...

'Would you like to stay up here on your own for a bit?'
she asked.

'I thought that was what I was supposed to be doing.
Can I look at your real jewellery, Aunt Tizzie?'

'No, not just now. I keep it locked away most of the
time.'

The child shrugged. 'I suppose it's what people have
pawned, anyway.'

'No, as a matter of fact, it's not. I wouldn't dream of
wearing stuff that's come through the shop – I might meet
the people who'd pledged it. I don't own all that much
expensive jewellery, but what I do have I've bought for
myself.

'Do you like it better that way than having a husband
earning all the money and buying things for you?'

'Yes, of course I do.'

'Then why have you taken that dwarf as a partner?
You'll have to share all the pawnshop money with him,
won't you?'

Steady, Tizzie warned herself. Elizabeth's attitude had
set a small memory bell tolling inside her head, but she
couldn't have said what it was she remembered. 'Mr
Jellicoe is very clever, Elizabeth. He knows as much about
the business as I do.' Full marks for restraint, she told
herself.

'But he's *horrible*! He's like something from a freak
show on the wakes!'

Before she knew it, Tizzie's hand was raised to strike
the child's face. With a supreme effort of will she
controlled herself and dropped the hand to her side. She

found she was trembling, Elizabeth looking up at her with barely concealed fear. Ah – that was what she remembered! She was nine years old again and pouring scorn on the pawnshop – her father's business. But in her case, more than twenty years ago, her mother's hand had connected, giving her a stinging slap over the ear and several more on her shoulders.

Tizzie was silent for what seemed an eternity, while Elizabeth stared at her with eyes that seemed dark as evergreen leaves. At one time she herself had found Barney grotesque, so why be upset that the child saw him in a similar light?

'Mr Jellicoe was born like that, Elizabeth, just as some people are born hunchbacked or with a club foot. In his case, unlike some very short people, his mind hasn't been affected. He's clever and loyal and kind hearted. That's why I want him as a business partner. It's not what he looks like that matters – it's what he *is*. Does that help you to understand?'

'Yes. But I still think he looks horrible.'

So did most people, thought Tizzie wearily. 'He's a good man, Elizabeth,' she said with finality. 'Now, you can look in this drawer, and this one over here, but nowhere else. Is that clear?'

'Yes, Aunt Tizzie.' Elizabeth began poking around, eyes intent, her bottom lip caught between her teeth. Tizzie thought that for once the child *had* reminded her of herself at the same age . . .

Downstairs William was on his feet, waiting for her. 'Could you spare a minute for business talk, Tizzie? I'm sorry to bother you about such things on a Sunday . . .'

Everyone was occupied: Mary helping Johnny to build a tower with wooden bricks, and the older boys trying to play draughts. Tizzie led William to the little morning room that was fitted out as her office. He was somewhat on edge, she told herself, though whatever was on his mind, he'd concealed it very well up to now.

'Sit down, William. It's not often we come in here to

talk business.' The room was small and her brother-in-law very large. Even when seated he seemed too big for his surroundings, like a vigorous well-groomed animal penned in at the market. He clasped his hands between his knees and looked her in the eye. 'You know all about the alterations at the shop, don't you, Tizzie?'

'I know they're pretty drastic and far-reaching,' she admitted. 'Is there a hold-up on the work or something?'

'Yes, in a way. You'll have seen that there's scaffolding up all three floors? They're bringing the wall right out at the back, to extend the shop area and to give us more living space above it. Well, they've found rotten timbers between the floors and up in the roof, and they can't proceed without renewing them. Now, I've paid the Barnes brothers half the cost of the job in advance, but new joists aren't covered in the quote, so it's a case of holding up the work until I have the means to pay. At any other time of year I could raise it, but I've had to lay out in advance for my Christmas beef and poultry . . .' Colour stained his cheeks right up to his hair line. 'You once told me never to go to a moneylender until I'd spoken to you.'

'Yes. Yes, I did.' She hid her surprise. It had never occurred to her that he was cutting it so fine. His plans for the shop were ambitious, the talk of the Saltley tradesmen, but she could hardly credit that he'd left himself without a reserve. 'You're asking for a loan, William?'

'Yes, if you have it, Tizzie. Until, say, late January, when customers pay their Christmas bills. Most housewives pay cash, of course; it's the pie makers and eating houses who keep me waiting. I'm always a bit short in December and January.'

'But Mary never said anything. We were talking about Christmas trade only the other day.'

His eyes widened in surprise; she saw that the whites of them were dazzlingly clear, tinged with blue. 'Mary knows nothing of this,' he said. 'I don't bother her with finance. She has quite enough on her plate with the house and the children.'

Well, well. One surprise after another. She'd always seen theirs as an ideal marriage, a true partnership. It was a love match, no doubt of it, but it seemed that though they shared the marriage bed, they didn't share everything. Why on earth were women content to be treated as featherbrains once they had a gold band on their finger? Though to be honest Mary had always been a bit of a featherbrain. She might be highly competent as a mother and housekeeper, but she was never likely to win prizes for the keenest mind in Saltley.

William was forging on. 'My parents can't help, you see, now they're retired. Neither can my brothers – they've all got their own commitments. In fact I'm the wealthiest of us all, but only because your father's legacy got us off to a good start in the shop.'

Tizzie went straight for what she saw as the main issue. 'If you've only paid half to the Barnes brothers and you haven't enough to buy new timbers, how will you manage to pay the other half?'

William wriggled in the chair. 'This is just a seasonal thing. By the time the job's finished, money will have flowed back into the business. I can do it, I know I can. I just need a bit of help for the next six or seven weeks.'

'Of course I'll help, if I can. The trouble is, my assets are mostly in kind rather than cash – property and valuables. I'm a bit low at present because I've just completed a property transaction. How much do you want?'

'Thirty pounds, thirty-five if you can manage it.'

Once again she had to conceal her surprise. He was stuck for a mere thirty pounds? 'That'll be all right,' she told him. 'I can let you have thirty-five in cash by noon tomorrow.'

He sighed in relief. 'Thanks, Tizzie. Make out a proper IOU for me to sign, won't you, adding whatever interest you think fair. And look – would you mind not mentioning this to Mary? I don't want her worried.'

Tizzie gritted her teeth in irritation. He didn't want

Mary to be worried about money; Mary didn't want him to be upset about the gossip regarding her and Barney, or about anything else, for that matter. What they both needed – what everybody needed – was a bit of straight talking, never mind all this hole and corner rubbish about 'don't say this' and 'don't mention that'.

Beneath her impatience, though, unease was nagging. 'William,' she said, striving to avoid a censorious tone, 'people tell me I have a keen eye for business – for finance and so forth. If ever you should want to talk things over regarding your affairs, in confidence of course, you only have to say the word.'

She watched him from under her lashes. He might be lacking in prudence but he was no fool. Awareness of what she was really saying showed in those clear brown eyes. He gave an awkward little shrug. 'Happen I should have talked it over with you before I got started,' he said.

'Happen you should,' she agreed quietly.

CHAPTER SEVEN

Tampering and Tears

The company flag thudded against its post on the tower of Jericho Mills, its golden trumpet and deep-red rose crusted with snow. The wind was rising, turning a snowfall into a blizzard, but inside the mills it was warm and noisy, the air thick with Jericho's permanent smells of hot engine oil, cotton and human sweat.

Joshua and Sam climbed the stairs of the tower, heading for West Side spinning room. As they opened the door the one o'clock blower sounded, announcing the end of the week's work. Driving belts slapped to a halt as machinery was switched off; everyone knew that five minutes later the mill engines would be shut down for the weekend.

Scantily clad men and boys stood barefoot on the oily floorboards, murmuring with satisfaction at the arrival of their employer. One grizzled spinner laughed and whispered to his fellows, 'Can't have this, lads – he's all of five seconds late!'

Joshua's punctuality was legendary among his workforce. 'Set an example,' he'd said often enough to his sons in their youth. 'If you shut folk out of the mill for arriving late and make 'em lose half a day's pay, the least you can do is to keep good time yourself.'

Joshua nodded to the overlooker, a lifelong friend. 'Now then, Joe.'

Joe Whitehead nodded back. Respect was there, but no subservience. 'Mr Schofield,' he said, 'an' Mr Sam.' It was always Mr Schofield in front of the men, never Joshua.

Sam looked from one white-haired figure to the other. He could hear the wheeze of the overlooker's breathing from four feet away. Joshua eyed his old friend keenly. 'A special day, eh, Joe? We were expecting my grandson to join us, but he's developed an interest in machinery, so I reckon he's down in the engine house. Still, we won't delay for a young lad.' He nodded to the head spinner, an amiable, bull-necked individual.

The man stepped forward and spoke with well-rehearsed confidence. 'We wish you all the best for your retirement, Mr Whitehead, an' we hope for an improvement in your health. If every cotton worker had a man as fair as you in charge of 'em, the industry'd be the better for it. We've had our appreciation wrote out in this illuminated address. We thought you an' your missis could hang it on the wall or happen stand it on your mantelpiece.' He expelled a breath, relieved that the speech was over, and looked round. 'Mr Sam, if you please.'

Sam stepped forward and presented the framed address to the overlooker. Like his father, he could rise to an occasion with a touch of the show man. He shook Joe Whitehead by the hand and clapped him on the shoulder, pretending not to see the shine of tears in the older man's eyes. He led a round of applause and observed Charles, red faced, trying to sidle in unnoticed.

Then it was Joshua's turn, and the spinners fell silent. 'It's hard when you have to say farewell to a man who's not only a faithful employee but also an old friend,' he said soberly. 'Some of you will know that when we were little lads Joe and me lived in the same row of cottages out on the old salt road. We started in the mill together at seven years of age and we learned the trade the hard way. Joe here has worked for me since I bought three pairs of mule frames and rented floor space in the old Daisybank mill. I mean it as no reflection on any other worker when I say that from the first day he's been my best and most reliable man.

'Next spring it'll be fifty years since I paid Joe his first wages, but the state of his health will prevent him from staying at Jericho for his golden jubilee – prevent him staying till the Christmas break, for that matter. It doesn't mean we can't mark the occasion of him leaving in a fitting manner, though . . .' He opened the lid of a blue velvet box to show a splendid gold pocket watch and chain. 'Gold for a man who's pure gold,' he said with a smile. 'Joe, I'm pleased to present this timepiece in recognition of your long and faithful service to Schofields. You'll find it's inscribed according to my instructions.' He handed over the watch and shook hands.

The men roared their approval and stamped the floor with their bare feet, then really let rip as Joshua led them in three cheers. It was a happy moment, tinged with nostalgia for those early days of struggle and triumph. Joshua was about to leave him with his men when Joe said quietly, 'Can I have a word with you before I go?'

'Of course you can. I'm going straight back to my office. Come down as soon as you've finished here.' Joshua turned to Charles, who was gazing as if hypnotised at the countless spindles of the spinning frames. 'Come on, lad,' he said shortly. 'Machinery is the lifeblood of Jericho, I've always said it; but the muscle, the heart and the very soul of the place are the workers!'

There was some kind of rebuke behind the words. Intrigued but apprehensive, the boy followed his grandfather while behind them Sam kept a straight face. A lecture on punctuality was imminent . . . It would be easier on the boy if he wasn't there to hear it. 'I'll just go and see Saul Bracewell, Father,' he said. 'He's there till half past and I said I'd look at his figures for the week.'

Joshua waved a hand. 'Aye, off you go.' He watched Sam make for the East Side floors and then descended the stairs with his grandson. 'Why were you late, Charlie?' he asked quietly.

Charles blushed like a girl. 'It was so thrilling in the engine house, Grandpa. I just forgot the time.'

'Aye, it's thrilling in the engine house, right enough. They're two fine engines, the best of their kind, but they'll be here next week, next month, next year. They'll be here until they're out of date and have to be replaced. Mr Whitehead, on the other hand, won't be here at all as from now. After forty-nine years and eight months of working for me he's had to give up because of his bad chest. I arranged for the three of us to be there at one o'clock for his farewell presentation. Your uncle Sam and me were on time, Charlie.'

They had reached a landing and Joshua stopped and faced his grandson. 'Look, lad, if you follow your interests it's more than likely you'll be either a musician or a cotton engineer – what we used to call a millwright. I don't know much about a musician's life, but if you go into the manufacturing of cotton cloth there's two things in particular you'll have to remember. The first is that you treat your operatives with respect – you must have regard for their feelings. The second is that you never expect from them what you're incapable of yourself. That applies to being on time as much as it does to giving a fair day's work for a day's pay or to being honest down to the last farthing. Is that clear?'

'Yes, Grandpa.' The boy looked up with his straight, dazzling gaze. 'I'm sorry.'

'All right, we'll say no more about it. Now, we might be here another half hour or maybe longer. Do you want to run off to Meadowbank or hang on here and go back with your uncle Sam and me? We'll be in the carriage as the weather's bad.'

Charles looked out of the window to see snowflakes whirling against a yellow-grey sky. From far below he could hear the dull thudding of clogs on snow as workers streamed out through the gates. 'Mama doesn't let me play in the snow at home,' he said thoughtfully. 'I'll go now, if you don't mind.'

'Go on then. Tell Lilah we'll be at the table by – let's see – half past two.'

'All right Grandpa, see you later.' Charles gave him his wide, sweet smile and sped away down the stairs. His grandfather followed at a more measured pace, asking himself why Joe could be wanting to have a word. Happen he felt like five minutes' talk about the old days.

In his office he said, 'Come in, Joe, and sit yourself down. I know you're not a drinking man, so could you do with a ginger cordial? It'd keep the cold out till you get home.'

Joe accepted a glass of cordial and perched on the edge of a big, leather-covered chair. 'Thanks, Joshua, for the watch,' he said sincerely. 'I'll feel a right swell with that across me middle. The missis'll be pleased, an' all, when she sees the words.'

'We've come a long way since we were both seven, Joe.' To Joshua there was nothing incongruous in linking himself with his employee. He was the owner of Jericho because of a keen brain, a wife in a million, years of hard work and smiling good fortune. Joe worked for him because of a slower brain, a certain lack of enterprise, just as much hard work but rather less good fortune. In most respects they were equal. Joshua saw that he was shifting his shoulders uneasily. 'Is there anything special you wanted to say, Joe?'

'Aye, there is. I can't leave Jericho without having a word. Years back I let you down by not telling you that Harry Lingard messed about with the weavers, but that was because I didn't really believe it an' anyway I had no proof. I've got no proof now of what's on me mind. It's more what you'd call a feelin', like . . .'

'Come on, then,' urged Joshua good-humouredly. 'Spit it out!'

'You recall we've had five different repairs on the driving belts in the last few months?'

'Yes, you mentioned it last week. It's a nuisance, but not unheard of, surely?'

Joe wiggled a hand. 'Hold on, hold on. We've had a right series of ups and downs, as a matter of fact. Nothin' I'd bother you with in the normal way, nothin' really out of the ordinary, but they all kept mountin' up, like. Then this mornin' I realised that somebody had been in my cabinet.'

Joshua sat up straight. The cabinet was in effect the overlooker's desk; a tall set of drawers that held his work records, his notes on the output of individual spinners and his precious sample hanks of yarn, the work of his most experienced men.

'Was anything taken?'

'No, but you know how it is – you keep things in a certain order, an' that. I'm quite sure somebody's been through every drawer, an' I'm just as sure it's nobody from the spinnin' room. Then when we switched off this mornin' there was a belt off. Again. It's happened a few times lately. It were only a minute or two's delay, but it caused bad feelin' on the floor.'

'So what are you saying, Joe?'

'I think you've got somebody tamperin',' said Joe soberly. 'I'm sorry, I know it sounds daft . . . There was that affair with the reservoir a couple of months back, don't forget.'

'But we decided that must have been children, messing about with the sluicegate.'

'Aye, an' so it coulda been, but it delayed firin' up for a good couple of hours, didn't it? Then there was that do when the hotplates hadn't been switched on, yet the boiler man swore he'd done it.'

Joshua remembered that only too well. Many of the workers brought their dinner in basins to be warmed up on vast metal plates that were heated by hot water from the boilers. It had been a cold day in late October and they hadn't relished cold dinners. He had thought it just another omission, a mistake. What if he'd been wrong?

Joe was in deadly earnest. 'I'm sorry, Joshua,' he said awkwardly. 'I can't put my finger on anythin' special, but

I just have a feelin' that things aren't right. Everythin' that's happened could be the work of an outsider – a man unskilled with cotton. I know you have a good night watchman, but he can't be everywhere at once, can he? I reckon if you question your overlookers an' your floor managers you might hear of other upsets here an' there.'

Joshua looked into the shrewd grey eyes and heard the wheeze of lungs clogged with cotton dust. Had this man tumbled to something that he himself had been too blinkered to see? In his own mill? 'I'll look into it,' he promised, 'and thoroughly at that. Thanks for telling me, but try and put it out of your mind for now; Nellie will be waiting for you at home. Off you go, Joe, and I'll let you know what happens. Take this paper and write down everything you can think of that's struck you as odd. Put it in this envelope and give it to anybody who passes your house on their way to work on Monday morning. Tell them to just hand it in at the office.'

From his window Joshua watched the overlooker cross the yard for the last time. All this was too much like the missing order book at Mosley Street, the book that was later found in the Irwell, its pages a sloppy wet mush. Was there a link with those poor consignments of cotton a while back? There was a dull ache in his chest as such possibilities and their implications registered and refused to be dismissed. He would have to talk to Sam, but not until they'd had their dinner. His brain wouldn't function when he was famished.

It was steak and kidney pie, one of his favourites, taken out of the oven five minutes before serving, the way he liked it. Lilah was a treasure. The three of them had second helpings, followed by baked apples and cream. Sam watched his father enjoying the meal and wondered why, when he ate just as much as when his mother was alive, the flesh should now be so spare on his bones; in earlier days he'd been thickset and as well fleshed as a wrestler. Happen it was just advancing years, because it was a fact that muscles lost their bulk with age . . . but no, instinct told him that his father's lean frame was somehow connected with his emotions, as if good produce fed him as it had always done, but no longer gave true nourishment.

Apron crackling, Lilah brought in the coffee, her plain face flushing when Joshua complimented her on the pie. 'It'd be a poor do if I couldn't make a bit o' pastry, Mr Schofield,' she said briskly.

'Aye, I suppose it would, but there's pastry and pastry, Lilah. Has Hannah done the baskets?' Food still went out from Meadowbank to the needy, as it had done since the days of the cotton famine in the sixties. The staff accepted it as a normal part of their duties.

'Ellie's puttin' her shawl on now to start deliverin', Mr Schofield.'

Joshua frowned and breathed out heavily through his nose. 'Have none of you seen the weather?' he demanded irritably. 'Zacky's standing by to take the carriage out, and Ellie must go with him. She isn't the size of two penn'orth of copper; if she sets out on foot she'll end up under a snowdrift, baskets and all!' He pulled at his whiskers and glared as Lilah marched out to deliver his instructions.

Sam eyed his father carefully but Charles, oblivious, was scraping his plate with the fervour of one habitually starved. 'Grandpa, why is the food so much nicer here than at home?'

'We have a good cook in Lilah, that's why. She's up to Alice's standard, and Alice was trained by your grandma.' That, to Joshua's mind, made further comment superfluous.

Charles helped himself to a chunk of Cheshire cheese and crammed it on an oatcake. 'We have a lot of different cooks at home, not just one,' he observed. 'They're always changing.'

Aye, because nobody'll work for your mother if they can get taken on elsewhere, thought Joshua. Aloud he said, 'It isn't always easy to keep domestic staff, especially out in the country.' Three pairs of blue eyes exchanged looks, but no more was said about the cooking of food. Charles finished his meal and asked permission to go upstairs and play his beloved trumpet.

Joshua shut the door after him. 'Right,' he said, 'listen to this, Sam.' He repeated almost word for word what Joe had told him. 'What do you think?' he concluded.

'I think it makes you and me look a bit daft if he's right – an employee pointing out what we've missed.'

'Joe's a bit more than an employee, though, isn't he? He's no fool, Sam.'

'No, I know he's not. What do *you* think?'

Joshua gave his son an odd little smile. 'I'm not quite in my dotage, Sam, nor do I need protecting all of a piece. Your brother spoke his farewell words to me, don't forget.'

Sam sagged in his seat and then leaned across the table, open-mouthed. 'You mean *Ralph*? You think it might be him?'

'Not being a numbskull, yes, it had occurred to me. When the order book went missing at Mosley Street my first thought was that Ralph had come back and started to play little games, though it was inconceivable that he'd entered the place in daylight without being recognised. Don't forget we'd already had that to-do with the three bad consignments. Then when nothing else happened for a bit I thought – I wanted to think – that I'd been jumping to conclusions. All these little happenings that have disturbed Joe, they could be innocent enough or they could be the work of Master Ralph. No doubt in time we'll find out which.'

'You speak of his farewell words, Father. Could you tell me what he said?'

Joshua smiled thinly. 'Oh, he said plenty . . . That your uncle Charlie and your mother had been lovers; that Charlie had bribed him to keep his mouth shut about it; that he *had* killed Charlie but that I'd never prove it, that I was deranged. . . Regarding Jericho, though; when I told him I was sending him to Australia, he said, 'I'll set up in business. I'll make a fortune and then come back and buy you out – you and your precious Jericho.'

Sam tried to laugh it off, but his brother's words echoed unpleasantly in the big, comfortable room. 'That's high finance, though, not like pinching the order book or opening the sluice on the reservoir,' he pointed out.

'I know. But happen he hasn't made a fortune. And even if he has, nobody could buy into Jericho just like that, now could they? Ralph was always clever – cunning, you might say; he could always play a waiting game. I've been thinking he could start off by causing unrest, then by making us look incompetent, then by affecting the quality of what we produce so that people lose confidence in us.' Joshua looked Sam in the face. 'It's my life's work, is Jericho, especially since I sold the mine, but I'm not such a fool as to think it's impregnable. There's many a solid firm gone bankrupt in the last few years.'

Sam leapt from his chair, ready for battle. 'What's the first move, then? To find out everything that's gone wrong in the mill during the last six months?'

'Yes. Then decide whether they're acts that could have been perpetrated by Ralph – with or without help. Then proof or no proof, we'll take on extra watchmen.' Absently he cut himself a piece of cheese. 'No doubt he's aged a bit, like the rest of us, but even so he'd have been noticed at once if he showed his face in Saltley . . .'

'Wait!' Sam broke in suddenly. 'Harry Fairbrother said something last week . . . It didn't make much impact on me at the time, I just thought it a bit odd, you know. He said they'd been having trouble with the carding machines at Greenbank. Nobody could work out why they kept going wrong. They'd had the engineer on to it and he'd demanded to know who'd been messing about with them. It couldn't be connected with our little lot, could it?'

'It's possible, I suppose, though I doubt whether the town's operatives have enough grudges to turn machine breakers. Still, if John Fairbrother's having trouble as well, it might mean I'm worrying needlessly about Ralph. See what you can find out, Sam, without giving too much away. We'll get to the bottom of this lot or my name isn't

Schofield.' Restlessly he walked to the window, halting when from upstairs came the high, clear notes of a trumpet. It was a simple air, played with what seemed to both of them a smoothness and depth of feeling far in advance of what Charles could be capable of.

Joshua listened with his head on one side. 'I didn't get round to telling you I called in on his teacher yesterday,' he said thoughtfully. 'I decided it wouldn't be treading on Esther's toes or anything, seeing as I'm still paying for the lessons.'

'What did he say?' asked Sam with interest.

'He said that Charlie shows outstanding talent. He said he's remarkably gifted.' Joshua gave a rueful little smile at his own tone of voice. He had sounded amazed, yet apologetic. 'I can't seem to take it in, that he has this ability,' he confessed, staring out of the window. 'Just a minute!' He peered out to the garden at the side of the house. 'There's a child out there in the snow, Sam, crouched under the hedge. I do believe it's Matthew's girl, young Rosie, still as a statue. What are they thinking of, letting her hang about in this weather?'

Sam was already on his way to find out. He snatched his big caped coat from the hall and made for the garden. The wind moaned softly, but there was no other sound apart from the trumpet, clearly audible out of doors, high and sweet and oddly compelling. That was it – she was listening to Charles. He glanced up at the bedroom windows and saw that one of them, his own, was a few inches open. Well, well.

'Rosie,' he said quietly.

The child shot to her feet, clutching an enormous plaid shawl around her. Her face looked pink and warm amid the thick enveloping folds, but it was clear that she was highly embarrassed. 'I – I just happened to hear the trumpet,' she gabbled, 'as I were passin', like.'

Sam smiled. 'Don't be frightened, Rosie. My father saw you out here and we were worried that you might not feel well.'

She was looking into his face intently, as if expecting to find something displayed on his features. 'I'm all right, Mr Sam. Truly I am.'

'But where are your parents?'

The child bit her lip and looked uneasily towards the side gate. 'They're doin' the buyin' in at the market. They always go on Saturday afternoon. Me dad won't let me mam carry it all on her own. Sometimes they leave me here.'

'Ah. And that's when you come out here and listen to Charles playing his trumpet?'

She shook her head and a few flakes of snow drifted down from the shawl. 'Sometimes I do,' she muttered unwillingly.

Sam recalled some sort of fuss about her being forbidden to play with Charles. They'd thought Esther a bit high-handed about it, but in Saltley a boy in Charles's position didn't ever play with a gardener's daughter, so they'd let it slide.

'Does Charles know that you listen?'

'No,' she said quickly, then blushed. 'Well, p'raps he might guess.'

'And do you like it when he plays?'

Rosie smiled. She was a pretty little thing, he told himself. 'I do an' all,' she said simply.

'Look, Rosie, don't you think your mother and father will be upset if they know you're out in the snow like this, listening to him?'

'Yes,' she muttered. 'Will you tell 'em?'

'No, not if you go indoors right away and shake all the snow off your mother's shawl. Go on, off with you.'

The spherical bundle dipped towards the ground, and he deduced that she was dropping a curtsey. 'Shall I tell Charles that you were listening?' he asked.

The brown eyes widened in amazement at the offer, then lifted to the bedroom window. 'Yes, please!' she whispered, 'though I s'pose he might already know.'

He stood up and waved her away. 'Off you go, then.'

'Thanks, Mr Sam.' She made for the stable yard, her small booted feet sinking in the snow and the shawl swaddled around her in a great bundle.

Back indoors his father said, 'She was listening to Charles, was that it?'

'Yes. She was a bit frightened she'd been seen, I think. She seems a bright little thing. Do you think we should have let Esther get away with putting a ban on her and Charles playing together?'

'I don't know. I'll give it some thought.' Joshua's mind was occupied by other matters. He gripped Sam's wrist and said heavily, 'Do you know what question I ask myself every day of my life?'

'No, what?'

'I ask myself why? Why, why, why?'

'Why what?'

'Why was Ralph like that? What made him so different from the rest of us? Where did we go wrong? Was it something we did or didn't do? Was it perhaps in his blood? It wasn't that he was a slate short, it was more a complete absence of any moral sense.'

'I've wondered that myself,' admitted Sam. 'Heredity is still a bit of a mystery, Father, but we know that madness and certain illnesses can be passed down through the generations, don't we? Maybe Ralph had a – a state of mind, a lack of principles and proper care for others, that had come down from some ancestor or other. It's possible.'

'Aye,' agreed Joshua wearily, 'happen it is. Now, you won't forget to find out all you can from Harry Fairbrother, will you? I'm off for a quiet hour in front of the fire in the little sitting room. I feel – I feel a bit tired.' He said it in a tone of such disbelief that Sam would have laughed if he hadn't guessed the reason for his tiredness.

The snow had gone, apart from frozen black slush in the gutters, but a keen north wind blew from the hills, warning of more to come.

Tizzie walked briskly down Farthing Lane, heading for a certain shop beyond the Old Cross and then on to the network of streets that led to the pawnshop, where she would leave Christmas presents for Barney, Albert and Gideon. She now limited her visits there to three a week; the main business meeting with Barney taking place in the little counting house on Saturday mornings. It was bitterly cold but she was so full of energy she relished the prospect of a long walk, dressed as she was in her warm hooded cloak and comfortable boots.

It was Christmas Eve. She wasn't sure why that should depress her, but it did. Everyone else was so obsessively busy. For days Mary had been running round like a woman possessed, organising presents for the children, helping with the pies and cooked meats in the kitchen behind the shop, and up in her own domain baking, baking, baking. It seemed to Tizzie that her sister presented cakes and pies to half of Saltley at Christmas time.

On a far grander scale it was the same with Sarah up at Alsing. She had supervised the sending out of Christmas baskets to the cottagers and estate workers, chosen gifts for every last member of the household staff ready for their party on Boxing Day, entertained the county aristocracy to a grand dinner and had a hand in fund raising for the infirmary.

Even in Tizzie's own orderly house a kind of frenzy lay beneath the calm. Rebecca was expecting her daughter Naomi for a three-day visit and was as near to excitement as Tizzie had ever seen her. Tizzie walked on, shaking off her low spirits and letting her mind dwell on Naomi. It was understood that her true home lay with her mother and Tizzie; it had been so ever since Rebecca had applied for the post of Tizzie's housekeeper at the pawnshop and thrown in the services of her daughter as an added inducement. A bright, biddable child she had been; undernourished but so eager to learn . . .

'Miss Tizzie!' It was a high-pitched squeal from across Farthing Lane. A small figure hurtled over the cobbles, causing a carthorse to rear in the shafts and the carter to curse aloud. Tizzie stared. It was Annie, the part-time mother's help from Mary's, wearing her indoor cap and apron without so much as a shoulder wrap. The girl's mouth was agape, taking in air. She looked both sweaty and cold, her pale eyes wide and staring.

'Miss Tizzie – I'm to find you an' take you back. Come quick, Mrs Hartley wants you!'

Tizzie yanked the child to the safety of the flagstones. 'Calm down, Annie! What's the matter?'

'Come quick!' Saliva spattered from the girl's mouth. 'Oh, come *on*!'

Tizzie crushed a faint stirring of dread. '*Annie!*' Nobody ignored that tone of voice. 'Tell me what's wrong. Is it one of the children?' All the town knew that fever was raging in the hovels of Gallgate and that it could spread.

'No, no, it's Mr Hartley! He fell off the scaffoldin'. Come *on*, Miss Tizzie!'

Tizzie lifted her skirts and ran down Farthing Lane, her cloak billowing, the fur-lined hood bouncing up and down behind her neck and pins falling from her hair. Annie ran with her, silent now and intent only on speed.

Outside Bennison's jewellers Tizzie paused to scan the little square around the Old Cross. Sometimes a cab could be found there, but not today. She grabbed Annie's arm and ran with her past the railings of Albion Chapel and on past the new post office into Peter Street. People turned in amazement as they sped along, perhaps telling themselves that for once Tizzie Ridings had forgotten to stand on her dignity.

A carriage pulled into the pavement ahead of them and a broad, familiar figure leapt out. 'Can I help?' asked Sam Schofield briskly.

Tizzie gulped with relief. 'Please! My sister needs me!'

He asked no questions but helped her into the carriage and lifted Annie in behind her. 'Hartley's butchers, Zacky,' he said, 'and be quick!'

Tizzie flopped on the seat next to Annie. There was

surprise on Sam's fair, rough-hewn features, but whether at her running through the streets or his own reaction she didn't know. 'Thank you, Mr Schofield,' she said limply. 'There wasn't a cab to be seen.'

'It's urgent, I take it, Miss Ridings?'

Beneath the heat of the moment she was keenly conscious of their formality. Once it had been Tizzie and Sam – in fact it was still first names in front of the Schofield family. Next to her Annie was shivering, her teeth rattling like dried peas in a jar. Quickly Tizzie draped part of her cloak across the thin young shoulders, telling herself they could do without the child collapsing from exhaustion or a chill.

'This is Annie, Mary's little maid,' she told Sam. 'She's just run all the way to Farthing Lane and by good fortune met me on my way to the shops. She says it's William – he's had an accident. Annie, tell me properly, is he badly hurt?' The noise of the wheels on the cobblestones drowned her words, so she repeated them, almost shouting. 'Is he badly hurt?'

There was a film of sweat on Annie's brow but still she shivered, staring at Tizzie in bafflement. 'He fell off the scaffoldin'.' She spoke the words loudly and very clearly, as if addressing a dullard.

'Yes, yes. I'm asking if he's badly hurt.'

Annie folded her arms and hugged her chest, looking from Tizzie to Sam and back again. 'He's dead,' she said flatly. The carriage rattled noisily over the cobbles and they both stared at her blankly. *'He's dead!'* she bellowed, and burst into tears.

Sam was shocked by the sound that issued from Tizzie's mouth. It was a howl of pain, of anguish. Her eyes were fixed unseeingly on his, her lips drawn back over her teeth. 'Mary!' she groaned. 'Oh Mary, Mary, my little Mary!'

He stared at her, his mind reeling. Will Hartley dead? That prime example of health and well being? And Tizzie here, hard-headed Tizzie, howling like a dog on hearing that her sister was bereaved. 'I'll help,' he said, grabbing her hands. 'I'll stay as long as you want me. The carriage is yours to use as you will!'

She looked down at their joined hands and he saw the top of her head. The hair was unpinned, spiralling in wild unruly waves from the centre parting. It was still crisp and red-gold, but for an instant he fancied that it looked less bright, that it had given up its lustre ... He swallowed hurriedly. Once before he'd thought that, hadn't he? Long years ago, when he hardly knew her. Awkwardly he released her fingers.

At that she raised her eyes. Behind the translucent green irises he imagined that he could actually see her mind taking over from her emotions, deciding what her first task should be, how she could be of most help. They were slowing down outside the shop where a small crowd had gathered on the flagstones. Tizzie was now very pale; he thought she looked all eyes and mouth and hair.

'Stay until I've seen Mary?' It was a request. He nodded and helped her from the carriage, then leaned in and plucked Annie from the seat, keeping her in his arms. She was weeping and shivering, close to collapse.

Billy came pushing his way out through the crowded shop, dry eyed but tense as stretched wire. 'Aunt Tizzie,' he said abruptly. 'Come on through. He's in the back.'

She waved a hand at the throng of customers. 'Why are this lot still here, Billy?'

'Mother says they're to be served. We must stay open to fill their Christmas orders.' The boy glanced at Sam and the helpless Annie without curiosity.

Sam thought he had the stiff, unnatural movements of a mechanical toy. 'I'm here to help for a bit,' he said reassuringly, but Billy ignored him and went ahead of them.

Tizzie turned and looked at Sam just once. She dreaded seeing Mary in case she was like their mother had been when their father had died: irrational, unbelieving, fondling the corpse, kissing the dead lips – it had been repellent. She had believed those memories to be banished for ever, until just now when Zacky stopped the carriage outside. All at once they returned in all their horror; she could hardly force herself through the shop.

'I'm right behind you,' he said, sensing her reluctance. 'Go to her – and God bless.'

She paused for only an instant, but he saw her shoulders straighten. He wondered why he had spoken those old words of blessing; instinct, he supposed, or a case of not knowing what else to say. Then, still carrying Annie, he followed Tizzie and her nephew to where William's body was lying on the great wooden block where they sawed up the beasts' carcasses. Two sides of mutton lay on the floor, no doubt thrown aside to make room for him. A doctor was fastening up his bag and preparing to leave.

Only Sam's words, the sight of him behind her carrying Annie, had given Tizzie the strength to proceed, to find that Mary wasn't at all like their mother had been. Stunned, yes; heartbroken, without a doubt, but so controlled it was clearly affecting the children. There wasn't a tear being shed, not even by Johnny.

Of necessity her own grief at the sight of William lying dead on his cutting block had to be set aside; there wasn't time to bid an unspoken farewell to the big, genial man she'd grown so fond of, nor to marvel that he looked much as he always did, with his apron still tied around his middle. There was no visible sign of the broken neck. Instant death, the doctor told her sombrely; unusual in a fall of less than thirty feet, but not unheard of . . . it was all to do with the way a person landed.

Sam was horribly aware of intruding on a family bereavement but he couldn't bring himself to leave until he knew they didn't need him. He watched as Tizzie gathered her sister in her arms, while Billy picked up young Johnny and stood next to Abel and Elizabeth. None of them was weeping; it was as if they were all suspended without speech or feeling . . . Tears were still to come, he thought, and the sooner the better. Over her sister's shoulders the woman he once thought he loved was looking at the children . . .

Tizzie held Mary close and felt a distinct tremor running through her sister's body; it was constant, like a well-tuned machine being driven to its utmost capacity. Over her shoulder she saw the children standing there, bewildered that their mother wasn't in a torrent of tears, not quite taking in that their father would never play with them again. In that instant two separate facts impinged on her above all others: one, she must take charge of things before Mary's control cracked; two, she must watch over the children until their mother was capable of doing it herself. Responsibility for the five of them descended on her like a lead weight. She shifted her feet in an effort to brace herself for the unseen burden.

The builder's men were still in a huddle, waiting for Richard Barnes to arrive from Droylsden. They told anybody who would listen that Mr Hartley had climbed the ladder to the platform at the top of the scaffolding, as he'd done many a time before. They'd been about to knock off for Christmas and he'd wanted to see for himself that they'd left the building weatherproof. He'd stumbled as he stepped from the ladder, they said, then grabbed at a pole, missed it, and fell to the yard behind the shop.

Tizzie listened in silence but her mind was crying out loud in protest. Did he *have* to go swarming up the ladder in the middle of the busiest afternoon of the whole year? Had he been ensuring that the money she had lent him was being properly spent? How could the life of a big strong man be wiped out by missing the step at the top of a ladder?

And then things began to speed up. It seemed only seconds before the undertaker and his man arrived and between them carried William upstairs to a more dignified resting place, only minutes before his parents came, deeply shocked but both with tears blessedly flowing, tears that seemed to spread naturally to Johnny and Abel and then Billy. Of the four only Elizabeth remained dry eyed, her wary gaze noting all that went on, her mouth set in the familiar mutinous line.

Then in ones and twos came the rest of the Hartleys, their noisy good humour silenced, the menfolk having to leave almost at once to attend to their Christmas work. And all the time customers thronged the shop wanting their joints of meat or their poultry or their jellied pies, many of them not knowing about William until they saw the announcement that she'd chalked on the blackboard.

The two young assistants sweated as they hurried to and fro, weighing birds, cutting joints, answering questions and sometimes forgetting to cross off names in the order book. The elderly man on the cooked meats table was grim faced behind his scales. 'I've known Will since he were a lad,' he kept saying, 'since he were a little lad.'

Tizzie found her mind becoming clearer, but amid the turmoil only one person seemed to share her need for order and method – Sam Schofield. He was a godsend in that first awful hour; brisk, calm, capable. He went to tell Barney what had happened and at the same time took Albert and Gideon their Christmas bonuses; he called at Farthing Lane to inform Rebecca, he took Annie home to her mother and even brought the minister from Bethesda Chapel to say a prayer over William.

Tizzie scribbled a note to the shop she'd been heading for regarding the gift she'd ordered from them: two leather-backed clothes brushes for Barney, one for his coats, one for his hats, on an embossed leather tray – a luxurious, masculine sort of gift, made to her own design. The tradesmen hadn't known who it was for and she certainly hadn't enlightened them. All at once, in the midst of death and chaos, it didn't seem to matter who knew or didn't know that she'd bought Barney an expensive Christmas present.

She didn't even wonder what Sam might think of it. 'I was about to collect a present for Barney Jellicoe from Simister's leather shop,' she told him. 'Would you take this note for me? It's asking them to deliver it to the pawnshop before closing time and saying I'll settle with them as soon as – as everything's finished here.' She found she couldn't

frame the words 'after the funeral', nor explain that she
didn't want Barney to be without a present from her on
Christmas morning.

Sam merely nodded and took the note, wasting no time
on words of comfort but in some measure giving it by his
presence. When he came back she was busy on the cash
desk in the shop, accepting payments, making out bills and
jotting down notes about anything that puzzled her. He saw
that she had scraped her hair back behind her ears, where
it still managed to look wild and unruly. She had regained
some colour, as well.

'I have to go now, Miss Ridings, on a matter of
business,' he said abruptly. 'I'll call in again at six thirty to
see if there's anything I can do.'

After years of exchanging words only for appearance's
sake in front of his family, such helpfulness seemed almost
unreal. 'You're very kind, Mr Schofield,' she said quietly.
'Thank you.' She didn't want him to go – oh, she didn't.
He was polite, he was formal, but in the seething, gas-lit
chaos of the shop he was like a strong anchor in a storm-
tossed sea. He raised his hat and strode out into the
darkness, but by then two women in weavers' aprons and
shawls were in front of her, jostling as to who was first in
line to pay for their goods.

'Forget him and buckle to,' she told herself. Business
was business after all. It was what she was good at; but all
she really wanted was to look after Mary. That task,
however, had been taken over by two of the Hartley wives,
while another of them had accompanied William's parents
back home.

'I'm all *right*, Tizzie,' Mary had told her tightly.
'Everybody must have their Christmas orders – William
would have wanted it. So if you can keep an eye on things
in the shop, that will help me more than anything. Then,
when we're closed and the children are in bed we'll talk,
just you and me.'

So it was all activity. No lack of helpers, no lack of
goodwill and sympathy. All that was needed was an

organiser, which inevitably had to be her. No sooner had Sam Schofield departed than a short familiar figure appeared at her side. Barney was dressed with care in his best black coat, white shirt and a grey necktie. He removed his hat and gave an odd little bow; she knew at once that such correctness was for the benefit of all those in the shop. His dark eyes observed her with care. 'Are you all right, Miss Tizzie?'

'Yes,' she said, 'though things are a bit busy, as you can see.'

He nodded grimly. 'That's no surprise, today of all days. What about Mrs Hartley and the children? Are the family here?'

'Yes. Mary wants me to keep an eye on things down here until they close. Barney, she's horribly controlled – unnaturally so. No tears – she's hardly batted an eyelid.'

He considered that. 'Tears'll come, no doubt of it, so you'd better make sure you're with her then. I've been round to see Rebecca. Naomi's arrived and they'll both be here at any minute.'

'I was going to send for her anyway. About tomorrow, Barney—' Gossip or no gossip she had long ago declined Mary's invitation to share their Christmas and instead had asked Barney to spend the day at Farthing Lane. 'I'll have to be here, of course, so I think I'll ask Rebecca to come round and take charge in the kitchen for a few days.'

'Good,' he said at once. 'That's what they want, both her and Naomi. I'll have a quiet day at home.'

'But Barney—'

'No arguing,' he interrupted, unaware that for once he was giving the orders. 'I can't join you here, I'd be out of place in a grieving family. Uh – I see young Mr Schofield was helping out earlier?'

'Yes. He gave Annie and me a lift in his carriage and then did some errands. He's gone off on business now.' She was aware of Barney looking up at her intently. His eyes were always guarded, but she imagined she could discern satisfaction in them; that, or maybe a kind of acceptance. She shook her shoulders impatiently. There wasn't time for imaginings.

'Will he be coming back here?'

'Yes, at half past six,' she replied promptly. Then she had to make out a bill for a sirloin of beef and reckon up the price of a newly weighed capon. There was hardly time to say farewell, but through the shop window she saw Barney struggling through the crowds on the street outside.

Half past six came and went with no sign of Sam Schofield. Gradually the marble slabs in the window were emptied of meat and the ceiling hooks of fowl. Trade slackened, and every time the shop door opened snowflakes swirled inside and melted on the damp sawdust that covered the floor. She was very cold. Rebecca had brought her a cup of tea and a barm cake but they hadn't warmed her at all. She was irritated by her own disappointment at Sam Schofield not keeping his promise, telling herself that he must have other things to do on Christmas Eve besides helping out in a house of mourning.

By eight o'clock all orders had been collected; only scraps of cooked meat and a few jellied pies were left. Through the window she could see a huddle of dark figures waiting. They were the very poor who usually gathered at the top of Rope Street, drifting now from shop to shop as they closed in case there was food to be had.

Tizzie looked at the gaunt women and their undersized children and sighed. Rebecca and Naomi had looked like that when they came to the pawnshop for work; taking them on had been her first real act of charity . . . How could she go upstairs to a dwelling that was warm? Where there was ample food in the larder? Though to be sure there was also a dead body laid out in the dining room. 'What would Mr Hartley have done for these people?' she asked the assistants wearily.

'He'da given 'em what's left,' said the oldest one.

She took coins from the drawer and replaced them with money from her purse. 'Share the food out and this as well, so they can buy stuff on the market. Then get off home as soon as you've cleaned up in here.'

She emptied the contents of the drawer into a cash box and made for the stairs, unnerved at feeling so very exhausted. Turning, she surveyed the empty shop; stripped of its produce it looked dark and desolate, very much in tune with her mood. That was what came of being fool enough to expect Sam Schofield to come back, she told herself.

The noise of high, overwrought sobbing met her as she set foot on the stairs. She gritted her teeth; it sounded like Elizabeth ... Happen the pouting mouth and the wary green eyes would show genuine feeling for once, or maybe she just needed somebody's undivided attention.

It seemed that the child wanted her mother, who was in the bedroom having a wash. Johnny and Abel were asleep, Billy was perched on the fender warming his hands, Rebecca was standing uncertainly by the kitchen door and Elizabeth was throwing a spectacular tantrum.

'Come on,' said Tizzie, crushing the desire to give her a slap. 'Let's get you washed and ready for bed, then I'll come to your room and brush your hair while we talk. I expect your mother is tired out.'

The answer to that was another howl and for good measure Elizabeth stamped her feet. Johnny woke up and joined in with the mournful wail of a young child whose sleep is disturbed. It was bedlam. At that moment there was a knock on the door. Elizabeth's cries rose to an outraged scream at the prospect of someone else arriving. She clutched at Tizzie's dress just as she wrenched open the door.

Sam Schofield stood on the landing, hat in hand, caped coat dusted with snow, his hair gleaming under the lamp. 'I can see I've called at a bad time,' he said quickly. 'It's just that I'm sorry. I couldn't help it – I was delayed.'

Behind her Mary appeared and pulled her daughter from Tizzie's side, holding her tightly by the hand as she went to deal with Johnny. Tizzie gazed anxiously after her sister and then turned to Sam Schofield, too weary to pretend she hadn't cared when he didn't come back. 'I needed you,' she admitted, 'but don't worry about it. Thanks for all you did.'

For once he seemed lost for words, standing there with his vivid blue gaze fixed on her. 'I think we'll be able to manage now the shop's shut,' she told him. 'My sister is taking it very well up to now.'

She thought his manner extremely odd. He was blinking and shaking his head in a circular motion like a man awakened from sleep. 'In that case I'll be off,' he said. 'Goodnight, Miss Ridings.'

'Goodnight,' she replied, then watched as he dragged his hand along the balustrade and walked to the top of the stairs. She couldn't seem to bring herself to go in and close the door.

On the fourth step down he stopped and looked up at her. 'I'm sorry, Tizzie,' he said quietly. 'I'm really sorry.'

The way he spoke the words made her wonder if he was sorry about something else besides William's death and the fact that he had been delayed, but there was no way of knowing. It was enough that he had called her Tizzie. She put a tired hand to her cheek and looked down on him. 'So am I,' she said simply.

When the children were all settled Mary busied herself arranging their presents ready for morning, then flopped down in a chair. 'Thanks for bringing Rebecca over, she's a wonderful help,' she said. 'I'm ready for bed now, I think. Would you like to stay and sleep with me, Tizz-wizz? I can lend you a nightie. Two of us in the same bed ... it'll be like the old days, won't it?'

Not quite, thought Tizzie grimly. In the old days we didn't have your husband's dead body on the premises. 'Of course I'll stay,' she said. 'Come on, let's go up. We always used to talk in bed, didn't we?'

She watched her sister in bafflement as they undressed. Such composure wasn't at all what she would have expected: Mary adored her husband. For years her every conversation had been larded with his name: 'William likes, William says, William thinks . . .' She herself had never been at ease in their bedroom. To her the room and everything it contained held the essence of their physical closeness, their devotion to each other. Now she had no option but to sleep in William's place in the marriage bed, put her head on the pillow where his head had rested. What made it even worse was Mary behaving as if everything was quite normal and ordinary: plaiting her hair, buttoning her nightgown, fastening the ribbons of her lace cap. Her plump little sister, always so ready to laugh and to cry . . .

Then all at once things weren't normal and ordinary any longer. Mary threw back the bedclothes and in William's place was his folded nightshirt of blue and white striped flannel. For what seemed an eternity she stared at it as if she'd never seen such a thing in her life. Tizzie watched as her face changed colour and the smooth, chubby features became ugly with grief; her mouth stretched, eyes wide with horror and then streaming with tears. She clutched the nightshirt and kissed it again and again. 'He's dead!' she cried, as if Tizzie might not be aware of it. 'William's dead! That's just his body in the dining room. He's dead, Tizzie. He'll never hold me again!'

That was the beginning of a night of agony for them both. Tizzie recalled that Barney had told her she must be there when the tears came. Well, she was here, and Mary was weeping as if she would never stop. She held her in her arms, whispering little words from their childhood, kissing her, stroking her hair, finding her fresh handkerchiefs.

It was daybreak before Mary fell into a fitful doze and by then Tizzie was beyond sleep; she lay awake and watched the light of reflected snow behind the curtains. Outside was the unique quiet of Christmas morning; at any moment the children would be awake. She braced herself for the day to come and edged silently from the bed. Rebecca was here already, Naomi would be round to help, the Hartley family would come and go . . . There wouldn't be a moment to themselves. Time enough to think of the future when they'd got through today.

CHAPTER EIGHT

Precautions

The Schofield men stood at the front door of Meadowbank House, bidding farewell to a group of cotton masters after an informal meeting over supper.

Luther Dobbs put on his hat and gave the melancholy twist of the lips that was as near as he ever came to smiling. 'Thanks, Joshua,' he said. 'You've had the sense to bring it all out, in the open. The rest of us were that busy pretending everything was all right in our own mills it never occurred to us that there might be others in the same boat.'

Joshua laughed, and his sons exchanged looks; there was relief in the sound and they knew the reason for it. 'We're all aware now that there's something going on, Luther,' he agreed, 'so we'll have to keep our eyes open. It can't all be accident and coincidence.'

John Fairbrother took his coat from Ellie. 'No, but we mustn't jump to conclusions,' he warned. 'I'll be interested to see if the Bluebell and Boulton's keep free of trouble.'

One by one they went out to their carriages, leaving the Schofields to reflect on what had been revealed over supper.

'Come on,' suggested Joshua, 'let's have half an hour in the little sitting room.' When they were settled round the fire he looked from one to the other. 'Now, what do you make of it?'

'That we can stop worrying our heads about Ralph being involved,' replied James promptly. 'If all those here tonight have had tampering in their mills, even in a minor way, then it must rule out Ralph once and for all.'

'Aye, thank God,' said Joshua heavily. 'If he wanted to harm anybody it would be us, not half of Saltley. The only question we're faced with now is who's behind it. Walton and Boulton are the only ones who haven't admitted to trouble, but we mustn't forget they're neither of 'em fools. If they wanted to harm their competitors I can't see they'd be so obvious as to set men to damaging other folk's mills and at the same time leave their own untouched.'

'Me neither,' agreed Sam. 'There's another aspect to it, as well; cotton's been up and down a bit lately but at present there's enough demand to provide orders for everybody. That being the case, why should they try to damage the competition? Let's just tighten up at Jericho for a bit and see how things go, shall we? And it might be prudent to speak to Matthew and the others about keeping an eye open for strangers around the place.'

His father flashed him a glance. 'You think something might happen here at home, Sam?'

'Let's just say I'm wary. If there's a mischief maker on the loose it's better to be sure than sorry.'

Joshua was pulling at his whiskers. 'I'll have a word with the household staff and those at the institute,' he promised. Then, as if obeying an order, they all three fell silent, Joshua sitting in the blue armchair that he'd given his wife for her fortieth birthday. It was his habit to stroke the arms whenever he sat in it, to such an extent that the velvet there was completely bald.

Across the hearth James was deep in thought, his mouth tight. Sam watched him with compassion and wondered what life was like up at High Lee. Was Esther giving him a bad time? Would he ever again assert himself as he must have done when he fathered Charles? In recent weeks he had taken to staying the night at Meadowbank after trips to Manchester, rather than travelling on to High Lee. The severe weather had been good enough excuse, as indeed it had for Charles, who was openly delighted whenever the roads were too bad to make the journey home.

Sam smiled at the thought of his nephew. There was a satisfaction in dealing with the boy, a fascination in watching the development of that gentle personality. As for his interest in music, it now equalled his passion for things mechanical, maybe even surpassed it. What was more, a streak of independence was surfacing in him from time to time, hinting that he might not be so very like his father after all.

Thoughts of his nephew led to memories of the fatherless Hartley children. Sam hadn't seen them since Christmas Eve when he'd called on Tizzie with his apology; on that occasion they had been making themselves heard in no uncertain fashion. He had been delayed at Mosley Street, having gone there at his father's request to check in person that the premises were secure for the Christmas break. To his astonishment he had found Nathaniel Lee and the two young clerks lolling over their desks bleary-eyed and incoherent from drink, a half-empty bottle of Madeira the only visible means of intoxication. The men from the warehouse and the teetotal Alf Grimshaw had already left for home, but if late customers had happened to walk in they would have found three drunkards in charge.

Sam's first reaction had been relief that his father wasn't there to see the flouting of a strict company rule: no alcohol to be consumed at work, either there or in the mill. Still on edge after his time with the Hartleys, he felt like banging their fuddled heads together. Instead he locked the big front doors, rummaged furiously for home addresses for the three of them and then bundled them into cabs and sent them home to their respective families, resolving to deal with them on his next visit. Drunkards nauseated him; they embarrassed and amazed him. How could anyone allow their brain to be addled to that extent?

He saw off the last cab from the side door and went back

inside. It was only then, in the echoing emptiness, that unease took him. He eyed the wine; was half a bottle of Madeira enough to render three men almost insensible? Even if they were more accustomed to ale, or even gin? He didn't think so. And where had it come from? A note on the table answered that one; it said, 'A merry Christmas to Mr Lee and the young gentlemen, from a grateful customer.' He nodded thoughtfully. They would all have been helpful and obliging; it was company policy.

Then, from somewhere on the floors above came a soft thud, as if a door had closed, followed by a creaking of floorboards. The hairs at the back of his neck lifted. Everywhere was dark except for a couple of gaslights in the outer office and an oil lamp here and there. It was very quiet.

Suddenly he thought of Ralph at eighteen: clever, chillingly self-absorbed, lacking in any humane principle; as foreign to the family as a hyena among English ponies. Could he really have returned to Manchester with none of them the wiser? The very idea seemed far-fetched . . . Still, his father had asked him to check the premises, not to stand gazing into space. He grabbed a lamp and marched to the stairs, determined to start at the top and to search all five floors. If there was anybody hiding up there he would damned well find them and throw them out.

His uncle Charlie had lived on the top floor years ago, but now the big rooms were empty except for a few pieces of dust-sheeted furniture. He looked in the wardrobe and cupboards, searched the kitchen; everything was in order. The next floor down was where sample bales of raw cotton from the shippers were sometimes stored, also consignments of spun yarn for specialist weaving mills. The lamp cast shadows on the whitewashed walls, but he looked behind every bale of cotton, examined every bundle of yarn. All at once he felt an absolute fool, clambering here, there and everywhere just because he'd heard a creak or two. Building timbers were never silent, after all, and everybody knew that Manchester was swarming with rats.

Grunting with exasperation, he went down again to the third floor where rolls of cotton cloth were stacked ready for export to all parts of the world. The arteries and heart of the Schofield company, his father called it, but then he said that about Jericho, too. It was neat and clean, the men saw to that, but somehow he always felt sick on that particular floor. From these hoist doors his uncle had been pushed to his death; grease from the wheel of this winch had been on Ralph's sleeve – his mother had seen it and realised its significance, then tried to keep her suspicions from his father . . .

Grimly he had inspected every window, looked behind every stack of cloth, then moved to the winch and the hoist. Feeling more foolish than ever, he held the lamp high and trod with care; he might feel like a fool but he had no intention of becoming Mosley Street's second corpse.

Then he saw that the iron bar that secured the hoist doors was missing, leaving them free to be opened from inside or out. Disbelieving, he swung round and saw the bar balanced on some rolls of fine poplin. Once again the hairs rose on his neck and he felt a similar prickle on his forearms. The men would never have left it there, he told himself; it was always slotted straight back as soon as the doors were closed.

It seemed to him that, balanced so nonchalantly on his father's finest cloth, the heavy bar mocked his efforts at security. In the light of the lamp it gave off a dull gleam, as if highly satisfied with its years of being handled. Angrily he slung it into place across the doors and headed down to the second-floor yarn room, where hundreds of hanks of Jericho's spun yarn were displayed for inspection. Nothing there to arouse suspicion, so down again to the first floor sample room with its mahogany display shelves and tables. This was where customers could examine pattern books before placing their orders – Alf Grimshaw's domain, with not a single thing out of place. Suddenly a current of ice-cold air blew across the tables and the moan of the wind became louder. Somebody had opened the door to the street!

He ran for the stairs. Fool that he was, he should have started from the cellars upwards. That way he might have cornered whoever it was. He found the side door swinging in the wind, mocking him again; the street was deserted, snow drifting to the opposite pavement and leaving bare the area just outside the door, so that no footprints could be seen. He went back inside, furious at his own lack of foresight. It was plain that somebody had wanted Nathaniel and his clerks insensible. His mind raced. He would get that Madeira examined, analysed; happen it was laced with laudanum or some such ...

But the bottle had gone. So too had the note, or the greater part of it. All that remained was a torn-off scrap holding the opening words of the message: 'Merry Christmas'. In pencil had been added an exclamation mark and a jaunty sprig of holly.

At that his mind became crystal clear. Time for little games, was it? Well, two could play games. For a start he would take the ledgers home with him, every one of them – unless the game player had beaten him to it?

Thank God, they were all in the safe when he unlocked it. He piled them up and ransacked drawers for anything else of importance, then wrapped the lot in a length of hessian and fastened the bundle with rope. He locked the doors meticulously, signalled for a cab to take him and his bundle to Victoria and then stopped off on the way to report the intruder to the city police.

The hours had flown, right enough. By the time he took another cab from Saltley station to go and see Tizzie it was half past eight. Now he kept wondering if she'd known what he meant by that final apology, because his words had come from instinct rather than thought. At the time he had been conscious only of a deep, unfathomable regret; a sense of waste and futility. He had thought himself grieved that Will Hartley's life had been smashed away on the stones of his own back yard.

Much later, lying awake in the snow-white early hours of Christmas morning, he had turned the years over layer by layer in his mind, like the pages of a book that has long remained closed. True, he'd been sorry he was late; deeply, startlingly sorry. Also true, he'd been sorry about William, sorry for his wife and children.

But observing Tizzie as she dealt with that hysterical child, recalling her howl of anguish on hearing that Mary was widowed, seeing the way she had buckled to in the frenzy of the shop, he realised that more than anything he was sorry for the wasted years, for the pride that had made him reject her, for – yes, he might as well admit it – the jealousy that had prevented him tackling her about her regard for his father . . .

'Well, we're a fine trio, aren't we?' said Joshua suddenly. 'Busy with our own thoughts and not a word for each other. Shall we sort out what we should do at Jericho?'

Sam brought his mind to the present. They discussed at length how best to use extra night watchmen at Jericho, but all the time he was wondering why he should still be asking himself whether Ralph had come back to England.

His father knew all about the bottle of Madeira, all about the intruder at Mosley Street. He couldn't have kept that from him, even though he'd wanted to. But he couldn't bring himself to declare that he was still worried about Ralph. He couldn't take away the relief that now softened his father's mouth and eased the deep grooves between nose and jaw. What he could do, though, was mention two other matters that were plaguing him. He spoke out abruptly, interrupting James in mid-sentence. 'We should increase our fire precautions at Jericho, Father.'

Joshua shot him a look. 'I agree, but we're well insured, don't forget.'

'I haven't forgotten. Another thing – what do you both think of me going to live in Uncle Charlie's rooms at Mosley Street? I've been fancying it for some time. A man of my age should have his own establishment rather than be under his father's feet.'

They both stared at him, and he sensed his father's

reactions: surprise, then dismay, followed by unease; at any moment he might guess the real reason behind the suggestion. All he said was: 'What, and travel to Saltley every day?'

'Why not? I travel to Manchester twice a week as it is.'

James was openly perplexed. 'But I always thought you liked living at home, Sam?'

'I do, but I fancy a change.'

'But could you be happy at Mosley Street after – after what happened there?'

'I don't see why not. My own memories of Uncle Charlie are happy ones. I think I could settle in those rooms – they're lovely. Since that do with the poor consignments of cotton I've been thinking that I should show my face more often at the Exchange and the docks.'

His father was watching him closely. 'Did anything else happen on Christmas Eve?' he asked. 'Anything you haven't told me?'

Careful, Sam warned himself. Thankfully he was able to speak the truth: 'Nothing, Father.' The only thing he'd kept to himself was a feeling rather than a happening.

'Look, lad,' said Joshua, 'if you really want to set up at Mosley Street then go ahead. I'll miss having you here, but you'll leave home anyway when you get wed. If it's just to keep an eye on things, though, dismiss it from your mind. We'll employ a full-time night watchman and make the place secure. No, say no more for now. Think it over and we'll talk about it again after the weekend. Oh, I nearly forgot – I've ordered a wreath from the family for Will Hartley's funeral.'

'That's good,' said Sam. 'I'm sending one of my own, as well. I was at the shop within minutes of it happening, after all.'

'How is she?' asked James quietly.

'Tizzie? Coping, I expect. She's a capable woman.' Sam saw his father's alert blue gaze go from one of them to the other.

James shook his head. 'I was meaning Mary. I wonder

how she'll be fixed financially, with four children to bring up.'

'Tizzie will see to all that,' said Sam with certainty. 'She thinks the world of them.' He stared sombrely into the fire. Whether she thought the world of anybody else, apart from Barney Jellicoe, he had no way of knowing.

The kitchen of Meadowbank's garden cottage was all steamed up; it was a wet day outside and washing day inside. Having been up since half past five, Martha was already busy with the lading can emptying the set boiler when Matthew came in at midday. He detested wet Mondays, he told himself, but at least Martha always managed something hot for him rather than the cold meat and pickles or bread and cheese that was Monday dinner for most of Saltley.

Cheeks pink, her big apron damp from the morning's work, she gave him a little quirk of the lips and ladled water from the boiler into the tin bowl for him to wash his hands.

'Had a lazy mornin', then?' he asked, straight-faced.

'Oh aye, same as you,' she retorted, and marched to the fireplace to get the dinner.

'I haven't had a lazy mornin',' said Rosie. 'I had to write names on the board when Miss Hardman left the room.'

'And could you spell 'em all?' asked Matthew.

'I only had to write the names of them who were *talkin'*!'

'And how many was that?'

'Two,' she admitted, 'but I could spell 'em both.'

Matthew sat down and gave her a kiss. 'If you carry on at this rate you'll be able to do all the writin' for your mother an' me,' he said proudly, 'all our letters an' such.'

'But you an' me mam don't write any letters.'

'Oh yes we do. I wrote to your aunties in Devon a few months back, now didn't I? I sent them the latest news of Miss Rosie Raike.'

She laughed, her dad always made her laugh. She wriggled on her chair and felt happy, even though it was washing day. She didn't like wet washing days because she couldn't see the fire for wet clothes and her mam put lines up across the room. But she did like mutton broth, specially when her mam put tiny little dumplings in it just for her, as well as the big ones for her dad.

Matthew ate his meal with pleasure. 'Mr Schofield had a word with me an' the lads this mornin',' he told them both. 'There's been meddlin' in the mill, he says, so he wants us all to keep an eye open for strangers around the place, in case there's somebody out to make mischief in Saltley. Rosie, you haven't seen anybody you don't know hanging around near the big house, have you?'

Rosie cut a dumpling in half with her spoon; she always did that because sometimes her mam hid a nice bit of mutton or a few peas inside one as a surprise. She considered her father's question and wished she could have told him something startling, such as she'd seen a sailor with an eye patch and gold buttons on his coat in the garden. 'I've only seen a man at the top of the buttercup field,' she said in apology. 'He was there when I was makin' me snowman. He looked black against the next field.'

'That was before Christmas Day, now, wasn't it?' asked Matthew casually. 'Did you know him.'

'No, but once I saw him walking down the road from Holdwell.'

'An' what does he look like, this man?'

Rosie chased a dumpling round her bowl. 'He's not as tall as you, an' he's dressed like a – a labourer. When it's rainin' or snowin' he has a sack over his shoulders – he hasn't got a waterproof or a big umbrella.'

'Is he young or old, would you say? Dark or fair?'

Rosie's bright eyes observed her father intently. Why was he pretending it wasn't important when his face told her that it was? She finished the last spoonful of broth and was able to give the matter her full attention. 'He's old –

older than you,' she announced gravely. 'His hair's black and grey and his face is . . .' She eyed them both warily. 'I know it's rude to say it, but it's true – he's ugly! His chin's all blue an' bristly an' his eyes are very little; they're black an' round like the buttons on your best boots, Mam. He doesn't like me.'

Martha's small face became very still. It went without saying that nobody would hurt a child of Rosie's age, but all the same . . . She made herself speak lightly. 'Has he talked to you, love?'

Rosie shook her head and thought for a minute. Grown-ups didn't understand when she told them about the messages on people's faces . . . Even her dad only pretended to know what she was on about. 'He didn't like it when I saw him in the buttercup field,' she explained carefully, 'an' one day he looked angry that I'd seen him on the path when I were runnin' home from school.'

'The path?' said Matthew sharply. '*Our* path?' All the staff at Meadowbank thought of the short cut from the town and the institute as their path. 'What was he doin' up there?'

'Lookin' at the house,' said Rosie. 'People stop an' look at it because it's nice, don't they? Specially in summer because of the garden. But it wasn't summer, of course, it was winter.'

Martha wasn't annoyed, she was worried. 'You never told us anything about this man, love.'

'I thought he was one of them without a home,' said Rosie defensively.

It was true; vagrants did come down into Saltley from the hills. Some of them walked miles every day looking for work. This man, though, sounded different. 'It's all right, love, don't worry,' said Matthew. 'I'll talk to Mr Schofield about him. If you see him again though, don't say a word; pretend you haven't noticed him and come and tell me as quick as you can.'

'What if you're at work?'

'Tell Davey or Zacky if they're here. If not, come and find me at the institute. If I'm not in the grounds I'll be in the greenhouses or the carpenter's shop – you know, the big hut with the green door.'

But Rosie wasn't going to be fobbed off just like that. 'Is he a bad man, then?' she asked with interest.

'This particular man might not be bad at all, but Mr Schofield wants to know if we see anybody round here that we haven't seen before. We must always try to please Mr Schofield, mustn't we? He's my boss, after all.'

'Mm. An' because you work for him you think you've got the world in a bant, don't you?'

Matthew stared at her, half amused. 'What?'

Rosie coloured slightly. 'It's what Becky Cropper said last week when I wrote her name on the board for talkin'. She said, "You think you're everybody, you, Rosie Raike! Your dad thinks he's got the world in a bant just because he works for Schofield."'

Matthew covered her hand with his, taken aback at the spite behind the words. 'Did Becky say anythin' else, liddle love?'

Rosie squirmed on her chair, but when he looked at her like that she knew she must tell him everything. 'She said, "He's from foreign parts, your dad, an' he's takin' work as belongs to Saltley folk."' Her dad looked weary at that, as if he'd heard it all before but didn't expect to hear it again. Her mam was going to say something but he shut her up without a word.

'If she says that again,' he said, 'tell her I work hard for my wages and in any case Mr Schofield himself offered me this job and this house to go with it. Tell Becky that.'

Rosie beamed with relief. He could always make things right, her dad. 'You *are* a foreigner, though, aren't you?' she persisted.

'Less of a foreigner than all the Irish in the town,' said Martha. 'Your dad came to Saltley because he knew a man who lived here as a lad. He worked his way here all the way from Devon, on his own. Tell that to Becky!'

Rosie gave a satisfied little wriggle. 'Is there any cake?' she asked.

*

Tizzie anchored the black velvet hat to her hair with two
long pins and for the first time in days studied her face in
the looking glass. Her cheekbones had always been
prominent, but never more so than now. Could she really
have lost weight in the space of four days? She must have
done; only that morning she'd had to tighten the draw-
strings of her stays. Evidently the upheaval of William's
death had taken its toll on her flesh as well as her
emotions.

She looked at the clock and stopped hurrying when she
saw there was half an hour to go before she need set off for
Mary's, though of course she could arrive early – there
would be plenty to do before the funeral carriages set off.
Then she checked herself. The tea was being prepared by
the Hartley wives, who were a tower of strength on
domestic matters. Financial matters, needless to say, were
being left solely to the woman with a head for business . . .

Tizzie stood by the window, undecided. Usually she
relished action and activity but all at once she craved a time
of quiet and reflection, just for herself. No, she couldn't
delay . . . Mary would be ready to fall on her neck again as
soon as she appeared. She thought for a moment and self-
preservation won. Deliberately she removed her hat and
coat, then sat in front of the bedroom fire with her feet up,
letting the events of that afternoon fill her memory.

Already it seemed like weeks, months, *years* since
Annie shouted out that William was dead; centuries since
Mary behaved with such unnatural calm. Since that awful
night when they shared the bed her sister had been unable
to eat, to sleep, to look after her family; it seemed that her
sole function was to weep. Well, she couldn't weep for
ever, thought Tizzie grimly. Sooner or later she must
answer to the needs of her children.

She stared into the red heart of the fire. There hadn't
been time to think about Sam Schofield; the days had been
so busy, and the nights were merely spells of exhausted
sleep broken by worry over Mary. Even now she didn't

know where the Schofield carriage had been heading when he'd seen her and Annie running along Peter Street. It was ironic that it had taken a tragedy to make him speak to her other than in the small talk that was their common discourse in front of his family.

Why, why, *why* did she find him so compelling? Why did all other men seem like faded watercolours compared to the bold, vibrant oils in which he was painted? He wasn't startlingly good-looking like Sarah and James and the absent Ralph; his features were roughly hewn, as if hacked from the stone of the Pennines. Admittedly, he had the dazzling blue eyes of the Schofields and the golden hair, but even that was darkening year by year. And he wasn't remotely elegant; his build was reminiscent of a prizefighter on the wakes.

Tizzie had first been drawn to him because he was the exact opposite of Edward Mayfield. Not to put too fine a point on it, Edward had been dissolute and completely unprincipled, tempting her to every physical intimacy but the ultimate one; the fact that they'd stopped short of that wasn't through lack of persuasion on his part. He had become engaged to Sarah even while fathering a child on a young servant and taking Tizzie to a house of ill repute in Manchester ... By contrast Sam Schofield had been restrained and honourable, devoted to his sister and like greased lightning in her defence. He had been resourceful, he had been kind; but above all he had been wholesome.

Since the end of her infatuation with Edward, Tizzie had been kissed by one man and it wasn't Sam Schofield. One man in eleven long years. He had been a dealer in precious stones from the other side of Oldham and he'd wanted to marry her. Others had proposed marriage, but he was the only one who had kissed her: a chaste brushing of her lips with his. He was a decent man, intelligent, hardworking, but with nothing about him to make her relinquish her cherished independence.

Sometimes she wondered whether the passion she had shared with Edward had spoiled all other men for her, but the truth was that she could hardly remember what had taken place between them. It had been madness, a fever of the blood, fuelled by youthful curiosity as to what went on between men and women and a conviction that life was passing her by. No, it wasn't her sexual encounters with Edward that had spoiled other men for her, it was the wholesome Sam Schofield, who had never touched her except to shake her hand; Sam Schofield of Jericho Mills ... the most sought-after bachelor in Saltley. At the town's social events she had seen eager mothers parade their daughters in front of him like heifers for sale at the market, but his sister had told her that he never came close to an engagement, let alone marriage. Whether, like many a man in the area, he availed himself of the women in Manchester, she didn't know. She didn't want to know.

Rain poured down on the cobbles of Farthing Lane, causing the better off to huddle under umbrellas and waterproofs and the poor to make do with shawls and sacking. In the house Tizzie still sat in front of the fire, wrapped in her thoughts. There was a tap on the door and when it opened the coals shifted noisily in the grate.

'Miss Tizzie, are you all right? The cab'll be here in a minute.' It was Rebecca, dressed for the funeral and wondering why her employer was still in her bedroom.

Tizzie jumped up. She would be of no use to Mary and the children if she drooped around harbouring pointless recollections. Apart from the fact that he hadn't left a will, that he had overspent on the extensions to the shop and that he had swarmed up and down ladders like an overactive monkey, her brother-in-law had been a good man. She must do her best for his family.

It was a fine funeral, said the people of Saltley, the best for many a month. Bethesda Chapel had been packed to the doors and folk had walked out in the rain and lined the path to the grave. A pity about the weather, but you couldn't expect much better at the turn of the year. The man who swilled out the slaughterhouse in Bushell's Yard every day had known William for years and he put it differently. 'It's just as it should be,' he declared. 'The heavens are weepin' for a good young fella, an' in my opinion it's no more than his due.'

Sam had received a letter from Tizzie, written on behalf of her sister, thanking him for his 'invaluable help' and inviting him to join the mourners at the funeral or, failing that, to pay his respects at the service. 'However,' she concluded, 'my sister will quite understand if pressure of business or other commitments prevent you attending in either capacity. Once again, Mr Schofield, my sister's warmest thanks and, needless to say, my own.' She had signed it Tizzie Ridings.

Carefully worded, he decided, so that he would feel no obligation to attend and could refuse without causing offence. Well, it was a fact that she didn't need him among the mourning party, because Hartleys would be there by the dozen. Maybe she didn't need him at all. Whether that was the case or not, he wanted to say a proper farewell to Will, both in hymn and prayer. And dammit, he wanted to see how she seemed. He kept remembering her looking over Mary's shoulder at the children.

Sam went straight to the service at Bethesda, sitting quietly near the back. The pews were filling up rapidly when a short figure came quietly down the aisle. Barney Jellicoe hesitated, looking for a vacant seat. Sam gestured to him and made room in the pew, concealing his surprise that the other man wasn't with the mourners. The big white face with its dark eyes lifted momentarily to his; both of them nodded in mutual regard and then sat in silence.

Moments later the congregation rose as the minister walked in front of the coffin and its bearers, calling out loud from the scriptures, 'I am the resurrection and the life ...' The mourners followed in procession, Tizzie supporting Mary, who leaned on her so heavily she might as well have been carrying her.

As they passed, Sam instinctively stretched out a hand to help. Next to him two short arms jerked forward for the same purpose, then fell to the dwarf's side. Why couldn't one of the Hartleys have supported the widow, Sam thought angrily. Tizzie, unveiled and dry eyed, was deathly pale, her hair like a flame beneath the black hat. Mary was tottering, close to collapse. Behind them came the three older children, holding hands. Abel was crying.

There were so many mourners they filled the front half of the chapel. When the last one was seated, a late arrival edged quietly into their pew and Barney leaned backwards to let the newcomer sit next to Sam. It was James. Sam was surprised again. He had thought his brother to be busy on estate work at High Lee.

Then it was hymns and prayers, with the minister saying flattering things about the dead man: 'a young life cut down in its glorious prime,' 'a devoted husband and father', 'a tireless worker for the chapel', and 'a son of one of the town's most respected families' ...

Sam joined in the hymns and half listened to the words. Will Hartley hadn't been much older than him, but when he died he had something to show for having lived, hadn't he? Years of loving marriage with a good woman and the fruits of that marriage – four fine children. If he dropped down dead tomorrow what would *he* have to show? That he'd been a loyal, hard-working son? Not much to compare with Will Hartley, was it?

And then the service was over. Everyone stood as the mourners followed the coffin back up the aisle. This time two sturdy Hartleys supported Mary. Snuffling, Billy and Abel walked behind their mother; Tizzie and a subdued Elizabeth came next.

As she passed them Tizzie looked along their pew. Sam thought that her face seemed all cheekbones and eyes; eyes that widened on seeing him and James and Barney Jellicoe. She gave a little nod of the head. That, for now, would have to be enough, he thought.

CHAPTER NINE

Strangers

Things were improving, Tizzie told herself cautiously. The previous day Mary had been out of bed in time to see the children off to school and had announced that by the end of the week she might tackle some cooking. Annie was coming in full-time, the Hartley wives were doing the washing and baking and Elizabeth had started to help in the house, managing several small tasks without sulking.

To Tizzie, more important than domestic issues was the matter of supporting her sister's family. Mary had given her a free hand to look into William's affairs, but when she tried to talk to her about it a few days after the funeral she would have none of it.

'Money, money, money!' she cried, 'is that all you can think of? William would never have left us unprovided for! Never!'

But William *had* left them unprovided for, and in property against which he'd borrowed money. Tizzie had been staggered when she'd found the IOUs, dismayed to open Mary's letters of condolence and find among them demands for repayment of debts. How often had she warned him against borrowing? When he'd borrowed from her she had thought it was for the first time; now she suspected he'd turned to her only because he couldn't raise money elsewhere. She was unable to tell Mary that – it would be too cruel, so she was going against her nature, which favoured straight talking rather than subterfuge. The Holden Street shop remained closed and she gave the men two weeks' pay in lieu of notice, then asked Mr Hartley and William's brothers round to Farthing Lane for the evening.

Decent, good-natured, hard-working men, it was clear why they weren't up among the town's wealthiest business families. Country born and bred, skilled in the slaughtering of livestock and in butchering, shrewd when it came to selling meat and poultry, they knew nothing at all of more complicated finance. Once again she found herself unable to reveal the full details of William's affairs; his family just took it for granted that the Barnes brothers had been paid for work done and that there was money to finish the job. Not one of them wanted to take on the shop, even as a tenant.

'We're all well set as we are,' said the eldest earnestly, 'in a small way, admitted, but then our Will was always the one with big ambitions, like. When he bought the shop outright, we knew he musta been well off.'

Fortunately Tizzie had ideas of her own but at that point hadn't wanted to enlarge on them. They agreed that she must deal with everything because Mary was in no state to make decisions. 'Do what you want, Tizzie,' she had said limply. 'I'll sign something to give you authority. We can't stay here, I know that. I don't want to, anyway; I couldn't bear it. I can't think about the future, my mind's in a whirl. You handle things, you're so good at business.'

Handling William's affairs was like wading through treacle, Tizzie told herself in the days that followed, but difficulties had always brought out the best in her. She called on the lawyer, Kenworthy, to warn him that she might need his services before long; she settled bills, sent out forceful reminders to William's debtors and conferred at length with Richard Barnes, to that gentleman's ill-concealed astonishment. Finally she consulted her own personal lawyer and the leading property dealer in Saltley.

The relief of being a wealthy woman in such a situation was deep and satisfying, though admittedly she was wealthy in property rather than pounds. Wealthy enough to support a mother, four children and possibly a little maid? she asked herself. For years and years? Yes, wealthy enough for that, if Mary would accept such help. Knowing her sister's obstinate streak, she thought it likely that when Mary was herself again she would refuse it.

Day after day, Tizzie spent the afternoons and evenings round at Holden Street, then came home and worked until the early hours, making plans, totting up figures, examining specifications. She'd always thrived on challenges, but she found it unexpectedly wearing. There was nobody to talk to except the man whose discretion was absolute and who knew as much about her affairs as she did herself – Barney.

In her weaker moments she imagined discussing things with Sam Schofield. He would listen, she thought; solid, dependable, *concerned* ... or maybe he wouldn't. Perhaps regretting their brief closeness on Christmas Eve, he was keeping his distance. She hadn't seen him since the funeral. Day followed busy day and she was forced to banish him to the fringes of her mind, turning instead to the man who never failed her.

She arrived at the pawnshop by cab at nine o'clock one morning to find Albert up the ladder and Barney at the desk in his shirtsleeves and waistcoat. He slid awkwardly from the chair and stumped towards her. 'Miss Tizzie! This is a pleasure!'

Tizzie didn't waste words. 'Good morning. I need to talk, Barney. Can you come round this evening?' He hesitated for only an instant, but she flipped an impatient hand. 'Gossip can't rule my life, you know, not when there's things to be done! Anyway, I've had an idea – and not before time.' She looked up, 'Albert!'

Barney's assistant clutched the sides of the ladder and slid down without touching the steps. 'Yes, Miss Ridings?'

She gave him a straight green stare. 'I expect you know

that there's talk in the town about Mr Jellicoe and me?'
Next to her Barney shuffled his feet and grunted as if
punched in the stomach. She ignored him.

Albert gaped at her and coloured up. 'Ee, Miss Ridings,
I don't know what to say—'

'You've been here long enough to have made up your
own mind as to whether it's true. Do you think it is?'

'Nay, nay, course I don't. It's wicked!'

'Thank you. Now, I need Mr Jellicoe at my house on a
matter of personal business. Could you accompany him to
protect his reputation – and mine? Stay as long as he stays;
Rebeccca will give you your supper. I'm prepared to pay
you for your time.'

Albert ran an agitated finger inside his collar. Miss
Ridings was one on her own, he told himself. He thought
of his bare little house and the constant temptation to visit
the warmth and company of the Salters' Arms when he got
home from work. He would be glad of a change of scene.
'I need no pay if it'll help you an' Mr Jellicoe,' he told her,
'specially if I get me supper.'

'Thanks, Albert. Barney, will you both come round as
soon as you've closed up?'

'Yes, Miss Tizzie.' The dark eyes were watching her
closely. 'Do you want me to bring anything from here?'

'Only Albert,' she replied with a faint smile, then went
out to the waiting cab.

It was good to talk to Barney again in the comfort of her
sitting room. There was so much to tell him, so many
things about which to ask his advice, that before she knew
it she was gabbling.

When she paused for breath he said, 'Well, nobody
could accuse you of wasting time. Mr Hartley didn't
borrow the full value of the property, then?'

'No, but he's mortgaged it as far as he can – to about
two-thirds the value. The trouble is I simply can't tell
Mary. She thinks that though money's short, he didn't
leave them in debt. I can't believe it of William. He always

seemed so sane and level-headed.'

'He isn't the first to have got out of his depth, now is he? There's many a one comes to pawn just because they've overreached themselves. His shop was a success, so given time I reckon he'd have cleared his debts. What have you in mind, then?'

'I can't do anything until Mary sanctions it, of course, but I thought I'd put the idea to her as soon as I've got an option on the place. That empty house at the top of Peter Street – you know, the one with the walled garden. There are eight or nine bedrooms and it needs some work . . .'

'A bit big, isn't it?'

'Yes, for the family. But I thought she could take in lodgers. It's near the Theatre Royal, and I've found out that stage people are always glad of respectable lodgings. Mary's a good hostess and an excellent cook. I'm settling a sum on her to be paid out monthly, but it won't keep them. I thought this other idea would provide income and a degree of independence, because she has a practical streak that's never been fully explored. In money matters William treated her like a dimwit. What do you think, Barney?'

He eyed her as he'd often done in the past, like a proud parent observing a precocious child. 'You were never short of ideas, Miss Tizzie. I reckon Miss Mary'll agree. She'll be able to earn and won't be entirely dependent on you. Have you put in an offer?'

'Not yet. It's with a Manchester firm. I wanted to find out what you thought before I go and see them tomorrow.'

Barney shook his big grey head. 'You don't really need me to give you an opinion, now do you? You could always sort things out for yourself, not to mention manage your own money. Are you thinking of paying cash?'

'Of course. I'll have to sell something, needless to say; I thought maybe two or three smaller properties. I've got out my title deeds, so will you go through them and give me your opinion on what should bring a quick sale? And will you stay for a bite of supper, Barney?'

It pleased her to be able to ask the routine question again after so long a lapse and to see his smile as he accepted. 'Barney,' she said, 'if Albert will agree to chaperone us, shall we go back to our Friday nights? We're partners, after all, and in spite of what you say, I do need your opinions now I'm responsible for Mary and the children.'

There was a long pause before he answered. 'In that case we'll go back to our old arrangement, Miss Tizzie.'

She would have had to have been blind and deaf not to sense his reluctance. She fiddled needlessly with the tape around the title deeds. Was this to be the pattern of her future, then? The highlight of her week a business supper with a man no longer at ease in her company? Bitterness filled her chest and caused an ache beneath her ribs; she could almost taste it. She was a fit, healthy woman, for goodness' sake, barely into her thirties . . .

Matthew walked home carrying an unlit lantern. A full moon was rising, outshining the early stars and giving light to the path. Behind him was the institute and the roofs of the town; to his right and below lay the vast bulk of Jericho, windows still ablaze, the company flag hanging limp against its post in the still, frosty air.

For the first time in years he had left work early, the truth of it being that they'd worked themselves to a standstill: greenhouses long since scrubbed out ready for the sowing of seeds, spring-flowering beds planted and ready, herbaceous borders immaculately dormant and the paths cleared ready for relaying. Inside the institute every conceivable aspect of maintenance was so up to the minute he was hard put to find enough for the three of them to do. He'd told Mr Schofield as much weeks ago. His employer had seemed to pay attention like he always did, but Matthew thought that a one-eyed halfwit could have seen that his mind was engaged elsewhere. He had waved his stick dismissively, saying, 'I reckon I can trust you and your men to get through your work, Matthew; Davey as well, here at the house – he treats your orders like holy writ, he does that. Now look, in no time at all it'll be spring and you'll all be working every hour God sends, so I'm not going to kick up a fuss if you knock off early now and again at this time of year.'

Then he'd gazed blankly at the forest of mill chimneys that formed the skyline of Saltley, tapping his stick on the ground. 'I'll have a word with my sons,' he'd said at last. 'A while back we talked about extending the reading room at the institute, so happen we'll come up with something of that kind to keep you occupied. In the meantime carry on, carry on.'

It had been funny, had that, because Mr Schofield was always one for having his workers well organised; he was known as a fair master who paid good wages but demanded hard work in return, yet he hadn't seemed bothered that three of his men were short of work. The very next day, though, he had sent for him and all the household staff, telling them that there was meddling and mischief making going on in the town's mills, so would they all keep an eye open for strangers around the place, just in case somebody with a grudge should attempt the same sort of thing at Meadowbank. Brisk, businesslike words which for Matthew explained his employer's preoccupation the previous day.

Everyone was put on their guard. There were new locks on the doors, new catches on the windows at both Meadowbank and the institute, where the live-in caretaker was joined each night by a man who sat in the main hall and walked the building every half hour. 'If it costs good money to keep my premises secure then so be it,' Mr Schofield had said. 'I'll not be intimidated by some hothead who gets a thrill out of damaging other folk's property. If we catch him I'll have him up in court, I won't part!'

Within days of that Matthew had reported Rosie's account of seeing the man, though it seemed nobody else had set eyes on him. At work, the three of them took things a bit easier but they didn't knock off early. Billy and Jonas were reluctant to go as far as that. 'Mr Schofield might be a good boss,' Billy protested, 'but it stands to reason he'll have second thoughts if he calls in one day and we've all gone home at half past four or summat. Let's stay till six like the rest o' Saltley.'

This they had done, all of them, until tonight, when at five o'clock Matthew had left the other two putting up a new tool rack they'd made. He'd done it on impulse because he wasn't easy in his mind about Martha, who'd been under the weather for the past few days; pale, she'd been, and very quiet. He had thought it might be her monthly bothering her, but she didn't usually have trouble of that sort. She was pleasant enough and insisted she was all right, but at dinner time there'd been something about the set of her mouth . . .

It would be a surprise when he walked in early. She'd be all flustered and her cheeks would turn deep pink. He liked it when that happened – she looked young and uncertain rather than like his prim, capable little wife. Deep in thought he walked on, his trousers brushing the tall, frost-dry grasses at the path's edge.

From a distance of ten yards or more he saw the man standing motionless in the birch grove, his coat and hat dark against the massed silver bark of the trees. He could just see the pale blur of his face and his bare hands – hands that were holding something up to his eyes. Scarcely breathing, Matthew stared at him; he was looking through a spyglass – a telescope such as was used at sea or by commanders in the field of war.

Was this the man who Rosie had seen? His spyglass was focused on Meadowbank House, down beyond the butter-cup field. In one snatched glance Matthew saw the big yard illuminated by the lamps on the stable wall; a distant figure who could only be Zacky harnessing the horse to the carriage; a woman carrying a bucket of kitchen waste from the house to the midden.

Matthew turned back but by then he had seen the lighted window of his own kitchen facing the field. Behind that window Martha would be busy and Rosie helping her or maybe doing her spelling. He saw the man adjust his telescope and was swept by a red-hot rage that he should spy on his wife and child and all those going about their business at Meadowbank House. The rage ebbed as suddenly as it had flowed, leaving him cold with anger. Quietly he put down his lantern and launched himself at the man, knocking him to the ground and pinning his arms behind his back. 'Don' 'ee move!' he snarled in the man's ear, then sat squarely on the small of his back.

No sooner had he done it than he knew he was faced with a fight. There was nothing with which to tie him up and he was bucking and heaving like a demented bullock. Matthew looked for something to stun him with but there was only the tussocky grass and the bare trees. The telescope had been knocked out of reach.

'What you doin' spyin'?' he asked, but the man was in such a frenzy to escape he didn't even hear. Matthew saw curly hair that could have been fair or ginger. The body beneath him was long and tough as whipcord, so this couldn't be the man described by Rosie. He writhed around and with a cat-like wriggle freed his arms and jerked something ice cold up into Matthew's side.

Matthew cursed himself. He should have expected a knife. The trouble was he'd been softened up by years of plenty. The man was still half beneath him but he'd managed to stick a knife in his ribs. He could feel the warmth of blood wetting his waist. He grabbed the man's wrist and twisted it so that he dropped the knife. He himself was lean and hard, but the man was harder; with a gigantic heave he threw Matthew off and rolled sideways, then aimed a vicious upward kick.

Matthew heard a crack inside his head and felt a dull weight in his jaw. Soft fool that he was, he hadn't expected such savagery. Salty vomit rose in his throat and he spat it out, his head whirling. He saw a heavy boot raised above his face. He shifted but it stamped down on him and pain shot from his neck to his shoulder. He groaned, and through a black mist of pain and bitterness saw the man snatch up his hat and the telescope and run off into the darkness. All at once there was silence.

'Home!' he told himself weakly. 'Don't worry 'bout the hurtin' – stop the bleedin'!' He pressed his hand to his side and leaned against a tree trunk to help him to his feet. He knew he was almost at the top end of the buttercup field, so he could do it. He would do it if it killed him.

It almost did, but not quite.

The carriage pulled up at the front steps of Meadowbank. Father and son alighted, still deep in the conversation that had occupied them since boarding the train at Manchester. As the carriage pulled away, Joshua paused on the top step before going indoors; he liked to view Saltley from his own front door and then cast an eye over Meadowbank itself. He was turning to go in when over the top of the side hedge he saw somebody crawling through the back gate of the yard. Even as he watched the man crashed to the cobbles and lay there motionless. 'Sam!' Joshua bellowed. 'Zacky – stop!'

Sam came out again at a run and Zacky reined in the horse.

'Quick! There's a chap collapsed in the yard!' With the speed of a man half his age Joshua leapt down the steps and raced round the hedge, closely followed by the other two.

Sam bent over the man. 'God above, it's Matthew,' he said, stunned. 'He's hurt! Hurt bad!'

'Get the others,' said Joshua to Zacky. 'No – you and Mr Sam carry him inside.'

'Wait!' Sam showed caution. 'We mustn't hurt him more. Zacky, get a board – a couple of planks, an old door, anything. He's unconscious.' He ran into the kitchen and waved an arm at the big scrubbed table, clear except for a tray of crockery and a freshly baked fruit cake. 'Get ready to help,' he told the women. 'Matthew's hurt. We'll put him here on the table. Zacky will fetch the doctor.' Sam stared at the women. 'He's bleeding. Can you help him?'

Lilah spoke up. 'I know a bit, Mr Sam, from me mother. I'll see to him till the doctor gets here. Ellie, shift them pots. Hannah, get them clean puddin' cloths out o' the top drawer.'

In less than a minute Matthew was lifted onto the table, his face green-white in the gaslight. His hand lay still against his side, the fingers dark with blood. Ellie stared at him and burst into tears, so Hannah gave her an impatient shake. Next to them Sam swallowed, his throat suddenly dry. A second man laid on a table in less than a month. God grant that this one didn't end up like the first.

Joshua paced up and down, impressed by Lilah's calm command and impatient that he himself was idle. He watched her undo Matthew's coat and ease away his blood-soaked shirt. 'Warm water,' she said to Hannah, 'there's some in the kettle.'

The wound was like a pursed mouth low on his ribs, steadily oozing blood. Calmly Lilah washed it, then folded a snowy pudding cloth and held it against the cut. 'Press on that, Mr Sam,' she said, turning to examine Matthew's head and shoulders. 'His jaw's broke, I reckon, Mr Schofield. I'd better let the doctor see to that. And there's summat the matter with his neck – I think the collarbone's gone.' She thought for a minute. 'Happen we should get his things off while he's unconscious – to spare him, like.' Sam helped her to remove the shirt and coat, while from some deep pit of pain and sickness Matthew moaned in protest, but he showed no other sign of consciousness.

Joshua was almost dancing with impatience. 'Shouldn't his wife be told?' he demanded. When nobody made a move he glared at them all. 'Right. I'll go myself!'

He strode across the yard and hammered on the door of the garden cottage. Rosie answered it and dropped a hasty curtsey when she saw who was standing there. He warned himself to keep calm and speak quietly. 'Is your mother here, Rosie?'

She stared at him. Something bad had happened. It was written all over his face. 'Me mam's not so well,' she said, amazement at such a thing showing in her tone. 'She's in bed.'

It didn't occur to Joshua to get one of the women. 'Take me up to her, love,' he said.

Rosie ran ahead of him up the stairs and dipped her head in apology at the bedroom door. 'Will you wait here, Mr Schofield, while I see if she's fit to see you?'

Admiring such tact in a child, Joshua waited obediently at the top of the stairs. This was a right to-do, he told himself. Sam could do with being out searching, never mind holding bandages at the kitchen table.

'She says to go in,' Rosie told him, so he entered the spotless little room. The gas was lit at the wall bracket but turned down low. Even so he could see Martha looking small as a child in the high double bed, and still in her working clothes. He was relieved to see her wide awake and alert. 'What's this, then, Martha?' he asked, 'aren't you well?'

'What's wrong?' she asked fearfully. 'It's Matthew, isn't it?'

Joshua sat on the bed and took her hand, noticing even in his distress that it was a very small hand but hard as iron. 'We think he's all right, Martha, but he's – he's been hurt. He's in the kitchen across at the house.'

She let out a low moan. It was bad. It must be bad or Mr Schofield would never have come to the house himself; he would never, never have come up to the bedroom.

'The doctor's coming. He's – we think he's been stabbed, Martha. Attacked on his way home. I thought I'd better tell you.'

She shook her head from side to side, then found it made her neck ache because she couldn't seem to stop. She edged her hand from his grip. 'Thanks, Mr Schofield.'

'If you're too poorly to go across he's being well looked after, I can assure you of that.'

She stared at his lips as if trying to fathom a foreign language. 'If you'll excuse me I'll just get out of me bed, Mr Schofield. An' will you send our Rosie in?'

He went downstairs but Rosie was nowhere to be seen. No doubt she'd heard what he'd said and was already across at the house. He returned to the bottom of the stairs. 'I'm sending Ellie to help you, Martha,' he shouted and went back across the yard.

In the bedroom Martha stood next to the bed, pain wrenching at her pelvis. She reached for another folded cloth and lifted her skirts, her fingers trembling so much she could hardly pin the cloth to her shimmy. At least she wasn't losing as much blood, she told herself. She put on her slippers and went downstairs very carefully. She'd been thinking that a miscarriage was the very worst thing that could happen to her until Mr Schofield came into the bedroom and told her about Matthew ... She put on her shawl and walked painfully across the yard. Ellie came out just as she reached the steps to the kitchen.

Later that evening Joshua sat in front of the fire in his study, annoyed to find that he was tired out. Anybody would think he was a dodderer of eighty-five, he thought irritably, rather than a man just past his prime. Sam had gone round to Jericho to check on the night watchmen, so there was nobody to talk to about what had happened. Restlessly he rang the bell. When Ellie appeared he told her to ask Lilah to come and see him as soon as she found it convenient.

Minutes later there was a tap at the door and the cook came in, wearing a small white pinafore instead of her big crackling overall. 'I'm a bit on edge, Lilah,' he confessed without preamble. 'Daft, I know, but I'm that worried about Matthew.'

A faint colour edged into Lilah's thin cheeks. She nodded her head at him. 'It's not daft at all, Mr Schofield. He were bad, you know, but he's bein' well looked after an' he's fast asleep now. I've had to promise Martha I'll send across for her if there's any change. Young Rosie's been backwards and forwards across the yard like a shuttle on the loom.'

'Will he be all right, Lilah?'

'Aye – so long as he doesn't mortify. He's lost blood, as you know, so when he's on the mend he could do with

plenty of good red meat and a glass of stout every night, an'
so could Martha. We can't do more than we're doin' now,
Mr Schofield.'

'How is Martha?' he asked cautiously.

Lilah looked down at her pinny. 'She's restin'. She's a
bit weak, like.'

Neither of them mentioned the sudden haemorrhage that
had turned the kitchen into a blood bath. A sight that had
been, Lilah told herself – husband and wife losing their
lifeblood side by side, and the child flatly refusing to leave
the room. She was a little madam, was that one, but her
heart was in the right place.

Mr Schofield was still looking at her, waiting to hear
more. If she hadn't had a feeling for him, a respect, she
knew that as a single woman nothing could have made her
speak of such things. 'I've never carried a child, Mr
Schofield, but I've had dealin's with many a woman who
has. Martha thought she was expectin', but because of her
age an' such she wasn't sure of her dates. The doctor says
she was three months' gone, an' happen there'da been
somethin' wrong with the baby if she'd managed her full
time. She's been spared a poorly child, maybe one with
somethin' lackin' – who can say. We'll look after her, never
fear.'

Joshua found he was listening with no trace of embarrassment, much as he would have done years ago with
Rachel. He waved Lilah to a chair, but when she didn't so
much as move he was suddenly impatient, shouting, 'Sit
you down, woman – I have something to say to you.'

She remained standing and said stubbornly, 'It's not
fittin' I should sit, Mr Schofield. An' I'm not deaf!'

He sighed. 'No, of course you're not. I'm a bit on edge.
I just want to say how I admired the way you dealt with
things down in your kitchen, and to say thanks. You're a
remarkable woman, Lilah. We're lucky to have you.'

She made no reply. She couldn't, not without shaming
herself by weeping. She was a remarkable woman, was
she? So remarkable that no man had ever offered her

marriage, never even offered her his bed without the benefit of a ring. She was forty-eight years old and she'd been taken with many an unavailable man in her time; the one she was taken with most, though, was sitting here, across the room from her, telling her how he admired the way she'd dealt with a man and his wife who'd bled all over her kitchen.

With a supreme effort she managed a small smile. Better he admire her for that than for nothing ... 'Thanks, Mr Schofield,' she said quietly. 'Is there anythin' else?'

'No, Lilah, that'll be all. Goodnight to you.'

'Goodnight, Mr Schofield.' She closed the door behind her and went back to her clearing up.

It was cold but very sunny, so Tizzie ignored the line of cabs at Victoria Station and set off on foot for St Ann's Square. She was wearing her black: a long, full-skirted coat over her heavy woollen dress, with the half-veil pulled down on her hat. She hated veils, preferring to see the world clearly rather than through a crisscross of black, but as it was only three weeks since the funeral she'd decided to observe the proprieties, especially as she was using public transport.

Manchester was busy; it seemed as if the entire population had been brought out of hibernation by the sun. After the events of the last few weeks, all of which had taken place in appalling weather, it seemed to her that the crowded sunlit streets had a festive air, like those around the market at Saltley Wakes.

Festive or not, the scene did little to raise her spirits. Wearily she told herself it was lack of sleep that ailed her, because following Barney's visit she had spent her worst night since sharing a bed with Mary after William had died. Never one for wild imaginings, she had been startled by her own mental images. Over the years she had convinced herself that she had forgotten the physical intimacies to which Edward had introduced her. Now she wasn't so sure. Had she perhaps merely buried the memories? Buried them deeper than the level where conscious thought ruled the mind? Buried them because Edward had cared nothing for her? Nothing for any woman, come to that …

She was well aware of what was unsettling her. It was the moment of bitter insight last evening when she'd seen what her future might be; that, and a sudden overpowering hunger for the feel of a man's arms around her. A man's arms? Any man's?

She walked briskly up Market Street, eyes wide behind the veil, scorning such pathetic attempts at self-deception. She didn't want the arms of any man, she wanted the arms of Sam Schofield. That day at Mary's when for long seconds she had been held against his chest in that idiotic game of blind man's buff … She had smelled him – a warm, clean, unscented body smell, overlaid by the damp worsted of his coat and a faint whiff of cotton. But she'd been released at top speed and then snubbed, hadn't she? On Christmas Eve, though, surely there'd been a change in him? Those brilliant eyes had been raised to hers as he'd descended the stairs from Mary's landing. 'I'm sorry, Tizzie,' he had said, 'I'm really sorry.' He hadn't said what he was sorry *for*, but she herself was sorry for the years without him; the long, long years when her bank balance increased while her personal life stagnated.

Deep in thought, she almost forgot to turn into St Ann's Square and had to warn herself to concentrate on the matter in hand. Between expensive shops she found an imposing building that housed several business establishments, among them Messrs Walker and Bland, one of the city's top property agents. Climbing the steps, she squared her shoulders ready to face the inevitable amazement that a woman, a young woman, should question the price of and make an offer to buy a sizeable dwelling house with her own money.

Ten minutes later she emerged with her spirits rising a little. She had been given a three-day option on the Peter Street House, at a price well below what had been asked originally. All that was needed now was to put it to Mary and for her to agree. She descended the steps and as she reached the pavement a pieman hurried past with his great wicker basket of hot pies, heading for King Street and the business houses there. It was almost noon and she knew that in winter the clerks would come out to buy pies for their dinner.

A passer-by swerved to avoid the man's basket and in doing so bumped into Tizzie. She dropped her big velvet purse and the man picked it up, handing it back without apology. From behind the fine lattice of her veil she saw lank dark hair under a tall hat, a pockmarked oval face and a pair of blue eyes, deep cornflower blue, observing her without a trace of expression. She was taken aback. The eyes were flat, dead, like pebbles in a pond. He merely nodded, not even raising his hat. Slightly nettled, she was about to walk on when from the top of the steps someone called, 'Miss Ridings!' It was the agent's young clerk, waving an envelope.

She turned, but not before she saw the dead blue eyes widen and the man put up his collar and walk away. A chord of memory sounded in her mind. Where had she seen that odd, mechanical walk? A walk with little movement of the arms?

'Miss Ridings!' The young clerk touched her sleeve. 'Mr Walker says I'm to give you this postage-stamped envelope for your convenience when contacting us again. I apologise – it was my omission.'

Well, well. The overweight Mr Walker was making up for his momentary disbelief that a woman of her age should want to buy a property for cash . . . She thanked the young man and put the envelope in her purse, staring thoughtfully after the surly, pockmarked man. It wasn't his gait so much as the eyes that were familiar . . . a deeper blue than Sam's – more like Sarah's – but with a strange lack of expression.

She shrugged. All at once she felt hungry for the first time in weeks and on impulse headed for a small restaurant that she liked, close by the Royal Exchange. It wasn't every day that she took an option on a nine-bedroomed house for her widowed sister, she told herself, so as Rebecca wasn't expecting her home for her dinner she would have a splendid meal and try to cheer herself up. Accepting a table in the window she studied the bill of fare. It felt good to be away from Saltley.

She was eating her dessert, a flaky apple turnover with cream, when it came to her that the blue-eyed man had something about him of Ralph, the absent Schofield son, the one who was never mentioned, the one who had gone to Australia within hours of his mother's funeral. It had been so strange the way the man put up his collar and turned on his heel when the young clerk came out with the envelope. Not that he'd seemed to recognise her behind the veil, even when they were almost face to face, but he might have heard her name and noticed her hair ... Hair! What was she thinking of? The man's had been dark and greasy while Ralph's was golden, almost as pale as Sarah's; he was a beautiful young man, more lovely than many a woman. Oh, what did it matter? She finished her apple turnover and decided to order a pot of coffee and watch the world go by.

After a leisurely look round the shops Tizzie boarded the three o'clock train back to Saltley, somewhat irritated to find herself still thinking about the pockmarked man. Hadn't she once heard a whisper about the way Ralph had left the town so abruptly? She recalled long-ago hints that he was the family black sheep, but she'd ignored them out of an inborn dislike of tittle-tattle and a respect for the Schofield family. If he was back in England, though, why hadn't he been home? Or perhaps he *had* been home. Perhaps Ralph was the reason she'd seen nothing of brother Sam.

Tizzie sighed. Perhaps, perhaps, perhaps. Soon she would be in Saltley, ready to tell Barney about the option. As for Ralph Schofield being back home, she might find out more from Sarah when she went up to Alsing. Only that morning she'd had a letter urging her to spend a weekend there as soon as she was able to leave Mary.

*

'So when will you speak to Miss Mary?' Barney was as eager as she was to get it all settled.

'As soon as I can. She gets very upset, so if she's crying I'll have to leave it for a bit.' They were in the little counting house with the door wide open, as was their custom. Tizzie perched on the edge of the table where they reckoned up the takings and asked, 'Barney, do you know anything about Ralph Schofield – the son who went to Australia?'

'No more an' no less than anybody else. It's you who's friendly with his sister, Miss Tizzie.'

'She never speaks of him, so of course neither do I. This isn't idle curiosity, though. I saw a man in Manchester who didn't look a bit like him and yet in some way he did. He bumped into me outside Walker and Bland.'

'Did he recognise you?'

'No. I just had a—' she smiled in apology at saying something so out of character, 'a bad feeling about him, that's all.'

He considered that. 'We don't repeat gossip, you an' me, Miss Tizzie, but I do recall there being talk years back when he went off to Australia. He'd never been liked in the town, you know. Everybody said he was a bad 'un.'

'What did *you* think, Barney?' She knew that very little escaped him.

'I think they were probably right,' he said quietly.

That was as far as she could go; more questions would smack of disloyalty to Sarah and the family. She glanced round the shop. 'Is everything in order?'

'Everything's all right here, Miss Tizzie.'

'I'm off, then. Wish me luck with Mary.'

'I always wish you luck,' he said, 'not just with Miss Mary.'

It wasn't luck, thought Tizzie the next day, it was maternal instinct that had brought her sister back to a kind of normality.

Mary had given her a great hug when she'd arrived at Holden Street the previous evening. 'Thanks, Tizz, for everything,' she'd said simply. 'I don't know what on earth I'd have done without you. You can stop worrying about me – the weeping and wailing's over. Life's terrible, but it has to go on for the sake of the children.'

Tizzie had looked into her eyes and seen acceptance there. 'What's happened?' she'd asked in relief.

'Johnny started wetting himself again after being dry for months. Then yesterday Abel was sent home from school after being caned by the headmaster for being disobedient – Abel, mind, always so good. His bottom was sore from the stick. As for Elizabeth – well, I can never make her out, you know that, but she's really odd. She insists on helping with the housework though she hates it like poison and she keeps on asking whether we'll have enough money to live on. They haven't got a father and I've been in such a state they haven't had a mother, either. I can't let them fall apart like that, Tizzie, so here I am, back in harness.'

After that it had been easy to tell her. They had talked and planned until eleven, then this morning Tizzie had taken Mary to view the house, managing to give the impression that she, Tizzie, could buy it without having to add a great deal to what would come from the sale of the shop.

Almost light-headed with relief at the success of her plans for Mary, she let her mind dwell on her own concerns and Sam Schofield in particular. Things had been happening at Meadowbank House. News was spreading that Matthew Raike had been set on and half killed on his way home from work.

What had the Schofields made of that? she wondered. Neither Sam nor his father was likely to sit and twiddle his thumbs in such a situation; from past experience she was sure it would be better for any man to have Sam as a friend rather than an enemy. She imagined what it would be like to have him by her side now, walking home with her ... That man climbing the lane up ahead could almost be him:

the same broad build, the long forceful stride, the fair hair showing between his hat and his collar ... It *was* him, heading for her house. She had to stop herself from breaking into a run.

But he didn't knock on the door. He merely pushed a letter through the box and turned on his heel, coming back down the lane to face her. 'Tizzie!' he said blankly.

She couldn't think of a single word to say, not even a greeting. He looked good. There was a kind of glow about him, like a sunlit picture done in shades of gold and silver and bronze. He removed his hat and faced her bareheaded, shifting his feet noisily on the flagstones. 'It's nearly a month,' he said, 'so I've put a letter through your door.'

Her customary acumen deserted her. What did he mean? She gazed at his fair, uncovered head and recalled the lank dark hair of the pockmarked man in Manchester ... Once, years before, she had been unsure whether to tell Sam something and had acted with speed. She had given him unpleasant news and he'd been grateful. All at once she wanted him to be grateful again. She needed him to stay for a minute, rather than go striding away down the hill.

'I was in Manchester yesterday,' she said rapidly. 'I thought I saw your brother Ralph.'

It was Sam's turn to be stuck for words; he simply stared at her. She gave an awkward little shrug. 'No doubt you'll have seen him already if he's back in England.'

Silence fell between them, heavy as a bolt of calico. She was making a fool of herself, she thought, drivelling on about his brother when he might not want to speak of him. 'Don't let me detain you,' she said lightly. 'I'll go indoors and read your letter.'

'No!' He grabbed her arm. She could feel the heat of his hand through her sleeve. 'Why did you only *think* it was Ralph?'

'Because he was dark haired and pockmarked,' she said shortly. 'Unrecognisable, really.'

'So what brought my brother to your mind?'

'His eyes. They were a cornflower blue – very striking.

Darker than yours, almost like Sarah's, but they were blank, like a blind man's eyes. And he walked without moving his arms.' Heavens, it sounded like the ravings of a madwoman. He was still staring at her, grasping his hat like a battle shield. 'A clerk called my name,' she added defiantly, 'and at that he turned up his collar and hurried away.'

Sam was cursing silently. He'd been right then – Ralph was back. Tizzie didn't imagine things; those vast eyes of hers saw life as it was: complex and often unpleasant. He should be grateful to her for confirming his suspicions, but all he could feel was resentment that Ralph should interfere with what he had planned to do, which was apologise to Tizzie and then set about wooing her.

He gritted his teeth irritably and she saw it. Nothing had changed, she told herself bleakly; he was standing here against his inclination. She turned towards her gate.

'Tizzie.' Her name seemed to be dragged from deep inside his chest. 'Can I come in for a minute?'

Ralph had captured his attention then, even if she herself couldn't manage it. She opened the door and picked up his letter from the mat, then beckoned him inside. Rebecca hurried towards them, wiping her hands on her apron. Dipping her knee she took Sam's hat but sensing the strain between them edged backwards to her kitchen.

Sam barely noticed her; his attention was on Tizzie. He should be questioning her about Ralph, but he couldn't take in anything except those eyes and the flawless skin showing up like cream against her mourning clothes. How could he ever have thought her bony? Or hard? Her bone structure was wonderful, elegant, more striking than ever since she'd lost weight. She was so slender he guessed that his two hands could circle her waist. He flexed his fingers but kept them firmly by his sides.

He didn't even notice the comfort of her sitting room with its graceful furniture and unfashionable lack of clutter; an opportunity had presented itself, and he was damned if he was going to waste it.

'Will you have a seat?' Tizzie asked, indicating a normal chair rather than one of those sized down to fit Barney. Sam shook his head and, still in their outdoor clothes, they faced each other across the width of a jewel-bright rug. She tapped his letter. 'Need I open this now that you're here in person?'

'No. I wrote to say that I hoped you were well and could I call on you.'

'To what end?'

'To talk.'

His manner was peculiar, she thought; hesitant and yet aggressive. In anyone else it might have betrayed nervousness, but that would hardly be the case with Sam. He wanted to talk, did he? After eleven years of silence? She gritted her teeth and waited. It could only be a matter of business.

He looked her straight in the eye. 'Do you recall that many years ago I had a certain regard for you, Tizzie?'

He didn't bandy words, but then neither did she. 'I recall that you *seemed* to have a regard,' she agreed cautiously.

'It was a true feeling,' he assured her, 'and I've come to realise that I've never lost it. I'm not going to ask whether you could have a feeling for me – it would be an impertinence. I just want to tell you that I was on the point of proposing marriage when I saw, and believed, that you were setting your cap at my father.' He'd said it now, the thing he should have challenged her with and which had eaten at him ever since.

Those eyes were watching him, green as leaves in summer. 'I know you believed that,' she said. 'I knew it at the time.'

'You knew it yet you didn't protest? Are you saying it was true?'

Years of independence protected Tizzie like armour. Deliberately she unpinned her hat and removed it, then she took off her coat to reveal her black woollen dress with its tiny jet buttons and black silk sash. 'Those are deep questions to pose within two minutes of inviting yourself inside my house,' she said coolly. 'What makes you think I want to answer them?'

'Nothing,' he admitted, 'but you see, I've always been uneasy at not tackling you about your feelings for my father. I suppose I was frightened that I might have been wrong. Then on the day William died I spent hours in your company. I think I saw the real Tizzie then, and I bitterly regretted the years I'd wasted. I told myself I must wait a full month before I approached you, busy as you were with your concerns and responsibilities, but this morning I found I couldn't wait any longer.'

There was an odd sensation in her chest, as if a rope that had been bound tight around her ribs was being severed, strand by strand. His honesty deserved honesty in return. 'It was true that your father fascinated me,' she admitted. 'He had so much that I admired: power, wealth, brains, principles ... and sheer masculine attraction.' Sam's eyes widened at that. Truth, she urged herself, give him the plain, unvarnished truth. 'Later I came to acknowledge that because you are so much alike, I had seen in your father what you would be in thirty years' time. I showed open admiration for him and he didn't even notice. My mistake was that I didn't conceal it from you.'

He was staring at her. 'I was as jealous as hell,' he said, 'and guilty, I suppose, because it was my father and I thought the world of him. I still do.' He kept his hands pressed tightly to his sides. 'I'm sorry, Tizzie.'

There was a world of regret in those two words. The rope around her chest was loosening ... 'So am I,' she said.

At that he stepped forward and grabbed her. No preliminaries such as 'Can we get to know each other?' or 'May I embrace you?'; he simply crushed her to his chest, bent his head and kissed her on the mouth. His lips were warm and eager and *right*, but she stood there unresponsive, her mind racing. She didn't know whether to allow it or to protest. It was ironic; the most self-possessed woman in Saltley wasn't sure how to deal with an uninvited kiss. Instinct won; she put her hands against his chest and pushed.

At once he released her. She caught a look of dismay in his eyes but it was his mouth that held her attention. A ten-second kiss from those lips and she was a mindless ninny, breathing as if she'd run a mile. She might have longed for Sam's arms around her, but not this way, without a by your leave. 'Do you seriously think you can walk in here and kiss me like that when you've all but ignored me for years?' she demanded.

'I didn't think at all. I just couldn't wait any longer.'

She glared at him. 'I've been kissed once,' she said, '*once*, since Edward threw me aside for Sarah, so don't think I kiss all and sundry, no matter what you might hear. No man is going to hurt me again, Sam.'

He shook his head in bafflement. 'What are you *talking* about? I wouldn't hurt you, Tizzie. I want to look after you, to cherish you. I would never hurt you. How could you think it?'

She didn't know what she thought and that was a fact; her mind was whirling. 'You know what they say in the town?' she asked. 'That I have unnatural relations with Barney Jellicoe.'

He expelled his breath in amazed exasperation. What a woman! Who else would have come out with that? 'I know quite well what they say. It's rubbish, started by those who envy your success and independence. I'm not interested in gossip, all I know is I want you.'

'I could never be any man's mistress,' she said haughtily.

He gaped at her. 'What?'

'You say you want me. Hard lines. I could never be your mistress.'

'God above, woman, I should hope not! I want you in marriage, Tizzie. I love you.'

'Oh,' she said.

'This is a proposal. I'm asking you to marry me!'

'Oh,' she said again.

'Is there anything else you'd like to clarify?'

'Lots of things, but I suppose they can wait.'

'And what about an answer?'

'That can wait as well.'

Sam eyed her carefully to see if she meant it. He hadn't expected to win her in five minutes flat, had he? He was all set to court her, to woo her, but dammit, he simply had to kiss her again in the hope she'd be less like a block of marble. 'May I kiss you?' he asked.

'Yes.'

He lifted his chin impatiently. 'This doesn't mean I'm always going to ask permission.'

'You expect it to happen often, then?'

'All the time,' he told her, and threw aside his overcoat.

He took it slowly, laying his mouth gently on hers, but at once passion sparked between them into a low, purposeful flame, burning more fiercely with each mingled breath. Tizzie wondered why she'd ever thought she'd been kissed before – *really* kissed. She had harboured an ugly little fear that the wild excesses of her time with Edward might make other men seem lacking in desire, but that could never be said of Sam. With his mouth on hers, his arms around her, his body giving off heat and the clean, male-animal smell that she loved, he banished for ever the spectre of that elegant, red-lipped, dissolute man.

Freed from the thought of Edward, a mature woman now rather than the wilful, inexperienced girl she'd been all those years ago, Tizzie stood on tiptoe and put her arms around Sam's neck, kissing him back with eager delight. Deep in his throat he groaned with pleasure, but he carried on kissing her while their bodies swayed together as one and her feet left the floor.

At last he set her down and lifted his mouth from hers, laying his cheek against the curl and spring of her hair. He'd known it already, he told himself, but now it was confirmed a hundredfold: he wanted to spend his life with her. Much of what she did was unknown to him – she was a woman of business, after all; but in their sense of values, the length of their love for each other and now this new physical bond, they were as one.

Sam put her from him and said soberly, 'I love you, Tizzie. Can you forgive me for wasting the years? If you'll have me, I swear I'll spend the rest of my life making you happy and trying to be worthy of you. Will you marry me?'

The last strand of rope fell unnoticed from around Tizzie's chest; she was conscious only of a new, heart-shaking exhilaration that at last they'd finished waiting. They were standing on the rug in her sitting room and it was noon on a winter's day, but she, the least fanciful of women, imagined that they were up in the cloud-strewn heavens, heading out past the moon and the stars to the wild and distant galaxies where the skies were always blue.

Sam saw that her cheeks were flushed with rare colour, her eyes bright but free of tears. 'Yes,' she said, 'yes, yes, yes!'

CHAPTER TEN

Reactions

Sam might have wasted years, but now nobody could accuse him of wasting so much as a second. Always swift and decisive herself, for the first time in her life Tizzie found what it meant to be swept off her feet. There was hardly time to speak, let alone think.

They had to stop kissing when Rebecca tapped at the door to ask what time she should serve dinner. 'Postpone it,' Tizzie told her, 'but have yours.' She was still stunned by Sam's closeness; she had actually swayed on her feet when he put her away from him.

He stood back, straightening his necktie and running a hand over his crisp fair hair. 'Shall we go and tell my father?' he asked. 'He'll be home for his dinner and James is down from High Lee, so we can tell them both at once. As for Sarah and Francis, would you like to surprise them up at Alsing? And what about Mary? Is this likely to upset her?'

Tizzie thought about her sister. 'She's pestered me for long enough to get married, so I think she'll be pleased. We mustn't make too much of it, though, because it might come hard that I'm gaining a husband when she's just lost one; I'd hate her to slip back from the state of mind she's in at the moment. I'll go round on my own, this afternoon. I'm more concerned about telling Barney as soon as I – as soon as we can.'

Sam was curious. 'How will he take it?'

'He'll be pleased,' she assured him. 'He told me once that there was only one sure way of silencing gossip about him and me.'

They picked up a cab in Old Square and stopped off at the pawnshop on the way to Meadowbank House, finding Barney alone while Albert was out for his dinner. 'Miss Tizzie!' he said in surprise, 'an' Mr Schofield.'

Later she told herself she must have imagined that he lost colour when he saw them walk in together. He was always pale, so it could have been winter sunlight through the window that made him look so ghastly.

'Barney,' she said, 'I want you to be the first to know. Mr Schofield has asked me to marry him and I've accepted!'

Perhaps twenty seconds of silence followed, but to her it seemed longer. She could hear her own breathing, the ticking of the clock on the wall, the hoof beats of a passing horse. At her side Sam was silent, observing Barney carefully.

Then, with the aplomb of a man well versed in social niceties, Barney held out his large hand and shook Sam's, smiling in congratulation. 'That's the best news I've heard in months, if not years,' he said warmly. 'You're a lucky man, Mr Schofield, you are that; an' I say it as one who's known Miss Tizzie since she were a young lass. Happen when you have the time you'd both do me the honour of joinin' me in a little celebration here in my rooms? An' you'll let me know when you settle the date of the weddin'?'

Barney hardly looked at Tizzie, but she knew they would have time to talk later. Something made her offer him her hand before they left. 'I'm glad you're pleased, Barney,' she said. No matter how delighted she was to be with Sam at last, Barney's approval seemed to set the seal on it.

He held on to her hand for an instant and his dark eyes met hers. 'I'm pleased to see you happy,' he said simply.

'I could never be any other, now could I?'

Sam and Tizzie hurried out to the cab and drove up past Jericho to Meadowbank House. Sam was in a ferment until he had told his father. At the news Joshua took Sam in his arms and kissed him on both cheeks, turning to Tizzie somewhat abashed. 'You'll be thinking you're marrying a Frenchman with that sort of carry on,' he laughed, 'but I'm that pleased. Come here, Tizzie, and give me a kiss. It's taken you both long enough, that I will say, but better late than never.'

He gave her a hug and kissed her warmly on the cheek, concealing an emptiness inside him that Rachel wasn't here at this unique moment in their son's life. Tizzie was thin as a rake, he thought in alarm as he let go of her. He must warn Sam to keep an eye on her diet ...

'I'm delighted,' he told her. 'I can see now where Sam sloped off to without a word to anybody. You'll stay and have your dinner with us? We've got James here; he's upstairs having a word with my gardener – we'll tell you all about that to-do later on. Young Charlie will be here at any minute, as well, so we can all celebrate together.' In high good humour he announced that he was going to have a word in the kitchen and then go down to the cellar to find the champagne he'd been keeping for years, ready for just such an event.

Sam sat Tizzie on the sofa, gave her a quick kiss and then ran upstairs to find James, slowing down only when he recalled his own reactions on hearing of James's engagement to Esther, twelve or thirteen years back. He'd certainly put a blight on that little event, but he'd been proved right in the end. He wished to God he'd been proved wrong, for Jimmy's sake ...

He met him coming out of the room where Matthew was being cared for. 'He's asleep,' James whispered, then looked into Sam's face. 'Hey, what's going on?'

'Come downstairs,' said Sam, eyes glinting. 'There's somebody I want you to meet.'

Intrigued, James hurried behind his brother, halting in

perplexity when he saw who was in the sitting room. 'Why, Miss Tizzie – this is a pleasant surprise.'

Sam took her hand and pulled her to her feet, presenting her at arm's length as if to a theatre audience. 'James, meet my future wife!'

James gave a laugh of sheer delight. 'Wonderful!' he beamed. 'Sarah and I have often wondered how long it would be – or if it would happen at all!'

Tizzie decided to think about that remark later; for the time being it was all bliss, pure unalloyed bliss – which after all was something of a novelty in her life. Charles blushed and gave a formal little bow, muttering, 'Welcome to the family, Miss Ridings,' a remark that set his grandfather chortling with pride.

The meal, like everything she'd ever eaten in that house, was excellent, the size of the men's helpings, to her eyes, enormous. Her spirits were soaring; this was a family she had always admired, always respected, and here she was, about to become part of it.

Lilah brought in the pudding, her thin cheeks pink as she gauged her employer's reaction. It was a baked ginger sponge with the words 'Good Wishes Sam and Tizzie' piped across it in butter cream that was already starting to melt. The men laughed; Sam slapped the table, and Joshua gave Lilah a conspiratorial nod. Tizzie, though, felt her throat tighten at the hurried little gesture of goodwill. It gave her a warm, cherished feeling unlike anything she'd experienced before, even with Barney. Her eyes sought Sam's to find his vivid blue gaze sending an unmistakeable message . . . *I love you*.

They were eating the pudding with a splendid egg custard when Joshua leaned across to Tizzie. 'I said we'd tell you about Matthew Raike, didn't I? Happen you know him – he's my head gardener and he lives in the cottage across the yard. He was attacked on his way home from the institute yesterday – stabbed in the side and bones broken, at five o'clock in the afternoon, mind, long before the blowers sounded. We have the police on to it, of course, but the scoundrel got clean away. There's been interfering going on in the town's mills, you know, and we think it might be connected.'

Opposite her Sam was suddenly tense. She could see it in the set of his mouth and his fixed gaze. What was – but Joshua was waiting for her reaction.

'How is Mr Raike now?' she asked. 'Will he get better?'

'We think so. The doctor seems satisfied for the moment, and he's being looked after here at the house until he's stronger. It's a worry, Tizzie, it is that. You're an employer yourself, so you'll know the feeling of being responsible for your workers.'

Tizzie regarded her future father-in-law with warmth. In speaking those words he accepted her as a businesswoman in her own right, which of course was exactly the case, but how many men in his position would think like that? She and Barney employed two people; Joshua Schofield employed twelve hundred, yet his words had made them equals.

The meal finished and congratulations at an end, Sam handed Tizzie into the family carriage, kissing the palm of her hand in farewell. 'The best of luck when you tell Mary,' he said quietly. 'If you don't hear from me to the contrary I'll pick you up at six to go to Alsing.' Then he braced himself and managed a smile. 'Back to business now, for a while . . .'

Once indoors he found James and his father putting on their coats ready to walk down the road to Jericho. 'Hold on a minute before we all set off,' he said, 'I want a word, Father.'

Joshua shot him a look. 'We'll go in the study,' he said, 'though if it's about your marriage you know you have my blessing.'

'It's not about that.' Sam hustled them both into the study and closed the door. 'I should sit down if I were you, Father.'

Joshua stood quite still for a moment, then sat heavily

in his big leather chair. It seemed to Sam that all at once he shrank from being a lean, ageing man to one who was thin and old and very tired. He knew! He knew what was coming. 'Let's have it, lad,' he said.

Sam looked away. He couldn't watch his father's face, not yet. He cleared his throat. 'Ralph *is* back,' he said bluntly.

Joshua sat forward, eyes narrowed, the grooves from his nose to his jaw deeper than they'd ever been. 'How do you know?'

'Tizzie saw him in Manchester.'

James put a protective hand on his father's shoulder. 'Tizzie? Was she sure it was him?'

'No. She only thought it was.'

'*Thought*?' repeated Joshua. 'Didn't she recognise him?'

'Not at first. He was badly pockmarked and his hair was dark. It was the eyes – remarkable, she said, similar to Sarah's but blank, like a blind man's.'

'Did she know we'd been worried whether Ralph was back?' asked Joshua.

'No, of course not. She met the man face to face, but when somebody called her name he put up his collar and hurried away. She said he walked without moving his arms.'

At that Joshua sank back in his chair as if he'd been pushed, but James was shaking his head, still dubious.

'Tizzie doesn't imagine things,' Sam told him impatiently, 'she sees what's there. It was Ralph, I feel it in my innards. She told me before noon, but I put it to the back of my mind until we'd dealt with more personal matters.'

'This has spoiled your day,' said Joshua heavily, 'and mine as well, I can tell you. But if Ralph's back, could it have been him who attacked Matthew?'

James was getting edgy. 'We don't know, do we? All we've found out is that Matthew was coming home early and presumably that's why the man was still up there, not expecting to be seen. Matthew couldn't even talk to the police, could he?'

Joshua stood up. 'We'll have to see if he'll talk to us then.'

'And we'll tell him about Ralph?'

'Not unless we have to. But listen, if it has to come out in the end then so be it. I might set store by what's written round the dome of the Exchange, in fact it's always been my creed, but if our good name has to go, then *so be it*!'

Sam almost groaned. A quotation from the Book of Proverbs was inscribed around the great dome: '*A good name is rather to be chosen than great riches, and loving favour rather than silver and gold.*' His father had lived up to that, he hadn't part.

More important at that moment was what had come to Sam at the dinner table, causing him to curse himself all through the meal. Tizzie had accepted him – accepted a man who was brother to a murderer – because she hadn't known about it. Suppose she changed her mind when she knew? He felt ill at the thought of it. 'Father,' he said urgently, 'can I tell Tizzie what Ralph did?'

Joshua expelled breath as if it was heavy as lead, while James looked from one to the other, his face grim. 'It's up to you, Sam,' said Joshua. 'Your brother here chose not to tell his wife, but Francis knows; he knew before the wedding. Tizzie has a head on her shoulders, a handsome head, but she uses it for something else besides putting her hat on. She's entitled to know what she's marrying into – so if you want to tell her, go ahead. Now come on, let's go and see Matthew.'

Matthew eased his shoulders against the pillows, telling himself that though his mind was clearing and his body easing, the feeling of weakness was something awful.

It was a fine room he was in here in the big house, with windows tall as any door and patterned paper on the walls. The womenfolk were powerful kind in caring for him, though he'd been overfaced when he came to his senses and found them attending to his personal needs. But all the kindness in the world was as nothing against his one overriding concern: where was Martha? He was positive that she would be looking after him herself if something wasn't preventing her.

He could remember, now, that the man with the spyglass had been watching Meadowbank – watching the lighted window of his little kitchen with Martha and Rosie unknowing; safe, so they thought, in their own house . . . How long was it since he'd fought with the man? His head ached when he tried to remember; it might be fifteen or sixteen hours, maybe longer. In that time he'd had visits from Mr Schofield and his sons, the family doctor, another doctor who was an expert at setting bones, two policemen, the womenfolk who worked in the house and Rosie, sitting like a solemn little guardian angel next to his bed, spoon-feeding him liquids through lips that could barely open because of his strapped up jaws. Oh yes, a positive procession had come through the bedroom door, but not his wife.

He had questioned as best he could, signed and gestured and mumbled, but all he managed to get out of them was that Martha 'wasn't so well'. There was a frightening picture in his mind of her on the kitchen floor here at the house, with everybody rushing around; a hazy kind of picture, like when he used to gaze through steamy shop windows as a boy. He'd looked down on her, yet he didn't recall standing there; he thought he'd been lying on something, with a great pain in his shoulder when he moved and his head feeling ready to burst . . . He'd been worried about her before this, of course. That was why he'd been going home before time, when the man might well have judged himself safe from discovery, before the blowers sounded.

The bedroom door opened quietly and he tried to lift his head in case it was Martha coming in, but it was Mr Schofield with Mr James and Mr Sam. They looked relieved that he was awake, but he turned his head away in bitter disappointment that it wasn't Martha. He loved her, of course he did, yet he'd never thought to miss her as much as this . . .

'Well, Matthew,' said Mr Schofield awkwardly, 'this is a bad do, it isn't part, but the doctor seems satisfied with you and we thank God for that. Now, can you hear me? We want to get to the bottom of who did this to you. Can you nod your head? Can you speak, Matthew?'

Matthew looked into his employer's eyes and, as always, felt drawn to do his best for him. He moved his tongue experimentally; it felt twice its normal size, as if it was wedged inside his tight-strapped mouth. He attempted to form words without moving his lips and managed, 'I can try.'

'Good lad,' said Mr Schofield, exchanging a satisfied look with his sons. 'Now listen, Matthew, we want answers, vital answers to our questions. I'll phrase them so you need say only yes or no.

Matthew narrowed his eyes. He wanted answers, did he? Well, he wasn't the only one. Matthew Raike wanted answers as to why he'd been half killed; why his wife hadn't been to see him, and why she and Rosie had been spied on by some madman who had a grudge against the Schofields, or their mill, or their fine house. He waved his free fist in the air and grated, 'Martha! Where be 'er to?'

Joshua realised he was mishandling him and flashed a wary glance at his sons. 'Martha had a bad turn,' he said gently. 'She collapsed, and the doctor ordered her to bed for forty-eight hours. Hannah and Ellie keep going across and Rosie's being a good little lass ... Martha will be all right after a spell in her bed, the doctor's assured me of it.'

That eased Matthew's mind a little, but he was still resentful, he still wanted answers. 'Spyin'!' he said through his teeth. 'On my wife an' child!'

Joshua decided that this wasn't going to be easy. Matthew was more concerned about his family than about providing information, and rightly so. He drew up a chair and sat very close. 'You're bound to be upset at what's happened,' he said, 'but listen to me, Matthew – you can't be any more upset than I am, and that's a fact! As for Martha and Rosie being spied on, I think you can take it that it's my family and my house that they're spying on, not yours. We think it's all to do with this meddling in the mill – what I warned you about a while back. Now please, Matthew, answer yes or no. Was the man using a spyglass to watch the house?'

'Yes.'

'Did you recognise him?'

'No.' He saw Mr Schofield's shoulders slump forward at that, as if in relief.

'Was he tall?'

'Yes.'

The catechism went on. As Matthew struggled to give answers his anger evaporated. Mr Schofield was trying to find the culprit – he had to. Matthew was in a fine feather bed here in Mr Schofield's house, being treated like a lord; Martha was at home in their own bed, being looked after by Mr Schofield's servants. What had happened had happened, and it wasn't Mr Schofield's fault. There was no call to be angry any more. The three of them had got their answers – a full description of the man, but there was more he could add. He held up his hand and at once they fell silent. 'Hard man,' he managed. 'Rough – used to fightin'.'

Sam leaned forward. 'We'd already worked that out, Matthew. He must have been a hard man to do what he did to you – you're one of the strongest men in my father's employ. We'll leave you now to try and nod off for a bit, because the doctor says rest is essential when you've lost a lot of blood. Rosie will be in to see you after school, I expect.'

They went out, leaving him exhausted by his attempts to communicate. So that was it – Martha had collapsed. Because she was worried about him or what?

When Rosie crept in, still in her school pinafore and shawl, he was sitting up, willing himself to keep a clear head. She squeaked in delight when she saw him looking better and climbed onto the chair, covering his free arm with little kisses. Better not touch his face, she warned herself; it looked all purple and yellow and horrible, with whiskers growing on top of the bruises. His eyes were the same, though; dark brown and shiny, like treacle toffee. 'Are you feelin' better, Dad?' she asked, looking up with her lips still against his arm.

'Yes, liddle love,' he mumbled. 'Where be your mother? Where be 'er to?'

Rosie blushed. Nobody had told her what to say if he asked that. All she knew was that he mustn't be worried. Well, he would be worried if he knew her mam had been bleeding all over the floor . . . Her heart sank when she saw his face. Above the funny stiff bandage he was looking at her in the way that meant she must tell the truth and keep nothing back. He didn't speak and she was glad about that because he sounded so funny. Instead he moved his hand as if he was writing and looked at her enquiringly.

She beamed at him and hurried from the room, returning with her pencil and slate. She held it at an angle for him and he wrote, 'Is your mother poorly?'

'Yes,' she answered, blushing again because his eyes still had that look.

Then he wrote, 'What is wrong with her?'

Rosie squirmed and he tapped the slate impatiently, just as her teacher Miss Hardman did when she was getting angry with somebody in the class. She looked at the bedroom door; it was closed, so nobody could hear her. 'I don't know,' she muttered. 'She was in bed with a stomachache when Mr Schofield came across an' told her you'd been set on. I ran over here to see you an' left her in bed.'

'Yes? What then?' Matthew forgot he was supposed to be writing his questions.

'She came across the yard an' – an' she was doubled up, like. I was busy lookin' at you, Dad, but all at once there was blood all over the floor, comin' from under her skirts, an' then the doctor arrived. Hannah tried to bundle me out but I wouldn't let her. Me mam was on the floor an' she'd gone all white an' the doctor said, 'God in heaven, I don't know which of 'em to see to first!'

Rosie gave a little wriggle of satisfaction at being able to repeat such forbidden words, while Matthew stared at her with his eyes very wide. 'They didn't tell me what was wrong,' she went on, 'but I heard the doctor say, "Over three months, or I'm a Dutchman." Did he mean she'd been poorly for over three months?'

Matthew grunted a denial and waved his hand to tell her to continue.

'Then they said she had to rest an' they took her home, an' now Hannah an' Ellie keep comin' across to see to her. Lilah sends her beef soup, an' all – it's lovely, Dad. She always gives me some, an' she wants to know all about you. I have to tell her everythin'.' She fell silent, knowing she should have felt bad, telling him all that when he mustn't be worried, but she didn't, she felt a lot better. She felt happy.

Deep in thought, Matthew patted her head. A miscarriage ... His little Martha had been expecting a baby, but she hadn't said a word. Maybe she wasn't sure and didn't want to tell him until she was certain. She was thirty-seven, of course, going on thirty-eight, and no longer as regular with her monthlies ... When she'd been off colour in the dinner hour perhaps she'd wondered then if she was starting to lose the baby. His little Martha, struggling across the yard to be with him ...

Hurriedly he rubbed his writing off the slate with the sleeve of his nightshirt and wrote on it in capitals 'I love you.' Then he signalled to Rosie to take it to her mother. 'Quick!' he mumbled. 'Be quick, my liddle love!' When she had gone he flopped back against the pillows, tired out. Would he and Martha ever conceive another child? This one might have been a boy – a boy to make up for the one they'd lost.

He thought he heard the slam of the cottage door as Rosie arrived home with his message.

It was dark and cold and gloomy in the secret place

between the back of the stables and the hedge, but to Rosie
it was the most exciting place on earth because nobody
knew about it except her and Charles. It was a lot better
than their old place under the hedge that bordered the road.
One afternoon he had caught up with her as she walked
home from school. 'Between the bottom hedge of the
buttercup field and the back of the stables,' he'd muttered
hurriedly as he'd passed her. 'Get in behind the hawthorns
at the far end – ten o'clock in the morning.' Then he'd
walked on ahead of her, tall and straight and golden haired,
carrying his books and his trumpet case.

The next day, a Saturday, had been cold and sunny.
She'd helped her mother after breakfast as she always did
and then asked if she could go out to play in the buttercup
field. 'What a child,' Martha had said absently, 'you'd want
to go out an' play if the heavens fell, wouldn't you? Wrap
up warm, mind, an' be sure an' come when I shout you.'

She'd met Charles in the darkness of the tunnel for the
first time. They called it a tunnel because that was what it
was like – a long narrow tunnel with a roof of crisscrossed
bare branches. Charles had brought an old rug from the
stables to sit on and a freshly baked oven-bottom muffin
that Lilah had given him. Oh, it had been lovely.

Ever since then it had been their secret place, a perfect
hidey-hole away from grown-up eyes where they could
play guessing games and talk about what they would do
until they were old enough to get married. Charles told her
about going to hear the Halle orchestra in Manchester and
about his trumpet lessons. Rosie in turn related how she'd
been asked to read her composition out loud to the class
and how Miss Hardman had sent a letter to her mam and
dad with a list of books that they should buy for her or try
to get from Mr Schofield's library at the institute. Failing
that, there was the prospect of a new town library being
built in the next year or two. 'Rosanna has an aptitude for
the English language far in advance of her years,' Miss
Hardman had told them.

Now, after taking the slate in to her mother and getting

her a clean handkerchief when she cried about it even though she said she was happy, Rosie ran round to the tunnel just in case Charles was there. It was almost dusk and the hawthorns were tipped with frost; the sun had gone but when she caught a glint of gold in the undergrowth her heart gave a joyful lurch. He was there, holding his trumpet as he always did when he waited for her.

She slipped through the gap in the bushes and crouched down next to him. 'I'm glad you're here!' she said breathlessly. 'Me dad's in bed in your grandpa's house, do you know? Somebody's stabbed him an' broke his jaw an' his collarbone. An' me mam's in bed poorly!'

Charles knew all about it because he'd heard the grown-ups talking, but he let her tell him every detail. He in turn knew something, as well. 'My uncle Sam's going to marry Miss Ridings from the pawnshop!'

Rosie was pleased about that. She liked weddings and she liked Mr Sam; as for Miss Ridings, she was the lady who always looked cool when it was hot, and warm when it was freezing; she was Elizabeth Hartley's aunt, every-body knew that. But Rosie saw that Charles's mouth was tight, like when he was worried about something. 'Aren't you glad?' she asked in puzzlement.

'Yes, I'm glad,' he said slowly. 'But as soon as Papa comes in we're going home and then we'll have to tell Mama.'

'Ah.' There was no need for explanation. Rosie knew at once that his mother wouldn't want to be linked to the pawnshop through her husband's brother. 'Miss Ridings is very rich,' she comforted. 'She's clever as well; Elizabeth Hartley told me.'

'I know,' he said, producing the small, worried smile that always gave her a little pain in her chest. 'If Mama doesn't like it there's nothing she can do to stop them getting married.' His tone carried no conviction and they both knew it.

'P'raps your dad will tell her off,' said Rosie, trying to offer a shred of comfort.

'Perhaps,' he agreed dubiously. 'Uncle Sam kissed Miss Ridings, you know, when he thought nobody was looking. He sat her down on the sofa and kissed her on her mouth.'

Rosie looked at him curiously. What was so odd about that? 'Me dad kisses me mam all the time,' she said apologetically. 'I think some people do.' She wondered if that information would tempt Charles to kiss *her*, but it didn't.

'Not my parents,' he said. 'They don't like each other.'

Rosie took his hand between her small, cold palms. 'Try not to worry about it,' she advised gently. 'Grown-ups are a bit funny sometimes. I expect your mam will be pleased when you tell her about Miss Ridings and your uncle.'

Charles knew she was wrong about that, but he didn't say so. He just let her carry on holding his hand in hers. It gave him a warm sort of feeling.

Sarah, Countess of Soar, was taking tea with her husband in her sitting room at Alsing. She loved that little room; it was pretty rather than grand: chairs upholstered in dull-pink velvet, curtains made from her father's finest cloth, wallpaper patterned with leaves and rosebuds, and a pale-green carpet that had been woven in Staffordshire, not far from one of the smaller Soar properties. They seldom visited that particular house; it was the home of Francis's mother, a woman implacably opposed to her daughter-in-law.

Francis, the gentlest and kindest of men, had been amazingly brisk at bundling his mother out of Alsing and into her own establishment. 'She's not like you, my love,' he had told Sarah before they were married. 'She tolerated my father because of his title, then produced me as a duty and ignored me throughout my childhood and teens. She's incapable of affection and I doubt she's ever heard of love. That house will suit her very well; it's on the outskirts of the town rather than in the country like Alsing, so she'll have ample opportunity to do what she likes best – flaunt her rank.'

If anyone else had said that about their mother, Sarah would have thought them hard, maybe even cruel, but she couldn't ever think that about Francis. She had trusted his judgement on the matter, feeling guilty at ousting his mother from the ancestral home but knowing that she had never received a kind word from her in all the years of Francis's courtship.

Now, with the lamps lit early and the frost-silvered lawns fading into the dusk beyond the curtains, they sat and talked of the day's events. Francis was usually too busy to take tea with her, but of late, whenever she was at home in the afternoon, he would sit here as if he had all the time in the world. Her heart swelled with love for him. He knew she was trying to be happy for her maid Polly, whose baby was due any day; he also knew that she was sick with envy because it was Polly who was about to give birth rather than her.

Sarah was touched by his concern but also, to her shame, resentful. She didn't want to be treated with care, like a piece of porcelain in one of Alsing's showcases; she wanted to help with the birth and use her own hard-earned midwifery skills – it was the least she could do for her dear Polly. Then, the baby safely delivered, she would hope, long, pray to be in labour herself before the year was out.

She offered a plate of little cakes to Francis, but instead of choosing one he set the plate aside and took her hand, turning it over and pressing his lips to the inside of her wrist. 'I love you,' he said quietly.

'I love you, too.' She leaned forward and planted a kiss on the end of his nose.

The door opened and someone cleared their throat. It was accepted by the army of servants that they never entered a room suddenly when their master and mistress were alone together. A footman came in, bearing a letter on a silver tray.

'For you, m'lady,' he murmured, offering it to Sarah. 'The coachman will wait for an answer.'

She flashed him the smile that had long since earned her

the goodwill of the entire household. 'Come back in five minutes, will you?' She glanced at the envelope. 'Oh goody, it's from Sam!' Reading the contents she said, 'Francis, he wants to know if we're free this evening. He has something to tell us.'

Francis smiled. He liked Sam. 'Tell him to join us for dinner,' he suggested. 'Will he be alone?'

'He doesn't say.' She jumped to her feet. 'It'll be Zacky who brought it – I'll go and talk to him.' She sped out of the room and past the waiting footman towards the great entrance hall. Zacky was part of her growing up at Meadowbank, when they were all together as a family . . .

Back again with Francis she picked up her teacup. 'Zacky was a bit peculiar,' she said in aggravation. 'I couldn't get a thing out of him except "I really couldn't say". Anyway, I've asked him to tell Sam we'll expect him for dinner. Francis, you don't think there's anything wrong at the mill, do you, after what Papa was saying about putting men on guard through the night?'

Francis leaned back in his chair and watched her, purely for the pleasure of seeing her with the lamplight shining on her hair. Joshua Schofield had adored the mother, he thought, just as he himself adored the daughter. Sarah was so very like her mother, both in looks and character, though if anything even more beautiful. 'We'll soon know,' he said, 'but if it concerns Jericho surely Sam would be more likely to call on James than to come here?'

'Not if he could help it. He doesn't like High Lee Court, and we know how he feels about Esther, don't we?' She thought of her eldest brother and, as always, her spirits plummeted. 'Poor James,' she whispered.

'All men aren't as fortunate as I am,' Francis agreed soberly.

Fortunate? Sarah told herself for the hundredth time that having no child seemed to worry her far, far more than it did Francis. How often had he said, 'I would rather have you than fifty sons, my love.'?

Outside the windows the frost-laden dusk turned to

darkness while they sat in front of the fire, holding hands.

Esther was at her embroidery frame in the drawing room when James and Charles arrived home. She carried on with the fine needlework, lifting her head for an instant to say coolly, 'You're late.'

'Yes, a little,' agreed James pleasantly. 'I'm sorry about that.' He always strived for an air of normality when Charles was present. 'We've brought good news, Esther – Sam's to be married!'

At that she pricked her needle into the fine linen and gave him her full attention. She was clearly aggrieved. 'I didn't even know he was paying court to anyone. Who is it?'

'Tizzie.'

Esther's mouth fell open. 'Tizzie? Tizzie Ridings?'

'Yes. We don't know any other Tizzie, do we?'

Charles looked from one to the other, his eyes guarded and wary, but Esther ignored him and concentrated on her husband. 'What does your father think about this?' she asked tightly.

'He's delighted, of course, and so am I.'

'Well *I'm* not delighted,' she snapped. 'Have you all gone out of your *minds*?'

James had gone very still, very quiet. 'What do you mean?'

There were two bright spots of colour high on his wife's cheeks. She was tapping the floor with the toe of her shoe. 'Charles, leave the room!' she said.

Charles made his escape, fumbling clumsily with the door handle.

'Close it; close it behind you!' she said irritably, then turned back to James. 'I would be unwilling to be linked by marriage to the Saltley pawnshop,' she said, enunciating her words slowly and clearly as if to a young child, 'but I absolutely refuse to be connected to a woman whose name is a byword in the town for lewd behaviour.'

It was James's turn to gape. 'Esther!' He stepped back

a pace. 'Surely you don't believe all that rubbish about her and Barney Jellicoe. He's a decent man, very intelligent – he thinks the world of her.'

'I'm sure he does.' Esther nodded her fluffy, kittenish head. 'He *would* think the world of the woman who uses him for her perversions. Who else would touch such a lump of deformity? Everybody knows he's been well paid for it with a partnership in the business.'

'But—' James was almost speechless, 'my father has always received Tizzie at Meadowbank. You've been in company with her there and at Alsing many a time.'

'Maybe, but you must have seen that I never fell over myself to be pleasant to her.'

With an effort James held back the obvious reply that she never fell over herself to be pleasant to anybody except her social superiors. Instead he said, 'If you feel so strongly why haven't you refused to sit in the same room as her? Why haven't you declined invitations if you knew she was to be present?'

Silently she glared at him, her delicate little nose suddenly sharp, like a beak. She chewed her lips with her tiny, very white teeth.

'Hah!' James nodded his head in sudden comprehension. 'You didn't protest because she *is* received at Alsing – she's a friend of Sarah and Francis. That's it, isn't it? You've put up with what you call a lewd woman because she's welcomed by the aristocracy. Well, they're better judges of character than you, madam. You're despicable!'

She gaped at him. 'How dare you speak to me in that tone?'

James smiled but it was more a baring of his teeth than a relaxing of his lips. 'I don't usually, do I? But that's because I dislike acrimony, as you well know. Don't be fooled, Esther. I may not say very much, but I think all the more.'

'You think a load of rubbish if you think I'm going to stand by and watch that insufferable brother of yours bring the Schofield name down by marrying a trollop – and a pawnbroker into the bargain!'

'I can't imagine that even you could prevent my "insufferable" brother marrying whoever he wants. He has impeccable judgement when it comes to choosing a wife.'

Esther was openly scornful. 'I see no evidence of it.'

There were beads of sweat along James's upper lip, the only visible sign of his hatred of arguments. 'I say his judgement is impeccable because long ago he warned me not to marry you. Fool that I was, I ignored him and I've regretted it ever since our wedding night.'

'Oh, we're on that tack again are we? I thought as much. Listen, I've always known that Sam didn't want me to marry you – he made it abundantly clear. As for our wedding night, I'm sick of telling you that you have the appetites of the byre, the stable and the sty.'

'Aye,' he said wearily, 'and cows, horses and pigs have natural God-given instincts, which is more than I can say for you. But don't get alarmed, any desires I might have harboured in the past have been killed off long since. You'll not have forgotten that I once threatened to leave you if you didn't allow me a husband's privileges? Well, I don't want those privileges now, Esther; I haven't wanted them for years – at least not from you.'

She stared at him as the implication of his words sank in. 'Are you telling me that you would go elsewhere? Visit a house of ill repute? A man in your position?'

'If I did I'd be joining some of Saltley's top business-men – men who are your father's bosom friends – grandfathers, some of them. I would also be joining a number of the landed gentry whose wives you entertain so eagerly at your little tea parties.'

Esther was blinking uncertainly but her voice never faltered. 'My friends' husbands are gentlemen,' she said flatly. 'They would never even think of using loose women.'

James eyed her in bafflement. She was razor sharp, alert to every aspect of social distinction and keenly aware of the class divisions in both country and town. Surely she couldn't be as naive as she sounded? What did she talk about with her lady friends? The latest fashions? The weather? The gossip of the town? If she'd listened to the gossip about Tizzie her afternoon teas couldn't be all that innocent . . .

All at once he'd had enough. To talk with Esther of all people about such matters was more than he could stomach. He made for the door. 'I'll dine in my room,' he said, 'and Charles can join me. I'm thinking very seriously about moving back to Meadowbank. With Charles.' He left her standing by her embroidery frame, for once quite speechless.

When his father crossed the hall Charles slipped silently from the next room and headed for the rear stairs. He hadn't been able to hear all that they said but one thing was clear . . . Rosanna had been right in what she'd forecast. His father *had* told his mother off! With a spring to his step he clattered up the stairs and made for his room. He had a book on great engineers that he wanted to read. After that, he would light the lantern and head for the loft above the stables where he practised playing his trumpet. He hadn't got his latest set of scales quite right . . .

By the time Sam went round to Farthing Lane he was sick with apprehension. How could he have neglected to tell Tizzie about Ralph when she herself had mentioned him? How *could* he?

He was early but she was ready and waiting, wearing a pearl-grey velvet dress, very plain and tight waisted, subdued half mourning which had the effect of making her hair and eyes appear more colourful than ever. She was as near beautiful as he had ever seen her.

Tizzie noticed at once that he wasn't the forceful, self-confident man of earlier that day. He didn't attempt to kiss her, not even her hand. 'Is everything all right?' she asked.

'Please sit down, Tizzie.' He stood facing her with his hands behind his back and his feet together.

She found herself getting irritated; he looked like a

schoolboy brought before the headmaster – not at all how she wanted to see her future husband. She gave an edgy little laugh. 'What's all this about, then?'

'Tizzie, I've done you an injustice,' he began.

God! He'd changed his mind! Her head whirled and her cheeks went ice cold as they lost colour. She gripped the arms of the chair to prevent herself falling forward to the floor. She took a deep breath. No, of course he hadn't changed his mind – he couldn't have done, not after the way he'd kissed her, the way he'd presented her to his family. She managed to speak calmly. 'An injustice? In what way?'

'It's my brother Ralph, Tizzie. I put him out of my mind because I didn't want the thought of him to spoil what was happening between you and me.'

'I could see you didn't want to talk about him,' she agreed cautiously. Ralph had been an odd youth, she recalled, self-obsessed and somewhat arrogant. Had he got some girl into trouble? Or was it gambling – they said it was the scourge of Manchester . . . Worse, was it embezzlement, or even full-blown fraud? Behaviour of that sort would hit the Schofields hard; Sam no doubt felt he must reveal it to her before she joined the family. She recalled Barney saying that Ralph was a bad 'un and was suddenly apprehensive. 'What about him?' she asked. 'You can tell me, Sam. You can tell me anything.'

He looked into those concerned green eyes and told her. 'He committed murder.'

Tizzie heard something issue from her mouth, a weak, ineffectual noise like the mewing of a kitten. At once she was ashamed of it, shaking her bright head as if to disown the sound. 'Go on,' she said, struggling with disbelief.

'My mother found out about it and tried to keep it from my father. The strain of it killed her, but not before he realised the truth of it for himself. After the funeral he disowned Ralph and had him transported to Australia without a rag to his back or a penny to his name.' Sam stared down at the rug. He had lived with those facts for years, yet they sounded utterly far fetched when put into words.

'Who did he murder?' she asked, still incredulous.

'My father's best friend – his business partner, Charlie Barnes. Ralph hated him and wanted his job. He pushed him out of the hoist at Mosley Street. You might remember the case – his death was recorded as an accident. I should have told you all this before I asked you to marry me.'

She flashed him a cool green stare. 'Yes, you should, but you're telling me now, so don't get in a state about it.' Flicking an impatient hand at the sofa, she said, 'Sit you down and let me think for a minute.'

Her mind raced but her emotions merely swirled and eddied like water trapped behind a dam. It was no use saying it didn't matter – it mattered terribly that the Schofields, the lovely, clever, golden Schofields, were family to a murderer, whether free or convicted. She would be linked to a murderer by marriage. If indeed it had been Ralph she'd seen in Manchester, she had looked into a murderer's eyes. Those eyes ... sky blue and dead as stones ...

'Who knows about this?' she demanded.

'James, Sarah and Francis. And now you.'

'Not Esther?'

'No. James chose not to tell her.'

'But you chose to tell me.'

'I love you,' he said abruptly.

There was silence between them. She noticed his hands clenched tight on his knees as he sat opposite her. She thought of Joshua Schofield, banishing an eighteen-year-old boy to the other side of the world; of Sarah, never ever mentioning her brother; of James, keeping a secret from his wife for years and years ... Sam here obviously thought she might turn him down now that she knew. 'You never batted an eyelid at people saying that I keep Barney as a grown-up catamite,' she said thoughtfully.

'I never batted an eyelid because it isn't true,' he pointed out. 'All this about Ralph *is* true.'

She was tapping her foot on the floor. 'Do you think Ralph is behind all this interfering in the mills?'

'Yes.'

'And the attack on Matthew Raike?'

'Yes. I'm almost certain he's behind that as well.'

'Then it looks as if you're going to have a fight on your hands.' She was silent again for a minute, a small defiant smile touching her mouth. 'You once told me I was a fighter. Do you remember?'

'Of course I remember. It was in Peter Street, outside the bank.'

'Well, I'd better sharpen my sword and gird on my armour, hadn't I? You're going to need all the help you can get.'

Sam closed his eyes for an instant. 'You mean you don't mind marrying into a murderer's family?'

'Of course I mind, but I'll be marrying you, not your brother!'

'Tizzie, oh Tizzie! What a woman I've got myself!' He pulled her to her feet and whirled her round the room in a mad dance of joy and relief. Her skirts dipped and swayed, her feet left the floor, but his arms were like iron. He planted her down and kissed her parted lips hard.

Outside in the frosty lane Zacky got down from his seat to walk the horse. Mr Sam had said, 'I'll only be five minutes, Zacky.' Some five minutes!

The carriage sped along the road to Alsing with Tizzie and Sam side by side under the rug. Sam had his arm around her shoulders, holding her so close they swayed as one at each bump of the wheels.

Tizzie was still excited by the day's events and still stunned by the revelations about Ralph. She wasted no energy on agonising. It was done, in the past. If he was back in England and about to cause trouble, then she would be right there next to Sam and his family. And she would fight. That was that.

'We're not putting a blight on the evening by telling

Sarah and Francis about him,' Sam had said flatly. 'I've written them a letter to be handed over in the morning. That little swine has spoiled enough of today for us.'

Tizzie agreed. She was savouring the closeness of the man she had loved for years, and compared to that Ralph seemed like a side issue. She was deeply thankful; Sam had come to her – *he* had made the move, without any scheming or encouragement or even expectation on her part. The physical attraction between them was intense, yet he had done no more than kiss her, comprehensively it was true, but with respect. She felt the most overpowering relief about that; it would have been more than she could have coped with if Sam had made the same sort of demands as the half-forgotten Edward.

All he had done with his hands was to hold her close – by the waist or by the shoulders. This must be what real love was all about, she told herself: a linking of thought and feeling, while physical desire – a burning, desperate desire in their case – was kept under control until it could be fully expressed in marriage. And their particular marriage was going to be soon.

'Don't keep me waiting for long,' Sam had begged before they'd set off. 'What about your time of mourning? Will we have to wait because of that? How has Mary taken it?'

'She's pleased, I think. She was a bit quiet, but for some reason she's under the impression it should have happened years ago.'

'Tell me the old, old story,' he said, somewhat put out. 'But what about fixing a date?'

'We can hardly have a big wedding within a few months of William dying, but if we keep it fairly quiet I don't think she'll object. After all, she married William a fortnight after my father died, though admittedly he requested it in his will.'

The carriage sped on its way with Sam asking what sort of engagement ring she wanted and Tizzie pointing out that she owned a jeweller's shop and had contacts in the precious stones trade, so she could get him a good discount.

He laughed out loud at that. 'I'm marrying a woman of business, so I might as well take advantage of her experience! What shall it be, then? Diamonds, emeralds? No – emeralds would suffer by comparison with your eyes ... He kissed her eyelids and traced her lashes with his tongue.

It seemed no time at all before they reached the vast stone bulk of Alsing. 'I can't wait to see their faces,' Sam grinned. 'I wonder if they'll guess when we arrive together?'

A footman took their coats while Sam had a word with the butler, handing over the letter about Ralph. 'We hope to surprise Lady Soar on this visit,' he told him, 'so just announce me and not Miss Ridings, will you?'

Sarah and Francis were in the small sitting room, looking forward to seeing Sam. 'Mr Samuel Schofield,' announced the butler, with the formality that was customary even when a guest arrived for a private dinner.

Always one for a touch of drama, Sam made Tizzie wait outside while he entered the room straight-faced. He kissed Sarah and shook Francis by the hand, but his sister knew him too well; their minds had been linked through childhood and teens. 'Sammy!' she laughed. 'What's going on? Are you on your own?'

'No,' he said, 'I've come with my future wife!' With a bound he returned to the door and brought in Tizzie, who stood there smiling as if she would never stop.

Sarah shrieked with delight and tried to grab them both in her arms at once. 'Lovely, lovely,' she was gabbling. 'So *this* is why Zacky was so secretive. Isn't it wonderful, Francis? Isn't it marvellous?' Her husband was already ringing for champagne, then he came and kissed Tizzie and put an arm around Sam. 'Congratulations, both of you.'

'Don't say it,' warned Sam.

'Say what?'

'What everybody else has said, "Not before time".'

Francis laughed. 'All right, I won't say it – I'll just think it. I'm so very, very pleased.'

Sarah's eyes were shining like jewels. Sammy – her darling Sammy and her dear, dear Tizzie. It was what she'd prayed for every night for years and years. There was a kind of radiance about them ... not unusual in Sam's case, he had always given off the glow of health and well being, but this was something that encompassed them both. It was an aura of happiness, of course, but beneath it simmered an unmistakeable physical excitement. Only to be expected, she told herself firmly; they must have acknowledged their love for each other that very day.

She patted the cushions on either side of her. 'Sit here and tell us every single thing. When did all this happen?'

Sam hesitated and Tizzie held her breath. What had happened was theirs alone, surely, but he and Sarah were so very close ...

'Steady, Funny Face,' laughed Sam. 'Some things aren't for open discussion.'

Their eyes met, a brother and sister so in tune they had often read each other's thoughts without even noticing. Sarah gave a little nod. Sam had known when to bow out of *her* life, he'd done it when she'd married Edward, but he had come back into it quickly enough when she'd needed him. Now it was her turn to bow out, and she was glad for him. Looking at Tizzie she saw her green eyes lowered and a small smile on her lips. She had registered the switch in Sam's priorities.

They dined in the adjoining room, where Sarah and Francis often took meals when they were alone, Sam handing Tizzie into the seat opposite with barely concealed reluctance. There was much talk and laughter; Sarah even managed to forget Polly and her expected baby. She told herself firmly that she was delighted about Sam and Tizzie, though she wondered if she might miss being the most important woman in his life. That wasn't why she found it difficult to look at them both; it was because of the passion that held them – the sheer physical desire for each other that was making her and Francis seem like intruders. It emanated from Sam like a lava flow. She almost expected to see scorch marks on the table. They didn't touch each other unless it was with their feet but their gazes locked almost constantly. Sam seemed to be watching Tizzie's every mouthful of food. Once, he pursed his lips in a kiss when he thought she and Francis weren't looking.

Sarah concentrated on her undercut of beef in wine sauce and tried to calm her mind. Sam was her brother; she had never imagined, let alone seen him in any kind of sexual situation; she had merely accepted that he liked women and was attractive to them in a wholesome, well-balanced kind of way, like their father. Now, though, under Tizzie's glowing regard, he positively exuded desire, his eyes dark in the light of the candles as he watched her every move, his lips parted. He looked as if he could have eaten her.

Across the table Francis was being the attentive host, fond of his guests, attentive to their needs. From time to time Sarah saw him glance at her, oh, so calmly. Didn't he see the barely disguised passion that dominated the table? Didn't he sense it? Didn't he feel it? Watching him, she ached with love. He was so good to look at these days. Not handsome or distinguished, just *good*; straight and tall and serious, with his honest brown eyes and fine hair that always flopped over his forehead no matter how much he brushed it back.

All at once she ached to be in his arms, being kissed until she was dizzy; but that wasn't likely to happen because he was always so very gentle. When they made love he all but apologised for reaching his climax. In the early years of their marriage she had been touched by such treatment, knowing he would die rather than make her live again the hell of her brief marriage to Edward. Much later, she had ventured to say, with a laugh, 'I'm not made of glass, Francis, I won't break,' or, very gently, 'I'm a healthy young woman and I love you. Don't hold back.'

It hadn't changed him. 'I can't bear to hurt you,' he'd replied simply. 'You're so very lovely, so very delicate. I feel like a great blundering bear when we make love.'

Gradually it had dawned on her that he might be insecure or lacking in confidence after his loveless upbringing, or maybe he had some deep-seated problem that damped down his passion when it should have been burning white hot. She had even wondered if their sweet, gentle, considerate lovemaking was the reason there were no babies, but her medical knowledge refuted such an idea. Babies were made whether the partners were eager or unwilling, passionate or lethargic . . .

She was ashamed to find herself relieved when at last Sam and Tizzie made their farewells. Sam hadn't even noticed that she was quiet, she thought, where once he would have tuned in to her feelings and shared them. That was good; it was as it should be. Her heart swelled with love for them both as she kissed them goodbye and arranged to visit Tizzie to discuss the wedding. She and Francis waved them off from the main doors of the house, but once back in the small sitting room she was too restless to sit and chat, pacing back and forth behind the sofas.

'Are you quite well, sweetheart?' asked Francis. 'You were a little quiet during the evening, I thought.'

'I'm fine, really I am,' she told him. 'Sam and Tizzie are very much in love, aren't they? Did you notice?'

'Yes,' he said quietly. 'I noticed.'

'They'll be well matched, won't they? Physically, I mean.'

'Yes,' he said again.

'Francis,' she said urgently, 'do you ever feel like that about me? As if you can't bear me out of your sight, not even for a minute?'

He stared at her for what seemed an age. 'Sweetheart, I want to kiss the ground you walk on,' he said gently. 'How can you doubt it?'

'I don't. But we're so – so sort of restrained, aren't we? So subdued. I – I just wondered if you ever, ever feel – oh,

I don't know. It doesn't matter.' She couldn't say more, it would sound like criticism.

Dismay was in his eyes. The skin around his nose had gone very white. It gave his face a pinched look, as if he hadn't eaten in days. 'Sarah,' he said, 'are you telling me that I don't satisfy you? Is my lovemaking not to your liking?'

She hurled herself into his arms and buried her face against his chest. 'Of course it is!' she gasped. 'I love you! You're always kissing me and holding me and it's gorgeous, but when we really make love I have the feeling that you – you won't let go. It's as if you're forcing yourself to be gentle.'

He pulled her arms from around his neck and stepped back from her. 'You've had one brute to deal with,' he said shortly. 'I'm quite sure you can do without another.'

'But you could never remind me of Edward,' she protested. 'Never!'

'I'm glad of that,' he said, but he didn't look glad at all.

Constraint had fallen between them for the first time in almost seven years of marriage. She didn't know what to do, what to say to make things right again. She thought back to her mother, the source of so much wisdom. 'If you're uncertain what to do, follow your instincts,' she used to say. 'Instinct is always better than intelligence in a tricky situation.'

A picture came to her, then, of her parents in their bedroom. Once she had rushed in without knocking, anxious for her father to go downstairs and receive Edward, who was ready to ask for her hand. Bursting in, she had found her father tightening her mother's stays, laughing as he did it. What she remembered about the scene was the easy intimacy between her father and mother. Without knowing it she sighed. There was little intimacy in the bedroom with a maid and a valet hovering. 'I think I'll go up now, Francis,' she said. 'You won't be long?'

He managed his usual good-natured smile. 'I'll be up in ten minutes, my love.'

She sped upstairs. The young maid who had replaced Polly was waiting to undress her and see her into bed, while in Francis's dressing room his valet was ready to prepare his wash bowl and put away his day clothes. She had always accepted such service as normal in a great house like Alsing, but her mother hadn't had a personal maid, her father had no valet. His clothes had been looked after by her mother and the women servants.

'You can go to bed, Lucy,' she told the maid. 'I'll see to myself tonight.'

'But your hair, my lady?'

'It's all right, I'll see to it, and my gown has front fastenings.' She went through to the dressing room. 'Hamer, I'll see to his Lordship's clothes, and he can make his own preparations for bed. We shan't need you again this evening and we'll ring for you in the morning.'

With both of them gone she looked uncertainly round the room. It was all very well relying on instinct, but what happened when instinct failed? Common sense took over, she told herself, and looked in the mirror. Instinct told her not to undress completely; it would be too blatant. Common sense told her to remove her dress and petticoats and to unpin her hair. Francis loved to see it loose.

When he came in she was wearing a silk wrap over her underclothes, brushing her bright hair in front of the mirror. She looked at him gravely through the glass and saw that he still looked pale and ill at ease. 'I've given them both the night off,' she told him. 'I thought we could relax better if we were completely alone.'

His eyes were on the gleaming mass of her hair. He smiled slightly. 'I've often wanted to brush your hair,' he said, 'but Polly was always there, and then Lucy.'

She handed him the silver brush. 'I don't have to have a maid,' she said, 'and you don't have to have a valet.'

He brushed her hair, and the novelty of being alone was such that it was almost as if they were newly married. Francis undressed on his own, returning in a velvet robe over his nightshirt. She shook out and hung up his clothes and folded his linen ready for the laundry, then she slipped out of her wrap and smiled. 'If I don't have a maid you'll have to unlace my stays, Francis.'

Silently he fumbled with the laces and the twelve steel hooks until at last he laid the pretty white stays to one side and she stood there in her shimmy and long frilly drawers. She removed the shimmy and bared her round white breasts. Then she stepped out of her drawers and shook back her waist-length hair. He had never before seen her naked. Modesty was what he had always seemed to want. She herself had wanted it, at first.

He didn't move.

Her cheeks flamed. Squirming, she dug her toes into the carpet. She was embarrassing him! So much for instinct. What should she do?

She didn't have to do anything. He uttered a sound that was half sob, half laugh, then picked her up in his arms and laid her on the bed, throwing aside the velvet robe and the fine lawn nightshirt and showing himself to her. That also was for the first time.

She said, 'You're a fine figure of a man, my love,' and lay there ready for him. He bent over her and kissed her from the top of her silver-gold head to the tips of her toes, then pulled back the covers and lifted her on to the sheet.

He was like a man set free from captivity: joyous, earthy, passionate and almost delirious with desire. His hands were everywhere and so was his mouth. 'You won't hurt me,' she whispered against his lips. 'You won't, I promise you!'

So for the first time in their marriage the Earl of Soar made love to his wife without restraint, and for the first time in her life the Countess of Soar knew the heights of sexual arousal and fulfilment. They slept naked in each other's arms, wakening again and then again for longer, slower loving, until at last they fell asleep exhausted.

At the first sounds of activity in the house, Sarah opened her eyes to find Francis still asleep with his arm across her thighs, his hair tousled and beard growth darkening his jaw.

She kissed his neck and then his ear without disturbing him. Two separate thoughts were struggling for prominence in her mind. One was that they had made love three times without her once wondering if she would manage to conceive. The other was that Sam, her darling Sammy, had performed a service for both her and Francis by his direct if unwitting display of passion at the dinner table.

It couldn't possibly have been that he had known about her and Francis? Of course it couldn't! But it was as if his thoughts and feelings had joined hers for one last time before separating for ever, he to go to Tizzie, she to Francis, with a thankful heart. So real was the image that she could almost see her beloved companion of thirty years disappearing into the future with the sun shining on his hair. How often had she watched that broad, well-loved figure striding through life with a smile?

'Goodbye, my Sammy, and thank you,' she whispered silently, then turned to her husband and snuggled against his chest.

CHAPTER ELEVEN

A Visit from Ephraim

Joshua stood in his dressing gown and slippers by the sitting room window. It was early but he'd been awake for hours, tossing and turning and finally leaving his bed to come down and watch the lights going on in the town.

The gas lamps on Jericho's tower flared into life under the flag and seconds later the clock behind him chimed the threequarters. He nodded in satisfaction; his orders were that on dark mornings the flag was to be lit up by a quarter to six so as to be visible to the workers as they approached the mill gates.

Behind the tower reared Jericho's chimney, the tallest in Saltley, belching red-tinged smoke as the boilers were fired up for setting on the engines. He could see the glow from more of them down in the town – a satisfying sight, he told himself; chimneys issuing their own evidence of prosperity. In a matter of minutes there would also be the evidence of his ears: the ring of clog irons on flagstones as thousands of workers made for their mills.

The spinning and weaving of cotton was what gave impetus to his life, but he had to admit that the impetus had slowed a bit in the last few weeks. And why? Because his youngest son had come back from the other side of the world.

He sighed. For years he had kept the facts about Ralph

in his heart like a cold, heavy black stone that he could manage to carry as long as he didn't examine it too closely. But since the affair of the missing order book at Mosley Street he had been forced to examine the stone daily, sometimes hourly, and now the weight of it was taking away his sleep, robbing him of the ability to concentrate his mind on his family and his business.

To be sure there had been a week or two of respite after his meeting with the other cotton masters. The bliss, the exquisite relief of hearing that he wasn't the only one to be having trouble in his mill ... He had convinced himself then that Ralph wasn't implicated, because if he had been he would have wanted to damage only Jericho rather than the mills of all and sundry.

Now Joshua clicked his tongue in self-disgust. He should have remembered how Ralph's mind worked; he was devious. Red herrings were his favourite fish. Leaving Boulton's and the Bluebell out of it had been a red herring, designed to make him suspicious of two mill owners he had little time for. Spreading the vandalism over a period of time had been another red herring ... but not the attack on Matthew. That had been an accomplice, a man who stuck at nothing to prevent himself being captured; the fella seen by young Rosie was probably another. One thing was sure, though, they would be paid accomplices. Ralph spun a lonely thread; he had never been one to draw folk to him. He hadn't had a friend in the world apart from that young lad in Liverpool – Richard something or other. His own son without a friend ... what an idiot he was to let that hurt him still.

The clatter of clogs was gaining volume in the distance. Few clog wearers went past Meadowbank; it was too far from the crisscrossed dark streets that housed the workers. Joshua stared out at his mill, his mind on Ralph. He still found it hard to believe what his own son had done ... God only knew he himself wasn't perfect, but he could recognise the difference between right and wrong. He didn't thump the Bible at Albion, nor stand up and prate at prayer meetings, but he was a believer, just as Rachel had been. Between them, though, they'd produced Ralph.

Believer or not, he knew he could never be like the father in the parable of the prodigal son, nor for that matter would Ralph have wasted his substance on riotous living – he'd left home without any substance at all. There'd be no fatted calf for Master Ralph, no falling on his neck and kissing him. The only ones to greet him would be a gang of watchmen protecting Jericho, two brothers on the lookout for mischief and a father determined to protect the family name.

Yesterday he'd said to Sam, 'If it has to come out, then so be it,' but since then he'd had second thoughts. If they could keep it dark for nearly twelve years they could keep it dark for ever that they had a murderer in the family.

The wail of the mill blower sounded, then another and another, joining in strident warning over the dark town. Thoughtfully he eyed his flag. For days past it had hung limp in the still, frosty air, but now it streamed out in the wind with the smoke from the chimney behind it. He saw the change as symbolic, his flag encouraging him to take action to protect Jericho.

Irritably he jerked his shoulders back. What ailed him, moping around like some decrepit old dodderer? He had his family behind him and twelve hundred workers. It was a poor do if that lot couldn't guard against Ralph and a couple of henchmen.

There was a tap on the door and Lilah looked in. 'Mornin' Mr Schofield. How soon do you want your hot water? Ellie's ready to take it up.' By her tone it might have been a regular occurrence for her employer to be standing in the cold sitting room in his dressing gown before the house was astir.

'I'll have it right away, Lilah. I'm going up now.'

'An' your breakfast, Mr Schofield?'

'The sooner the better,' he said. 'There's a lot to be done today.'

*

'I'm going to take a good walk through this morning,' he told Sam as they ate. 'In view of what's happened I feel I've got to check everything myself.'

Sam was in high spirits, full of thoughts of Tizzie. 'I could send the runners round to tell everybody to report to you in your office,' he suggested. 'It would save you time and energy.'

'What's the point of saving energy?' asked Joshua sharply, 'I'm not in my dotage!' He helped himself to smoked haddock and a poached egg and slapped them on a plate.

'Nobody said you were,' pacified Sam. 'I'll come with you, if you want, so we can discuss every aspect of security. Regarding Tizzie, Father. As she has no parents we're going to put our own announcement in the papers, both here and in Manchester. Have you any objection to that?'

'Of course I haven't, but at the moment I'm thinking about a family get-together.'

'A celebration? A party?' Sam was highly pleased. 'Yes, that would be good . . .'

Joshua bit back another sharp retort. The lad was in love, his head in the clouds. 'Aye, a party,' he said hurriedly, 'a real good do, but before we get round to that I'd like a get-together with you and James and Sarah and Francis, aye – and Tizzie. We've had a man half killed and if that young devil's back in the country—'

Sam was contrite. 'You're right, Father. We need to map out a plan of campaign – a strategy. I can't seem to get my mind on anything except Tizzie at the moment. Sarah's hankering to stay close to home until Polly's given birth, mind.'

'Does she know about Ralph?'

'She will as soon as she reads the letter I left for her and Francis.'

'I reckon they'll want to talk about it, then. See what they think about us having a family conference up at Alsing. As for an engagement party, your mother would have wanted us to have it here.'

They finished the meal in silence, Sam watching his father in concern. Sometimes he had a disconcerting way of referring to his mother as if she'd been dead for only a matter of weeks. This morning it was evident that Ralph was preying on his mind; he looked eighty if he looked a day. Sam thought he must insist on taking over more of the work. His suggestion of living at Mosley Street had come to nothing, which was just as well seeing how things had turned out. He would have been spending all his spare time going to and fro on the train in order to see Tizzie ...

In the mill he would have welcomed congratulations about the engagement, but the news wasn't out yet. Side by side Joshua and Sam walked the floors, and it was almost noon before they were satisfied that the place was as secure and fireproof as they could make it. Twenty-four able-bodied men – two on each floor of both buildings – had authority to challenge anybody they didn't recognise on their particular floor or who behaved suspiciously. They in turn were answerable to a foreman who was known to all and sundry as 'the safety man'. Six more men patrolled the yard and the reservoir, and all thirty were relieved by a smaller group when the workers had gone home. A tidy wages bill to keep a Schofield off the premises, as Joshua had remarked more than once. Add to that the men at the institute and the two watchmen at Mosley Street, and their total pay was indeed a tidy sum.

No sooner were they back in the office than Joshua's elderly clerk came in. 'Mr Buckley's here, Mr Schofield. He says could he have a word – in private, like.'

'Mr Ephraim Buckley? Send him in, send him in.' The small, energetic figure of Esther's father appeared in the doorway, his neat features set and his jaw jutting. 'Now then, Ephraim,' said Joshua. 'What can I do for you? We don't often see you at Jericho.'

The other man nodded briskly and looked round for somebody to take his hat and coat. Finding nobody, he shrugged out of the coat and placed it with his hat on

Joshua's desk, at the same time darting a look at Sam. 'I'd like a private word, Joshua – just you and me.'

As always, that antagonised Joshua. 'There's no secrets between Sam and me, Ephraim,' he said shortly. 'I'm sure you know he's my right-hand man here at the mill. Now, sit you down.'

'It's more of a personal matter,' said Ephraim Buckley firmly.

Personal? Here at his place of business? Joshua backed into his big leather chair. It couldn't – it couldn't concern Ralph? 'Well, perhaps this once,' he conceded. 'Sam, can I ask you to leave us for a minute?'

Sam shot a keen blue glance at the older man and walked out very slowly, his lack of speed saying more clearly than words that he was reluctant to leave. Joshua eyed his son's broad back and turned to the visitor. 'Now, Ephraim, what can I do for you?'

'I've just had a visit from Esther. She's upset, very upset, and she's got cause.'

Joshua tried for a jocular tone. 'It's James she's married to, Ephraim, not me, but I'm sorry to hear it. What's she upset about?'

Ephraim Buckley leaned across the desk, his eyes very wide behind his wire-rimmed spectacles. He reminded Joshua of a small but vicious bird. 'Tizzie Ridings joining her husband's family, that's what!'

'Oh, I see.' Joshua was deceptively calm. 'And what's her objection to my son's future wife?'

'She's a hussy – a trollop! Worse – she's a pervert. I can't credit you gave your permission for such a match.'

'Sam came of age years back,' said Joshua calmly. 'He makes his own decisions.'

'Ah! So you're not in favour, then?'

'Of course I'm in favour; it's what I've wanted for years! Are you trying to tell me you believe all this dirty talk about Tizzie and Barney Jellicoe?'

'Oh, I believe it,' said the other grimly. 'There's no smoke without fire.'

'You can get smoke from hot air if you try hard enough. Now, listen to me, I've known Tizzie for years – she's a good friend to my daughter and to my daughter's husband. I notice Esther doesn't refuse to go to Alsing when Tizzie will be there. What does she do? Pretend not to see her? Or is Tizzie's reputation suddenly restored when she's with the aristocracy?'

'There's no need to brag because your daughter's made a good match after that disaster of a marriage to Mayfield. Everybody knows he carried on with Tizzie Ridings before he took up with your Sarah!'

Joshua got to his feet. 'When it comes to disastrous marriages I'd keep quiet, if I were you. It's my considered opinion that James's marriage is almost as big a mistake as Sarah's to Edward Mayfield.'

Ephraim gaped, his mouth open like the beak of a bird. 'How dare you say such a thing about my Esther? She could have had the pick of the county when your lad proposed, she could that.'

'Could she indeed? It's funny she set her sights on James and clung to him like a limpet, then. Listen to me, Ephraim, your precious daughter makes my son's life a misery. He had to threaten to leave her before she'd give him a child – a child who's scared to death of her at that. If she doesn't alter her ways I haven't the slightest doubt that James will leave her.'

Ephraim moistened his narrow lips. 'You what?' he asked faintly.

'You heard me. He'll sell High Lee Court and come back to live with me. What's more, he'll bring his son with him – the lad asked me only last week why he couldn't live at Meadowbank all the time instead of only two nights a week. So tell that to Esther. As for Tizzie Ridings, she's more of a woman than your little madam will ever be.'

Ephraim was gripping the desk as if he would like to throw it across the room. 'Well,' he said venomously, 'my little madam, as you call her, won't come to the wedding!'

'Happen she won't be invited,' replied Joshua, but the

other wanted the last word, his lips twitching as he tried to think of something sufficiently cutting.

'You don't give a toss, then, if you son marries a harlot?'

'I would give more than a toss if such a thing was going to happen. As it's not, I have no objections whatsoever to the marriage. What's more, if I learn that you've connived to ruin Tizzie's good name, I'll encourage her and Sam to take you to court. They do say that anybody charged with slander needs an impeccable reputation themselves or personal immorality will lose them the case.'

'Eh?'

'You should have looked at yourself before you came bellyaching to me on Esther's say-so. Does she know you're a regular at the stews of Gallgate? At places no man with more than a shilling to his name would be seen dead in? Do they know about it at St Joseph's, where your daughter had the wedding of the decade? What's up? Are you in such a hurry you can't wait to get to Manchester to find yourself a drab, or don't you want to lay out on train fare? You've kept it dark, I grant you that. I only found out myself by accident, and it was safe with me because you're James's father-in-law. In fact this is the first time I've had cause to mention it, but as you've come here preaching morality to me maybe I should think again . . .

The eyes behind the spectacles were wet with tears of either rage or humiliation, Joshua didn't know which. 'Nay, nay, let's not be hasty,' Ephraim protested. 'We could talk this through. You can't have lived like a monk yourself since Rachel died.'

He stepped back hurriedly at the expression in Joshua's eyes. 'Don't speak of my wife,' Joshua said quietly. 'Don't let me hear her name on your lips again.'

Ephraim attempted a shrug. 'We all have our sins. It's the devil finding his way through the armour of the Lord.'

'Well, in your case he won't have much trouble – he'll be on a well-worn path,' said Joshua shortly. 'Now, it's time I went home for my dinner, though I seem to have lost my appetite all at once. Look behind you, Ephraim.'

Obediently, the other looked over his shoulder. 'You see the door?' asked Joshua.

'Yes, of course I do.'

'Then get through it, and don't forget your hat and coat.'

Ephraim's nose was more prominent than ever as his jaw sagged. He didn't say a word as Joshua rang for his clerk and told him, 'Mr Buckley is just leaving. He doesn't seem well, so see him to his carriage.'

With the door closed behind them Joshua sat down again, his mind racing. Should he mention this or what? No, he decided; he'd silenced Ephraim, so why take the edge off his son's happiness? He was going through his yarn book when Sam came in again and looked at him enquiringly.

'Just a quick visit,' said Joshua vaguely. 'Esther's a bit on edge, he says.'

Sam grunted. Esther's father had called at the mill for the first time in ten years or more because she was on edge? She was always on edge about something or other. He looked at his father's bent head and felt a surge of love so intense he had to clasp his hands to prevent himself touching the white hair. 'It was about Tizzie, wasn't it, Father?'

Joshua sighed. Sam's gift, if such it could be called, was a damned nuisance at times. 'Aye,' he admitted, 'but he's gone home less cocky than when he arrived. Forget it – it's over and done with.'

'Not for me it isn't,' said Sam tightly. 'Does Esther object to my marrying Tizzie?'

Joshua lifted his shoulders. 'Yes.'

'Because of the gossip?'

'Yes. They're short of something to talk about in Saltley, so they repeat whatever rubbish is going the rounds.'

Sam sat on the edge of his father's desk. 'You'd put your head on the block to protect the Schofield name, yet you really don't mind about this, do you?'

'I mind about the truth,' said Joshua flatly, 'not about lies. There's always talk of one sort or another in a place like Saltley – usually started in malice or envy. When I was younger it was common talk that Francis's grandfather kept a string of women up in the attics at Alsing. Nobody had ever seen them or heard them, but there was envy because he was one of the richest men in Lancashire.

'Then years back there was a tale going round that Joe Whitehead had fathered a child on a young woman in the card room. It nearly finished him off, did that, not to mention his wife and the young lass and her husband. I put my mind to it and discovered it had been started by a man Joe had sacked for knocking his piecers about. There's rumours all over the place, Sam, all over England, and most of 'em false. The Queen herself has had to put up with it – look at all the talk about her and John Brown.'

'But this about Tizzie ... it's about perversions and such. It's bad – it's evil. Does old Buckley believe it?'

'He says he does, but I don't think he'll repeat it in a hurry. I've given him a bit to think about regarding his own behaviour and told him a few home truths about his dear little Esther.'

'Well, well. Such as what?'

'I said I reckoned James would leave her before long and come home to Meadowbank with Charlie.'

'You don't wrap things up, do you?'

'Not when a little snicket like Esther plays the goody-goody yet makes my son's life a misery and the same with my only grandchild. I see now I should have opened my mouth years back. She'll get short shrift from me in future, she won't part, and so will her father. And there's another thing, Sam. It's obvious that Esther tittle-tattles to her father about anything that upsets her; therefore I thank God that James chose not to tell her about Ralph. I thought at the time it didn't say much for their marriage, but I see now it said a lot for his judgement.

'We'll still have that family talk, though, just to exchange viewpoints and check on precautions. It's possible that with Matthew seriously injured Ralph and his accomplice will lie low for a bit. There's not much we can do but wait . . .' He closed the yarn book and stood up. 'Come on, let's go and get our dinner and find out what the doctor's said about Matthew.'

Tizzie was at her desk surrounded by paperwork. The Barnes brothers would soon have finished at Holden Street and she was all set to put the property on the market. As for Mary's future home, they had spent hours round at Peter Street in the last few days with young Johnny in tow, deciding what alterations were needed.

'Tizz, are you sure there's enough money for all this?' Mary had asked, waving a hand at the dingy interior. 'I know I can't take in boarders with it looking so grubby, but can I afford to put in extra doors and walls and redecorate the entire house?'

That was exactly what Tizzie had in mind – to transform the place in one fell swoop. She could visualise the big, old-fashioned rooms cleaned and repainted, some of them divided into two, and then the whole house done out with carpets and curtains to her own unfussy taste. She'd had to remind herself more than once that the house would be her sister's . . . It was for Mary to choose colours and patterns, to decide whether the big front room would be a sitting room for guests and whether the kitchen could double as the family dining room. She was getting more and more involved now. The distraught young widow who had been insensible to the needs of her family was fast becoming the dignified, grieving young mother with an eye to the future.

Now, at home in Farthing Lane, Tizzie was listing what work needed to be done before seeking estimates. She had decided not to approach the Barnes brothers this time, reasoning that to use the firm connected with William's death would be a poor start to the new venture. In any case, Richard Barnes irritated her with his barely concealed amazement whenever she showed a spark of intelligence.

Sam wasn't like that. He approved of her business
ability, admitting that most of the young women he had
known over the years had bored him silly. 'They were after
a meal ticket for life and they hadn't a brain between
them,' he'd laughed. 'At least you think for yourself,
sweetheart. You're like a breath of fresh air after all those
overdressed little madams.'

He hadn't specified what he thought of *under*dressed
little madams. That would come later, she imagined, with
herself the little madam in question. For now it was all
activity and arrangements: they had fixed the date of the
wedding for three months ahead. A business friend of hers
who dealt in precious stones had sold Sam a superb oval-
cut diamond which Bennison's were making into a ring for
her. Announcements had been placed in the papers and an
engagement party was to be held at Meadowbank.

'It sounds lovely,' she had said when Sam asked her
about it. 'Will all the family be there?'

'All of us, including young Charles,' he told her, 'and
I thought we could ask Harry Fairbrother – we've been
friends since infant school. You must invite whoever you
like, Tizzie. Mary wouldn't come, I suppose?'

'No, not so soon after losing William. I have no other
family, of course, but I'd like to ask Barney. Will that be
all right?

He looked at her carefully. 'Of course it will. I wish to
God you had dozens of relations so we could show them
all how pleased we are to have you in the family.'

Now Tizzie recalled his expression when she had
mentioned Barney. It had been intent, analytical, a shade
puzzled. Some time very soon she must explain to him why
Barney meant so much to her. It was something she never
spelled out, even to herself; it was to do with knowing that
he cared about what happened to her . . .

She heard Rebecca answer the door bell and a moment
later Elizabeth entered the room, wearing her school coat
and everyday bonnet.

'Hey, this is a surprise!' said Tizzie. 'Take your things

off, Elizabeth. I'm just about to have afternoon tea. Would you like to join me?'

The child stood there in her school pinafore, considering. 'Yes, please.'

'Then run and tell Rebecca to bring another cup and some extra cakes. We'll go in the other room in front of the fire.'

Elizabeth chose a little iced cake and nibbled it daintily. Tizzie thought that she was enjoying the novelty of afternoon tea but aiming to give the impression that it wasn't a novelty at all. No doubt she had a purpose in calling and would come out with it when she was ready.

It didn't take long. 'Do you like being engaged to Mr Schofield, Aunt Tizzie?' she asked suddenly.

'Yes, I like it very much.'

'And Mr Schofield? Do you like him as well?'

'Of course I do. I wouldn't have agreed to marry him if I didn't like him, now would I?'

Elizabeth shrugged and eyed her aunt over the top of her tea cup. 'He's rich,' she said, as if that could explain any amount of strange behaviour.

Tizzie refrained from smiling. 'Yes, he's rich,' she agreed mildly, 'but I'm not exactly destitute myself.'

Elizabeth chose another cake and then sat staring at it. 'I expect you'll have babies, won't you, Aunt Tizzie?'

'I hope so.'

The lower lip jutted in the familiar mutinous pout and she jiggled her cup on its saucer. 'Who's going to look after us when you have children of your own?' she burst out. 'Suppose my mother doesn't make any money out of this lodging house.' She spat out the two final words.

Now they were getting down to it. Tizzie forced herself to be calm and pleasant when she would have liked to dish out a few facts about who was paying for the lodging house. 'I only help to look after you,' she said gently, 'and I'll carry on doing that, of course I will. Since your father died I feel that I share responsibility for all of you with your mother.'

'She's only worried about Johnny and Abel,' said Elizabeth, twisting her ankles together. 'She doesn't care about me!'

Tizzie watched her in consternation. Was this another 'me first' outburst or something much deeper – a cry for help from a fatherless child? The pouting lip began to wobble. Tears appeared in the green eyes and edged reluctantly down her cheeks. Tizzie was alarmed. Apart from a couple of temper tantrums, Elizabeth hadn't shed a tear since William died.

'I don't like having no father!' she wailed, her mouth stretched wide. 'I don't like hearing my mother crying when she thinks we're all asleep. And I don't want to live in a lodging house!'

Tizzie moved fast. She picked Elizabeth up from her chair and cradled her on her lap, cuddling and kissing her as if she was the same age as Johnny. 'We love you,' she crooned, 'we all love you. Your mother cries because she loved your father and she misses him.' Elizabeth clung to her and sobbed like a toddler seeking comfort, while Tizzie rocked her back and forth and murmured little words of consolation. At last the child stopped weeping and stuck her thumb in her mouth, something she hadn't done in years.

'We're going to make the house so beautiful that famous actors and actresses will reserve their rooms months in advance,' Tizzie promised, 'and you'll be able to choose your own curtains for your bedroom and maybe a couple of rugs. Your mother's a good cook and she knows more about running a house than I do, so she's sure to make a success of it. Just think – you'll live in the biggest house of anybody in your class.'

Elizabeth removed the thumb. 'D'you think it'll be better than living over a butcher's shop?'

'Infinitely better,' Tizzie assured her.

At that the child slid down from her lap and smoothed her pinafore. 'When can I choose my curtains and rugs?' she asked briskly.

Tizzie breathed out heavily. 'Next Monday,' she said. 'Samples and pattern books are being sent round to your mother.'

Elizabeth ate her cake standing up and gulped a last mouthful of tea. 'Thanks, Aunt Tizzie,' she said, bestowing her rare, radiant smile. She stood on tiptoe in front of the mirror to put on her coat and bonnet and then headed for the door. 'I don't *usually* suck my thumb,' she said.

Tizzie leaned back in her chair. What a child! One minute she irritated her intensely, the next she touched some deep, half-buried chord of memory. There was a strange, guarded affection between them: kindred spirits bound by the ties of family blood.

Elizabeth wasn't easy. Mary herself admitted that she didn't understand her, while the child spoke of her mother with ill-concealed antagonism. Tizzie would have to put Elizabeth right on that ... she would have to put her right on lots of things, but how to do it? Behind that alert young mind was an iron will, a streak of self-interest that rejected the views of other people if they didn't agree with her own.

Tizzie's irritation faded when she thought of how Elizabeth had cried and sucked her thumb. Was there a forlorn little girl behind that alarming self-possession? If so, she needed to be shown that she mattered. She sat up straight. Of course! Why hadn't she thought of it before? Sam had said invite whoever you like, so she would take her to the party at Meadowbank. She wouldn't be the only child because Charles would be there. Excellent! Barney and Elizabeth would be her guests. She must make sure that Elizabeth knew she was to treat him with respect. But in all the excitement she hadn't yet invited him. It was likely he wouldn't want to go; he disliked social events and felt ill at ease on other people's chairs or at their tables. She stared into the fire as she finished her cup of tea. She wouldn't try to persuade him, he must make up his own mind; but oh, she wanted him to be there. It wouldn't be the same if he wasn't.

The thought was the deed with Tizzie. She jumped up and took the tea tray back to the kitchen. 'I'm going round to the shop to have a word with Mr Jellicoe, Rebecca. I'll go on foot, but I might pick up a cab to come back. I won't be long.'

She was out on Farthing Lane in her hooded cloak and walking boots when it occurred to her that Rebecca had been very quiet. Come to think of it, hadn't she been a bit subdued ever since Sam had proposed? Pleased, yes; even delighted, but not quite herself. Of course she was devoted to Naomi, her one surviving child, who was now employed as governess to the daughters of a cotton broker in Liverpool. It was a position that made Rebecca immensely proud of her, but also grateful to her employer for educating her daughter ... No, she would have said if she was worried about Naomi. Surely she couldn't be uneasy about her job? They would need a housekeeper in their new home, wherever that might be. She must put Rebecca's mind at ease about her future.

There was a spring to Tizzie's step as she faced the wind; her cloak billowed and her cheeks stung with the cold as she crossed the Old Square and headed along Peter Street. Life was good, she thought, though that might not apply to the coming evening. She was to go to Alsing with Sam and his father for a 'get-together about Ralph'. It was hardly likely that a deep discussion about the family black sheep would be a time of untrammelled joy.

When she arrived Barney was coming up the stairs from the dolly shop wearing a hessian apron, and she was put in mind of the days when he used to emerge through a trap door in the floor like an underground animal. It hadn't taken her long to put a stop to that, but still he wanted to be involved in menial tasks – it was one of the things they argued about.

'Mrs Siddall's here this afternoon,' he said. 'Could I offer you tea and cake, Miss Tizzie?'

She didn't think of refusing, though it was barely twenty minutes since afternoon tea at Farthing Lane. She led the way up the familiar stairs and the housekeeper dipped her knee when she saw her. 'If I might wish you well, Miss Ridings,' she beamed. 'Mr Schofield's a fine young fella – the best in Saltley – an' everybody's that pleased . . .'

Barney nodded his big grey head approvingly and made small talk until the tea tray arrived and Mrs Siddall had left the room. 'I was goin' to send Gideon round to ask about tomorrow evenin',' he said, avoiding her eyes. 'With it bein' Friday.'

'Why? Can't you come?'

He smiled slightly. 'Oh, I can come. It's just I thought you might have other plans – be seein' Mr Schofield or somethin'.'

'I'll be seeing him for most of the weekend, house hunting,' she said. 'I've told him I always spend Friday evenings with you on matters of business. I don't want that to change.'

Still he avoided her eyes. 'You don't want that to change,' he repeated. 'Right, then, as long as I know.'

'I've come to invite you to Meadowbank House as my guest.'

'As your guest?'

'Yes. It's a big family do – a party to celebrate our engagement. Mary won't be there, of course, but if I'd had a dozen brothers and sisters I'd still want you there, Barney. Will you come?'

'A party to celebrate your engagement?'

He was repeating everything she said. It wasn't like him at all. Tizzie eyed him narrowly. She fancied there was an odd twist to his lips but she couldn't guess what was causing it. 'Sam's set on it,' she told him, 'and so is his father. There's no date finalised yet – we're waiting until Matthew Raike's on the mend. The family are upset about him being attacked on their land.'

Barney ignored all that. 'No date,' he murmured.

She was getting impatient with his attitude. 'No,' she said briskly, 'but of course it won't be a Friday. Will you come, Barney?' She imagined she could see him framing

words of refusal and asked herself if she was going to have
to plead. No, she wouldn't do any such thing! She heard
him sigh; a long expelling of breath as if he was
unutterably weary. At once she forgot her resolve. 'Barney,' she urged, 'please say you'll come.'

At that he finally looked her in the eye. 'Of course I'll
come,' he said with a bright smile. 'It'll be my pleasure.'

Highly relieved, she told him, 'My guests will be you
and Elizabeth.'

'Miss Elizabeth? She'll enjoy a party,' he said mildly.
'It'll do her good. You'll let me know when you settle the
date?' He picked up his untouched tea. 'Happen I'll make
my own way to Meadowbank House. Arrive separate,
like.'

She opened her mouth to protest that they must all three
arrive together, then closed it again. There was little that
escaped his notice, so he would be aware that Elizabeth
found him distasteful. In sparing the child's feelings he
was also sparing his own. 'Just as you like,' she said gently,
'so long as you *come*.'

The announcement was published simultaneously in the
Saltley Chronicle and both the *Guardian* and the *Courier*
in Manchester. The cotton men of the city showed an
interest, but in Saltley there was a fever of excitement. The
Chronicle was on sale by noon, and by the time the engines
were switched on for the afternoon's work every man,
woman and child in Jericho knew that Mr Sam was to
marry Tizzie Ridings.

The weavers wrote 'Congratulations' on a spare piece of
calico and tied it to one of the iron beams; Saul Bracewell's
spinners made up a rhyme as they walked back and forth
at their frames and arranged for one of their number who
wrote a good hand to set it out on parchment. The office
staff clubbed together and ordered a bouquet of flowers to
be sent to Tizzie at Farthing Lane with a message of
goodwill. It seemed that everyone in Jericho Mills was
delighted.

In the town itself feelings were mixed. There were those who said, 'Trust Tizzie Ridings to land Sam Schofield without even a courtship when many another has tried and failed!' Others were admiring of Sam, saying, 'He's weighed 'em all up for long enough but he's picked himself a right bobby-dazzler in the end – money as well as looks!'

Those who had half believed the gossip now dismissed it, reasoning that a Schofield would never wed a woman who had messed about with a dwarf. Others had never believed it anyway, pointing out that she was a bosom friend of Lady Soar, who was above reproach. Tizzie was thought to be fair in the pawnshop, she was a member of Bethesda Chapel, she had all but carried her sister and the family since Will Hartley's death and was known to support good causes and to give to the destitute. Everybody talked, but those who had no voice in the town, who lived in the hovels and cellars of Gallgate, remembered that Tizzie Ridings had given a new start to Rebecca Drury and her last surviving child when she was barely of age herself.

Yes, everything considered, the folk of Saltley approved the match, with the exception of those who had started the gossip in the first place ...

Eleanor Boulton told herself that only the Almighty had prevented her going down with a seizure when at three o'clock Bessie struggled up the front steps waving a copy of the *Chronicle* at arm's length like a matador with his cloak. 'Have you seen it?' she yelled from outside the house. 'Have you *seen* it?'

Highly irritated, Eleanor had waited until she was shown in. Everybody knew that Bessie was going senile, but it seemed that for once she was reliable – it was there in black and white on the printed page that Tizzie Ridings had landed a Schofield. Fury caused Eleanor's temples to throb until her head was fit to burst; she regretted having her new stays laced so tightly. They had to ring for the tea tray at once, but when it came she needed more than tea. She got out Ezra's whisky and gave them both a good tot in their cups. 'We need this Bessie,' she said heavily.

They talked and talked. It didn't seem to matter if Bessie
lost the thread of what she was saying, Eleanor could say
enough for both of them: 'A daughter of two nobodies . . .
a carrot-headed hussy . . . she only caught Sam Schofield
because she battened on to Lady Sarah, and Sam doted on
his sister . . .' It went on and on until at last they agreed that
they deserved each other – Tizzie with her over-painted
pawnshop and the Schofields with their dolled up mills,
their swimming baths and that ridiculous institute. Bessie
vowed to take the wind out of Tizzie's sails at the next
infirmary meeting. . . In the end they consoled themselves
with the thought that Sam Schofield would have plenty of
time to change his mind – with Tizzie in mourning they
couldn't possibly get married inside a year.

Martha found it a relief to talk to somebody who wasn't
from the house. Jessie Lane had looked after her when
she'd first entered the weaving shed and they'd been
friends for years. Now she'd called round to ask after her
and Matthew. Rosie was in bed, so Martha brewed a pot of
tea and then had to sit down, her head spinning. 'It's over
a week now, Jessie,' she said wearily. 'How long do you
think it'll be before I pick up a bit? I've had a letter from
our Bella saying she'll come if I need her, but her first
grandchild's due any time, an' it's a long way from
Grimsby. If only they'd still 'a' been in Rochdale she could
have come over for the day. I'm that tired, Jessie.' Large
and capable, Jessie shook her neat grey head. 'It's not just
miscarryin',' she said gently. 'From what you tell me you
lost a lot of blood. They do say it replaces itself in the
veins, like, but it takes time. Red meat, liver an' watercress,
that's what you need after bleedin'.'

'I know. That's what they gave Matthew at first –
minced liver an' stout, but when he took a turn for the
worse the doctor stopped it. I'm that worried about him,
Jessie. I had to turn awkward with 'em over at the house
– I carried on like anythin', shoutin' an' screamin' an' said

I wasn't bein' kept in the dark about him any longer.'

'Has Matthew turned septic, then?' asked Jessie, trying not to show dismay.

'No, they say there's no sign of mortifyin', an' his bones are settin' all right. He started bein' short o' breath an' he was that drowsy. Then he started vomitin'. The doctor thinks it's his kidneys.'

Jessie stared. 'Was he kicked in the back or summat?'

'No, it's to do with losin' a lot of blood – the doctor says the kidneys can be affected. I've been sittin' with him a lot, but half the time he's asleep.' Dread clouded Martha's eyes and she kept her head bowed, as if it was too heavy for her neck. 'I didn't see him at all for two days after it happened, you know – I nearly went mad. Then Mr Schofield wouldn't let me climb the stairs. He made Davey carry me. At the time I didn't care as long as I saw Matthew, but the next time he did it I felt a fool, so after that I pretended I was all right. They've all been good across at the house, but I do wish I could look after him meself.'

'If there's able-bodied women nursing him I should leave him where he is for another day or two, till you're stronger,' advised Jessie.

Martha stared into the fire. Jessie would think she was daft if she said she didn't want other women pulling up his nightshirt and putting him on the chamber pot. It was a wife's place to see to her husband ... She made herself change the subject. 'What's happenin' at Jericho, then?'

'Well, you might guess everybody's been all of a doodah about Mr Sam an' Miss Ridings. He walks the floors with a smile that won't wash off.'

Martha knew that if things had been different she would have been thrilled to bits. As it was she had to struggle to summon any interest. 'They're goin' to have a party here in a week or two to celebrate. Mr Schofield says they're postponin' it till Matthew's on the mend.'

Jessica leaned across and patted her hand. 'I call that thoughtful of him, Martha.'

'Aye, so do I, but if Matthew was attacked by a fella

who's got it in for the Schofield family, happen he thinks it's the least they can do. Ellie told me Mr Schofield was goin' to Lady Sarah's last night with Mr Sam an' Miss Tizzie. They set off just after the doctor told us all about Matthew's kidneys an' I saw 'em gettin' in the carriage. Mr Schofield – ee, he did look grim. Mr Sam was holdin' his arm as if he thought his legs might give in.

'An' I've been surprised at Miss Tizzie, Jessie. I never liked her all that much; I thought she was bossy an' stuck up – a bit hard, like – but she called here the other day when I was havin' me lie down. She has no side to her, you know, considering she owns property all over Saltley. When I wished her all the best for her engagement she said they'd be able to enjoy it all the more when Matthew's himself again. I thought that was nice.'

Jessie nodded. She had a married daughter whose husband liked his ale and so was a regular at the pawnshop. 'They say in the town that she's makin' a good match, but I reckon Mr Sam's not doing so bad for himself either.'

CHAPTER TWELVE

Congratulations

Joshua marched through the house determined that nothing would spoil the evening: not lack of preparation, thoughts of Ralph, nor his own recurring low spirits. As for uninvited guests, he had two men patrolling the gardens against intruders ...

It was a fortnight since the family get-together about Ralph, and he'd never had the misfortune to be involved in a more stilted, unproductive affair. What annoyed him was that it had been his own fault: he'd been shaken by what the doctor had said about Matthew and worried sick that he might not pull through. The family had seen the state Joshua was in and been so anxious not to upset him further they'd talked platitudes and pleasantries like a bunch of old women at a sewing bee rather than the family of an unconvicted murderer. The mollycoddling had reached such a pitch he'd half expected them to spoon-feed him his supper ... Even Tizzie had lost her tongue, sitting there silent and uncomfortable as if she wished she was some-where else.

Things had improved, though. In the last week Matthew had turned the corner, partly due to good nursing and his own iron constitution, maybe – who could say? – as a result of desperate appeals to the Almighty, but in the main because of a new wonder cure for the kidneys called jaborandi. The doctor had mentioned it, saying it had only been available for a year or two. A year or two, a month or two or twenty-four hours – what did it matter if it was well thought of? He'd insisted that it was bought for Matthew and it had worked; already he was up and about and getting stronger every day. So for the first time in what seemed an eternity Joshua was going to stop worrying and enjoy himself.

He eyed the big table critically. It was ready to be loaded with food, its floor-length cloths swathed and swagged and caught up with ribbons and greenery. It was so long since he gave a big party he'd forgotten how much he used to enjoy such events. For this particular event no detail had been too small for his attention. 'Hire extra help if you need it,' he had told Hannah and Lilah. 'As for how many will be coming, at first we thought a dozen or so – just the family and two or three friends, but it's risen to thirty-odd and four musicians for a bit of dancing. D'you think you can cope?'

Lilah had served as scullery maid, kitchen maid and then cooks' help in a far bigger house than Meadowbank before running the kitchens of a country manor up in the Pennines. She would cook a banquet single-handed if it would please her employer, but of course she didn't say so. 'We'll cope, Mr Schofield,' she'd said briskly. 'We'll pull together like we always do, an' Miss Tizzie's sending Rebecca round every day. It'd help if you could give me some idea of what you have in mind for the food – what effect you're after, like. Do you want it hearty, or elegant, or dainty, or what? An' how about cost? Must I keep inside a certain sum?'

'Nay, I'll not skimp on it, Lilah, not when I've waited this long to have my son choose himself a wife.' Joshua thought fleetingly of Rachel's calm expertise when it came to planning meals, then brought his mind back to the present. Domestic matters baffled him, but at least he knew what he was talking about when it came to food. 'I want a good do,' he'd said firmly. 'Good to look at, good to eat.

I'm not one who worries over much about what other folk think, but in this case I don't mind admitting I want to impress, for the sake of my son and his future wife. Nothing dainty or fancy, mind; elegance is what I'm after, but something you can get a knife and fork into. Look, plan a menu and we'll go through it together, then you must order whatever you need to be sent down from the farm or from the shops in town. I'll give you a free hand . . .'

Now he nodded in satisfaction. The kitchen was a scene of organised activity and the house was immaculate, glinting and gleaming in the gaslight and decorated with flowers from the hothouses at Alsing. Sarah had spent all afternoon on them as happy as a lark. She looked well this last week or two, she didn't part – more like her mother every day. She'd begun to take on the soft inner radiance that had been one of Rachel's most lovely attributes – a sort of deep-down tranquillity. It was funny he'd never noticed it in Sarah till the last couple of weeks . . . a time when he would have expected her to be eaten up with envy of Polly and her fine baby boy.

Thoughtfully he turned back to the table. He'd been a bit stunned by Lilah's suggestions for the meal. If it turned out to be as good to eat as it had been in writing then he'd underestimated her. He thought of what he paid her. She wouldn't have taken the job if he hadn't offered her enough – or would she? In her time off she was always nipping round to see her elderly mother who lived with a married sister only half a mile away; no doubt that had been an incentive to work at Meadowbank. Happen he should give her a rise. Aye, if tonight was as good as it promised he'd up her wages – see if that would bring forth a smile.

There was something about his cook that appealed to him and the good Lord only knew it wasn't her looks. She called a spade a spade, the same as he did, and she wasn't frightened of hard work – he could picture her running six looms at Jericho without batting an eyelid. She answered back when the fit took her, yet she had a way of looking at him when he made a remark as if he was giving out the

wisdom of Solomon. He'd always flattered himself that he
could read folk, but he couldn't read Lilah – she was one
on her own.

Joshua shook his head and went out to the yard through
the lobby rather than the busy kitchen. It was very cold,
with a half-moon riding the scudding clouds. The dark
figure of a man appeared at his side and muttered, 'Did you
want me, Mr Schofield?'

'You and your colleague know what's expected of you,'
he answered quietly, 'and there'll be a hot supper for you
at ten o'clock. You can have it one at a time in the kitchen.'
The man touched his cap and edged silently into the
shadows while Joshua crossed to the garden cottage and
tapped on the door.

Matthew himself answered it, his eyes glinting with
pleasure above the still strapped up jaw. By now accustomed to using gestures instead of speech, he stepped back
and waved an arm, inviting Joshua to enter. Martha jumped
to her feet as he walked in and Rosie ran to plump up the
cushions on her father's big wooden chair.

'Will you take a seat, Mr Schofield?' asked Martha.

'Nay, I'm not stopping. It's just that I've got two men
patrolling the gardens, so don't get worried if you see
somebody sneaking about in the shadows. They're both
wearing dark heavy coats and checked caps with scarves
over the top. Now, you'll not forget I want you over at the
house for when I propose the toast at nine thirty? There'll
be various drinks for those who don't want champagne. All
the others will be there, just for ten minutes or so – Davey
and his wife, Zacky, the women in the house and Mr
Whitehead from Jericho and his wife.'

Martha hid her surprise that he should imagine they
might have forgotten such an invitation, while Rosie felt
put out that he hadn't mentioned her staying up late, nor
noticed her dress. She'd noticed what *he* was wearing – he
looked like somebody out of an illustrated paper in his
smart evening clothes. Ignoring her mother's warning
glance she gazed up at him and held out her skirts. 'Look,

Mr Schofield, I'm wearin' me best dress!'

'Ah, so that's it – I was thinking you looked very grand.'
There was a flutter of pink ribbons among her dark curls
and Joshua touched them gently. He'd seen a lot of her just
lately, and he had to admit he'd got a soft spot for her; he
wouldn't have said no to a granddaughter half as lively.
Should he tell her what was happening later on, after the
toast? No, better not. He might not agree with forbidding
her and Charlie to play together, but there was no point in
actively encouraging their liking for each other.

When he had gone Matthew eyed his wife and daughter
with pride. Rosie looked a picture in her best blue dress
with the pink sash and new blue slippers; Martha was in her
dusky pink and had gained a bit of colour in her cheeks at
last. She'd worn curl rags all day and had scooped the
resulting ringlets into a cluster on the crown of her head.
It was a style that could have looked too young and
frivolous but somehow managed to appear comely and
dignified.

They both saw the pride in his eyes. Rosie gave an
excited little skip and kissed his arm, while Martha quirked
her lips in place of a smile and allowed herself to slip a
gentle arm around his waist. He was getting better. What
was a lost baby compared to that?

Tizzie was happy. She was beginning to think that until
Sam had asked her to marry him she'd never known what
happiness was. Everything was different, life itself was
different – so brightly coloured, so *clear*, so sparkling
compared to the misty grey existence before Sam had said
he loved her. She stood between him and his father,
greeting friends of the family – the Dobbs, the Fairbrothers, the Lawtons of Rochdale and their sons and
daughters. They all brought gifts – in Saltley it was the
custom to give something for the 'bottom drawer' on an
engagement – and as she and Sam received them she knew
that she was both at ease and at home in this big, beautiful
house. She had often thought that Sam's father didn't do

things by halves and here was the proof of it – a party arranged at short notice but with no expense spared and no detail overlooked.

She had wanted to wear yellow, the colour of spring and new life, of sunshine and happiness . . . the colour she always associated with the Schofields, but even at a private party it was hardly the colour for a woman whose sister was in deep mourning. In the end she had chosen a gown of ribbed silk in a muted sage green, bought in Manchester at a small, exclusive establishment on Oldham Street, not far from the string of shops owned by Mr Affleck and Mr Brown. It was in her favourite style, the panelled princess line, with a low square neckline and tight elbow-length sleeves.

Sam was so proud of her he told himself he would like to eat her off a plate. He had seen her shoulders and bosom before, of course, at social events up at Alsing and once, years ago, at a grand ball in Saltley Town Hall. He couldn't understand why he'd never been kept awake at night thinking of that smooth creamy skin and the hint of high firm breasts. He must have been blind not to have been stunned by such a sight.

Now the subdued green of her dress made her eyes seem brighter than ever and her hair glowed like a flame. Next to the frills and bustles of the older women and the crinolined skirts of the younger ones she looked understated and supremely elegant. Her only jewellery was a pearl-studded tortoiseshell comb anchoring her hair, a string of milk-white pearls – his father's gift – around her throat, and of course the diamond ring. He was well pleased with that. It was magnificent, the glittering oval stone showing to perfection on her very slim hand.

Joshua looked on benignly as they greeted more guests and received their congratulations, but he kept an eye open for James . . . If Esther prevented the three of them coming he would never forgive her – never. There was no sign of Tizzie's business partner Barney Jellicoe. He found it a bit odd that she could manage to invite only a nine-year-old child and a dwarf . . .

The child Elizabeth was a self-confident little soul if ever he'd seen one, sitting on a window seat deep in talk with the Dobbs' young granddaughter, who had been invited solely as company for her. It had seemed to him overoptimistic to expect young Charles to entertain a girl he didn't even know. Ah! His heart lurched in relief. Here they were! Evidently Esther had given in and decided to come. It was amazing what a bit of straight talking to her father could do – he should have tried it years ago.

Tizzie smiled as Sam's brother approached with his wife and son. There was no doubting James's pleasure in the engagement ... Charles also had welcomed her without being prompted. Esther, though, was different. They hadn't exchanged more than a dozen words in all the years they'd known each other. She was wearing a silvery dress with a full crinoline, her pretty little face wreathed in smiles but her eyes assessing the sage-green silk.

'*So* lovely to have you in the family, Tizzie dear,' she cooed in her high, light voice. 'We really must get to know each other better. How slender you look in your neat little dress ... You must take care not to lose too much weight, though, it's so very ageing, isn't it? And how sensible of you not to buy an expensive gown when you're still in mourning. Charles, our little gift for Miss Ridings, if you please.'

Apparently unmoved, Tizzie smiled serenely. This little bag of bones could give lessons to Eleanor Boulton when it came to undiluted spite. There was no need for Sam to look as if he was about to witness a battle royal – she would deal with her later.

With an embarrassed bow Charles presented a parcel as his mother said, 'I thought some really good table napkins would be useful. You can't very well offer calico to your guests, can you? Even if your husband does work in a mill!' With her tinkling laugh she moved on, heading for Francis and Sarah and leaving James, tight lipped, to shake his brother's hand and give Tizzie a kiss.

'We're not the last to arrive, are we?' he asked.

'Almost,' Sam told him. 'There's just Tizzie's friend Barney Jellicoe still to come. We'll be doing the rounds chatting to everybody as soon as he arrives.'

But Barney didn't arrive. Tizzie couldn't understand it. He might not have jumped at the invitation but he'd accepted it, and with Barney his word was his bond. She and Sam left their place by the door and mixed with everyone. They listened to the soloist, a small, earnest tenor who sang Verdi arias magnificently, they laughed with Sarah and Francis and talked politely to Esther, who after her initial bout of ill feeling was on her best behaviour in front of the Soars. The four instrumentalists played light classics quietly, and there was much talk and laughter, but all the time Tizzie kept an eye on the door. She couldn't believe he had let her down like this, but she could hardly leave the party and go searching the streets for him.

Sam was watching her. 'I expect he's delayed at the shop,' he murmured consolingly, 'a difficult customer, or something. You know how conscientious he is.'

She shrugged and managed a smile. 'I'm not going to let the evening be spoiled by him not being here. Let's watch the conjuror.' She looked round to check on Elizabeth and saw that though she was still with Minnie Dobbs, her gaze was fixed intently on Charles, sitting with his grandfather and laughing at something his uncle Francis had just said. She looked deceptively demure in her full-skirted grey velvet with its white lace collar and black ribbon bow. It was the collar and the bow that had reconciled her to the dress, which she'd thought excessively boring. Typically, she had said as much, to her mother of all people. It had been left to Tizzie to explain that though she herself might edge round the conventions of mourning at her own engagement party, it simply wasn't possible for a young girl in her position to wear a brightly coloured dress so soon after her father's death.

Then the conjuror began his performance, and Elizabeth reverted to a wide-eyed little girl, amazed at the man's sleight of hand and laughing at his jokes. Tizzie relaxed;

she'd wondered whether it had been a good idea to have her mixing with people so much better off than her own family. There would be little point in giving her a special treat if it filled her head with unattainable dreams ...

Joshua was enjoying himself. It did him good to see Charles having a laugh in the same room as his mother – something hitherto unknown. Everything was going well. He told himself that all you needed to get folk enjoying themselves was to make them welcome, put them among kindred spirits in pleasant surroundings, provide top-class entertainment and give them good food and drink. He wasn't too bothered about the drink being alcoholic – his Methodist roots held him if not to abstinence at least to moderation, but the food must be good. He did hope that Lilah would have done them all justice.

He needn't have worried. He'd asked for elegance and he'd got it. Spiced beef soup in little lidded pots that hadn't seen the light of day since Rachel died; cold cuts served on the big silver platters engraved with the letter *S* that he'd sold during the cotton famine and bought back again in 1866. There was glazed duck, chicken galantine, cold turbot with lobster creams, open pies, vast winter salads, crispy bread rolls in the form of lovers' knots ... The table was so loaded that the beautiful desserts had been placed on a side table until there was room for them.

Sarah was wide-eyed. 'Look at this, Francis! Isn't it *lovely*! Papa, surely Lilah hasn't done all this? Has she had professional help?'

Joshua was silent for a moment as he thought of the years of training that lay behind the preparation of such food, the hours of hard work here in his own kitchen. 'It's all Lilah,' he said simply. 'Her ideas, her planning. She's a remarkable woman.'

The guests did justice to it, helping themselves, with Hannah and Ellie in attendance, then sitting at small tables that edged the room and filled the hall. In the big drawing room Davey and Zacky were busy moving back the chairs to leave the polished oak floor ready for dancing.

Tizzie was impressed by the atmosphere; there was an air of luxury to the evening and yet not the slightest degree of pretension. She was trying to push Barney's absence to the back of her mind. Perhaps she'd expected too much in inviting him? She was so used to his handicap that sometimes she forgot about it. He could never forget it, though; he had no option but to spend his life looking up at every adult but facing children eye to eye. She resolved to mention the party when she saw him but not on any account to reveal how crushingly disappointed she was that he hadn't showed up.

She was sitting with Sam and his father at a table for three in the window arch. Joshua was enjoying his food and at the same time keeping watch to see if everybody else was doing the same. Esther, he saw, was positively glowing as she talked to Arthur Lawton's wife. She might say she despised trade, but the friendship of the wife of one of the wealthiest men in Lancashire was evidently worth cultivating . . .

Tizzie leaned across to him. 'Thank you for this lovely, lovely party, Mr Schofield.' She touched the necklace at her throat. 'And thanks again for the pearls.'

'Thank *you* for accepting Sam,' he replied quietly. 'Not to mention my family's problems.' For an instant it was as if they were sharing an intimate supper for three rather than being part of that noisy, good-humoured gathering. Joshua cleared his throat. 'Er . . . Tizzie,' he began.

Sam's eyes widened. He sounded unsure of himself! What was coming now?

'I never knew your father all that well,' Joshua continued, 'though I've heard he was respected as a man of his word. Now I've no wish to try and take his place in your affections or anything of that kind, but if ever you should wish it, and – and when you feel ready for it – I'd be proud and happy for you to call me Father.'

Sam's jaw sagged but he managed to keep his mouth closed. This was approval with a capital *A*! He was touched and delighted.

So was Tizzie. To her mortification, tears rushed to her eyes and hung on her lower lashes. Sam thought he had never seen anything so lovely, but he quickly offered his handkerchief. She dabbed her eyes and blew her nose, while Joshua watched uncomfortably. He hadn't expected tears . . . he'd never thought her to be one for weeping.

Tizzie knew she should thank him and agree because she had always admired and respected him; but first she must have time to relinquish that scrawny, shrunken, undemonstrative man – her own father, who in his lifetime had brought from her only impatient scorn and, after his death, what? Love? Affection? No, merely remorse and very real gratitude that he had left her his thriving pawnshop before she even came of age. If she was a prosperous businesswoman now, she had Abel Ridings to thank for it.

But Sam's father was waiting for an answer. She longed to laugh and kiss him and say something like, 'Very well, then, Father it is from now on!' but she couldn't do it. The evening had been all take on her part and no give. She couldn't take this as well – not without a time of remembering her own father. 'Thank you,' she said. 'That means a very great deal to me. I'd like to use the name Father, but not right away – shall we say from our wedding day? I'll always remember that you asked me at our engagement party.'

Joshua hid his relief. For a moment there he'd thought she was going to refuse and make him look a sentimental old fool. He could see Hannah setting out the sweet course. He knew what there would be because he'd approved Lilah's list: wine jellies, nut meringues, chocolate creams, fruit vol-au-vents, layered sponges, cheese cakes, russes and her special candied cakes. He consulted his watch. Good; the timing was going to be right for nine thirty.

He got up to have a look at the sweet stuff and to check that chairs had been set out for the household staff. It was a touch that pleased him. In his experience it was rare to see servants take part in a toast and unheard of to have them

seated, however briefly, in the same room as their employers' guests. Well, he'd always liked doing the unheard of;
he'd arranged with Sarah for two footmen from Alsing to
appear on the dot of nine thirty to serve the drinks for the
toast, reasoning that Hannah and the others could hardly
relax for ten minutes if they were rushing about with
bottles and glasses. They all worked hard, and he liked to
show his appreciation now and again; in any case, Zacky,
Hannah and Davey had known Sam since he was a lad. As
for the Raike family, he had a lot to make up to the three
of them.

Rosie hardly ever stayed up so late, but she told herself that
she didn't feel even a teeny bit sleepy. She sat between her
mam and dad while a man she'd never seen before brought
them drinks in special glasses on a silver tray – it was
lovely. She'd chosen raspberry cordial but her mam and
dad had asked for ginger. The others all had glasses of
Madeira or ale, except Lilah, who was holding a glass of
champagne. All the servants looked as if they really liked
sitting down at the party, though Ellie kept blushing.

　　Lilah seemed different without her cook's cap, but the
message on her face was clear. It said, 'I'm jiggered. I can
hardly sit in my chair for tiredness, but it's been worth all
the work.' She never looked at anybody else when Mr
Schofield was there, though her face showed no messages.
Everybody liked him, but happen she liked him extra
specially because he always told her when he'd enjoyed his
dinner.

　　Charles was sitting at a table with his mam and dad and
Lord and Lady Soar. He had sent her a message of
welcome just by widening his eyes and she'd done the
same to him. They'd talked about it in the tunnel and
decided that if his mother was there they wouldn't even
smile at each other. It was very hard not to, especially when
Elizabeth Hartley leaned across from her place at the
Dobbs' table to say something to him. He made a reply and
nodded his head politely. It wasn't fair – Elizabeth was a

butcher's daughter, and a butcher was no better than a head gardener, but if she wanted she could talk to him in front of all these people. No, she couldn't ... His mam seemed to be smiling and patting her hair, but behind her hand she was giving Elizabeth one of her looks.

Oh! Fancy that! Elizabeth was staring back at her without blinking, just as if she was a grown-up. She liked herself, did Elizabeth Hartley. She was bossy – everybody at school said so. They said she thought she'd got the world in a bant because her aunt Tizzie had plenty of money.

Her mam was whispering in her ear now. 'Rosie, remember what I told you about only takin' a sip of your cordial. You'll need it for drinkin' the toasts. Watch how much me an' your dad drink.'

Martha saw Mr Schofield go to stand in front of the musicians. The pianist played some loud chords and everyone fell silent ready to listen. 'My Lord Soar, Lady Soar, Mr Mayor, Madam Mayoress, ladies and gentlemen,' he began. 'Please be upstanding and raise your glasses to drink the health of our gracious sovereign, Her Majesty the Queen!'

Everybody stood up and said, 'The Queen!' Rosie sipped her cordial and tried not to sigh. The room was warm and she would have liked to have emptied her glass. Matthew also drank with care. His jaw was still strapped up and he had no wish to dribble ginger cordial down his best shirt. Martha took a reluctant swallow. It had annoyed her mother before her and now it annoyed her when everybody made a fuss about the Queen. She might have had nine children but there were women in Jericho who'd had a dozen or more with only a week off their work at each confinement. She knew women who'd lost their husbands as well, but they'd had to go on working, never mind shutting themselves away for years and years with armies of servants waiting on them hand and foot.

'Let the Queen come here an' bake a dozen o' flour!' her mother used to say when they lived in Ledden Street. Then her uncle Jack would chime in. 'Half her country's wealth comes from Lancashire, an' what do we get for it? She visits Manchester, they spend a fortune dollin' the place up an' she gives her say-so to callin' the Exchange "Royal"!'

Matthew eased himself into his chair as Mr Schofield began to speak of his son. What a father he was, to be sure. He had a way with words, just as old Peggy-oh Luke had had during Matthew's Devon childhood. What stories Petty-oh had told of his travels, what tales of his home town of Saltley ...

'... my right hand man in business,' Mr Schofield was saying, 'who has the welfare of every worker at heart and who knows as much about cotton as any man in Saltley, or Manchester for that matter. Why, I remember ...' He lost the thread of what he was saying when a short, thick-set figure edged into the room and stood against a wall. Matthew saw it was the dwarf, Jellicoe, whose name was linked to Miss Tizzie's in lewd comment throughout the town. He looked very smart, his clothes the equal in quality to those of any man in the room. Would Mr Schofield ignore him and carry on? No, he raised a hand in greeting. 'Welcome, Mr Jellicoe. You've been delayed, I know, but sit you down and take up your glass – you're in time to join in the toast!'

Barney hitched himself up on a proffered chair and accepted a glass of champagne, holding it awkwardly between bent knuckles. His dark eyes sought out Tizzie, still sitting with Sam at the table in the window arch. He lowered his head once, and she knew it was his apology; she was so pleased to see him she missed what Sam's father was saying. For a moment there was a silent communion between her and Barney that excluded the man at her side. She put up her hand and touched the tortoiseshell comb in her hair, just in case Barney hadn't seen it. He had given her many small gifts since he'd become better off, but few of them had been personal. The comb was one of the few that were; a tasteful, expensive hair ornament given, so he said, to seal the bargain when she'd made him her partner in the business.

From across the room she saw his jaw tighten as it always did when he was upset, and she gritted her teeth impatiently. She'd thought he would be pleased that she was wearing it … The man was a mystery – she hadn't been able to understand him at all during the last few weeks. She turned in her seat to listen to Sam's father.

'I've waited a long while for this day, and so have the rest of my family,' he was saying. 'For years Tizzie has been a good friend to my daughter and now I couldn't be happier to welcome her as my son's future bride. I have their permission to tell you that the wedding is to be on Easter Saturday, the fourteenth of April, so raise your glasses, friends, and join me in drinking the very good health of Tizzie and Sam.'

Sam was holding her hand as everyone echoed their names and raised their glasses. His eyes blazing with triumph, he opened her fingers and laid his lips on her palm; she could feel them, hot and eager and loving. This, thought Tizzie, was what was meant by being radiantly happy. It was as if the light of a thousand candles was illuminating the present moment and the years that lay ahead.

'Now, before we all circulate and prepare for a bit of dancing,' Joshua went on, 'we have another entertainment – a special tribute to them both. I'm proud to present to you my grandson, Charles Joshua, who'll give us a trumpet solo, *"Un di felice"*, which I've no doubt you'll know means "One Happy Day", from Verdi's *La Traviata*.'

With a smile he beckoned to Charles. He could have explained that this was the lad's first public performance, but it might have sounded as if he was asking them to make allowances and that wasn't the case at all. They were lucky to hear him and he would have liked to have told them so.

Clasping his trumpet, Charles stepped forward, blushing and very nervous. He tuned his instrument with the piano and, turning to the company, put the trumpet to his lips. Before their eyes his nervousness disappeared and he began to play with a sweet, lyrical ease that somehow complemented the natural clear, piercing sound of the trumpet.

Rosie wriggled with satisfaction. She'd known he was going to play this – he'd told her all about it in the tunnel. He said his teacher had transposed it from the score of the opera specially for him. He'd been worried about – what was it? – a French word; it meant when he put his lips to the trumpet. *Embouchure*, that was it – he'd spelled it for her. Because he was only a beginner the muscles of his lips got tired when he was playing slow pieces, and he was worried that he might play out of tune or go wobbly. But it wasn't wobbly at all – it was lovely. She was so proud of him she longed to blow him a kiss, but of course she couldn't. His mam didn't look proud, though. She thought brass instruments were common and had flatly refused to even consider buying him a cornet so he could play in a brass band.

It was a lovely tune, though it seemed too sad to be about a happy day. Charles had told her that a tenor and a soprano sang it in the opera, but with the best singers in the whole world it couldn't possibly sound better than on his trumpet. She looked around and it was clear that everybody liked it. Then by chance her eyes alit on the face of Miss Tizzie's dwarf, and Rosie gasped in dismay. What was hurting him? What had he lost? She had never seen so sad a message on anybody's face. It was pain and loss, and – what? Some grown-up sort of feeling that was beyond her.

And then it was over and everybody clapped. She could tell that Mr Schofield was relieved but not a bit surprised as he joined in the applause and whispered something in Charles's ear. And then he *was* surprised because Charles nodded and stepped forward to speak. 'Thank you very much, ladies and gentlemen,' he said. 'Now I'd like to play another short piece.' He twitched his shoulders and lifted the trumpet to his lips again.

Rosie was astounded. He'd never told her he was going to play twice. At the opening notes her heart gave such a leap she thought it would fly out of her chest, while those listening gave a soft, collective sigh of pleasure and recognition. It was 'The Last Rose of Summer' from *Martha* – the piece he had played specially for her when she had been listening out in the snow that day; the one he played when he practised in his uncle Sam's bedroom.

In that perfect, magical moment she saw Charles's hair shining gold in the gaslight, his blue, blue eyes looking at her over the top of his trumpet; she saw the pianist staring at him in surprise, his grandfather Schofield blinking as if he was taken aback by what he was hearing. Charles was playing it for her – she knew it. She felt a blush burning her cheeks and bent her head so his mam wouldn't see.

Once, towards the end, he wobbled and lost the note – that would be his *embouchure*, she thought, watching his eyes widen as he tried to keep in tune. He regained control, and the last few notes were perfect. He gave a rueful smile, relieved that it was all over, then when the applause continued he bowed very low and turning in her direction, gave her the faintest suggestion of a wink. She was frightened that people would see, but he had his back to his mam. She clapped until her hands hurt, so excited she could hardly stay in her seat. She saw his dad saying something to him and nodding. Even his mam looked a bit pleased.

'Dancing will begin in ten minutes, friends,' announced Joshua, then went to have a word with his staff. 'Thanks for joining us, all of you,' he said. 'I'll be in to have a word when you have your own do tomorrow. Lilah – just a minute before you dash off.'

The cook stood before him in her grey checked dress with the white collar, her mouse-brown hair pulled behind her ears and her long face pale and tired. 'Well done,' he said quietly, 'and thank you.' She pressed her lips together but didn't reply. 'I very much appreciate the way you've used your skills,' he went on. 'Now – I'd like to see you in my study at ten o'clock in the morning. Can you manage that?'

'I should hope so, Mr Schofield, seein' as I'm always up at six.'

'That's all right, then,' he said equably.

Barney stood in front of Tizzie and Sam, colour staining his neck but his face pale as ever. Tizzie nudged Sam to remind him not to stand, but instinctively he stretched out a hand to shake Barney's. The dwarf ignored it, giving a stiff little bow and fumbling a small package onto the table at Tizzie's side. 'Just a little somethin' for you both,' he muttered, then put his hands behind his back. 'I'm sorry I was late, Miss Tizzie. Somethin' cropped up at the shop, but I'll tell you about it later.'

She observed him carefully. He was immaculate: newly shaved, his clothes brushed and pressed, his hair a pelt of well-cut grey curls. His appearance declared that nothing was wrong; she suspected otherwise, but it wasn't the time to fire questions at him. 'I knew there must be a good reason for you to be late,' she said easily. 'I'm glad you arrived in time to drink our health.'

He gave a small, tight smile. 'So am I, Miss Tizzie. Well, I'll go an' find a spot where I can watch the dancin'.'

'My father has saved you a seat near the musicians,' Sam told him, 'but if you haven't eaten perhaps you'd like some supper?'

'No thanks. I reckon I'll just sit an' watch the party for a bit.' He turned to go, and at that moment Tizzie's suspicion became certainty. The air in the room was filled with the smells of a party: food and drink, flowers, scents and pomades, all on top of the constant household smells of wax polish and gas jets; but Barney smelled of smoke – he reeked of burnt worsted and wet ashes. It came – yes, it came from his hair!

'Wait!' she said, standing up. He had tried, she told herself . . . Oh yes, he had washed and shaved and put on his best clothes, but he hadn't washed his hair. 'Where was the fire?' she asked.

He stared up at her blankly. 'What fire?'

'Barney,' she snapped, 'you've arrived very late, your hair smells of smoke and there's evidently something wrong with your hands. I say again, where was the fire?'

Sam was looking from her to Barney and back again. Tizzie had told him that she was one for facts and certainties rather than instinct and intuition, but he knew there was something between her and Barney that was far beyond fact and certainty. It was akin to what he had shared with Sarah – a bond, an unbreakable tie. He didn't know why he hadn't been as jealous as hell when he wanted to have Tizzie all to himself and never let her go, yet he'd felt no jealousy of Barney – up to now. Physically the man was no rival, of course, but what about mentally? Emotionally?

Sam saw that guests were watching the confrontation, so he hustled them both out through the door that led to the kitchen passage, where a hired woman was pushing a trolley of dirty dishes to the scullery.

'What's happened?' asked Tizzie again.

Barney sighed. 'I didn't want you to know, Miss Tizzie – not tonight. We've had a bit of a fire at the shop, that's all. There's no need to worry, it's out now – I've checked an' double-checked.'

'What about Albert and Gideon?'

'They're all right. They're still there, clearin' up.'

'And the stock?'

'Damaged, some of it, but we're well insured, aren't we?'

Tizzie was clutching her skirts, ready to lift them and hurry away. This might be her engagement party, but a fire at the shop? It was what she'd always dreaded, what they'd been at great pains to prevent, even in her father's time. Then she met Sam's eyes and collected herself. Barney said the fire was out, that he'd checked, so she could inspect the damage in the morning. Flashing Sam an apologetic look she let go of her skirts, and asked, 'Your hands, Barney? Are they hurt?'

Reluctantly he held them out, palms upward. They were blistered – raw in places, with the skin hanging. She groaned in horror. His hands – his best feature – his big clean hands were burned. Over the top of his head she looked at Sam.

'Doctor!' he said decisively. 'I'll write a note. Zacky will take you in the carriage, Barney. No arguing! I won't be a minute.'

He hurried away to find Zacky and left them together in the passage. All they could hear was the muted conversation of the guests and the clatter of crockery from the scullery. Tizzie's mind was racing. 'Barney,' she said, 'was it deliberate?'

He stared up at her, eyes narrowed. 'It mighta been,' he admitted. 'Gideon says a stranger came in the dolly shop just before closin' time and pledged a coal scuttle. When he'd gone the lad locked up an' went to help Albert, seein' as I was comin' here – in fact I'd just that minute gone upstairs to get changed. Then they got a whiff of smoke from the cellar and found the rack of beddin' an' curtains smoulderin'. They called up to me an' the next thing we knew flames were lickin' up the cellar steps an' goin' along the coat racks.' He stopped and sighed.

Tizzie glared. If he sighed once more instead of telling her what had happened she would bat him over the head with her bare fist. Then she thought of how he must have used his hands and was consumed by anger rather than the sympathy and gratitude that she knew to be his due. 'Did you have to use your *hands*? What about the fire buckets?'

'We'd emptied 'em,' he shrugged. 'Albert did well; he grabbed a rug an' kept smotherin' the flames. Ee, Miss Tizzie, if I hadn't come here you'd have known nothin' of this until the mornin'. I didn't think you'd cotton on, like. I shoulda known better.'

'Yes, you should,' she agreed shortly. 'This man, did Gideon say what he looked like?'

'Shortish, black hair goin' grey. Little dark eyes. I really don't see it coulda been somebody connected with Eli Walton, Miss Tizzie. He wouldn't be that daft.'

'It's not Walton I'm thinking of,' she told him, 'but I can't say more just now.'

Sam hurried back. 'The carriage is outside,' he said, 'and Zacky's got your hat and coat. He'll wait for you while you're with the doctor and then take you home.'

Belatedly, Tizzie said, 'Thank you, Barney, for coming here and for putting the fire out.'

He gave her a long look. 'You'll come round in the mornin' to look at the damage, then?'

'Of course I will. We'll have to work out compensation for anybody who's lost their goods. And Barney, ask Albert or Gideon to stay the night with you in case you can't manage on your own with bandaged hands.'

She watched him go and then turned back to Sam. 'It was Ralph,' she said bluntly.

He didn't seem surprised. 'What makes you think that?'

'A stranger was pledging in the dolly shop just before the fire started. He could have put a match to the curtains and bedding when Gideon's back was turned. His description sounds like the man Rosie Raike saw hanging about.'

Sam stared ahead of him unseeingly. Tizzie fancied she could hear him gritting his teeth together. 'It has the earmarks of Ralph,' he agreed bitterly. 'He must have heard about the party. He couldn't get at Meadowbank because it's under guard, so he got at the pawnshop instead. I'm sorry, Tizzie.'

A moment ago she'd been all set to leave the party and dash off to the shop, but now, seeing his expression, she simply wanted to go back through the door and dance with him.

Sam said, 'He might have spoiled the party for us, but he won't spoil it for my father and James because we won't tell them.' He took hold of her upper arms and kissed her on the mouth.

Gently she pushed him away. 'Ralph knows everything that's happening in your family,' she reminded him.

'Aye, he has the advantage over us. He knows the town and he knows where to find us, whereas we haven't the faintest idea where he might be. I keep trying to fathom how I can arrange a confrontation with him.'

She took hold of his hand. 'That isn't his way, though, is it?'

'No, but it's mine,' he retorted grimly. 'Come on, let's go back and lead off the dancing. We can tell my father and James in the morning.'

Tizzie's eyes gleamed in approval. She was going to marry a fighter. What more could she ask? They were still holding hands when they opened the door.

Sam arrived at Farthing Lane by cab early next morning. Tizzie was waiting for him, wearing one of Rebecca's big aprons. 'Have you told your father?' she asked at once.

'He knew last night, love. He's always had eyes like a hawk and an instinct for when things aren't right – it's one of his assets in business. He was waiting for me when I got back from seeing you home.'

'He knew something was wrong?'

'He said he'd put two and two together and guessed that things weren't right with Barney, but he was trying to convince himself that it didn't have anything to do with Ralph.' He looked back on the real anguish of telling his father what they suspected ... 'It was hard, telling him. He's insisting on paying for any repairs to the shop – he sees it as his responsibility.'

'We don't know yet whether any repairs are needed, so let's go round there and find out.' Tizzie put on an old cloak and wrapped a scarf around her head, smiling slightly at his expression. 'There's no point in ruining good clothes if the place is a mess,' she said, holding back when he would have hurried her out to the cab. 'One thing, Sam. It's Barney's business as well as mine, so I think he's entitled to know our suspicions about who might be behind this. He's the soul of discretion and very observant. People in the town underestimate him and often talk openly in front of him, so he gets to know all sorts of things that might be useful to us. Do you think I could tell him?'

He barely hesitated. 'Yes, if he accepts that it's in confidence. You know, at first my father said, "If it has to come out then so be it," but with arson on top of grievous injury and murder, he's becoming more and more concerned with protecting the Schofield name.' For an instant he thought of the inscription around the dome of the Exchange – his father's favourite quote – then helped Tizzie into the carriage.

When they arrived the three gold balls were shining in early sunlight but the inside of the shop window was filmed by smoke – the only outward evidence of the fire. Inside was very different. The smell met them as they opened the door: singed cloth, wet ashes and burnt paper. The sound of scrubbing came from the cellar and in spite of his bandaged hands Barney was sorting through piles of clothes, with Albert checking each item against the records.

'Mornin' Miss Tizzie, Mr Schofield,' said Barney. 'We're gettin' a bit more sorted out so I can't see as you'll need to dirty your hands, Miss Tizzie. We can do all that's necessary.'

'I'm not frightened of a bit of dirt,' declared Tizzie, 'and I'm staying for the day, Sabbath or no Sabbath. Rebecca's coming over later on with stuff to make a hot dinner for us.' She took out her notebook and pencil. 'Right, let's see it.'

Sam was at her side as Barney showed them the damage. It was considerable, some items burned beyond recognition, others charred, the wooden slats of the dolly shop shelves blackened and stinking, the newly painted walls streaked. She sighed with relief that the little drawers holding jewellery and valuables were untouched.

'It's bad,' she admitted, looking round, 'but it could have been so much worse. You all did marvels to stop it spreading.' She turned to Sam, knowing he was anxious to check with the guards at Jericho. 'We'll be all right, Sam, if you want to get to the mill.'

'I'll be back to see you this afternoon,' he promised. 'Father's set on the family going to chapel and then having Sunday dinner together. I'm only sorry you won't be there as well.' Forgetting for a moment that they weren't alone he gave her a farewell kiss on the mouth. Something made him look over her shoulder at Barney, but the dwarf's gaze slid past his, bland and unrevealing.

The shop bell pinged as he was going out, and he saw a letter in the wooden box behind the door. 'Hey, here's a letter,' he said, taking it out. 'Look – it's addressed to both of us. No postage stamp, though ... It must have been brought by hand.' For long seconds he stared at the envelope, shaking his head when Tizzie put out her hand for it. 'I'll open it,' he said firmly.

The envelope contained a single sheet of paper. On it was drawn a heart, pierced not by an arrow but by a lighted match. Puffs of smoke surrounded it and underneath was printed the word 'Congratulations'.

It was far more elaborate than the little pencilled note at Mosley Street, the one that had said 'Merry Christmas', but there was no doubt in Sam's mind that it was from the same source. He crumpled it up but was faced by Tizzie's straight green stare and outstretched hand. Reluctantly he gave it to her.

Barney and Albert were watching with interest as she read it. 'Just a note of congratulations,' she told them lightly and handed it back to Sam. As she saw him out he whispered, 'Lock the door!'

She nodded and mouthed silently, 'I love you!' Then she rolled up her sleeves to start work.

CHAPTER THIRTEEN

Getting Back to Normal

'Spring must be in the air,' laughed Sam, taking off his top coat and slinging it over one shoulder. There was a touch of warmth in the sun, but though they were heading for Mosley Street at a smart pace Joshua kept his big caped coat buttoned up.

The truth of it was that he was feeling the cold more and more. He'd first noticed it about the time the order book went missing – his very bones had been chilled that day, and since then it was happening all the time. He found it depressing. In his youth and middle-age cold weather hadn't bothered him; Rachel used to pull his leg and say he'd got pea soup in his veins instead of blood, but now he was chilled at a mere puff of wind. He'd had to tell Ellie to light his study fire at midday rather than four o'clock as she'd been doing for years; he'd even turned so soft as to accept a hot bottle in his bed. What with that and his new crystal spectacles for reading, old age wasn't so much creeping on as galloping headlong towards him.

'Have you thought any more about showing Tizzie round Mosley Street?' he asked. Soon after the pawnshop fire she'd wanted to see Jericho and Sam had suggested that Joshua did the honours. 'The mill's your creation, Father,' he'd said, 'you know you like showing it off. Tizzie's a good listener — she's interested in everything.'

Joshua had been well aware of that, remembering how she had tackled him about overproduction years back in the aftermath of the cotton famine. She'd known next to nothing about the industry but she'd studied the markets and come to her own conclusions – which to his amazement had echoed his own. At that time many a cotton master had been so intent on using the expensive machinery they'd installed before the American war, they were running their mills round the clock. Sure enough, within the year the markets had been so swamped with cotton cloth you could hardly give it away, let alone sell it. One or two had gone bankrupt, and he himself had come perilously close to putting his workers on short time. It hadn't been all plain sailing in '66 – far from it.

She had her head screwed on, had Tizzie. He'd enjoyed showing her over Jericho. The weavers had done him proud, as well, every one of them dodging out to the gangways from behind their looms to wave to her; not dropping curtseys – they were too independent for that – but with their uncanny timing giving her three cheers against the deafening clatter of the looms.

She'd smiled and waved back but she hadn't been such a fool as to think they'd done it for her sake. Those green eyes of hers had shone like emeralds as she'd said, 'It's clear they think the world of their employers.'

Now, at Joshua's side, Sam was answering his question. 'I plan to bring her to Mosley Street as soon as we have time, Father, but she's been so busy with the aftermath of the fire, the alterations to Mary's house and now furnishing our place. Next week, though, she has to come and see a diamond dealer in Shudehill, so I'll show her round the same afternoon. She's always asking about the Exchange and what Bill Tetley does to earn his commission as our agent. I tease her and say she should have gone into cotton rather than pawnbroking.'

Joshua was well pleased at that. 'You're a fortunate man, Sam. You'll have a wife you can talk business with, the same as I did with your mother. I'll be more than content to leave Jericho in your hands.'

Sam shot him an astounded stare. 'Steady on! That day's a long way off, God willing.'

'Everything's in order,' Joshua went on as they turned the corner. 'Kenworthy has my will, and there's a copy in the top drawer of my desk at home.'

Sam was aware of a sinking feeling in his abdomen. He only just stopped himself clapping a hand to it. 'Are you feeling all right, Father?'

'Aye, of course I am – I don't know what brought that on. Happen I'm on edge because things have gone quiet with Ralph.'

'Would you prefer it otherwise?'

'No, but nor do I relish being the mouse while he plays the cat. No matter how I try, I can't seem to foresee his next move. If it was you or James I might be able to guess how your minds would work, but not Ralph. I never could read him, even as a child.'

They arrived at the big oak doors beneath the trumpet and the rose to be greeted by Nathaniel Lee, shiny faced and beaming. Joshua threw off his coat and they settled to the weekly routine of examining the books, invoices and shipping manifests. That accomplished, Sam went off to talk to Will Grimshaw in the sample room while his father, unusually quiet, made for the stairs on his customary tour of inspection.

Half an hour later Sam found him on the top floor, pulling his whiskers and gazing out at the rooftops through the small glass panel in the closed doors of the hoist. Part of that floor was walled off to form the spacious apartment that had once been the home of his uncle; the remainder was sometimes used to store special export orders.

Without turning round Joshua waved a hand at the apartment. 'Don't forget there's still a few good pieces of your uncle Charlie's furniture in there – things too plain for Esther's taste that we couldn't find space for at home. Happen you'd show Tizzie when she comes?'

It was evident to Sam that only a fraction of his father's

mind was engaged on such matters, but he could never manage to read his thoughts concerning Ralph. 'I'll show her,' he promised. 'Now, what's really troubling you?'

'I'm wondering how long before Ralph puts a match to Jericho,' said Joshua quietly.

'And I'm thinking that perhaps the pawnshop was his final throw,' retorted Sam. 'He couldn't get at Meadowbank nor Jericho, remember, so perhaps he's given up. In any case we can't do more than we're doing already.'

'Can't we? I wouldn't tell the police it might be my son and I haven't told the other mill owners that he's behind the vandalism. Outside the family we've only mentioned his name to Tizzie, to Barney Jellicoe and to two private investigators – neither of whom have come up with a scrap of information about him. I ask myself now whether I should put a notice in the papers.'

'What?'

'Should I announce that I've disowned him, that I accept no responsibility for any unlawful action he might take? Folk do that sort of thing when they disclaim responsibility for debts and such.'

'It wouldn't be true, though, would it?' asked Sam gently. 'You do feel responsibility, don't you?'

'Aye, I do. But do you know what I feel even more? In here?' Joshua thumped his chest. 'Guilt! Guilt that I fathered him and did nothing to stop him turning out like he is; guilt about losing my best friend's life to him; guilt that I didn't apply my mind earlier to the real cause of your mother's illness; guilt about Matthew being half killed; guilt about Tizzie's shop; and guilt that the run-up to your wedding's being spoiled. I'm swamped in it and I *don't like it*!'

'I never imagined that you did,' said Sam shortly, 'but for guilt substitute shame and resentment and you've got what *I* feel, so you're not on your own.'

There was silence for a moment, then Joshua looked him in the eye. 'I'm sorry, lad. Don't ever let me fall into self-pity.'

Sam clasped his forehead like a second-rate actor on the stage. 'I've never had to worry about it till today,' he said mournfully.

Joshua shook his head in admiration. Sam would raise a smile if the heavens fell. 'Come on,' he said, making for the stairs, 'let's get round to the Exchange. I don't doubt Bill Tetley'll be champing at the bit till he sees our faces.'

'Mam, can I play out for a bit?' Rosie tried to sound as if she was bored, which wasn't true at all. Miss Hardman had been giving her extra work since the end of February and she liked it a lot. Today she'd been altering sentences where the tense was wrong, then writing them correctly in an exercise book. Nobody else in the class did English at home in a special book, not even Hannah Bennett.

Eyes streaming, Martha looked up from peeling onions. It was Friday, cleaning day, so the house was like a new pin from top to bottom, and she was wearing a clean pinny over her working dress as she prepared to stuff onions ready for baking. 'Aye, go on then,' she said, 'an' wrap up warm. Now, do I need to say it?'

'No, Mam.' In the singsong chant she used for reciting her tables, Rosie repeated, '"Don't leave the yard and garden. Don't go outside the walls." I'll just play with me ball in the yard an' along near the side hedge, like I always do.'

An' look out for Master Charles comin' home from his lesson, thought Martha but didn't say it. She and Matthew couldn't have been the only ones to take in the significance of what he'd played at the party, yet she'd not heard a word about it from anybody, not even Ellie.

Rosie put on her playing-out coat and her head wrap, turning to Martha as she lifted the latch. 'Mam, is Billy Warhurst goin' to walk home with me dad for ever an' ever?'

'*Mister* Warhurst,' corrected Martha. 'No, it's just that Mr Schofield doesn't want anybody goin' along the path on their own. You should know that, Rosie, you've been told often enough.'

'I do know, but I heard Mr Schofield sayin' to me dad that things had gone so quiet everywhere he was hopin' that whoever it was had seen the error of their ways an' that we might soon be gettin' back to normal.'

'Little pigs have big ears,' said Martha, stirring mixed herbs into a bowl of breadcrumbs. 'Off you go then, an' mind you come when I shout you.'

'Yes, Mam.' Rosie went out with her ball, dutifully bouncing it on the flat area that bordered the cobblestones. After a few minutes she walked with apparent aimlessness to the far side of the big house, where she climbed nimbly over the rockery that bounded the drive, edged through tall bare bushes and then stood behind a stone pillar that marked the front corner of the grounds. There, hidden from view, she could watch the Holdwell Road as it climbed from Saltley Station and swept along Meadowbank's side wall towards the hills. Charles would come up from the town that way, rather than along the other road that ran past the institute and Jericho.

He had lessons three times a week now: trumpet practice on Tuesdays and Thursdays and music theory on Fridays. If he was a bit late he wouldn't be able to stay and talk, but if he was early he would come into the shrubbery and they would tell each other about school. Sometimes they went in the tunnel, but last time it had been muddy and her mam had told her off for having dirty boots.

She could see the lamplighter trudging up the rise, lamps gleaming in his wake like Miss Tizzie's string of pearls at the party. Children and housewives were out and about, but in late afternoon the streets were fairly quiet until the blowers sounded. Then, especially down in the town, they would be thronged with thousands of people going home from their work; the pie shops would do a roaring trade and the black-pea men would be at the street corners with their big iron pans and ladles. The girls at school said that Dolly Redfern had started selling tater hash and cow-heel stew from the back window of her eating house, but when Rosie asked her mam if they could have some she said the day hadn't dawned when she'd take a basin to Dolly Redfern's for a meal, thank you very much.

And then she could see Charles in the distance, carrying his book bag and his flat music case. All she could hear was the distant whistle of a train and the rattle of wheels on gravel as a carriage came up from the town towards Holdwell. Good – there was nobody to see if he came into the shrubs.

He climbed over the rockery in his slow, graceful way, his teeth gleaming and his hair shining under the neat peaked cap that matched his coat. 'Hello, Rosanna,' he said.

'Hello.' She beamed up at him from her hiding place. 'Did you get good marks for your theory?'

He grinned. 'Every exercise right, and he says my sight-reading is excellent.'

'Does that mean you could look at a sheet of music – even somethin' hard – an' play it right off?'

He laughed. 'I could read it but perhaps not play it. It's harder for me to play something difficult than it is to read the notes.'

She wasn't convinced by that. Hadn't he played just like a grown-up at the party? Didn't he play scales that went on and on when he was in his uncle Sam's room?

Charles scuffled his feet in the damp soil. 'I've asked my father again about coming to live here all the time,' he said. 'It's awful at home. It was bad enough when they hardly spoke to each other, but now they're always arguing. My father must be fed up – he was shouting yesterday.'

Rosie patted his hand consolingly. She remembered what it had been like when things weren't right between her mam and dad. 'What did he say? Can you come?'

Charles shook his head. 'He says it's not as simple as it seems. It would cause talk in the town, and he doesn't want anything to upset Grandpa and Uncle Sam so near the wedding. That's one thing; another is that he'd miss me. I'd miss him as well, Rosanna. I hadn't thought of that.'

'Did you tell him *why* you wanted to live here?' She knew he couldn't have said it was to be near her, though in the tunnel he'd told her that that was the most important reason of all.

He gazed dolefully over the wall at the road winding up into the darkness. 'I told him I don't like it in the country. Well, it's true. I know it's lovely and clean and everything, but I *like* the mills and the factories and the trains. I like engineering – bridges and canals and big machines.'

'P'raps he'll change his mind,' she said. 'Does your mam know you want to come here?'

His face took on the tight look that always made her chest hurt. 'Yes, she knows. She said she'd always thought I was a mental defective and that's proof of it. She said I'd be better off with a private tutor than coming into this appalling town every day.'

'Oh.' What should she say to that? His mam was really horrible. 'An' does she still try an' stop you playin'?'

'No,' he admitted. 'I think she liked it at the party when people were praising me up, but I still have to practise in the stables.'

'R–o–sie!' It was her mam, calling her in.

'I've got to go,' she said reluctantly, 'an' you'd better go in an' all, or they'll wonder why you're late.'

'Rosanna, will you be at the wedding?'

She stared at him. 'Me? Course I won't. Why?'

'Uncle Sam's asked me to play at the ceremony. He wants me to accompany the organ as Miss Tizzie comes up the aisle and to give a fanfare before the Mendelssohn when they go out as man and wife.'

She didn't know what the Mendelssohn was, but the messages on his face were clear as clear. This was very important to him; he was pleased to be asked, but a bit wary. 'Will you do it?' she asked keenly.

'Yes, because I like my Uncle Sam. It'll be the first time in public, though.'

'No, it won't,' she said, puzzled. 'What about at the party?'

'That was a private occasion – in a private house,' he explained. 'The wedding will be at Bethesda Chapel – a place of public worship. They've got a good organ there and the organist is my teacher's brother.'

'Well then,' she said, 'what are you worryin' about?'

He wriggled his shoulders, and then she knew what was bothering him. It gave her a warm sort of feeling, like her stone hot bottle in bed on a cold night. 'I'll be there,' she promised recklessly. 'I can sneak in at the back. I'll be there to listen, an' I'm sure your playin' will make it the best weddin' in the world. You'll have to practise a lot so your *embouchure*'s all right.'

Then, for the first time ever, he kissed her. There, in their meeting place behind the stone pillar, he bent down and kissed her on the cheek. It was *lovely* – but oh, she did blush.

Young Johnny strutted through the empty rooms at Peter Street, shouting and stamping and pretending to be a soldier. Tizzie watched him and laughed. 'Here's one of the family who's already at home. What do you think, Mary? Do you think you'll make a go of it?'

Mary nodded gravely. 'If I don't it'll be my fault, not yours, Tizzie. But considering I've already got advance bookings I think I can do it. Annie's keen to come in full-time, and I've booked her auntie to do the washing. Now we've got water piped to the outhouse she'll have a little laundry there and all the big back yard for drying it.' She gave Tizzie a gentle squeeze. 'A thousand thanks, Tizz. I'd never have managed without you, and all the while you've been getting your own house in order. I just don't know how you've done it.'

'Oh, well, you know I like organising,' said Tizzie, giving her a hug and trying to ignore the sharpness of Mary's shoulder blades. It wasn't surprising that she'd lost weight, what with grief and worry over the children and setting up the lodging house. But at least she was back in the role of mother – that was what mattered; she knew that her children needed her and that she must make this house a home as well as a means of earning money. The Hartley wives were all at the ready to rally round and help with settling in when the time came.

Tizzie eyed her sister and hid her concern. The old Mary had disappeared as surely as her husband had disappeared under the earth in his fine oak coffin. There was no bounce to her now, no giggles. She still had the dimples but as she so rarely smiled they were seldom in evidence. She was calm and quiet and determinedly sensible – a widow who would soon be a landlady on one of the town's most respectable streets.

'You can leave Johnny and me here if you want to get off, Tizzie,' she said. 'I want to put shelf paper in the larder.'

Such tasks bored Tizzie to distraction, so she buttoned her coat, eager to go and see what the newly laid carpets looked like in her future home. Mary caught at her wrist. 'Tizz,' she said quietly, 'you've never said anything about your wedding dress, or the ceremony, or – or anything. You've hardly even mentioned what's happening afterwards.'

'I know,' agreed Tizzie, somewhat on the defensive. 'I didn't think you'd want to hear every single detail.'

'Why not?'

'Why not?' She was suddenly aggravated. 'Because you lost your husband less than three months ago, that's why not! I've never been what you'd call the sensitive type, but I can fathom that one out!' She was annoyed with herself for sounding so aggressive, but did Mary think she didn't *want* to discuss her wedding? She longed to talk abut it, not just with Sam but with an interested woman. If she hadn't had Sarah to talk to she would have felt completely deprived.

Mary was staring at her with sombre brown eyes. 'Do you think I've forgotten how you helped William and me to have a lovely wedding?' she asked. 'How you dealt with mother being so peculiar and helped me to choose my dress, all in the middle of taking over the shop and sorting out father's affairs?'

'No,' said Tizzie, 'I don't think you've forgotten, love. It's just that I don't want you to be upset by me gaining a husband so soon after you losing one.'

'William's dead,' said Mary flatly, 'and my heart's broken, but life goes on – it has to. He gave me years and years of wonderful happiness and four beautiful children – that's more than some people get in a whole lifetime, isn't it?'

'Yes, I suppose it is.'

'Then can we talk about your wedding?'

Tizzie smiled. 'Of course we can!' It was as if clouds that had obscured the sun were being blown away, but outside it was still a dull March day. 'Listen, how about coming round to Farthing Lane for the evening. You could get Annie to see to the children. It'll be a change of surroundings for you and we can talk.'

Mary smiled – a real smile. 'Tizz-wizz,' she said, 'I do *want* to know about your wedding. I want to help you get dressed and everything. Do you think I could do that?'

'Of course you could. Rebecca's Naomi has arrived home suddenly – for good, so she says – so she could help with the children if you like.'

'I do like,' Mary assured her. 'Go on now, off you go to your fine new house.'

It was a very fine new house, Tizzie told herself as the cab rattled away from Peter Street. Situated on the road that led to High Holden and faced by the edge of the moors, it lay as far to the west of Jericho as Meadowbank was to the east, convenient for Sam to get to the mill and for her to have access to her various concerns in the town.

A property agent had showed it to them a few days after Sam had proposed. It had been the last of six on his list, newly completed by a firm known for their unusual designs. 'I like the windows,' she'd said as they'd driven up the lane.

'It's an elegant house,' the agent had agreed.

Sam had helped her down from the carriage. 'It's a family house,' he'd said thoughtfully, 'and stone built, at that.'

In addition to the arched windows and doorways it had an oval hall with polished oak floorboards, a curving staircase, eight bedrooms plus those for the staff and a superb drawing room with floor-to-ceiling windows onto a terrace at the rear. Tizzie had been thinking of colour schemes even as Sam had been examining the futuristic plumbing.

They'd bought it the same day.

Tizzie had planned to sell Farthing Lane in order to pay half the cost, her last proof of independence before she gave up her name, but there was no need. In the darkest days of the cotton famine, Sam's father, worried that he might end up bankrupt like many another, had put four marriage settlements into special accounts. Two of them had been handed over to James and Sarah; one, Ralph's, withdrawn and used to make good his embezzlements; Sam's settlement, with fourteen years' interest, was enough to buy the house outright. In six days, with the builder's men still finishing the coach house and out-buildings, they'd taken possession of the keys.

That afternoon, in the big empty bedroom that would be theirs, with the smell of paint and new plaster all round them, Sam had kissed her until she was dizzy. 'Just as well there isn't a bed in here,' he'd said with a grin, then he'd grabbed her again and danced her round and round the room in a mad, triumphant polka.

Back at Farthing Lane they'd tried to decide on a name for the house, then talked of furniture and curtains and carpets. Sam had left such choices to her. 'I like the way you've decorated this house,' he'd said seriously. 'It's amazingly bare compared to any house I've ever set foot in, but it has style. If our house is as good I'll be content.'

'It'll be better,' she'd assured him.

Now she unlocked the front door and knew that she'd

spoken no more than the truth. She saw the tall arched window at the curve of the stairs and the new leaf-green carpet curving upwards. She turned slowly to see each room in turn and felt a surge of joy that she was going to marry Sam and live in this beautiful, beautiful house.

It didn't spoil her pleasure in the least to know that above the coach house live Noah, a young man hired by Sam to be their coachman, though at present his sole responsibility was to watch over the house. Sam was playing safe, and considering what had happened to the pawnshop, who could blame him?

'Record deposits from High Lee, Mr Schofield, with remarkable figures coming up for the half year. I'll put it in writing that I guarantee the extra half per cent interest, and if I can be of further assistance, Mr Schofield . . . ' Pink face glistening, baby-fat fingers plucking at the air, Jeremiah Norton was repeating himself for the third time, bowing so low he was almost touching the floor. James rose to take his leave, but Norton was still talking. 'The estate is in capable hands, if I may say so, in very capable hands, and please convey my regards to your father . . . '

James edged past him to the door and tried to avoid shaking that damp pink hand. Norton knew his job – none better – but why on earth did he have to grovel? James extricated himself with only a brief, limp shake from the hand, emerging thankfully on Peter Street and telling himself that it was a poor do when you felt you needed a wash after ten minutes with a bank manager.

For a few seconds he hesitated, looking along the street to where the business premises ended and private dwellings began. That high garden wall in the distance marked the house where Mary Hartley and her family would begin a new life, but he was going the other way to collect some shoes he'd had made. The shop was at the bottom of Farthing Lane with other expensive establishments; a pity it wasn't acceptable to call unaccompanied on a sister-in-law to be – he could do with seeing a woman who talked sense rather than pretentious drivel larded with spite.

James's spirits sank lower as he thought of Esther. Something awful was happening to him where she was concerned; he was finding it difficult to keep calm in his dealings with her. He, who had never in his life hurt a living soul (it worried him to swat a fly or squash a beetle), had more than once needed all his control not to raise his hand to her.

It was as if the restraint of years was being ripped away by her attitude to Charles and by what she had said about Tizzie. He simply couldn't credit that she had believed such evil rubbish. Deep in thought, he crossed the Old Square towards the shoemakers.

Mrs Eleanor Boulton was crossing the square in the opposite direction, heading for the bank and in thunderous mood. Her knees were killing her, but it wasn't worth the intense effort of climbing back into her carriage to be driven forty yards or so. Not only that, she'd been to the infirmary meeting and once again failed to get a dig in at Tizzie Ridings, who had sat there cool as a cucumber, taking the minutes and flaunting that showy ring, all the while smirking at Lady Sarah and no doubt gloating about that great new house of hers. Then, the business dealt with, Eleanor had walked right round the big table to Tizzie's side, only to be given a look from those bilious green eyes and the news that she had to 'dash off' for a fitting at her dressmaker's.

It was infuriating. Eleanor had told Bessie and Eli that Tizzie would be married before they could turn round, her reputation restored; yet not a soul would have tackled her about her sinful behaviour with that grotesque little Jellicoe. It was never spelled out between her and Ezra and the Waltons, but it was understood that Eli himself wouldn't be the one to say anything to Tizzie's face. If he did, she was so bold she might well come out with a few home truths about *him*.

Bessie had closed her eyes to it for years, of course, but since she'd started losing her grip Eli had been getting careless. Age wasn't calming him down at all – not like her Ezra, who'd always been one for seemly restraint but now never so much as touched her hand. She'd heard that Eli's name was becoming a byword in Ancoats, not for associating with the drabs but with the women who plied their trade in comfortable houses.

All that was by the way, though. Eli was a man, and men were different; they lived by different rules. It was Tizzie who must be chastised and Eleanor was the one to do it; she felt that she owed it to the people of Saltley. And it must be soon, for once married to a Schofield, everybody would fall over themselves to forgive and forget.

Then, coming towards her, she saw James Schofield, tall and lean, walking with the brisk self-confidence of all his family. She gripped her stick more tightly as she negotiated a kerb. The Schofields were all so *active*, she thought in sudden rage; even Joshua could prance around like a thirty-year-old when the fit took him. His eldest son here looked as if he had the energy to run a mile, all dressed up like a tailor's dummy and with a great house in the country like one of the landed gentry. Still, word was going round that he wasn't getting on with Esther, a dolled up little madam who thought herself above the wives of the cotton masters. Wait a minute! The wife . . . of course!

'Good day to you, Mr Schofield,' she said, forcing a smile as she barred his progress. Mr Schofield indeed! Hadn't she known him thirty years ago as young Jimmy, a docile little boy always drooling over lost dogs and baby birds and such?

James halted. 'Oh, good day, Mrs Boulton. I'm sorry I didn't see you – I was deep in thought.' He would never have chosen to pass the time of day with her because they had nothing in common, but she looked so old and unsteady, like a top-heavy old ship struggling to cross a waterway.

She faced him, leaning on her stick. 'It won't be long now to the wedding, Mr Schofield.'

'No, indeed ma'am. Things are busy up at Meadowbank

and I'm sure the same can be said of Miss Ridings' home.'

'Your dear wife must be feeling quite relieved, Mr Schofield.'

'Relieved? About what, Mrs Boulton?'

'Why, about her concerns being without foundation.'

James didn't know whether to mutter a platitude and move on or to ask what she was talking about, though if it was a concern of Esther's it must be either money or social position. 'I'm afraid I don't quite follow you ma'am. What concerns are you speaking of?'

The cold grey eyes held his and gleamed in anticipation. 'I'm sure dear Mrs Schofield meant well, otherwise she would never have spoken – well, you'll know what I refer to, of course.'

He shook his head uneasily. Something in her manner was bad, rotten, like a cut of meat that smells just slightly tainted but underneath is a seething mass of maggots. 'You'll have to be more specific, Mrs Boulton,' he said briskly.

'Very well,' she agreed graciously. 'I mean that, with Tizzie about to join the family, Esther must be relieved that you are all prepared to dismiss what is common talk about her. I refer to her immorality.'

James stared at her, knowing that his mouth was open, seemingly wedged apart. This couldn't be happening, he told himself. This terrible old woman couldn't be saying such things at half past four in the afternoon, here in the middle of the Old Square. He gathered his wits. 'We have always dismissed such vile slander, madam, for the very good reason that it isn't true.'

'Well, of course you would say that,' Eleanor murmured forgivingly. 'But you see, Mr Schofield, I know for a fact that it was your wife who first warned the town about the depraved behaviour of Tizzie Ridings and her dwarf. I can't believe you didn't know that. Dear Esther was the first to speak out about it. We all congratulated her on her sense of civic duty.'

'And no doubt were at pains to exercise your own civic

duty in repeating it! Slander is an offence at law, madam. You would do well to repeat *that*, night and morning!' He stepped sideways to avoid her skirts and strode away across the square, anger fighting a losing battle with shame.

Eleanor Boulton continued her laboured progress, satisfied to have got a dig in about Tizzie and at the same time rattled a Schofield. James sounded as if he might well go home and have a sharp word with his stuck-up little madam of a wife. Of course, she'd been spoiled as a child by her father – a man whose morals could well give Eli some keen competition.

She arrived at the bank in better humour, all set to discuss her personal account with Mr Jeremiah Norton. Now there was a man who knew how to show respect to the most important lady in Saltley.

James marched on, his mind in chaos but with one fact quite clear. Mrs Boulton had been telling the truth. It shone forth from the murk of her malice; it echoed with certainty through the falseness of her tones. God in heaven, what should he *do*? That was it – he would go and see Tizzie and apologise, now, this instant! No – he couldn't do that; it might give rise to talk if he called at her house. Talk! Ugh! He looked around him, desperate for action, until he met the eye of the young flower seller under the lamp, her stall the twin of one run by her mother in Saltley market.

He marched up to her and pointed to pail after pail of daffodils; perfect, half-open blooms from the market gardens of Low Holden. Eagerly the young woman offered wicker baskets, filling them until the flowers surrounded his feet like a golden tide. Still beside himself, he called a driver from his cab and asked him to deliver them, writing down Tizzie's address and then scribbling a message on one of his business cards. He wrote, 'With respect and affection'. That said it all – for now.

Paying the girl and the wrinkled old cabbie, he watched the daffodils being loaded and then set off on foot for Meadowbank House, where his carriage would have

arrived to take him to High Lee. Thank God it was a
Tuesday – Charles would be staying the night at Meadowbank. He himself must talk to Esther before he spoke to
his father and Sam.

Trade had been slow on the floor of the Exchange, so after
confirming a few orders with the customary handshake
Joshua left Sam and Bill Tetley with the brokers from
Liverpool and went off to King Street to have his dinner at the
Reform Club. The food there was good, and several
members were old friends – cotton men with the same liberal
views as his own. He liked the atmosphere; it was orderly and
restrained. You could have an interesting conversation or
bury your head in the paper and nod off for a bit.

He went for a wash and then sat in one of the big leather
chairs, studying the day's bill of fare and smiling to himself
to see steak and kidney pie listed. He'd give that a miss . . .
The chef might be a marvel but he'd have his work cut out
to equal Lilah when it came to pastry.

She was an unusual woman, was that one. He'd thought
to please her, weeks back, when she'd come to his study
the morning after the party. He'd been a bit on edge
because of the pawnshop fire and she'd been crackling like
the devil in her stiff pinny, but apart from the touch of
colour in her cheeks had looked much as usual – plain as
a pikestaff.

He'd thanked her properly for the party food and said
something to the effect that he'd been reflecting on what he
paid her and had decided that she deserved a rise. 'I'm
giving you another five shillings a week, Lilah,' he'd said.
That was some rise, mind; it upped her pay to more than
sixty pounds a year on top of her room and board.

'I'm well paid as it is, Mr Schofield,' she'd said, abrupt
as anything, 'but I thank you. If it's all the same to you I'd
rather take it in kind – provisions, like – for me mam an'
our Abbie.'

'I see. Well, tell me a bit about them, then. They don't
go short, do they?'

She'd scuffled her feet like a child in front of the head teacher. 'Not all the time,' she'd said uncomfortably, 'cos I help 'em out. Me mam's gettin' on, an' our Abbie – that's me sister – she's been a widow since she were a young woman. Then three years back she had to give up in the card room at Boulton's cos of her rheumatics, so now she takes in mendin' an' ironin' an' scrapes hides for the tanner – anythin' to make a bit, like.'

He'd been put out to find that close relations of his cook were going short. It would never have happened in Rachel's time, a fact that made him a bit sharp. 'God above, woman,' he'd snapped, 'why haven't you put 'em down on the list for the baskets?' Food was sent out from the house every single day.

She'd looked down that long nose of hers. 'They've never took hand-outs in their life, Mr Schofield, thank you very much!' So, swallowing his irritation, he'd asked where they lived.

'They had to leave their cottage cos it belonged to Boulton,' she'd said quietly. 'But they do have a – a dwellin'. It's in Bushell's Yard.'

He'd been put out at that, as well. Bushell's Yard was in the oldest part of the town. It was where beasts were slaughtered, and the gutters ran with blood every morning. He recalled that there were dwellings round the yard, if you could call them such.

He'd looked anywhere but at Lilah, knowing she was too embarrassed to meet his eyes. 'Right,' he'd said. 'In your kitchen accounts each week put down five shillings for, say, extra provisions. Buy what you see fit with it, along with all the household stuff. Will that suit you?'

No, it hadn't suited her. 'Hannah will think it's funny if I do it that way,' she'd objected. 'We always do the accounts together.'

'All right, I'll inform Hannah that from now on you're having part of your wages paid in that way as you aren't always free to go running to the market to buy goods for your family out of your own money. I can make it clear that

the five shillings is extra to the household accounts. Will
that suit you?'

'Yes, Mr Schofield, an' thanks.' She'd nodded her head
at him and marched back to the kitchen.

Next morning he'd told Zacky to take him to the bottom
end of Holden Street, and then he'd gone on foot through
rutted dirt streets to look at Bushell's Yard for himself. It
had nearly turned his stomach to hear the squeal of the pigs
and see little lads picking over the piles of entrails, their
bare feet paddling in blood. He'd hardly been able to bear
to look at the hovels, let alone try to spot which one
belonged to Lilah's sister. So he'd given them a Schofield
house; one of those overlooking a stretch of grass in Mitton
Street. That was that, apart from having to witness Lilah
sobbing her heart out when he'd told her it was all arranged.

He'd told her to stop snivelling. He shouldn't have said
that, but it was bad enough seeing women weeping when
they were miserable without having to put up with it when
they were happy. Anyway, it always made him feel a bit
awkward when he was being thanked. The good book said it
was more blessed to give than to receive and it was certainly
easier . . . until folk started weeping with gratitude.

The steward was hovering at his side. 'Mr Luther Dobbs
sends his compliments, Mr Schofield, and asks if you
would like to share his table for dinner?'

He agreed at once. Luther wasn't much of a talker, but
when he did come out with something it was usually worth
listening to.

Joshua met Sam again as they emerged simultaneously
from different cabs at Victoria. Rain was coming down so
hard they didn't exchange a word until they were inside the
station, and even there it was all noise and bustle and the
hissing of steam.

Once aboard the train Joshua related what had passed
between him and the other mill owner. 'Luther says he's
decided to stop paying out on watchmen and John's doing
the same at Greenbank. He says all the others will probably

follow suit because as far as they're concerned things are back to normal.'

Sam smiled with a touch of bitterness. 'The same could be said about us, I suppose. It's seven weeks since the pawnshop fire.'

Joshua put his stick between his knees and leaned his chin on the handle. 'Luther didn't come out with it, but I've no doubt he wonders why we've hired such an army of watchmen. I suspect he'd have liked to ask what – or who – we're frightened of.' He looked at Sam from under his bushy white brows. 'How do you see it? Do you reckon we should ease off a bit on security?'

By nature somewhat reckless, Sam was now prudence personified. 'There's been no incident since the pawnshop,' he admitted, 'but with the wedding less than a fortnight away I say we don't ease off at all until we're back from our honeymoon.'

Joshua nodded without enthusiasm. 'Ralph didn't announce his return and he hasn't said goodbye, but that doesn't necessarily mean he's still in England, does it? I'll go along with caution, though: no cutting down on the watchmen until after your honeymoon. Now, let's enjoy a bit of business talk. What price did they accept for that last shipment of fine staple?'

James was surprised to find his father already home, waiting to talk to him about a conversation he'd had with Luther Dobbs. He knew he must stay and listen; to rush off to High Lee would be like shouting out loud that something was wrong.

He tried to make suitable comments, to sound intelligent, but the problem of Ralph seemed to lack urgency compared to what he'd learned only half an hour ago. He made himself pay attention. One minute he thought that the strain and uncertainty were telling on his father, the next those eyes gave him a look so razor-sharp it announced that Ralph would meet his match if he got up to more devilry.

At last his father said mildly, 'Well, I expect you've got

things to see to at home, James, so don't let me keep you talking.'

James hurried from the study only to meet Charles in the hall. 'I'm off home,' he told him, rushing past to pick up his hat. Then he turned to put a hand on his son's shoulder. 'How did the lesson go?'

Charles gave him his wide, beautiful smile. 'It was good,' he said simply.

At High Lee he wrenched off his coat. 'Where's your mistress?' he asked the maid.

With deep respect she bent her knee and he sighed impatiently. Esther insisted that the servants bowed or curtseyed every time they were spoken to. 'Madam is in her room, changing, sir.'

He would have to invade forbidden territory. Climbing the stairs he felt none of his usual distaste at the prospect of acrimony; his shame was beyond that. He entered the room without knocking and found Esther in a feather-trimmed robe, having her hair dressed. She stared at him in the looking glass as if the devil himself had appeared behind her.

'Please leave us,' he said to the maid.

The woman curtseyed but looked enquiringly at her mistress. Esther flipped a dismissive hand. 'Go on,' she said, tapping her foot, 'but stay within call.'

'No,' said James quietly. 'Leave the upper floor – I'll ring when I'm ready.'

The maid curtseyed again and left them, while Esther swung round in her chair. 'Have you gone quite mad?' she asked icily.

'On the contrary, I was never more sane.'

Her eyes flickered warily. 'Oh?'

'I saw Mrs Boulton today.'

Esther shrugged. 'What of it?'

All at once he felt weary. 'She told me that it was you who started the rumours about Tizzie and Barney Jellicoe. What have—'

'Tizzie?' she snapped. 'Huh! I might have known. What

has she *got* that makes everybody run round after her?'

'Integrity?' he suggested drily. 'Intelligence? The capacity for hard work?'

She glared at him, one eye obscured by ringlets that had not yet been pinned into place. She pushed them aside and her gaze wandered towards her comb and brushes.

'Esther,' he said tightly, 'this is of the utmost importance. Was it you who started those rumours?'

She wriggled her shoulders. 'What if it was?'

He shook his head. He was *married to her*, for heaven's sake! 'If it was you I shall have to apologise to Tizzie, to Sam and to my father. That will be my first action – the first of many. I ask again, was it you?'

Lips pursed, Esther was running a finger up and down the back of her silver hairbrush, evidently calculating how much to say. He knew bitterness so keen it tasted like acid on his tongue. That brush was one of the set he had given her as a wedding present. 'Quite pretty,' she had said, openly disappointed. That had been the first thing to go wrong in his marriage; the second had followed a few hours later.

'Tizzie was at your house week after week,' said Esther resentfully. 'Sarah was always with her, never with me. When she became countess she still clung to Tizzie, even though she was from a pawnshop! It wasn't fair!'

'Fair? She was Sarah's friend – she still is. Tizzie helped her to make a new life when she left Edward. You, I recall, tried to pretend it had never happened. Ah, I see it all now; you thought Sarah would drop her when there was talk of immorality. That was it, wasn't it?'

'You tell me – you're the one who's got it all worked out.'

'Yes, I believe I have. Months went past – years – with Tizzie still welcomed at Alsing. You were connected by marriage to a woman who was tainted with rumour – rumour you yourself had started!'

'And I'll be connected twice over a week on Saturday, won't I?' She was on her feet now, the pink feathers of her collar wafting with each expelled breath.

'You admit it, then?'

'Of course I admit it! She deserved it – her and that flea-ridden shop and that obscene dwarf. It's obvious he's besotted with her. She's insufferable, sucking up to the Soars and buying houses all over the town and living in that house of hers like a – a harlot!'

James could feel his control going. He wanted to smack her pretty, kittenish face; he could imagine her sinewy little neck under his fingers, his thumbs meeting . . . 'Be careful, madam, or you'll push me too far,' he warned, words so at odds with his nature they sounded artificial, as if they'd been written in a foreign language and spoken by a schoolboy.

Esther laughed. 'Push you too far?' she derided. 'And what would you do? Nothing – the same as always. You're pathetic. You and your precious family are all pathetic. You're a laughing stock, do you know that? Sam is nothing but an empty-headed clown, and as for your father – he must think he's in a Shakespearean tragedy or something, the way he goes on about your mother—'

James leapt the distance between them, snatched her up by the waist and threw her on the bed, face down.

She squealed in astonishment, then spat and gasped against the quilt. He held her down with one hand and with the other lifted her robe, revealing long silk drawers embroidered with rosebuds. She kicked her legs in fury and her feathered slippers shot across the room. Wiping out a lifetime of kindness and consideration, James pulled down the silk drawers. Her buttocks showed white beneath the edge of her pale pink stays. 'I'll tell my father!' she choked.

'Will you?' he asked grimly. 'Then tell him this, as well!' He leaned across her and picked up the silver brush then applied it with vigour to her neat little bottom. At the first stroke she gave an outraged scream. The maid was listening outside the door and on hearing the scream she smiled. Justice, she thought, and not before time!

The scream didn't make James stop. He smacked her with the back of the brush eleven times in all, each stroke releasing some of the misery inside him. Suddenly he paused with his hand upraised. She'd been wriggling like an eel and he was out of breath from holding her but that wasn't why he'd stopped. He was enjoying it! God above, he was enjoying beating his wife!

He threw the brush aside and she lay there, sobbing. After a while she turned over, covering her pubic hairs with her hands. 'You're mad,' she whimpered. 'You're insane!'

'I must be,' he agreed, 'to have stayed with you. This is the end, Esther, the finish. I'm leaving you at once. We'll sort out the details through the lawyers.'

She sat up and squealed at the stinging of her bottom. 'You can't leave me now!'

He smiled slightly. 'Give me one good reason why not.'

'Because the Cheveneys are coming to dinner!'

He shook his head. 'That's your problem, Esther. They're your friends, not mine.' He made for the door. 'Tomorrow I shall give the staff a month's wages in lieu of notice. We'll sort out later how many servants you'll be able to afford. Is there anything you want to ask me?'

'No,' she said defiantly.

'Not even about what will happen to Charles?'

'Not even about Charles,' she mimicked. 'You made me have him – you look after him!'

That was final enough. Tiredly he said, 'Goodbye, Esther.' She didn't reply. She was clutching at her robe, trying to cover herself. He walked out and closed the door behind him.

When he arrived back at Meadowbank he found his father sitting in front of the fire in the little sitting room. He didn't seem surprised to see him. 'Well, lad?' he said quietly.

'Father, I'm really sorry to inflict this on you so near the wedding, but I've left Esther – for good.' His misery was such that he sank to the floor, one hand clasping the worn blue velvet of his father's chair.

Joshua laid a hand on his head. 'You should have done it years back,' he said heavily. 'What's brought it on now all of a sudden?'

James was infinitely tired. He didn't think of his father being burdened already; it never occurred to him to keep silent about what his wife had done. 'I found out today that it was Esther who started the talk about Tizzie and Barney Jellicoe. She's admitted it and shows no remorse. I've thrashed her with a hairbrush. I wanted to throttle her. I'm sorry, Father.'

Joshua looked at his son, his good son, father to his only grandchild. He sighed just once. 'I didn't want her at the wedding, anyway,' he said.

CHAPTER FOURTEEN

The Letter

Hands were pulling at him; he could hear the crackle of burning timbers and the voice of his stepmother screeching his name. Soaked in sweat, Matthew writhed on the bed, reliving a day long gone.

At his side Martha waited for him to cry out. It was better that way, she remembered. To wake him out of the nightmare would leave him on edge for a day or more, but to let him reach the climax and *then* comfort him could ease the way to a limp, exhausted sleep that would wipe away his memories – until the next time.

Her heart ached with pity as he groaned and muttered, lost in the turmoil of his dreams. What had brought it on? It was years since the last time he'd been enmeshed in the horror of his little sister burning to death while he was drunk and insensible. Martha tried to hold his sweaty hand but he shook her off. A minute later he sat up and howled like a wounded animal. His eyes were open, blinking without comprehension at the candle she'd lit. 'Dorcas!' he called. 'My liddle girl!'

Martha took him in her arms, crooning soft, loving words of reassurance. 'You're at home, Matthew. It's all right. You're safe with me.'

Before, he had always buried his head against her small breasts, sometimes half sobbing but always trying to pretend that it wasn't really a nightmare. This time it was different and she didn't know why. He put her away from him and looked round the bedroom. 'Rosie!' he cried hoarsely. 'Where be 'er to?'

'Rosie?' she echoed in amazement, it was always Dorcas in the nightmare. 'Rosie's in bed, love,' she said gently, 'in the next room.'

His face shining with sweat, he jumped out of bed and grabbed the candle. Martha padded after him barefooted and found him standing in his nightshirt with the candle-stick held high, looking at the child, who lay on her side fast asleep, her cheeks pink and her mouth curved in a little smile.

'See, love, she's all right,' Martha whispered. 'Come back to bed.'

Matthew nodded, still confused. 'Twas powerful strange that he'd dreamed of Dorcas but wakened fearful for Rosie. He bent to kiss her cheek but Martha said, 'Just a minute – what's this?' The child was cuddling something between her neck and the pillow, trying to hold on to the object as Martha eased it from her grasp. It was a leather glove – brown leather – too big for her, too small for an adult. Martha's breath hissed through her teeth. 'Master Charles,' she whispered. 'It's his glove!'

Matthew was still on edge. 'Put it back,' he told her sharply. 'Leave her to her liddle secret.'

Martha obeyed him and together they tiptoed from the room, but once in bed she turned to him, his nightmare forgotten. 'This can't go on,' she said, worried. 'We'll have to talk to her. She'll end up gettin' hurt an' puttin' us all in the muck cart – it's always the way when girls look above their station.'

'A child of ours is every bit as good as the son of that woman up at High Lee,' retorted Matthew. 'It was her who objected to him playin' with our Rosie, don't forget, not his father and grandfather. Anyway, he's livin' here at Meadowbank now and from what we've heard, it's permanent.'

'I don't care if it is permanent, I'm not havin' her runnin' after a lad like Master Charles. It's not fittin'!' Martha blew out the candle and slammed her head back on the pillow.

Matthew would have liked to challenge her, but the nightmare had taken it out of him and he couldn't summon the energy. He stared into the darkness and after a minute found himself smiling. What if this childish attraction should last into their teens? Why shouldn't his little Rosie marry a Schofield? She was as good as young Charles any day, and what was more, Mr Schofield had a soft spot for her. You only had to see his face when he spoke to her.

He felt Martha's hand searching for his but with a touch of resentment he turned away, the terror of the nightmare still pulling at the fringes of his mind until at last he fell into a restless sleep.

Martha lay awake, wondering why there was always a bad side to the good things in life – to two things in particular. First, there was Rosie doing well at her schooling, really well; but she was putting them all at risk with her mad attachment to a lad who was far above her. Second, there was Matthew back at his work and taking up his woodcarving again, but it seemed that in the struggle to regain his health the loss of her baby seemed to have been swept aside. He cared about it, of course he did, but not like her; it was as if part of her had been severed and tossed away like so much rubbish.

She sighed and touched his sleeping back. He was alive and well again, that was what mattered. Happen in time she would get over losing what was no more than a scrap of her innermost tissue. As for Rosie, she would talk to her in the morning, no matter what her father might say.

With Matthew gone to work, Martha tackled her daughter as she sat down to her porridge, coming to the point at once. 'Rosie, me an' your dad looked in on you last night an' found you snugglin' Master Charles's glove. What have you to say to that?'

Rosie's eyes widened in alarm. She'd been cuddling the glove for weeks, but usually she tucked it under the bedclothes and next morning hid it in the space under her bottom drawer. She stared uncomfortably at the hearth rug. 'I like holdin' it in bed,' she said with a hint of rebellion.

'It's a leather glove,' said Martha shortly. 'They cost a lot of money. Where's the other one?'

'He lost it. He told his mam he'd lost them both an' he give me that one as a – a keepsake. It's all right now he doesn't live with his mam.'

'It's *not* all right!' snapped Martha. 'His grandad's the master of Jericho – the richest man in Saltley. He'll have his eye on some young woman of the gentry when Charles is old enough to get wed. As for you, lady, you're only just turned ten, so don't fill your head with silly ideas. You could lose your dad his job an' lose us this house. Do you hear what I say?'

Rosie eyed her warily. Her mam could be strict, more strict than her dad, but she was wrong about Mr Schofield. He would never sack her dad or make them give up the house. He liked her – she knew he did. He'd pulled her hair ribbon last week and called her a little keck-meg. She could read the message on her mam's face clear as clear, though. It said, 'I'll not be moved on this; it's important.'

Rosie picked up her spoon and stirred her porridge. 'I hear you, Mam,' she said meekly. 'I'm sorry I've been silly. I promise I won't do anythin' that could make us lose the house.'

'Right,' said Martha, slightly mollified. 'Just see you don't, that's all.'

Rosie ate her porridge with a clear conscience. She'd made the promise, but she could still be friends with Charles because she knew for certain that it wouldn't make them lose the house. As for being silly – it was her mam who was being silly for thinking such a thing.

It was nearly tea time and everything was grey. Grey sky, grey streets, grey mist hanging above the road to Holdwell, grey slates on the roofs going down to Saltley Station. There was even a grey drizzle of rain, but her mam hadn't seen it or she wouldn't have let her play out.

Rosie waited behind the pillar and squeezed herself tight round the chest. She wasn't cold, just excited because it was only three days to the wedding and Charles had played his special piece for her – the one he'd told her about when he first got his trumpet – the Air and Tune in C by Purcell. 'Will you listen to me this afternoon?' he'd asked. 'I know I said I'd play it just for you, but Uncle Sam and Miss Tizzie have decided on it for the wedding and Grandfather wants to hear it. Will you listen and tell yourself it's really for you?'

'Course I will,' she said, highly delighted. 'I'll be in chapel an' all, so I'll hear it twice over.'

He'd played it and oh, it had been lovely. She'd listened when her mam and dad had gone to do the buying in at the market. It had been loud as loud – fortissimo, Charles had called it – the sort of tune you could march to, a slow-stepping sort of march. She could hardly wait to hear it again with the organ.

Down the hill she could see two boys swinging on a rope tied to the top of a lamppost, and there behind them was Charles, carrying his trumpet. She watched him cross the road in front of Meadowbank and as he reached the kerb at the corner a dawdling coach pulled in at his side. A man leapt out – the man she'd seen up on the path. He grabbed Charles round the waist, trumpet and all, then threw him into the coach and jumped in behind him. At once the driver cracked his whip and headed the horses round the corner into the Holdwell road.

Rosie gaped in perplexity. It had happened so quickly it didn't seem real. She expected to see Charles on the flagstones, laughing and brushing himself down, but he'd gone. There was just a creaking and a rumbling as the little black coach gathered speed along the winding dirt road that led to Holdwell and the hills.

They'd kidnapped him! She let out a squeal of pure

terror and at the same moment wet her drawers. *Oh!* she hadn't done that since she was a *baby*, but she couldn't bother about it now, she must tell a grown-up what had happened. Wildly she looked from side to side, but there was nobody there. She would go and tell them in the house, then. No – she must see where they were taking him, follow them. She could run very fast and the road was all bendy. She would cut across the fields to keep up.

Scrambling over the garden wall she dropped to the road and began to run, holding her skirts high so she wouldn't trip. The coach was a long way ahead but she could see that the back window was covered – all the windows had been covered. Rosie was sobbing as she clambered over a wall and ran across the fields. She could see the top of the coach bobbing up and down, slower now because it was climbing. It must be the man who had tried to kill her dad, she thought desperately; it must be. If he'd nearly killed a man, he could easily kill a boy, even a big boy like Charles.

By now it was raining, not drizzling; there was mist lying behind the hedges and under the stunted trees. She could still hear the sound of hooves and the rattle of wheels, and as she scrambled over a hillock she saw the dark bulk of the coach below her, rounding a bend. She was keeping up with them! Triumph lent her a burst of speed, but minutes later the road levelled and she had to run harder and harder.

There were sheep all over the place, skittering away as she ran towards them. Her face was wet with tears and rain, so she caught at her pinafore and wiped her cheeks as she ran. It would soon be dark and then she wouldn't be able to see anything at all, but if she climbed higher and looked down she might be able to tell whether the coach was going on to Holdwell and High Lee or taking the road that led up to the faraway hamlet of High Holdwell.

Terror forced her on. She was the only one who knew where he was. If she lost sight of him they could take him away for ever. She might never see him again, never in all her life. They might tie him up and starve him. They might kill him. Grimly she staggered up the hill and saw the road below, dark and wet between the peaty green fields. Ridges and gullies and the absence of walls told her that she was on the edge of the moors. Gasping, she clutched at a gorse bush and watched.

Slowing down as if confident that he hadn't been seen, the driver steered into the left-hand fork of the road. Rosie sniffled with satisfaction. She might not have told the grown-ups what had happened but she knew now that they were heading for High Holdwell: a lonely, straggling sort of place with empty cottages that had once held hand-loom weavers, overlooking the plain that stretched to Manchester and beyond. People said there were caves in the rocks up there. She watched for another minute and then turned back towards home.

Charles was frightened. He was lying on the seat of the coach with his knees bent and his wrists and ankles tied. Round his mouth, effectively gagging him, was a strip of white calico. 'Jericho's grade one,' the man opposite had said mockingly as he'd tied it firmly into place.

There were two men inside the coach; one had little black eyes set close together and the clothes of a down-at-heel labourer; the other, the one who made his stomach start churning, was well dressed, with pockmarked skin and very blue eyes that were set in his face like two pebbles. The men were talking to each other in low tones, ignoring him as if he was a piece of baggage slung on the seat. At first he had shouted 'Help!', then he had asked where they were taking him. The little one had looked at the other for permission, then slapped him across the mouth so hard he had bitten his tongue and made it bleed. Then the pockmarked man had gagged him and made the remark about it being calico from Jericho.

His mouth was sore and his shoulder hurt where he had landed on it when he was thrown inside, but as they bumped along his mind was racing. The little one could be the man Rosanna had seen up on the path, and the driver might be the man who had attacked Matthew Raike. That was bad, very bad, but Rosanna might have been waiting for him in the shrubbery; she just might have seen them take him away. If she had, she would have told the grown-ups. At this very minute there could be carriages trailing them and maybe a black police coach holding a band of constables. They might be carrying firearms. They might blow the head off the pockmarked man. He felt a bit sick when he thought of that, so in his mind he changed it to they might shoot him in the arm. He tried not to look at his trumpet. If they realised how he treasured it they might throw it through the window or something.

They rumbled on, and at last he felt the carriage turn sharply. Then they were on a bad road, jolting over bumps and boulders. The two men had stopped talking and the pockmarked one was unfolding a sack. Without any change of expression the man grabbed Charles's bound wrists and pulled him upright. Then he dropped the sack over his head, saying sardonically, 'Just to keep those golden locks covered.'

They had stopped and it was very quiet. All Charles could hear was the steady drumming of rain and the snorting of the horses. Then he was picked up and slung over a man's shoulder, catching a whiff of stale sweat that made him think it was the little one who carried him. Would they bring the trumpet? He didn't know, and he was in no position to ask. Wary of another blow, he stayed limp and unresisting as he was carried along a path of some sort and then down steps to a place that smelled musty and was very cold. There he was tipped off the shoulder and left on the floor.

'Right,' said the voice of the pockmarked man. 'We're all blacked out? Go and send Slater on his way, then.'

A door closed. There was the sound of a lamp being lit and then the sack was pulled off his head. Charles blinked in the light. They were in a cellar, a dirty little cellar with a rusty stove in one corner and lots of pipes across the ceiling. There were cobwebs everywhere.

'Stand up,' said the pockmarked man, who was now lounging in an ancient armchair. He was still wearing his tall hat and big coat but on his feet were expensive riding boots.

Charles could hear his own heart thumping. The sound annoyed him because it stopped him from thinking properly.

The man crooked a finger. 'Come here where I can see you,' he said.

Charles jumped across the floor on his tied up feet while the man held up the lamp to examine his features. 'Quite the little Schofield,' he murmured. 'Grandpa's blue-eyed boy, in fact.' With a wrench he removed the gag. 'Am I right? You're Grandpa's blue-eyed boy?'

Charles licked dry lips. 'What if I am?' he asked defiantly.

The man tut-tutted reprovingly. Then he smiled, showing square yellow teeth. Without leaving his seat he leaned forward and struck Charles across the face with such force that his head rocked on his shoulders like an empty bobbin in the winding room. 'A civil tongue is advisable when speaking to me,' he said quietly. 'Otherwise the gag will be replaced and a blindfold added for good measure.'

His head swimming, Charles swallowed and looked at the floor. 'Could you tell me why you've brought me here?' he asked politely. 'And who you are?'

'I should have thought a bright boy like you would have worked out answers to both those questions. The first one – I've kidnapped you, for a ransom. The second – you aren't the only blue-eyed boy in the Schofield family. There's your saintly father, your clownish uncle Sam and—' With one hand he removed his hat to show his dark, greasy locks and with the other peeled the hair back from his forehead to reveal close-cut blond waves that looked as if they'd been dusted with silver.

Charles was more bewildered than ever. A wig? For a man?

'Come on,' said the other impatiently. 'They can't have kept my existence a secret.'

'Are you my uncle Ralph?' asked Charles, mystified. 'From Australia?'

'I am indeed. The black sheep of the family, returned to get his share of the grazing.'

The door creaked open and the little man slid inside and down the steps, addressing Ralph with wary deference. 'He's gone as arranged an' I've saddled the horse.'

'Right. I'll be off, then. Any nonsense from this one and you replace the gag at once. Untie his hands only for him to eat or to use the bucket and for goodness' sake keep him clean. I can't stand the smell of excrement.' With his empty blue eyes he observed the little man. 'I've warned you once and that should be enough, but I know your tastes and he's a pretty boy. So – no buggery. Later, maybe, if the old man doesn't jump to it, but for now just feed and water him until I get back.'

He picked up a waterproof cloak and went out, leaving Charles sick with relief that he was to stay with the little man. He was horrible, really horrible, but he didn't make his stomach turn over like the one who said he was his uncle. What had he meant about him being a pretty boy, though? And what was buggery? Was it a form of torture? People used the word bugger as a swearword. The boys at school said it, and so did his grandfather Schofield, when he didn't know Charles was listening . . .

Charles's face still stung and his shoulder was hurting, but in spite of his fear he felt the first stirring of excitement. He'd been kidnapped and he was being held to ransom! It was like a story in one of Rosanna's books. Would his uncle ask his father for money or would he go to his grandfather? He stared wide-eyed at the flickering lamp. Did the family know that his frightening, pockmarked uncle was back in England? Had they fathomed that he must be behind all the bad things that had happened?

The little man put a mug of water on a wooden stool and added a hunk of bread. He untied Charles's wrists and said, 'Fill your belly. There'll be nothin' else till mornin'.'

Obediently, Charles began to eat . . .

*

Martha ran into the kitchen with her shawl clutched under her chin. 'Have you seen our Rosie?' she asked the women. 'I've shouted an' shouted but she hasn't come in.'

Ellie gave a perplexed giggle while Hannah looked curiously at Martha. 'Have you been to the shrubbery at the side?' she asked gently.

At that moment only Lilah saw the implications of Rosie not answering her mother's call. She'd been putting a piece of smoked haddock to poach, but she laid it back on her board. 'Master Charles is due in, an' all,' she said uneasily. 'Have you looked under the hedge behind the stables, Martha?'

Martha flushed. 'They're neither of 'em there,' she said shortly. 'Our Rosie went out to play ball, same as always.'

'Yes, an' she always—' began Ellie, to be silenced by a look from Hannah.

'Ellie,' Hannah said, 'go with Martha an' check the stables an' the rest of the grounds. Take a shawl, mind.'

Together the two women looked through the stables and harness room and then ran round the perimeter of the garden and yard. Ellie scuttled into the shrubbery near the stone pillar and came back triumphant, clutching Rosie's little shawl. 'She was 'ere,' she gasped excitedly. 'D'you think they've run off, Martha? Rosie an' Master Charles?'

'No, I don't! Don't talk so daft!' Ellie wasn't the brightest of women, but seeing her chastened expression, Martha softened. 'Master Charles likes our Rosie,' she admitted, 'but that's all. She wouldn't presume any more – she's only ten years old!'

Lilah listened in silence when they returned with the shawl then told them that Hannah had gone across the road at the front to see if Charles was coming. 'He was due in ten minutes back,' she said, her long face holding an expression not of fear but maybe of foreboding. 'Get Davey!' she told Ellie, assuming a control that nobody thought to question.

When the gardener stood at the door in his wet coat she

asked, 'Have you seen Master Charles? D'you think he's called on Mr Schofield at Jericho?'

Davey shook his curly head. 'Not as I know of. Zacky's already set off for the mill, so Mr Schofield an' Mr Sam'll be back at any minute.'

Martha was losing patience. Why were they only talking about Charles? He was a great hulking boy but her Rosie was a girl and a dainty little soul – a puff of wind would blow her over. She looked at the kitchen clock and saw that there was half an hour to go before Matthew got home. She decided she couldn't wait that long. She was glad she was wearing her clogs because they stood up to the rain better than any shoes. 'I'm goin' out lookin' for me daughter,' she said, 'an' bringin' her dad home from his work. It's not long since he was half killed, don't forget, but that'll only happen to our Rosie over my dead body!'

They all stared at her in silence. 'She's not the size of six penn'orth o' copper!' she told them sharply. 'If she's back before me there'll be nothin' lost by me fetchin' her dad!' With a flap of her shawl and a clatter of clog irons she went out and set off along the road. It was raining steadily but she recognised the Schofield carriage speeding towards her. Without hesitation she stepped into the gutter and waved it down so that Zacky stopped almost at her side.

Joshua looked out curiously. 'Martha? What's the matter?'

'Our Rosie's gone missin',' she said, 'an' I'm goin' for Matthew. Master Charles hasn't come home, either.' She was so worked up she spoke as their equal.

The two men exchanged a look. 'Jump in,' ordered Joshua. 'We'll all get Matthew and then go home together.'

At the institute, Sam said, 'I'll bring him out, Martha, it'll be quicker.'

Matthew came at a run, his working shirt unbuttoned at the neck and his hat rammed over his eyes. 'Try and keep calm,' Joshua advised. 'The lad's no more than twenty minutes late and we all know they like each other's company. Happen they're playing in the stable loft or something.'

'No they're not,' contradicted Martha. 'Our Rosie's been told not to.'

Matthew glared at her. What did it matter if they played together morning, noon and night? She was missing, wasn't she? 'Did her go wanderin' off?' he asked abruptly.

Martha was indignant. 'D'you think I'm an imbecile? She was just playin' with her ball, like she always does. It wasn't rainin' when she went out.'

Joshua remained silent. It didn't strike him as odd that they were arguing in front of him; Rosie was their child, their only child. His glance met Sam's and he whispered, 'Don't get alarmed. It doesn't look as if Ralph's behind it. He might fancy getting his hands on Charlie but he'd never be bothered with the little lass.'

At the house Joshua told Zacky to keep the carriage waiting, and the four of them went inside. There was no sign of the children but the servants were in the hall, with Lilah holding Rosie's shawl. She addressed Joshua rather than Matthew. 'Wherever they are, Rosie left this behind, in the shrubbery.'

The three men looked at it as if they'd never seen a child's shawl before. His face pale, Matthew snatched it from her and held it pressed between his palms. He almost groaned aloud. God above – he'd wakened from his nightmare shouting for his little Rosie ... Suppose it had been a warning?

Joshua was moving into action, first of all sending Ellie running to fetch Zacky. 'Go down the road to Master Charles's music teacher,' he told him. 'If he's been delayed there you might meet him coming home; if not, ask what time he left and then come straight back.'

He turned to Matthew and Martha, knowing that between the three of them was once again the constraint of past hurts and past blame: a life-threatening attack and, long years before, the death of a baby boy ... 'Matthew,' he said, 'I can see you're on pins to get looking for her, so why don't you take Davey and check right round the field?'

'Me as well,' said Martha. 'I'm not stayin' here.'

Joshua eyed her. There was more to little Martha than met the eye. 'You must do as you see fit,' he told her, 'but stay together. Remember what happened the last time you were up there on your own, Matthew. If they're nowhere to be seen get your two men from the institute and bring them back here so we can organise a search of the immediate area.'

His face set, Matthew went out shouting for Davey. Martha followed him but the servants still hovered, waiting for instruction. They heard a cab pull up outside and James came indoors, back from an afternoon at Mosley Street. 'Ah, Father,' he said, 'd'you know what's happened at—' He saw them all waiting. 'What's wrong?' he asked warily.

Joshua hesitated but Sam spoke up. 'Charles hasn't come home and Rosie's missing as well. We think they must be together.'

James moistened his lips, then jerked his head at the study. 'Let's have a word.'

Joshua nodded. 'Ellie, Hannah,' he said, 'put your things on and go out round the streets. If you meet anybody, ask if they've seen the children, because most folk'll know my grandson by sight. Keep on reporting back in case they've come home – and stay together. Lilah, you're to stay here and be the link woman till they're found. Folk will be in and out of the house – you must pass on the latest news from one to the other and make hot drinks and quick bites to eat. We can't bring the police in yet – they've only been missing a half hour. Let's hope we don't have to do it at all.'

They went to the study and Sam closed the door. 'What do you think?' asked Joshua at once. 'Is it Ralph?'

James shook his head from side to side as if it was on springs. 'I don't know,' he muttered.

Sam was more definite. 'I think it is,' he said flatly. 'I feel it.'

Joshua sank into his chair. 'I should never have let him

come home on his own,' he said bitterly.

Sam bent over him. 'Did you ever think he might be in danger out on the town's streets? I certainly didn't.'

'No, not for a minute,' admitted Joshua. 'The attack on Matthew was because he caught somebody spying in a lonely place – I saw it as a kind of self-preservation on the spy's part. But there's one thing I should have remembered: Ralph hasn't much in common with me except that we can both recognise an opportunity when it stares us in the face. If he saw Charlie walking on his own, he might have snatched him on the spur of the moment.'

James was pacing back and forth. 'If we don't find him I'll have to send word to Esther.'

His father shot him a look and sighed. 'Aye, you will.' It was no use expecting much from James . . . Thrashing his wife and then leaving her seemed to have taken all the go out of him. He jumped up from his chair. 'Well, whether Ralph's behind it or not we won't find the children by sitting on our backsides. It's a possibility they've gone away from the town – happen up into the fields or somewhere. Let's take a look up the Holdwell road.'

Sam was already at the desk, scribbling a note. He had arranged to go down to Tizzie's at seven, but the way things were going he wouldn't be free by then, if at all. He opened the door and found Zacky coming through the hall. 'No sign of him, Mr Schofield,' the coachman reported. 'His teacher says he left at the usual time – just after five.'

'Stand by, then,' replied Joshua, 'in case we need you.'

'I need him now,' said Sam. 'Take this note to Mr Jellicoe at the pawnshop, will you? Tell him it's urgent. I've asked him to go in person to tell Miss Tizzie why I've been delayed. Come straight back here and follow us up the Holdwell road. We're setting off now.'

Zacky looked doubtfully at Joshua. 'Mr Schofield as well? It's a bit wet out there.'

Joshua snorted impatiently. 'Good God, man, I'm not in my dotage! Come on, you two – a drop of rain won't hurt us!'

They snatched top coats from the hall and left Lilah on her own, filling kettles and cutting bread for toast, all the while muttering in disapproval at Joshua going out in the rain.

Tizzie was in front of the big looking glass in her bedroom, almost laughing at herself for being so excited. Her wedding dress had just been delivered and she wanted to try it on without the dressmaker twitching and tugging at it.

Rebecca's daughter Naomi was helping her, flushed with satisfaction that her dear Miss Tizzie was to be married. Together they lifted the dress from its layers of soft muslin packing, Tizzie standing in her shimmy and stays and long silk drawers as they eased the ribbed ivory silk over her bright head. Naomi fastened the loops around the tiny covered buttons and eased the draping over Tizzie's slim hips. It had been made to her own design, the princess line again but with a simple front drape at thigh level caught up into folds at the back that gave just a hint of bustle; an elegant, graceful style – one for a bride who was sure of herself rather than a naive young girl.

Naomi sighed with pleasure. 'You do look lovely, Miss Tizzie, and with your flowers and all you'll be just like a picture from the fashion papers.'

Tizzie stared thoughtfully into the glass. She planned to carry a spray of apricot roses threaded with gold ribbon and to wear a cluster of the same flowers in her pinned back hair. Twelve years ago Sam had sent her roses in that very shade, tied with a trail of gold ribbons. To him they had been nothing more than a thank you for helping Sarah; to her they had been the first flowers she had ever received from a man. She hadn't told him what she'd chosen for her wedding flowers. Would he remember that long-ago bouquet? Probably not. At that time his mind had been full of Sarah's concerns.

'Miss Tizzie?' Naomi was repeating a question. 'Can I bring my mother up to see you?'

'Of course you can.' Mother and daughter had shared her domestic life for years, served her with devotion – it was fitting that they should have first view of the wedding dress.

As Naomi ran downstairs Tizzie heard the doorbell ring and a minute later she came back. 'It's Mr Jellicoe, Miss Tizzie. He says can he have a word?'

This was odd. Barney here at six o'clock on a Tuesday? 'All right,' she said, 'but tell him he'll have to wait.'

'He says it's urgent. He won't keep you a minute.'

Something was wrong at the shop! 'I'll see him now, then, up here – you must come up with him.'

Obediently Naomi went down again and returned with Barney lurching behind her as he manoeuvred the stairs. He was looking somewhat uncomfortable before he saw Tizzie, but at the sight of her in the gleaming silk dress, the colour drained from his face – he might almost have stopped breathing. Then she saw the telltale flush creeping along his jawline, evidence that he was upset. Fool that she was, she might have known that he would be touched to see her in her wedding dress, not to mention embarrassed at being up in her bedroom.

'I'm having a dress rehearsal for Saturday,' she told him lightly, 'but Naomi says you're in a hurry. What is it?' He was staring at the carpet as if he couldn't look up. Did he find the sight of her bed improper or something? There was no way she could tell what he thought of the dress.

He spoke in a singsong fashion as if he'd learned the words by rote. 'Mr Sam has asked me to bring a message in person, Miss Tizzie. He says he might not be able to come this evenin'.' His eyes flickered to Naomi, standing quietly in the doorway.

'You can speak in front of Naomi, Barney.'

'Aye, well, I was thinkin' you'd be able to sit down, like, but you're in your special dress . . .'

Tizzie felt as if the floor was tilting, a sensation that came to her only when she heard something awful. She held on to the edge of the wardrobe and said evenly, 'Quite right, Barney, it's silk and I don't want to crush it. Is – is Sam ill?'

'No, he's all right. It's Master Charles, He's – well – he's missin', an' so is young Rosie Raike. Only since a quarter past five, mind, but everybody's out searchin' round Meadowbank, so it's likely Mr Sam won't be here by seven o'clock.'

The floor straightened. Sam was all right. She felt light-headed with relief until the message registered. Charles missing? And Rosie Raike? 'Right,' she said briskly. 'I'll go up there as soon as I've changed my dress. Can I use your cab?'

'No. Mr Sam says you're to stay at home an' not go out.'

'He says what?'

Barney glanced at Naomi again and then stared up into Tizzie's eyes. 'He says the same folk might be behind this as were behind that do we had at the shop a while back.'

'Oh,' she said blankly and was ashamed to feel her lower lip trembling. 'Barney,' she said, 'oh, Barney – it's the wedding on Saturday.'

His big hand came out and clasped hers. Neither of them regarded it as familiar – they didn't even notice. All Tizzie knew was that comfort was coming from him – comfort and concern, the same as always. 'Can you stay for a while?' she asked. 'Have a meal with me and we'll talk?'

'Yes,' he agreed at once. 'An' – an' about your weddin' dress—'

She waited, trying to convince herself that it wouldn't matter if he didn't like it. He jerked his curly grey head and gave a tight little smile. 'I reckon it does you justice,' he said.

They ate beef patties with spiced beetroot, followed by apple fool. With Sam unavailable she found it bliss to be able to talk to Barney, to ask his views on this latest happening, to find out whether he thought the Schofield men should have guarded young Charles against abduction.

He shook his head. 'We don't know yet what's happened, but if he's been taken by force they could hardly have foreseen that he'd be snatched from a Saltley street at a quarter past five when it wasn't even dark. His father and grandfather can't be blamed for that.'

'But if he's been abducted then so has Rosie Raike. She's a nice little thing, Barney; sweeter natured by far than our Elizabeth. At the party I could see at a glance that they both liked Charles. Rosie's liking showed genuine affection but Elizabeth's – I'm sorry to say it, but she seemed overimpressed by the fact that he's a Schofield.'

'I've told you before,' he said gently, 'you were like her when you were the same age an' you're not so bad now. Give her time – she'll be all right.'

Tizzie poured more tea for them both and fidgeted on her chair. 'Can you think of anything I could do to help?' she burst out. 'Sitting here just waiting is making me feel ill!'

He considered. 'You want to help?'

'Of course I do! I've told you everything I know about what Ralph's done in the past – you know as much as me.'

He looked at her gravely. 'In my opinion he's a very dangerous man – an evil man. I suspect he's kidnapped Charles to hold him for ransom. If you want to help you can do it best by followin' Sam's advice – stay at home out of danger. Don't forget you recognised Ralph in Manchester and he might be holdin' that against you. He's killed once and got away with it so he might try it again. If you're safe Mr Sam can direct all his energy to findin' the boy without worryin' about you. His note to me said as much.'

That didn't appeal to Tizzie at all. Was she some sort of liability that she must sit behind locked doors until Sam swooped down to guard her? 'What do you think, Barney? Is that your advice as well?'

He gave that odd little smile again. 'My advice is that you keep out of danger, Miss Tizzie. Mr Sam says he'll send word as soon as there's any news.'

Soon afterwards she waved him off to go back to his

work at the shop then sat in front of the fire concocting audacious schemes to rescue a kidnapped child, her frustration mounting by the minute.

Joshua jumped out of the carriage and waved Zacky away. 'Come back in quarter of an hour to take me back to the others.'

The coachman trundled away to change horses and left his master climbing the front steps. Joshua hesitated outside the door for a minute, deep in thought. How often in his marriage had Rachel warned him not to walk around in wet clothes? Dozens of times, so for once he was doing what she'd always told him: he would change his wet shoes and put on his heavy old coat with the waterproofed shoulders. Happen Lilah would have a bit of news from the others and he'd get something to eat, as well. When he was famished his brain seized up like an engine starved of oil.

The smell of toast met him as he entered the house but Lilah didn't appear. The gaslight flickered in the draught from the door and he saw that nobody had thought to light any of the lamps nor to turn up the gas in the other rooms. 'Lilah!' he bellowed and slung his coat on a chair. He was half ashamed to be feeling so hungry when his grandson might be lying out in the dark fields or worse – aye, much worse, but that didn't stop him heading for the kitchen.

In the shadowed area at the foot of the stairs he tripped over what he thought was a bundle of wet clothes. Irritably he kicked at it and felt dread rise like bile in his throat. It wasn't a bundle of clothes, it was somebody on the floor. His heart leapt and juddered in his breast as he bent lower. God *above*, it was Lilah!

Joshua fell to his knees and willed himself to look before he touched. She was face down. Her white apron was hidden beneath her and her bony legs were splayed, the thick black stockings on view up to the knee. Hastily he straightened her skirts. There was no sign of injury, thank God; her long plain face was peaceful, as if in sleep, her white cap tilted over one ear. He fumbled for a pulse and let out a groan of relief when he found it beating, weak but regular.

He felt a drift of air on the back of his neck and stiffened. Were they alone in the house? He bent over her protectively, but there wasn't a sound apart from his own uneven breathing, the faint hiss of the gas jets and the rattle of a kettle lid as water boiled in the kitchen.

Gently he turned her over. It was then he saw the blood on her temple and a dark patch of it on the carpet, evidence that she'd been struck with some force. His restraint deserted him. 'Lilah!' he cried hoarsely. 'Don't die, Lilah! Oh, God, don't let her die! Lilah, can you hear me? Speak, Lilah, talk to me!'

He was suffering again the anguish he'd felt when Matthew had been injured, but this time it was worse, much worse; it had happened in his own home and to a woman, to Lilah, salt of the earth. It was Ralph's doing, he was certain of it. The taint of him was in the air around them. He could smell it.

In desperation he bowed his head and, still kneeling, challenged his maker out loud. 'How can you let this happen to a good woman?' he demanded angrily. 'What has she done to deserve it? You know as well as I do that it's Ralph's work! Well, let me remind you he's your creation as well as mine and Rachel's. We conceived him in love, and we'd been taught that you made man in your own image – so what about that, eh?' The bitter reflections of a thousand sleepless nights clarified as they spilled from his lips, muttered at first and then rising to a shout.

'Ralph's done this and he'll have to pay! No New Testament stuff like turning the other cheek; it'll be the Old Testament pure and simple – an eye for an eye. I'll report him to the authorities for killing Charlie Barnes – I don't care any longer about the family name, whether it's more to be chosen than great riches and so forth. Do you *hear* me? *Don't let her die!* If this good woman dies I'll never set foot in Albion Chapel again!'

He slumped against the newel post that Matthew had

once carved with such pride. His throat felt dry, and he
realised that he'd been shouting out loud, ranting and
raving at God when a woman could be dying in front of his
eyes. Remorsefully he patted her wrist and then touched
her cheek. 'Lilah', he whispered, 'it's me, Mr Schofield.
Don't die and leave me, Lilah.'

The eyelids flickered, opened for an instant and closed
again. He imagined that her lips moved in the semblance
of a smile, because for an instant he glimpsed her strong,
beautiful teeth. There was a faint pressure on his fingers
and he realised that he was still holding her hand. He left
her and ran for a cushion from the little sitting room,
coming back to slip it under her head. He patted her wrists
again, telling himself that that was what they did when
women fainted. 'Lilah,' he said again, 'it's me.'

She opened her eyes and saw his face only inches away.
'I'm all right,' she said faintly. 'He hit me, you know, he
hit me hard. Have you changed out of your wet things?'

He swallowed hastily. God above, he'd be weeping in a
minute! 'Who was it, Lilah?' he asked urgently.

'I come in the hall to turn the lights up an' I caught him
on the stairs. I shouted at him an' he hit me with somethin'
. . . just here.' She lifted her fingers a mere half inch, as if
believing she was touching her temple.

'Who was it?' he asked again. 'Did you know him?'

'No,' she said. 'I'd never seen him before, but he'd had
the smallpox.'

Rosie squeezed herself under an overhang of gorse and
new bracken and found to her surprise that it was sheltered
from the rain. She was desperately tired and her ankle hurt
so much she could hardly bear to put it to the ground. She
thought it was broken; she'd been thinking as much for
hours. It had happened soon after she'd turned for home,
jumping in weary triumph from clump to clump of the
tough grass, until she fell with a crash down a gully,
landing with her foot bent under her. The pain had been
awful, but it had got worse and worse every time she'd put

her foot down. She had cried; she couldn't help it.

Then, when she'd tried to continue her journey home, she had been terrified to find how little progress she made. If she didn't get home soon nobody would know where they'd taken Charles. For the first time she wondered what her mam had thought when she didn't come running when she called.

For what seemed an eternity Rosie tried to hobble across the bumps and boulders, watching out for dips and hollows. She couldn't see where she was going, and she was frightened that she would lose direction altogether. Suppose she walked in a ring and ended up going away from Saltley instead of towards it?

It was still raining and she was very cold, but beneath her wet bodice burned the urge to tell everybody where Charles had been taken. She knew she was getting confused, that her mind was mixed up, and she couldn't help crying again. Her pinny was all wet and horrible where she'd wiped her face and her eyes and her nose. It was then that she found the sheltered place and decided to stop for a minute. If she rested her ankle it might get better and then she could go on. Perhaps if she pulled tufts of grass and shoots of new ferns and things she could cover herself up and then, after a minute or two, carry on? It was very nearly dry under the overhanging gorse and heather. There was even a boulder or two to lean on, not that she would stay there, of course. She would never, ever go to sleep while Charles was in danger ... but it was hard to keep her eyes open when all she could see was the dark. Oh, if only her ankle would stop hurting ...

The doctor had been and Lilah was in her bed, being watched by Hannah in case her vision altered or she started to vomit, ominous signs that must be reported at once. Ellie was in the kitchen with Davey's wife, preparing food and drink for folk as they reported back from their searching.

Belatedly, Joshua made for his room to change his footgear, thinking that by now it might well have dried on his feet. James and Sam would be back soon, but already he had made his decision and talked to the police. In half an hour the chief constable of Saltley would arrive and in the meantime four policemen stood guard around the house. No more concealment, he told himself, no more sweeping things under the carpet, no more innocent folk being put at risk.

Wearily he opened the door to his room – his and Rachel's. The fire was still burning brightly; somebody must have made it up earlier. Not bothering to turn up the light he was crossing to his shoe cupboard when the coals shifted and he saw a shaft of gold leap from his bed.

He whirled round. Charles's trumpet was lying on the quilt, its polished brass reflecting the flames of the fire. He knew at once that it was both a threat and a challenge. This was why Ralph had been on the stairs – he'd had the gall to walk through the door, into the house, up the stairs and into this room! As surely as if his blood was being brought to the boil in a stew pan, Joshua felt anger run white-hot through his body. The arrogant young sod! If he wanted to play cat and mouse he'd damn well show him who did the stalking and who the running.

He grabbed the trumpet to see that it wasn't damaged and there, curled in the open end of the instrument, was a sheet of paper. A letter! With energy born of rage he leapt to the nearest gas jet and turned it up. Then he began to read.

'Here is the trumpet. The trumpeter will be delivered in instalments, to various addresses, unless these instructions are followed exactly:
1) If you have informed the police, fob them off with a feasible tale. There must be no bumbling policemen cluttering the scene. At present your little trumpeter is terrified but still in one piece.
2) Attend Messrs Hickory and Putnam, Solicitors, of Quay Street, Deansgate, at 2pm tomorrow. They have ready for your signature papers that make Ralph

Schofield the sole owner of Jericho Mills and all your visible assets. They also hold a new will, in case of your accidental death before the transfer goes through, disinheriting your other children in favour of the son you disowned and transported. These documents have been verified as being legal once your signature has been affixed and witnessed. No mention must be made of the fact that you are being persuaded to sign.

Quay Street will be watched to ensure that you arrive no later than 2pm tomorrow, a time that will allow you ample opportunity to reflect on the above. If you do not comply in every detail with these instructions, the first instalment will be delivered to an appropriate place at four o'clock tomorrow afternoon.

Do not doubt that I will carry out this threat. I dealt with Charlie Barnes and will do the same with his namesake, though in the boy's case ensuring a far more painful and prolonged departure.'

It wasn't signed. Sick with rage, Joshua stared at the impersonal, unidentifiable handwriting. Ralph had lost none of his cunning; no signature meant no admission that would stand up in a court of law. Joshua's neck began to ache and he found his teeth clenched so tightly that the tendons of his throat were standing out like ropes. Almost reeling with anger he made for the stairs. There would be plenty to talk about when Sam and James returned.

CHAPTER FIFTEEN

The Reply

James and Sam came in tired, wet and stunned, having heard from Zacky about the attack on Lilah. Joshua insisted that they consumed tea and eggs on toast before he took them to the little sitting room and showed them the letter. They read it together, heads bent intently.

'God in heaven!' said James, groping for a chair.

'The heartless swine!' roared Sam, pushing up his sleeves as if preparing for a bout of fisticuffs.

Joshua was pacing the floor, unable to keep still for a second. 'If he thinks I'll obey that lot he's off his horse and on a bloody donkey!' he said. 'For a start, the chief constable's due here in a quarter of an hour. And I—'

'Steady on,' interrupted Sam, rereading the letter. 'Let's not be hasty. Ralph's got Charles and he always was a cold-blooded devil. James, the boy's your son – read it again!'

Grey faced and haggard, James studied the letter minutely, as if expecting to find the key to a code hidden between the paragraphs. Joshua and Sam watched him, one still seething, the other increasingly grim.

Quietly James tapped the letter. 'Does anything strike you as odd about this?' he asked.

'Odd?' echoed his father. 'It's the work of a maniac, if you call that odd.'

James shook his head. 'There are two children missing,'

he pointed out, 'but there's no mention of Rosie. Ralph hasn't got her – he can't have, or he'd have used her as a pawn, a bargaining point, the same as he's using Charles.'

They both stared at him. Joshua stopped his pacing and sat down in the blue chair, stroking the worn velvet as he observed his eldest son. James had the closest blood tie to the boy and the gentlest nature of the three of them; there was no stamping and shouting with him, no aggression, yet in his quiet way he had seen what should have been obvious to Sam and himself. His very appearance betrayed his mental turmoil yet he'd been the one to think of the little lass.

Joshua shifted in the chair and felt a faint warmth ease its way around his heart, displacing the bitter anger. James would never set the world on fire, but he was good – hadn't he always known it? Hadn't Rachel said as much many a time?

'You're right, Jimmy,' Sam told him with remorse. 'How could we have missed that?'

Joshua laid a hand on James's shoulder. 'Thanks, lad,' he said. 'I can see it's time I calmed down and started using my head. Now, are we to call off the police?'

James spoke up again. 'Call them off for Charles, keep them on for Rosie.'

'The men could be moved from round the house, at any rate,' advised Sam. 'Have a word with the chief constable when he comes.'

Joshua pulled at his whiskers. 'I've known Nathan Makin since he was a lad,' he said. 'He's got to his position through honesty and hard work, the same as I've got to mine. I've a mind to tell him the truth.'

At once Sam thought of Tizzie. She'd vowed to stand by the family, to fight, but she was going to get more than she'd bargained for if it was made public that her brother-in-law was both murderer and kidnapper. 'You're going to tell him how Uncle Charlie died?' he asked, stunned. 'And that your son is holding your grandson to ransom?'

Joshua's eyes were sombre beneath the bushy white

brows. 'Aye,' he said simply, 'I'm going to tell him. He's got a brain, has Nathan; he'll not put the lad in more danger than he's in already. I'll talk to him and when he's gone we'll all discuss the terms of the letter.' He turned to James. 'Are you content to leave Sam and me in charge while you go up to High Lee to tell Esther? We'll take no action without you unless we're forced to it.'

James was going for his coat. 'I've asked Zacky to get me a cab,' he said. 'I reckon you'll need your carriage here.'

Joshua nodded grimly. 'I want Matthew and Martha brought back to see me. I'll have to tell them the truth.'

This time neither James nor Sam queried what particular truth he was going to tell. Their father's face declared that concealment was at an end. 'Sam,' he said now, 'I'd like a couple of minutes to prepare myself for seeing Nathan. Will you go and help Zacky to find Martha and Matthew and come back here with them? After that I want to talk to you – and to have a good think. I might have calmed down a bit but that doesn't mean I'm giving in, not by a long chalk.'

His father's expression reminded Sam of how he had looked in the days following the death of his mother. Then he had outwitted Ralph with no help from anybody. This time, though, Ralph held the winning hand: he had Charles. What option did they have but to follow his instructions and lose Jericho? With his heart lying heavy as a stone, Sam went off to see Zacky.

Minutes later, Hannah announced the chief constable of Saltley and Nathan Makin walked in, thickset and confident. 'Joshua,' he said, 'how are you?'

'Less than middling, Nathan; a lot less. Sit you down, I've got a few things to tell you . . .'

Sam and Zacky discovered the searchers scouring the hedgerows and coppices above the institute. They brought them back along with Billy Warhurst and Jonas Carter, who stayed in the kitchen for food and drink while Sam took Martha and Matthew to see his father.

Joshua offered Martha a chair, but she waved a dismissive hand. 'I'm sorry Mr Schofield, I can't sit me down. I'm that worked up, an' in any case I'm wet through.' Hoarse from calling Rosie's name, she was mouthing her words and using her hands as if she was in the weaving shed again.

Matthew also had reverted to earlier days, falling back on the speech of his native county. 'Have 'ee any news?' he asked impatiently. Mr Schofield had sent for them, hadn't he, pulled them away from their searching, so he must have a reason for that.

'I've just had the chief constable here,' Joshua told them. 'He advises us to call off the search of the countryside until daylight, but he's put his men out in the town, asking quietly round the streets. He thinks it unlikely that she's far from Saltley.'

'She?' pounced Matthew. 'Don' 'ee mean "they", Mr Schofield? What's agoin' on?'

Joshua let out a breath that was full of pain. 'We've had a communication,' he said heavily. 'My grandson's been kidnapped and he's being held to ransom.'

They both gaped at him. Martha sank to the proffered chair, wet shawl and all.

Joshua went on, 'The kidnapper hasn't mentioned Rosie at all, so we're almost sure he didn't take her.'

'Very thoughtful of him,' said Matthew. 'What did he do, then? Throw her away like a bag o' rubbish?'

Martha's little face was pinched and very white. 'If he didn't take her, then where is she?'

'They're both connected,' announced Matthew with certainty. ''Tain't no coincidence that the boy's been kidnapped at the same minute our liddle Rosie vanishes. Her wouldn't go awanderin' for no reason. Another thing: why's the constables goin' about it quiet? Why bain't they ashoutin' through the streets?'

'Because the ransom note says we're to call off the police,' said Joshua. 'That's one of the instructions. If we don't do as he says my grandson will be maimed and then killed.'

At that Martha let out a wail and Matthew dropped to his knees at her side, taking her cold hands in his. 'If they bain't together, she'll be safer,' he assured her, but Martha slumped in the chair, weeping with fear and exhaustion.

Still kneeling, Matthew asked, 'Who's took him? A madman?'

Sam was standing by the door and at his father's enquiring look he nodded, as if to say, 'Go ahead.'

'Mad or sane, the kidnapper is my son,' said Joshua quietly. 'The son I disowned some years back. His name is Ralph.'

Pictures jumped from Matthew's memory, clear and in sequence like paintings in a well-lit hall. It was the summer of '64 and his first day in Saltley. He'd been on the waggon that took raw cotton to Jericho Mills – the first American cotton to come through in years. Mr Schofield had been there to meet it with his four children, all dressed in their best. One, a beautiful blond youth, had followed his father around the mill yard, listening to his every word and watching his every move with eyes that were blue as cornflowers and as lifeless as two stones.

Matthew remembered asking himself if perhaps the lad was a bit lacking. Then all at once the empty blue eyes had been turned on him and he'd known that he wasn't lacking at all; just different – oh, yes, very different.

Now he looked with pity at his employer, feeling the familiar closeness, the desire to serve him. 'I'll do all I can to help 'ee get the boy back, soon as our Rosie's safe.'

Joshua nodded. 'I'll remember that. It's up to you both what you do next, but happen you should change your clothes and get some food inside you before you go out again. It's well into April so even if she's out in the open she's not likely to be suffering too much from the cold, only the wet.'

Martha got to her feet and trudged to the door, but Matthew turned back to Joshua. 'I be mortal sorry 'bout it bein' your son,' he said quietly.

Joshua eyed him gravely. 'I'm mortal sorry about young Rosie, as well. Let me know as soon as you find her, no matter what time it is. There'll be no sleep here tonight.'

Back in the cottage Martha poked the fire and set the kettle among the coals. She found some onions she'd boiled hours earlier and chopped up in milk, so she put the pan on the fire and after a minute added cheese. 'Come on,' she said quietly. 'Have a bowl of this an' a new muffin. It'll put some go in you.'

Neither of them remarked on what Joshua had told them; his revelation had merely added more unreality to an already unreal situation. Martha buttered an oven-bottom muffin and gave it to him, then brewed the tea. His dark eyes met hers and she shivered at the dread in them. 'We're not goin' to lose her!' she said sharply.

'Aren't we?' For the life of him he couldn't hold out hope. He shovelled the savoury mixture into his mouth and looked round the cosy little room in wonder. What were they doing feeding their faces when the child might be at death's door? She might be held in some house of vice in Manchester; she could be being bundled aboard a ship in Liverpool at this very minute; she could be being savaged by wild dogs out on the moors . . . And no matter what Mr Schofield might say, she could be being held captive by that mad son of his.

There was a knock on the door. They both rushed to answer it and found Billy and Jonas standing on the wet cobblestones. 'We're goin' home for some dry clothes,' said Billy, 'then we'll be back.' Weariness had settled on each of them like a cloak. They were no longer young, and they'd been on their feet since before six that morning.

'No,' said Matthew. 'The police have said we should stop searchin' the fields till it's daylight. Go back home, both of you, an' get a night's sleep. I'll send word right away if she's found. And thanks, lads.'

Martha stared after them as they left the yard. How she used to resent it in the early days when Matthew gave money to Billy and his family ... How impatient she'd been when they walked to the mill of a morning and he used to linger, staring down the long, crisscrossed streets in case Jonas was waving to him from under some distant lamp ... They were both so much older than Matthew, yet now he was their boss and they thought the world of him.

Matthew was putting on dry trousers in front of the fire. She bundled the washing-up into the slop stone and left it there, then found dry stockings and a different skirt for herself. 'Is Davey still helpin'?' she asked. 'He's got a better voice for shoutin' than either of us.'

Matthew was lighting a lantern. 'As long as he shouts for Rosie an' not Charles. For the boy's sake we don't want his uncle to mistake who we're lookin' for.'

It was still raining as they made for the fields again.

'He's *what*?' Esther was in the drawing room, her illustrated paper tossed to one side.

'I say he's been kidnapped. For a ransom.' James had dreaded telling her, but now they were face to face all he could think was that he should be at Meadowbank with his father and Sam, making decisions. He would give anything and everything to save Charles, but he knew that handing the mill to Ralph would be enough to kill his father. He told himself that Esther seemed devastated, so happen she had some feeling for the boy, after all.

'When?' she asked tightly. 'Why? How? Who's taken him?'

'Sit down, Esther,' he said gently. 'We think it happened on his way home from his trumpet lesson – just after five o'clock. We know why – for the ransom. How? In a vehicle, I suppose; folk would have intervened if they'd seen him being dragged through the streets. At first we weren't desperately worried – we thought he'd wandered off with Rosie.'

'Rosie? The Raike child? I knew it! That's what comes of living in that easy-going house. He's being allowed to mix with *her* again – a gardener's daughter!'

James flapped his hand as if brushing away a trouble-some fly. 'The girl is missing as well, Esther. I have to tell you that Charles's life has been threatened. If we make a wrong move he'll be mutilated, maybe killed.'

She blinked and clutched at the arms of her chair. 'What do you mean, a wrong move? Your father can pay the ransom, can't he? Everybody says he's the richest man in Saltley. It'll be no use asking Papa – I haven't seen him since just after you left me. How much do they want?'

'All my father's assets including Jericho Mills. He has to sign a new will, as well, disinheriting Sam, Sarah and me.' He fell silent and took a deep, uneven breath.

'In favour of who?' she asked keenly.

'My brother Ralph.'

'Ralph? In Australia?' She eyed him closely and clicked her teeth together, a sure sign that her mind was racing. He reminded himself that she could be uncommonly shrewd. 'Who's taken Charles?' she asked. 'Don't tell me Ralph – he's a nonentity.'

A nonentity ... in other circumstances James might have smiled. 'I wish he was,' he said soberly. 'It's Ralph who's taken him, right enough. He's been back in England for some months. We think it was one of his men who attacked Matthew Raike. He's been behind the vandalism in various mills, the poor consignments of cotton for Jericho, the books going missing at Mosley Street and such—'

'You never told me about that,' she said angrily. 'He must hate your father. What has he got against him?'

'He had Ralph transported,' James told her bleakly. 'That's how he went to Australia – under duress.'

Esther's eyes swivelled from side to side as if she was expecting somebody to appear and challenge what he was saying. 'You never told me,' she said again.

'No. We weren't communicating, even then.'

'Why did your father send Ralph away?'

James looked at her wearily. 'Because he had murdered my uncle Charlie.'

At that Esther's mouth stretched wide, baring her little white teeth. She looked like a cat halted mid-spit. James told himself he should feel sorry for her, having to hear such news when her son was missing, but all that mattered was that they were wasting time.

'I'm married to the brother of a murderer,' she said limply. 'I can't believe it – I simply can't believe it. Who else knows of this?'

'Until today just Sarah and Francis, Sam and Tizzie, Barney Jellicoe and me.'

She digested that, and hard, bitter creases appeared at either side of her mouth. 'Why the dwarf?'

'Sam thought he should know who set fire to the pawnshop.'

'Arsonist as well as murderer and kidnapper,' she said acidly. 'And why do you say "until today"?'

'Because my father may decide to tell the police about what Ralph did and then make it public knowledge. He's tired of subterfuge and guarding the family name. He wants to confront Ralph openly.'

'After Charles is safe or before?'

'I don't know yet,' he admitted. 'I came to tell you, Esther, and I've done that. Now I must get back.'

'Wait,' she said, putting out a small hand that was heavy with rings. He braced himself for her request to go back to Meadowbank with him. He could hardly refuse . . . Charles was her son as well as his. But what she said was, 'Have you had second thoughts?'

'About what?'

'About leaving me on my own in this great barn of a house.'

'You wanted the house,' he reminded her, 'and you're not alone – you have ten servants. But yes, I've had second thoughts, and third, and fourth and fifth.'

'You have?' If she was eager to know what they were, she concealed it very well.

'My thoughts are that I was right to leave you and a fool not to have done it years ago. I haven't regretted it for a single minute. In fact, I've been wondering whether there's any possibility of divorce. All that will have to wait, of course, until Charles is safe.'

'If ever he is,' she said venomously.

There was no answer to that. He walked out of the room in silence and boarded the waiting cab.

They were almost at Meadowbank before he recalled what she had said about her father. Had the doting Ephraim withdrawn his support after years of indulging her every whim? Happen he didn't like his daughter being a deserted wife. He would like it even less when she had to manage with a couple of servants in a modest little house ... and no doubt he would be apoplectic when he knew that her husband's brother had kidnapped her son.

James sat back and thought about the ransom demand.

It was half past two in the morning. James had gone off to his room saying he would try to sleep for an hour, but the other two knew quite well that he could never rest, let alone sleep. The truth of it was that he needed to get away from the endless discussion on the demands of the ransom.

Sam and Joshua were still arguing, each switching their opinion as they listened to the opposing point of view, then coming up with a fresh line of thought, then switching back again.

Sam eyed his father's ravaged face with deep concern. 'Why don't you go and get into bed for a bit,' he suggested. 'Even if you can't sleep it'll do you good to lie down, then when you get up you can have a bath and put on fresh clothes. It won't alter the situation but you'll feel a bit better.'

Joshua rubbed his hands over his face. 'It's a fact I could do with a change of clothes,' he admitted, 'but sleep? I don't sleep much at the best of times, Sam; I've not slept through the night since your mother died. Put some more coal on the fire, will you, then I might nod off in the chair for ten minutes. Not that we're much further forward, are we?'

'No,' agreed Sam, 'but like I say, I can't see we've any option but to give him what he wants.' Not for a second did he think that his father didn't care about Charles. He cared, oh, he cared, but he also cared for twelve hundred workers.

'Give way to Ralph and he'll think he's got the world in a bant,' he'd said earlier. 'He'll come to believe that he can get away with murder and abduction – that they're allowable. Listen, if he gets Jericho he'll sell it for ready money and the same will happen as happened to Johnny Darwell's mill at the other side of Hyde. A business consortium bought the Stronghold and turned it into a sweatshop overnight. His workers stayed on, eight hundred of 'em, because there weren't any other jobs in the town, but one by one the young ones found work elsewhere and moved away. The rest stuck it, falling ill and wearing themselves out for a pittance, and not a single law was enforced to protect them.

'They do a lot of prating in Parliament, a lot of putting new statutes on the books, but when it comes to the wellbeing of the workers, money still talks louder than fair play. I'm sorry, lad, but I can't stomach the thought of handing my workers over to Ralph. He'd sell them to the highest bidder.'

Sam agreed with every word, but he didn't see how they could juggle with Charles's life. 'I'm going for a wash,' he said shortly, 'then I'm going to see Tizzie.'

'It's a bit late for that – or early, whichever way you look at it,' protested Joshua.

'She has two women in the house to chaperone her,' retorted Sam. 'She'll be waiting up to see me – I know she will. I'll be back in an hour or so. Now, Ellie's sitting with Lilah and the others are snatching a rest, so shall I make you a pot of tea before I go?'

Joshua looked at him as if he'd offered to fly to the moon. 'Can you manage that?' he asked with interest.

Sam smiled for the first time in nine hours but concealed it behind his hand. 'Aye,' he said drily, 'if I put my mind to it.'

Having presented his father with tea and a piece of parkin, he saddled up and set off on horseback for Farthing Lane, blessing the day they'd decided to keep old Dancer as well as the two carriage horses. He rode with care over the deserted cobblestones, so intent on getting to Tizzie he didn't even notice that the rain had ceased, leaving a pale half-moon riding the departing clouds.

At Meadowbank Joshua was still sitting in the blue velvet chair, thinking, thinking, thinking. The white heat of his rage had long given way to a cold, deadly anger that filled his innards with the determination to fight, and to win. He knew why James had gone to his room: he couldn't bear to hear arguments for and against risking his son's life, but even he was leaving the final decision to his father.

Joshua recalled that over the last fifty years he had made countless decisions. They were part of his life and he didn't shilly shally about it. He would give a problem some thought and then do what he thought was right. In the main his decisions were proved to be correct – but now and again he'd been proved wrong and had had to put up with the consequences. Even then there'd been the consolation of having done what he believed to be right at the time.

Now he had to make a decision that was literally a matter of life and death: Charlie's life or Charlie's death. If he was wrong there'd be no consolation – ever. He groaned aloud and wrapped his arms around his middle, rocking back and forth in the chair. At last he became aware of what he was doing and, slightly ashamed, fell silent and kept still, willing his mind to clarity and calm. He wanted to pray, but it was only hours since he'd bellowed at God and tried to make bargains; he'd even thrown in a few threats . . . How could he pray after that?

All at once it came to him that throughout his working life one of his prime rules had been: Never pander to villains; never appease, never condone. He'd lived by that principle and it had served him well. Was he to abandon it for ever? He thought of his grandson when he'd given them an advance performance of his music for the wedding, blushing slightly yet proud of his skills, his lips to the mouthpiece of the instrument. That trumpet, that golden trumpet . . . a modern-day version of the biblical trumpet that was Joshua's trademark, symbol of a lifetime's achievement. No, he would *not* sacrifice his life's work to the one who had taken from him both his wife and his best friend.

Then he thought of Charlie's small, nimble fingers on the valves of the trumpet, his Schofield eyes bright with the excitement of playing at his uncle's wedding. Joshua let out another groan. Was it too much to hope that Ralph had left a loophole in the legalities at Messrs Hickory and Putnam? Of course it was. He stood up and was stunned by the weakness in his legs. Weak or strong, he was left with no alternative but to do as he was told. For the first time since he set up in business he would have to take orders instead of giving them.

Matthew sat in his chair and looked at his wife. Limp and exhausted, she had fallen asleep against the cushions of the wicker chair that had been her mother's. He had eased off her clogs and then her stockings, wrapping her small cold feet in the little blanket that had been first on Luke's cradle and then on Rosie's.

Martha looked young in sleep and he thought that was strange; she looked every one of her thirty-eight years when she was awake – more in fact, since Rosie had disappeared. Inevitably, his mind centred on his daughter again. What was it about him that brought disaster to the children he loved? There'd been Dorcas, burned to a stinking black cinder in the stable loft while her big brother lay senseless from drink. And baby Luke, named for the man who had meant so much to his father, overdosed with laudanum by the child minder while Martha worked in the weaving shed to support them. And why did she have to do that? Because her husband had lost his job for striking a dirty old man; lost his job, then lost his son and nearly lost his wife.

He sighed so deeply his chest hurt, almost as if his heart was being dragged from its casing of ribs and muscle. Now it was Rosie, his beautiful liddle girl; lost, stolen away, maybe lying in a peat bog on the edge of the moors, maybe – oh, God – maybe a captive in the hands of that dead-eyed lunatic son of the Schofields.

He sat staring at the red heart of the fire, waiting for day to break. When he heard the distant crowing of a cockerel he leapt from the chair and went to the back window. The sky was clear, washed by the light of a half-moon, while from the opposite side of the heavens came the faint pearly glow that heralded day.

Quickly he put on his boots and shrugged into his still-damp coat. Then, on impulse, he reached into a cupboard for the wide-brimmed felt hat that he had not worn since the long-gone day when the wakes had left Saltley. Martha was still deep in sleep, so he closed the door quietly behind him, fingering the soft black felt above his brow. 'Twas funny the way the hat suited his head, suited his whole being. It sort of gave him confidence, and God alone knew he needed it when he thought of the land that was still to be searched.

To save time he scaled the high wall of the stable yard and dropped to the road, the sky opening up above him like the heart of a creamy-pink rose. A blackbird began to sing among the hawthorns and at the same moment he saw a figure coming towards him in the half-light, stepping out briskly from the direction of the town. He waited, hoping it was somebody coming to search. It was Billy, grey and grizzled and stiff in his joints, up well before dawn to be here by now.

'How do,' was his matter-of-fact greeting. 'I reckoned she hadn't been found, bein' as I'd heard nothin'.'

Matthew gripped the older man's hand. 'Billy, why bain't 'ee abed?'

Billy shook his head. 'Could I sleep when she were missin'? I have a memory, lad, a long memory. Many's the time my childer woulda gone to bed hungry but for you.

You helped me when we had neither money nor hope, an' now it's my turn. Where're we headin'?'

'Up the road for a mile or two. The police might not be comin' – I'll tell you all about that later.'

They moved on each taking a side of the dirt road, zigzagging to and fro across the rough grass, calling Rosie's name and standing on boulders and hillocks to survey the surrounding land. Matthew stared dubiously around him as the fields gave way to the gorse and gullies of the moor. Could she have got as far as this on her own, in the rain, when it was going dark? 'Ro–o–sie,' he called, while Billy echoed him time and again from a distant rise.

It was getting lighter by the minute, the bright banners of dawn streaming across a pearly sky. He thought he saw Billy waving his arms and then heard him yell, 'Matthew – over here!'

Beyond the other man he could just make out the shape of an animal, dark against the tufted grass. Then Billy was racing towards the creature, leaping the tussocks like a boy, one hand grabbing at his cap, the other outstretched to keep his balance.

Matthew's heart lurched. It wasn't an animal, it was Rosie, half crawling, half hopping. She was hurt, but she was moving: she was alive! He crossed the rough terrain as quickly as if it was the smoothest turf, to be met by Billy carrying the child in his arms. She was crying weakly, wearily; Billy was smiling through tears, but Matthew laughed out loud with joy and relief.

Billy held her out to him like an offering. She was shivering visibly, her face very white and streaked with mud. Matthew tried to clasp her to his chest but she screamed in agony. 'Me ankle,' she said hoarsely. 'I think it's broke.'

If that was the worst that had happened to her, he'd thank God for it, Matthew decided; he'd put his hand on the Bible he never read and he'd say a prayer of thanks. Carefully they both held her while he took off his coat and wrapped it round her, only then allowing himself to cover her face in kisses. 'Don' 'ee worry, liddle love,' he said tenderly, 'we'll mend that old ankle soon as we're home.'

'Be quick, Dad,' she cried suddenly, 'I have to tell 'em.' Then she giggled. 'I heard you, Mr Warhurst. I heard you shoutin' an' the birds were singin'. I knew I'd got to come out of me hidey-hole or you'd miss me.' She looked at Matthew, her eyes amazingly bright. 'It was hot in there, Dad, near the fire. There was a big kettle like me mam's an' I were bakin' bread in the oven, but me ankle kept hurtin'.' She started to cry again and wiped her nose on her sleeve.

They were almost back to the road. Billy was stumbling alongside, still smiling, but Matthew looked at his daughter in alarm. She was rambling! He bent to touch her forehead with his cheek and found it hot against his face. She had a fever! Of course she had, he told himself stoutly, she'd been out in the rain all night. 'Twas nothin' that a day in bed wouldn't put right.

'Where's Mr Schofield?' she asked impatiently. 'I have to tell him. I saw where they took him, I saw it! I saw the coach!'

She'd seen them take the boy! 'Clever girl!' he said, holding her tight. 'Don' 'ee worry, just snuggle up to your dad.'

She let out a laugh that sounded like some full-grown woman out of Gallgate: raucous and triumphant. 'I saw 'em!' she cried, and fell fast asleep.

As if she'd known they were coming, Martha was at the door, shedding overwrought tears when she saw Rosie safe and fast asleep. She stroked the dark damp curls and then hurried to make up a place for her on the sofa. 'Praise the Lord,' she muttered over and over. 'Where did you find her, then?'

'On the edge of Holdwell moor. She's feverish, love, an' she's hurt her ankle. I want that doctor who dealt with me to have a look at her, but first I'll get Mr Schofield. He wants to know as soon as she's found. An' Martha, it was Billy here who spotted her.'

To both Matthew and Billy's astonishment, Martha

stood on tiptoe and kissed the older man's cheek. 'Come on in,' she said, 'an' I'll make you some breakfast as soon as I've seen to Rosie.'

He shook his head. 'Nay, you've enough on your plate without seein' to me. I can brew up when I get to work. What about the lad, Matthew? Do they want help findin' him?'

'I don't think so, Billy. I can't say more till I've talked to Mr Schofield.'

'I'll be off to me work, then,' said Billy. With a satisfied grin he marched out of the yard and headed for the institute.

Matthew ran across to the house and found Hannah laying a breakfast tray. 'We've found Rosie,' he said. 'Mr Schofield wants to know, no matter what time it is.'

'Ee, thank God,' said Hannah. 'That's one of 'em safe.' She jerked her head towards the hall. 'They've been up all night. Mr James an' Mr Sam are in the study, still talkin', but Mr Schofield's on his own. Come wi' me – I'm takin' him his breakfast.'

He followed her solid, capable form to the little sitting room and found his employer standing with his back to the fire, freshly shaven and immaculately dressed but looking so drawn that Matthew was thankful to be bringing good news. Hannah put down the tray and left the room, but Joshua made no move towards the food.

'We've found Rosie, Mr Schofield,' said Matthew quietly.

Joshua sat down with a thud. 'Thank God,' he said, 'thank God. Is she all right?'

'Feverish, an' her ankle might be broken, but otherwise she's not so bad.'

At once Joshua rang the bell and Ellie rushed in. 'Tell Davey to fetch the doctor for Rosie,' he instructed, 'and later on he might have to get a cab to fetch Dr Billings from Miles Platting. Just warn him to stand by.' He turned to Matthew. 'Where was she?'

'Up on Holdwell Moor. Billy Warhurst found her; we

went up there at daybreak. Rosie wants to see you, Mr Schofield. She says she saw where they took Master Charles. She's feverish, though, an' ramblin' a bit. I don't know if—'

Joshua was already through the door and heading for the yard. 'Let me talk to her,' he said.

They hurried to the cottage and found that Martha had stripped Rosie of her wet clothes and was giving her a wash as she lay on the sofa. When they both walked in Martha wrapped her in a big towel, covering her bare chest. 'She's had a hot drink' she said, 'an' I'll be settlin' her down when I've washed her legs an' put her in a warm nightie ...' She fell silent, realising that Joshua was interested in something more.

Rosie stared up at him, her cheeks now a bright pink and her eyes glittering. 'I saw 'em, Mr Schofield,' she said. 'I ran an' I ran, all across the fields. I kept up, I did, I kept up with 'em.' She sneezed and Martha bent down and wiped her nose as if she was an infant.

Joshua sat next to her. 'Did you see them take him, Rosie?'

'Yes. Charles crossed the road in front of the house an' I were waitin' in our secret place. He reached the kerb, an' then a little coach raced up.' Tears coursed down Rosie's hot cheeks at the thought of what had happened next. 'A man jumped out an' picked him up – that ugly man I saw on the path. He picked Charles up an' threw him inside.'

Matthew and Martha exchanged startled looks, but Joshua just nodded. 'I see. What happened then?' He spoke gently, quietly, as if they were having an ordinary chat about something that interested them both.

'The man jumped in after him an' the driver cracked his whip an' drove round the corner into the Holdwell road. You couldn't see inside the coach – all the curtains were drawn ...' Rosie fell silent for a minute, then suddenly, disconcertingly, began to sing, high and clear and true. It was a hymn for Palm Sunday that she'd learned at Sunday school. '"Children of Jerusalem ..."'

Joshua waited until she reached the chorus, then looked in appeal to Martha. 'Can you calm her?' he asked. 'I've got to find out if she knows where they took him.'

Martha wrung out the flannel and gently wiped Rosie's hot face. 'Mr Schofield's here, love. Do you remember you had somethin' to tell him? You know, you were out in the fields and it was nearly dark. You were following that carriage, weren't you?'

'"Hark, hark, hark, while infant voices ..."' Rosie faltered to a stop and looked at Joshua, the light of reason ousting the glitter of fever in her eyes. 'I ran an' I ran, Mr Schofield,' she said earnestly. 'I shoulda told the grown-ups first, I know I should ...'

'You didn't have time, though, did you? Not if you were to see where they were taking him.'

She gave him a small, approving smile and took his hand. 'I had to see, didn't I? I were frightened they'd hurt him like they hurt me dad, so I climbed up high where I could watch the road. They didn't see me, though – they didn't know I were watchin'.'

'No, of course they didn't.' Joshua was sending up prayers of thanks so fast he could hardly manage to frame the next question. 'So did they go right along the road to Holdwell and High Lee?'

Rosie smiled pityingly and then sniffled. 'Course they didn't. They turned of along the little road that goes to High Holdwell. I watched 'em go an' then I started to run home.' She thrust out her lower lip. 'I wanted to tell the grown-ups but I fell down a hole an' I couldn't run any more. I couldn't walk, either, though I tried for hours an' hours.'

Joshua looked up at Martha and Matthew. 'I thank the Lord for this child,' he said, 'I do that.' Then he bent and kissed Rosie's cheek. 'You might have saved his life, love. Now I know which way he's gone I can start trying to find him, can't I? You're a brave little lass, and Charlie's fortunate to have you for a friend.'

He made for the door. 'Davey's bringing my own

doctor,' he told them. 'He'll know if you need Dr Billings to see to her ankle.' He shot a last look at Rosie. 'Cut the boot off,' he advised. 'She'll have the best pair in Lancashire to replace them.' He went out and they heard him shouting for Zacky, then the house door banged shut behind him.

'"Hark, hark, hark,"' sang Rosie, '"while infant voices sing . . ."' She didn't notice that her mother was crying and that her father was kissing her. She only knew that she was very hot and very thirsty, but all at once just a little bit happy.

James and Sam were in the study, reduced to voicing what had already been discussed at length. They'd been expecting something unpleasant to happen, Sam told himself, but not this. It had been thrust on them at a minute's notice, whereas Ralph must have been planning it for weeks, months – aye, maybe years.

'No decent lawyer would accept business such as Ralph has put in the way of Hickory and Putnam,' he said for the tenth time. 'Father is too well known for a respectable firm even to consider such a transaction.'

'They might not be respectable,' James said wearily, 'but Ralph will have checked that they'll be acting within the law – he said as much in his letter. Even if our own lawyer finds a loophole these legal battles can go on for months, and we haven't got months, have we? God only knows what's happening to Charles at this very minute.'

They fell silent again and Sam stared at the fire with red-rimmed eyes. It had been like a breath of fresh air talking to Tizzie. She'd been waiting up for him, fully dressed at half past two in the morning, her mind sharp as a razor, her eyes as clear as if it was noon. She'd been so matter-of-fact, so positive, that in minutes he'd found himself dismissing all thoughts of relinquishing Jericho.

He had related the contents of the letter almost word for word. 'How can Ralph be sure that once Charles is safe we won't go back on the agreement?' he'd asked her in bafflement. 'Father could go to law and say that he signed under threat, and I'm sure it could all be made null and void.'

'Not if Ralph still has Charles,' she'd argued. 'He said nothing in the letter about when you'd get him back. And what about that mention of your father's accidental death? It's a threat, surely? He intends to get what he wants, one way or another.'

'You think we should just give in?' he'd asked unbelievingly.

Tizzie had tossed her head so hard she'd scattered hairpins. 'Did I say so? I want to fight, of course I do, but how? One thing I'm sure of, Ralph won't release him until it's signed and sealed and irrevocable. Couldn't your father turn up at Quay Street as instructed and then delay signing on some pretext or other?'

They'd tossed ideas around but it had done little except to clarify his mind. She'd been desperate to come back with him but he couldn't have that – not while Ralph had the nerve to walk in through Meadowbank's front door . . . He'd ridden home in the moonlight with his spirits actually rising until he'd been confronted by James's grey face. How could they fight, how could they conduct a battle of wits when Charles's life was at stake?

Now he was thinking that they should try to eat some breakfast, when his father burst in. 'Rosie's found!' he announced. 'She's all right apart from a chill and a bad ankle, but wait till you hear what she told me—'

At Jericho the blower was sounding its customary warning that the engines would be switched on in five minutes' time, but Joshua had sent runners to the engine house, to the floor managers and overlookers, to every room in the two vast mills, ensuring that this was one day when the driving belts wouldn't start turning at six o'clock. Sam and James and a group of helpers were at the gates, directing operatives to the front yard instead of letting them go to their floors.

Joshua himself was pacing the opening between the tall sliding doors of the first-floor hoist, while far above him the flag leapt on a fitful breeze and then lay still.

Behind him was a group of overlookers, all grimly on edge and communicating with each other by a shake of the head or a twist of the mouth. They had all decided that there could be only one reason for not switching on and for getting the workers together like this: Jericho was closing down; Mr Schofield was going out of business. He looked bad; he looked terrible – they'd all remarked on it, but nobody had dared to question him. Normally the most approachable of bosses, when he got that particular look on his face you didn't ask questions, you just jumped to it and did as you were bid. He'd been issuing orders as he'd stepped from his carriage and before they knew it he had been whirling around the place like greased lightning, outpacing even Mr Sam and sending the runners here, there and everywhere.

Now he turned to Saul Bracewell. 'We won't get 'em all in the front yard, Saul, so those who can hear what I have to say must tell the others. So must you and your colleagues.' He took out his pocket watch and nodded to a burly foreman from East Side. 'Right, blow your whistle!'

At the shrill blast, the muttering throng fell silent. All that could be heard was the scuffling of clog irons and the concerted wail of six o'clock blowers from all the mills in Saltley.

Joshua waited until they fell silent and then leaned forward, one hand gripping the iron bar that fastened the doors. 'There'll be no work at Jericho today,' he bellowed, 'but you'll all be paid and your jobs aren't at risk.' There was a collective murmur of relief at that, then they waited.

'I have to tell you that my grandson, Charlie, has – has been—' To his mortification, Joshua found that he couldn't bring himself to say the word 'kidnapped'. He'd *have* to say it – it was the only word that fitted. 'Taken' ... 'abducted' ... They didn't have the same punch. 'My grandson has been kidnapped,' he managed.

A sound came from the crowd below him; a strange sound, made up of sighs and disbelieving groans and the repeating of his words to those who couldn't hear. 'Master Charles is kidnapped.' 'No work today, but we'll be paid.' 'The young 'un's been kidnapped.' A strapping young girl from the card room started to shout a question but was hushed by the women around her.

Joshua held up a hand for silence. 'You'll appreciate that I can't have the mill working a normal day when my only grandchild is being held to ransom, but there's another reason for not switching on.' He looked down at them all, men, women and children, most of whom he knew by name. A free day off would be like gold to them, he thought. Women with babies could get them back from the child minder or just go home and put their feet up; men could tend their strips of garden or make for the bar top when the public houses opened, because they hadn't all signed the pledge, not by a long chalk. He'd look a right fool if his idea didn't come off, especially after he'd said to James and Sam, 'We have assets that Ralph can't aspire to – twelve hundred of 'em – so let's ask for their help.'

He held up his hand again. 'Those who want to go off on their own concerns are free to do so, and it won't be held against them,' he shouted. 'But those who want to help can join us in searching the countryside. They'll have to be good walkers, but they mustn't go wandering off on their own, nor entering caves and such. We've been told which way he was taken, so my sons will give you directions.'

'I'll search, Mr Schofield!' cried a man standing next to the weaving shed. Joshua spotted at once that it was Johnny Barnes. Sarah had tended him years back when he was a young lad with his shoulders ripped to shreds in the spinning room; she'd be glad to know he was the first volunteer. But now others were shouting from all sides, women among them. 'I'll go, Mr Schofield.' 'Me an' all!' 'Count me in, Mr Schofield.' 'I'll go!' 'An' me.' 'An' me.'

His throat tight, Joshua let out a strangled sigh. They

were offering in droves – dozens of them, maybe hundreds – yet he hadn't even mentioned what the ransom was. If he'd told them that the mill was at risk he would never have known for sure whether they were helping him because of their regard or because of concern for their jobs.

He could see Sam at the back of the crowd, waving his hat in congratulation. James was there as well, one hand touching the enamelled trumpet on the mill gate, his stance saying, 'What are we waiting for? Let's start looking!'

Joshua held up his hand for the last time. 'My sons and their helpers will direct you. Anybody who has food and drink, take it with you; we haven't had time to organise that. Don't set off until you've been told where to go. Anybody who's bad on their feet mustn't attempt to join the search; it's rough ground. Nobody must search alone – the kidnapper could be dangerous. Follow the instructions you're given. We'll direct the searchers from coaches and carriages on the road. And thank you all.'

'Who's got him, Mr Schofield?' It was one of the boilermen asking, his face grimy from feeding the boilers since five o'clock. 'We'll bring him back to you in chains, once the lad's safe. Who's got him?'

There was a sudden silence, then Joshua spoke up clearly, filled with the sense of throwing aside a damp, heavy cloak that had weighted him down for years. 'My son has kidnapped him – the son I disowned and sent to Australia when he was eighteen years old. Some of you will remember him as young Mr Ralph.'

There was another silence, a stunned silence, until one of the women spoke up. 'We never liked him anyway, Mr Schofield.'

Nobody echoed her; they all looked shocked or uncomfortable, or both, but a good number were nodding their heads in agreement. Joshua stepped back and waved a hand in the gesture that was familiar to them all. 'Carry on,' he said, 'carry on. And once again, thank you.'

He headed for the mill stairs, brushing aside any who approached him. He'd had hours of absolute hell, he thought, so now he would snatch two minutes of self-indulgence, of balm to the spirit. Doggedly he climbed towards his vantage point on top of the tower.

It was quiet up there, with only the sound of the flag flapping and a metallic drumming as more than a thousand pairs of clogs passed out through the gates.

He leaned over the parapet and saw them surging like a brown-black tide over the grey of the cobblestones. Some were hurrying off to their homes, but not that many – no more than one in ten, he judged. The rest were being sent on their way by Sam and James, heading for the Holdwell road beyond Meadowbank. In two minutes the yard was empty except for the security men tramping their endless rounds. He had decreed that as long as Ralph and his henchmen were at liberty Jericho should stay under guard.

Zacky was at the gates, ready to take Sam and James speeding to the front of the crowd. They'd wanted Joshua to stay at home – in safety, they'd said, no doubt seeing the implied threat against him in the ransom letter. He'd almost laughed that they should think he'd agree to such a thing. All he needed was a couple of minutes up here to prepare himself for whatever might come. Then he had to see Kenworthy and check on Lilah . . .

Sam was making for the carriage and, as if it was prearranged, he looked up and saw his father beneath the flag, outlined against the brightening sky. He'd known he would be up there . . . In better spirits now that he was taking action, Sam swept off his hat and waved it.

Joshua saw the bare blond head and waved back, remembering with a twist of the heart how one day last summer he had waved to Charlie from this very spot after seeing him touching the trumpet on the mill gates. 'Your little trumpeter,' Ralph had called him . . .

Slowly he turned full circle, seeing first the town and its forest of tall chimneys, then the road that climbed past the baths and the institute to Jericho, then the hill side behind the mill with its little copses of trees and the path – their path – now banned to any who were unaccompanied.

Further round still was the meadow – the buttercup field as Charlie called it, then Meadowbank, square and solid with its gardens and big walled yard – no doubt Ralph was aiming to get that as well – and beyond it the road to the hills, to the moors and caves and gullies in the high ground between Holdwell and High Lee.

Restlessly Joshua pulled at his whiskers, filled with a sense of expectation, of approaching change. It would be change all right if by this latest move he lost his grandson; but he'd made no more threats to his God, done no more ranting and raving at him. He was just using the brain and the instincts that he'd been given; it wasn't his fault that he was being forced to use them against his own flesh and blood.

For another minute he stood there, trying to empty his mind of tension and fear. This was where it was easiest to talk to Rachel, not in words but in the language of the spirit. In life they'd communed as if they'd shared one mind and one heart; death had intervened, but to his limitless relief the communion had continued. Tranquillity entered his heart as surely as if she stood at his side with her hand warm in his. Wordlessly he spoke: I don't know if I've done right, love, but I had to try. When Rosie told me what she'd seen I simply had to try. Do you understand?

After a minute he nodded and gave a little smile. She understood. He felt it. That would be his only consolation if things went wrong.

CHAPTER SIXTEEN

The Consequences

It was morning. Charles could hear birds singing when the men opened the door to change places. He knew their names now; to each other they were Bill and Dick, but his uncle addressed them by their surnames. The little one was Bill Dyson and the tall, curly-haired one who must have driven the coach was Dick Hamer. He could tell they didn't know each other very well; sometimes he thought they didn't even like each other. The previous evening he'd been lying awake staring at the lamp when his uncle came back, his clothes wet through in spite of the big cloak, but in apparent good humour.

'Was everything in order, sir?' Dyson asked.

'All according to plan. No problems here? The boy has been obedient?'

'Yes, sir. No nonsense from him.'

'Good. The coach is well hidden? And the horses?'

'Just as you ordered, sir.'

'I'm off, then. I'll be back at seven in the morning.'

Dyson chewed his lips dubiously. 'Suppose somebody comes? You'll be well away – sir – but we'll be holdin' the lad.'

There had been a touch of insolence in that 'sir' and his uncle gave Dyson an empty stare. 'Nobody will come, it's pitch dark and pouring down, but if anyone did venture up here you would see them coming – they'd be sure to use lanterns. So, as I've told you a dozen times already, you would gag the boy and hide with him in the trees at the side. Can you get *that* through your head?'

'Sorry, sir. Just wanted it confirmed.'

'Well, confirmed it is. Do as you're told and you'll get your reward.'

He had gone out with a wet flap of his coat. A minute later Hamer came in for the changeover and the two of them hurried to share a big meat pie. They muttered together about money and Charlie guessed they were talking about their share of his ransom. Once Hamer said, 'He's a cold fish if ever I've seen one. I'm sick to death of him. I've had months of it an' though the pay's good I'd never have stuck it if there hadn't been promise of a hand-out.'

Dyson just shrugged. 'He's talkin' big money. When you've earned two bob a day cleanin' out ships' holds at the docks, a spell like this is a rest cure. The thought of that money's more than enough to keep me doffin' me cap an' sayin' "sir" to his lordship. Cold fish or hot potato – it's all the same to me.'

Charles recalled that it had made him feel sick with hunger to smell that pie, though Hamer did give him a thick bread crust. Bread and water – that was what they always gave to prisoners . . . Later he'd had to use the bucket, and Dyson had watched him so closely he'd fumbled with his buttons and nearly wet himself. The man's little black eyes glinted like new coal as he'd carried the bucket out and brought it back empty.

Charlie had tried to settle down but a scattering of straw wasn't enough to make a stone floor comfortable. Not only that, he kept thinking of things, such as why were none of them worried about him seeing their faces? Was it because they didn't intend that he should live to tell tales? They'd have to hand him over in exchange for the ransom, wouldn't they? He'd have to be alive for that or his father wouldn't pay.

Once, in the night, Hamer was sitting in the armchair scraping his nails with a pocket knife, so Charlie decided to risk a question. 'Excuse me, Mr Hamer. Do you know how long I'll be here?'

Hamer mimicked his tone of voice. 'Until your nice, kind uncle decides to move you.'

Charles thought for a minute and was conscious of a feeling deep inside him – a feeling of strength. He wasn't as frightened as he thought he'd be – perhaps he was getting like his grandfather Schofield and his uncle Sam, who weren't frightened of anybody – not his mother or even his Grandfather Buckley. He decided that it wouldn't hurt to unsettle Hamer a bit. 'I expect you know that people will be looking for me, Mr Hamer. My father and grandfather will be organising a search party.'

Hamer gave a bark of a laugh. 'They'll have their work cut out, then! Nobody knows where you are or where you're goin'. Bill Dyson an' me don't know the next move. Your uncle keeps his plans to himself.'

'But you could both be charged with kidnapping, couldn't you? They'd put you in prison for that.'

'Aye, they would if they caught us. Prison, hangin', floggin', what's the odds? Listen, I've had nothin' all me life – nothin'! No grandad as owned a cotton mill an' sent me to music lessons, no big house with an army o' servants, no good clothes like you're wearin'. I've been treated like muck since the day I were born – so what's the odds? I can take a risk an' I can take the consequences.'

There had been a bitter bravado to his words. Charles had inherited his father's tender heart and saw something in the set of Hamer's mouth that made him want to cry. He'd bitten his lip and said quietly, 'I'm sorry you've been so unhappy, Mr Hamer.' He would have liked to tell him about his mother, how she hated him, but he knew he couldn't. It took him all his time to tell Rosanna. At last he said, 'I don't think my uncle Ralph will be kind to you, Mr Hamer. My grandfather Schofield never mentions his name, so he must have done something really bad.'

'Your Grandad's too busy makin' money to talk about his son, I reckon.'

'Oh no, Mr Hamer, he's a good man – everybody likes him. He looks after his workers and he pays them more than anybody else in Saltley.'

Hamer observed him carefully and tapped the pocket knife on his teeth. 'Go to sleep,' he said. 'Bill might slap you around if he finds you still awake.'

Obediently Charles lay down, telling himself that this one was a lot nicer than Dyson. On impulse he asked, 'Mr Hamer, do you think my uncle will kill me?'

'*Eh?*' Hamer stuck his head forward.

Charles propped himself up on one elbow so that the light fell on his face. 'I say, is he going to kill me?'

'No, course he isn't. Go to sleep.'

'Just one more question, Mr Hamer. What's buggery?'

'What?'

'My uncle said to Mr Dyson: "I know your tastes and he's a pretty boy – so no buggery. Later, perhaps, if the old man doesn't jump to it." Is it some sort of torture, Mr Hamer?'

'Aye,' the other said slowly. 'Aye, you could say it's torture, right enough, for a child. Don't upset yoursel' – nobody'll do that to you, neither Bill Dyson nor anybody else.'

He hadn't explained what it was, but all at once Charles felt safer. He pushed some straw into a semblance of a pillow and said, 'Goodnight, Mr Hamer.'

'Good – oh, go to sleep!'

When he peeped from under his lashes, Hamer was leaning forward in his chair with one hand under his chin as if he was thinking, or remembering . . .

It had been a long, miserable night, but now it was morning. That strong feeling was inside Charles again, a feeling that he must take action himself. If he saw a chance to escape he'd take it – he'd run away from his uncle Ralph. No wonder his grandfather never spoke of him – he was horrible.

*

Jericho's workers were spreading across the gorse-covered
slopes, examining every gully and prodding every clump of
new bracken. Sam and James and Francis were sitting in
the big coach from Alsing, heads together over a map, and
two of Francis's light carriages were waiting nearby, ready
to take messages and instructions up and down the dirt
road.

In the Schofield carriage, Joshua was speeding to join
his sons. Tizzie was at his side, wearing stout boots and a
wrap over her bright head. She had arrived at Meadowbank
on foot just as he was leaving. 'I must help or I'll go mad
with frustration,' she'd told him bluntly. 'Barney sent word
first thing about what's happening up on the moor – he
heard it in the shop. Please take me with you.'

Joshua had eyed her with approval. She had spirit, right
enough. 'Come on, then,' he'd agreed. 'No doubt they'll be
glad of your help in organising the search.'

Sam himself said little when he saw her, but he gave her
a swift kiss on the mouth and a hug, regardless of who was
watching.

With a lift of his brows in place of words Joshua asked
if there was any news. They shook their heads. 'Lilah's not
so bad,' he told them, 'though she keeps falling asleep all
of a sudden. And I've talked to Kenworthy. He says he has
no experience of kidnapping but he knows a bit about fraud
and extortion. He's put somebody to checking on Hickory
and Putman and he says that if Ralph's only half as clever
as he thinks he is he might well pull it off.' He climbed up
on the steps of the coach and stared thoughtfully at the
hundreds of men and women fanning out across the moor.
'He agrees with Tizzie that Ralph won't let Charlie go until
he's got everything he wants, including something in
writing to ensure that he'll never be charged.'

The three younger men listened but their minds were on
whether to direct searchers up to Holdwell Crags, where
the rocks were honeycombed with caverns. Tizzie edged
nearer to Francis. 'How's Sarah?' she asked quietly.

He turned from the others and flashed her a quick, joyous smile. 'She's sure, Tizzie – she's expecting right enough. She was so very happy until the message arrived about Charles. Don't say a word – this isn't the time, is it? In any case, she wants to give them the news herself.'

'Tell her I'm delighted,' she whispered, then joined Sam and James in studying a rough plan of the crags. 'I suppose you've put somebody to asking round those houses that are still occupied in and around High Holdwell?' she asked.

'Twenty women are heading there now,' replied James. 'Women are better at chatting to other women and somebody might have seen something.'

Tizzie looked around her. The sun was climbing a pale blue sky; a light breeze played across the grasses and groups of people were tramping across the moor. It could have been a public holiday rather than a life and death search.

Uncle Ralph was addressing Dyson and Hamer. 'The less you know, the safer for all of us, but I'll tell you this: the first move in handing over the ransom will be at two o'clock today – a signing of documents to transfer business properties to me. What concerns you is that there'll be provision to get my hands on ready money.

'It's a bright morning and people might be searching, so we'd better keep a keen lookout; not from the front porch, though – somebody might have glasses trained in this direction.' He jerked his head upwards. 'Dyson, you go inside. There's a ladder against the tall window so you can see for miles. Nobody can approach from the rear because of the rock face.'

Charles was listening intently. A tall window and a front porch? The cellar must belong to a big house, then. And what he said about transferring business properties ... Could his uncle possibly be after Jericho? Would he sell it? What would happen to the machinery? Twenty new looms had just been installed, the very latest models – Charles had seen them being tried out by the most experienced weavers.

But his uncle was talking again. 'We leave here at ten thirty so as to be near at hand for the signing. I have a man down there who's been acting on my orders – creating small diversions, shall we say. I've got rooms down by the Irwell near Quay Street where few will ask questions. The old man might need a shove, and we have the means to give him one . . .'

Charles guessed what that meant. He looked at Hamer for confirmation, but the man avoided his eye, following Dyson as he went out to keep watch. Charles could tell that neither of them wanted to be near his uncle; he guessed that they didn't like him, that they were even a bit frightened of him. His uncle sat down in the chair and started to read a newspaper; he was so calm he might have been in the library at the institute rather than in charge of a gang of kidnappers. Everything was very quiet when all at once the door crashed open.

'There's a band o' women marchin' on the village o'er yonder!' announced Dyson.

Charles's uncle let out a long, unbelieving breath and tossed the paper aside. 'How many?' he asked.

'Happen a coupla dozen. Hamer's got the spyglass on 'em.'

Before Ralph could reply, Hamer rushed in and descended the steps at a leap. 'There's folk all over the place!' he cried hoarsely. 'Headin' this way. Men, women and childer, scourin' the moor.'

'Give me the telescope,' said Ralph quietly, 'and gag the boy.'

'I don't like it,' declared Dyson. 'You said nobody would find us. You said nobody would guess we were here.'

'Shut your mouth and gag the boy. Tie his ankles!' The venomous hiss was more frightening than any shout. His eyes were like blue glass. He grabbed the telescope and ran up the steps.

Hamer reached for the rope but Dyson was almost dancing with alarm. 'How many are comin'?' he demanded.

'Hundreds, maybe thousands. It looks like the whole bloody town's turned out.'

Charles couldn't stop himself smiling. 'They'll be my grandpa's workers,' he said with certainty. 'There are twelve hundred of them. I expect my uncle Francis has got his men out, as well.'

Hamer was about to tie his ankles. 'Your uncle Francis?'

'The Earl of Soar. He lives at Alsing – out beyond High Lee. His countess is my Aunt Sarah.'

The men exchanged a look. 'I didn't bargain for this,' said Hamer. He bent down with the rope. 'Listen,' he whispered, 'I'm not tyin' this, I'm only wrapping it round. Take your chance when it comes, lad. I'm no saint, but your uncle's a bad 'un.'

Dyson was pacing back and forth, oblivious. 'I've done his biddin' for months,' he kept muttering.

Ralph came in again and the two men faced him. 'I'm leavin',' Hamer told him flatly. 'That lot out there are bad enough, without an earl as owns half Lancashire.'

'What about your money?' asked Ralph.

'Money?' echoed Hamer. 'With over a thousand men an' women on your tail? Give over! One thing, though. You'll harm the lad at your peril – there's too many as cares for him.' He shot a last look at Charles then turned on his heel and walked out.

Ralph stared after him, tight lipped. He flapped a hand at Dyson. 'Gag the boy,' he instructed.

'Gag him yoursel',' retorted Dyson, bold at last. 'You're a slate short if you think you can beat a belted earl as lives in a bloody great palace.' He swept off his hat in open mockery. 'Full marks for tryin', though.' With a hard little laugh he strutted out.

There was silence in the cellar. Charles decided that there would never be a better moment than this, while his uncle thought that his ankles were tied. He fiddled with the ropes as if they were too tight, then threw them aside and dashed for the steps.

His uncle leapt in front of him like a beast of prey. Teeth bared, he let out a sound that was both a howl and a scream. With a flat-handed blow to the head he knocked Charles to the floor and kicked him in the ribs. Panting, he trussed Charles's wrists and ankles and tied the gag so tight it dug into the corners of his mouth. 'Pray, little pretty boy,' he gasped. 'Just pray that the old fool signs!'

His saliva spattered Charles's forehead and the boy felt his stomach heave. He *was* mad, he told himself dizzily. Usually so calm, and now this!

Ralph tossed the armchair into a corner and the stool after it, then swept all evidence of their presence into a sack. He picked up the lamp and the bucket and took them to the door, then yanked Charles up the steps and out into the fresh air. Charles blinked and stared wide-eyed as they emerged. He was faced with a graveyard – an old, neglected place with only four or five of the graves cared for. He'd been here before, with his grandpa! It was a Methodist chapel above the village of High Holdwell, out of use now that the people it served had either died off or left the area. He stood there on his bound feet, fearful of another blow.

His uncle threw the rubbish over the wall, then with wild, pouncing energy advanced on a grave that was covered in newly opened daffodils. Charles stared. It was the grave his grandpa came to see – the one where his great-uncle was buried. Once when they came there had been a carpet of bluebells beneath the quiet old trees.

But Ralph was uttering cries that sounded like those of a crow attacking a newborn lamb. He was stamping on the daffodils. He tried to push the headstone over but it was set too firmly, so he snatched an iron bar from the cellar steps and struck at the name carved into the stone. 'Dog-faced old fool,' he panted, bringing down the bar with each word. He whirled round. 'Charlie Barnes lies here, did you know that? The man you were named after. It was his fault that I was sent to Australia.'

Wildly he jumped back and looked at the grave. The

flowers were ruined but the headstone showed little damage. He ran back to the steps outside the cellar and returned with more rusty iron bars and a rotting wicker basket, dumping them all on the ruined daffodils. That done, he suddenly became calm. 'The happy band of searchers will soon be here,' he said mildly, 'so we'd better leave the scene.'

He picked up Charles and slung him over one shoulder, then made his way through a coppice of trees and headed for a nearby field. 'You'll be travelling in a laundry basket,' he said in Charles's ear. 'Not much chance of escape from that, I assure you.'

The village itself had yielded no sign of Charles or his captors, so the three Schofields were ready to try anything. 'Search barns, outbuildings, empty farmhouses,' shouted James to the mill people. To his father he added, 'It was planned in advance – he'll have surveyed the moor.'

'The road goes elsewhere after the village,' Joshua reminded him. 'They could have carried on over the hills into Oldham, then through Failsworth to Manchester. Happen we're wrong in concentrating up here. If they're going to watch Quay Street somebody will have to be down near the Irwell.'

Sam was talking to a group of men who had been to the west of the village. 'Listen to this, Father!' he called. 'There's a deserted barn over yonder with access to the road. Horses have been kept inside and there's wheel marks from a coach!'

'Do any of the locals know the place?' asked James.

One of the men spoke up. 'I talked to an old fella, Mr James. He says that barn hasn't been used for ten year or more, since the farmer went bankrupt. There's a horse grazin' in the next field, an' all. Nobody knows who it belongs to.'

Joshua was rocking back and forth on his heels and toes. 'If it was Ralph, we've missed him,' he said heavily. 'There's no coach passed us this morning, so they must have gone out the other way.' He turned to the men. 'This is important news,' he said. 'You've done well. Stand by for a bit, will you?'

'Number twelve group are coming in,' said Francis, checking his list with Tizzie. 'They're the last lot from the outskirts of the village.'

Three men and three women were approaching and Joshua went to meet them. 'Did you have a look at the chapel up yonder?' he asked. It was a long shot, but there was a real link with Ralph – his victim's grave was there.

A man answered him wearily. He'd been stuck in a peat bog earlier on and his feet were wet and blistered; he didn't reckon much to being out in the wilds. 'We looked but there's nothin' there, Mr Schofield, bar a cellar full o' rubbish. The chapel's locked up but we could see through the window — there's nobody there.' He nudged the young woman next to him, reluctant to pass on the next piece of information.

She was shy in front of her employer and his sons. 'It's probably nothin', Mr Schofield . . .'

'We want to hear everything,' Joshua assured her as they joined the others. 'It's Annie Austin, isn't it? I remember your mother when she was in the winding room.'

She relaxed a little. 'There is one thing that's a bit funny at the chapel . . . It's Mr Barnes's grave . . .'

'Yes? What about it?'

'It's been – it's been knocked about, like. Desecrated. Trampled on, an' stuff piled on it.'

The four men stared at her. Sam felt the hairs rise on the back of his neck and his forearms. The air round them was fresh as young wine, but at that moment he imagined it to be foul as a midden. He met his father's eyes and saw pain there, pain and disgust. Tizzie took hold of his hand and he squeezed it as if he would never let it go.

The young woman pulled at the fringe of her grey plaid shawl. 'I were up at the chapel on Sunday with me mam, Mr Schofield, puttin' flowers on me granny's grave – she were born up here, you see. Well, Mr Barnes's grave were all right then. I said to me mam it were goin' to be a right picture when the daffs were in full bloom.'

Joshua nodded slowly. 'Well, Annie, that's the most important bit of information we've had all morning, and I thank you for it. Take a breather, everybody. There might be no need for more searching.'

He turned to the others. 'Take me up there. I've got to see this.'

'I'm coming as well,' said Sam, 'and so is Tizzie.'

'Me too,' said James. Francis just stood to one side, lifting a hand palm upwards as if to say that he would do whatever was needed. Tizzie, for once, was silent. She didn't like what she heard about Ralph. She didn't like it at all.

Joshua climbed into his carriage. 'Would you stay here, Francis, and take charge? Tell them all to wait here until we come back. By the looks of things they'll be able to have the rest of the day off.'

At the chapel he held up a hand as they approached the grave. 'Give me a spell on my own, will you? I have to think.'

Reluctantly, they left him and went off with two of the overlookers to go and find the barn, but Sam turned to watch his father standing alone among the graves. There were stone walls, he thought, there were trees. Ralph could be hiding nearby. 'I'll stay and keep an eye on him,' he told Tizzie.

'Me too,' she insisted, so hand in hand they lingered by the gate.

Joshua looked inside the cellar. Here was where they'd kept Charlie, he decided, signs of occupation or not. He went back and stared at the trampled daffodils. He touched the headstone, tracing with his fingertips the gouges on the lettering, knowing they'd been made by one of the iron bars. Until that moment he hadn't seriously thought of Ralph as insane. Bad, yes; twisted, peculiar, self-obsessed, a changeling ... lots of things and all of them unpleasant, but not actually mad. Now he wondered if any sane man would attack a headstone of a grave with an iron bar. God help the child, he thought. God help him, because we're making a damn poor job of it.

He sat on the low stone edging of the grave and thought of a long-ago day when he and Charlie Barnes were young men, out walking on a Whit Saturday holiday from their work. They had rested on the chapel porch and drunk water from a nearby spring. Charlie had taken him round the back to where his parents were buried, touching the bluebells with his foot and saying, 'This is where I'd like to lie, next to them. It comes to all of us, sooner or later.' It had come to him, right enough; his end might have been violent but he'd had the resting place he wanted, peaceful under the quiet trees – until today.

Joshua shook himself. Looking back would get him nowhere; he must look forward and try to anticipate Ralph's next move. Why had he stayed up here with the boy when he could have vanished with him in the streets of the city? There were hundreds, thousands of dwellings in Manchester where a boy could be taken by night and held captive – places within easy reach of Quay Street, at that.

Still seated, he put his stick between his knees and rested his chin on the handle, striving to read the closed book that was his youngest son's mind. Next to his thighs the crushed stems of the daffodils were weeping; he could smell them – fresh and green and faintly bitter, the very essence of spring. It seemed as if the scent seeped into his innermost being, slowing the thud of his heart and clearing the turmoil of his thoughts, until it came to him that there could be only one reason for bringing young Charlie to the place where his great-uncle was buried. It was to cock a snook at them all – to even the score. Yes, to get even with old Charlie. That was what it was all about.

Ralph and his men must have seen hundreds of folk crossing the moor towards them and they'd panicked and gone off in the coach. They'd taken time to clear the cellar, though; to remove all trace of their presence ... and yet they'd desecrated the grave.

Eyes narrowed in concentration, Joshua pulled at his whiskers. Attacking the grave was an act that spoke of Ralph's rare, ungovernable anger. As a child he would very occasionally turn into a wild thing, screaming with rage if he was thwarted. That was it – he'd been thwarted when he'd seen the searchers coming. He still hated Charlie Barnes; he still wanted to get even with a dead man. That was why he'd interfered at Mosley Street, stolen the order book, walked the floors at night . . .

Joshua raised his eyes from the grave and stared unseeingly at the walls of the chapel. Mosley Street! Could they have gone there? Aye, they could – it was all of a piece with bringing young Charlie up here to the graveyard! With a surge of energy he slung the iron bars and the rotting basket to one side and headed for the gate. Sam and Tizzie were there, backed by James and the two overlookers. 'He's been here,' he told them, 'thumbing his nose at us all. He'll be at Mosley Street now, with Charlie. I know it!'

Sam put out a restraining hand. 'It's Wednesday, Father. They can't drag Charles through the premises on a working day!'

James let out a strangled cry. 'I forgot! It's closed! I started to tell you when I arrived home yesterday but it went out of my head when you told me about Charles. The staff were ill – really ill, with vomiting and the gripes. All of them, Nathaniel, Will Grimshaw, the young fellows – aye, the watchman as well. I sent them home and put a notice on the door that the place was closed for the rest of the day owing to illness. I was going to suggest that we all three went down first thing this morning to open up. I just – forgot.'

'You did have other things on your mind,' Joshua pointed out drily, 'but as we've missed them here and I have to go to Quay Street anyway, there'll be nothing lost by calling at Mosley Street on the way. I admit that Ralph would be foolish to go there and whatever he is, he's no fool . . . but he's being irrational, as if something's thrown him off balance.' He smiled grimly. 'He could always plan ahead, could Master Ralph, but I doubt if even he would have expected to see hundreds of folk approaching his hiding place.'

Already Joshua was through the gate and heading for his carriage. 'I'll tell them all they can have the rest of the day off,' he said. 'James, Charlie's your lad, so you must do as you see fit, but I tell you I'm going to Mosley Street before I sign so much as a postage stamp. I'll see Nathan Makin before I set off. He knows we can't have open involvement from his men because we've been warned against it, but we should keep him informed about what's happening. I want him on our side.'

James and Sam exchanged glances. When their father was in this mood there was no stopping him. James turned for a last look at the mangled grave. An iron bar had made little impression on the headstone, but what if such a weapon had been used on his son? Dread was in him as he followed his father.

Back with the crowd, Joshua climbed up to the front of the big coach from Alsing and looked out on his workforce. 'You've found where my grandson was held captive,' he cried, 'and I thank you for it. The search will carry on elsewhere from now on, so off you go to your own affairs for the rest of the day.' For the life of him he couldn't add 'and back to your work tomorrow.' If anything happened to young Charlie, how could he start the engines ever again? With an effort he closed his mind to such a possibility and approached his son-in-law. 'Thanks for all your help, Francis. I'm off now, but Sam will put you in the picture about what's happening next.' His sharp blue eyes observed the other keenly. 'How's Sarah, then?'

'Fine,' replied Francis warily. 'Why shouldn't she be?'

'If she was well I'd have thought to see her here, giving support to her brother.'

Francis told himself that he should have expected Sarah's father to see her absence as strange. 'We had a difference of opinion about her coming,' he admitted. 'The fact is, she's expecting a baby. She's quite well, but I didn't want her out here on the moors and maybe – maybe seeing something to upset her.' His candid brown eyes looked into Joshua's. 'She did so want to tell you the news herself, but I can't have you thinking she didn't want to come.'

Joshua's sudden smile sat unnaturally on his ravaged features. 'I've seen a change in her of late,' he said. 'She's more serene; more content, somehow – more like her mother than ever.' In a rare gesture of affection he put an arm round Francis's shoulders. 'Congratulations, lad.'

That the 'lad' was in his mid-thirties and the Earl of Soar didn't make either of them see the word as inappropriate. There was mutual regard between them. Francis would have liked to reflect on what qualities their child might inherit from this strong-willed man, but there wasn't the time for daydreaming. 'Just tell me if I can help you,' he said.

'Have a chat with Sam, then go and let Sarah know what's happening. Paint a hopeful picture, mind. There's no use worrying her until we know a bit more. Tell her I'm delighted about the baby and that I think she was wise not to come.' His mind leaping ahead to what he would tell the chief constable, Joshua signalled to Zacky and made for the carriage.

Dosed with laudanum, Rosie was fast asleep in her own bed, her fever easing and her ankle strapped to a wooden foot cradle by the bone doctor. He had declared it to be a tricky fracture but dismissed her parents' fears. 'Young bones knit well,' he had said. 'She's a healthy little soul and I don't doubt she'll mend as well as her father did.'

Relieved and exhausted, Martha was asleep in the wicker chair at the side of the bed, but downstairs Matthew stood in front of the fire, restless and on edge. He had made a vow up on the moor, hadn't he? When he saw her alive he had promised to lay his hands on the Bible he never read and say a prayer of thanks to the God he wasn't sure existed. A vow was a vow – he accepted that more than many a man.

He went upstairs to where his Bible lay in its customary place on the chest of drawers by the double bed. He treasured that Bible, not because of its contents but because his name was written inside it in his mother's own hand, and he had loved her – oh, how he had loved her. Eight years old he'd been when she'd died and left him, the eldest of four. He carried the book downstairs and laid it in front of him on the scrubbed table, placing it so that a ray of sunshine picked out the words Holy Bible, tooled in gold on the worn black cover. He opened it and looked at his name on the flyleaf: Matthew Ezekiel Raike. The page was slightly greasy from years of fingering.

His mother had been a believer, he thought, so why not him? Deep in his heart Matthew knew that it was because his father had been a churchgoer and he hadn't respected him; he hadn't even liked him. He took hold of the book again and fell to his knees on the hearth rug, speaking out loud. 'I promised I'd say a word of thanks when my daughter Rosie was given back to us,' he said politely. 'I don't know if it was your doin', but I'm powerful pleased she's safe, an' I thank you from my heart.'

He felt it to be a stilted prayer, with the words falling awkwardly from his tongue. He knelt there and let relief wash over him like clear water, until it came to him what he must do next. He closed the Bible and took it back upstairs, checking that Martha was still asleep next to Rosie.

Moving almost without sound, he went down to the out shed and unlocked his cupboard, lifting out the muslin-wrapped carving of Jess with her hand outstretched and her feet among the flowers. For the very last time he looked at the finest work he had ever produced, aware that the pain of seeing Jess's likeness again was as nothing compared to the agony he'd known when they couldn't find Rosie.

He hesitated, then took a length of oiled cotton and swathed the figure in it, wrapping it again in a piece of sacking. Reluctance was slowing him down; he had to force himself to fetch his spade and to select a patch of earth under the lilac bush at one end of the back hedge, digging out the damp peaty soil with the easy, practised swing of a full-time gardener. The hole gleamed with moisture as he laid the bundle in it. He knew that the damp would get to the lime wood in time and rot it, but he assured himself it wouldn't bother him in the least. He mustn't linger – he mustn't allow himself the chance to change his mind. Hurriedly he filled in the hole and trod it down, then he looked over the hedge and out across the buttercup field. He fancied he could see the top of the birches in the little grove on the hill side … There was comfort of a sort in its nearness; his memento of Jess would lie within reach of the place where they'd made love. As to the whereabouts of the living Jess, he had no idea; but that, he told himself with finality, was as it should be.

Matthew cleaned his spade and his boots and went back indoors, feeling the call of sleep as soon as he closed the door behind him. He almost fell into his chair. Five minutes, he would have, and no more, he told himself, before crossing the yard to see how the search for young Charles was going. Never again would he think of the boy as 'Master' Charles. Hadn't his daughter risked life and limb to follow him and watch where he was taken? From now on, in Matthew's eyes at least, they were equal.

It was their first real disagreement since getting engaged: a brief, bitter exchange that left Tizzie fighting back tears as she watched the Schofield carriage drive away.

She had heard no discussion of it, but apparently Sam and James had decided to set off for Mosley Street with their father. Sam gave her a swift kiss on the cheek, saying, 'I'll let you know what's happening as soon as I can, love.'

She felt her jaw drop. 'I'm going as well.'

He all but laughed. 'Oh, yes? Talk sense, Tizzie.'

'But – you can't leave me here while you all go off to face Ralph!' It didn't occur to her that she wouldn't be able to sway him. She always won arguments.

To her amazement, Sam barely slowed his stride. 'Not

a hope!' he said over his shoulder. 'And you won't be left here – I've asked Francis to send you home.'

'Have you indeed? Like a brown paper parcel or a piece of left luggage?'

'Exactly,' he agreed, eyes glittering.

She planted her feet apart like a man. 'I'll follow you to Manchester,' she said.

Sam stared at her then and expelled a noisy, irritated sigh. What on earth was the matter with her? Couldn't she see that he hadn't the time to argue? He found he was grinding his teeth together in irritation and impatience. She could hear the sound they made; it was as if he had a ratchet inside his head. It made her feel slightly sick.

'Letter, parcel, luggage,' he snapped. 'I don't give a bloody damn what you call yourself, you're not coming to Manchester, and that's that! God above, woman, you're getting married on Saturday.'

'Not without you, I'm not.'

'I'll be there,' he said grimly. 'I'll be there if I have to drag Ralph behind me bound and gagged.'

She grabbed his arm, so eager to go with them that her words came out as a command rather than a request. 'Take me with you!'

Temper rising, he shook her off. 'Keep on acting the harpy and I might change my mind before I reach the altar.'

She gaped at him. A quiet little voice inside her head warned her to keep silent but her heart was thumping with fury. '*You'll* change *your* mind? *I'll* change *my* mind if you don't take me!'

'That's all right by me,' he said and marched off to join the others.

Francis pretended that he hadn't heard a word. 'Ah, Tizzie, can I send you home in one of the carriages? I'd ask you back to see Sarah but I expect you'll want to stay in Saltley until there's some news.'

She blinked. 'Yes, thank you,' she said stiffly. 'Your man can take me to the shop. I haven't the slightest intention of twiddling my thumbs at home.'

Barney was examining an emerald ring when she arrived. Polite as ever, he nodded his head and murmured, 'Good morning, Miss Ridings,' dispensing with the usual Miss Tizzie for the benefit of the customer, an elderly man who observed her with interest. People spoke of Tizzie Ridings as if she was some sort of wonder woman, he told himself, but at this moment she was pale and red eyed, with windswept hair and appallingly muddy boots. As for her and the dwarf, there was no sign of anything at all between them, let alone immoral behaviour.

The man dealt with, Barney left Albert in charge and led Tizzie into the little counting house, where from force of habit she sat in the chair and he stood at her side, their eyes level. 'You've been up on the moor, then?' he asked.

'Yes I have, in spite of your advice. I just couldn't stay at home waiting.'

He smiled slightly. 'They haven't found the boy, I take it?'

'No, but he'd been held at the disused chapel in High Holdwell. They've gone to Manchester now to see if they can trace him. If not, Mr Schofield will have to pay the ransom.' She was tapping the floor with the toe of her boot, still seething. 'Sam wouldn't take me, Barney. He wouldn't even hear of it!'

'Neither would I have, in his place,' he told her bluntly. 'No man would allow a woman they, uh, they respected to go where there might be danger. Now, shall I get Gideon to make you a cup of tea?'

'Tea!' she said scornfully. 'Why does everybody believe that a cup of tea will put everything to rights?'

'I for one don't believe any such thing,' he said quietly. 'I thought it might calm you down, that's all. You don't really need me to explain why Sam didn't take you with him.'

'I can think as quickly as any man in a tight corner,' she declared.

He gave that hint of a smile again. 'Quicker than most,

I'd say. Listen, Miss Tizzie, a hundred years from now women might be accepted as the equals of men, but not in 1877. You might not like it but that's the way it is, and there's no use coming crying to me because the man you've chosen to marry won't let you do everything you want. You'd soon lose respect for him if he was a doormat.'

She stared at him, her eyes still bright from angry tears. He was right. She would hate to have a doormat for a husband, or a man who didn't care if she exposed herself to danger. She thought of what she and Sam had said to each other about changing their minds and assured herself that it had all been in the heat of the moment.

'It's Wednesday,' she said briskly. 'I've been thinking that I might be a bit tied up on Friday evening.'

'The same had occurred to me,' he agreed mildly, 'it bein' Good Friday an' the eve of your weddin' day.'

'So have you the time now to go through the books and discuss business?'

'Here? Now? Of course I have.'

Tizzie took off her cloak. 'Good. Let's get down to it, then.'

Charles felt awful. He had cramp in his legs, the gag was hurting his mouth and it seemed as if every inch of his body was bruised. His uncle had known that the gag was hurting but he hadn't loosened it before he put him in this basket. They'd been in a big, dirty barn at the time and his uncle had pulled a great long knife from his boot and held the point of it against his chin. 'Not one sound,' he'd said, 'either grunting or banging the sides of the basket. If you try to attract attention in any way whatsoever, I'll slit your lips so you'll never play a trumpet again. Now, get in!'

What followed was a long, bumpy ride in the coach, then a stop at a stable yard – he could hear horses and the jingle of harness and such. Then the basket was put on a trolley and pushed to a railway station and on board a train, then to another station and on a porter's trolley to a cab, where he was slammed down on the floor next to his uncle's feet.

By the noise all around Charles knew they were in Manchester even before his uncle said, 'Quay Street by way of Mosley Street, and look sharp.' They rattled along cobbled streets and he felt as if the breath was knocked out of him every time they turned a corner.

'Stop!' said his uncle suddenly. Charles heard him jump from the cab and then come back to the driver. 'Up the street at the side there, and give me a hand with the basket, will you? It's overfull of my belongings. That's it, and now over to the hand lift in the corner.' His uncle must have paid the man then, because he said, 'You've never seen me or my basket, right? It's sort of a surprise for someone.'

And then Charles was being rattled about again, with a sensation of moving upwards. He felt sick and decided that he would never, as long as he lived, carry animals around in baskets or crates. Human beings didn't know how horrible it was because they never tried it themselves.

Then everything was quiet until Charles heard his uncle's footsteps on bare boards. He thought they must be in the premises at Quay Street. The rope around the basket was being untied and on impulse he closed his eyes and pretended to be unconscious, hoping it might make his uncle remove the gag.

With a curse he was lifted out of the trunk and his face was slapped, as if to bring him round. Then bliss, joy, heaven – the gag was removed. Charles gasped in relief but kept his eyes closed. His mouth felt like sandpaper.

His uncle was muttering to himself. 'More of a weakling than I'd thought ... but there's water turned on up here, if Maxwell followed his orders ...' He went out of the room and Charles opened his eyes. They were on the top floor of his grandpa's business premises on Mosley Street, the floor where his great-uncle used to live. His rooms were at the other side of that white-painted wall. He had come upstairs in the little hand-operated lift that was used to send packages between the floors; his uncle must have worked the ropes ... Next to him was a stack of cotton cloth, each roll stitched into a covering of striped ticking. That meant it was expensive cloth. Calico and such was sent out wrapped in sacking.

His uncle came back and handed him a mug of water, waiting impatiently while he drank. He had never tasted anything so good in his life. 'Planning,' said his uncle a shade smugly. 'Advance planning.'

Charles kept silent. What did he mean? Where were the staff? Mr Lee and Mr Grimshaw and the others? His uncle seemed to know what he was thinking, because he smiled, revealing his even yellow teeth. 'There's nobody here, little pretty boy. They were all taken ill yesterday, a detail I'd planned in case it came in handy. A few well chosen herbs in the tea caddy, a drop or two of ipecac here and there at dinner time. That's what I mean by planning ... but of course I had years to think about all this. One of my men has been in and out of this place for weeks, which doesn't say much for the watchmen, does it? We're going to spend an hour in the rooms here before we go to Quay Street. You can exercise your limbs before getting back to your comfortable mode of transport while I walk through the apartments that by rights should have been mine. It'll be just like old times!'

They left Victoria Station in two cabs: Sam and James in one, their father and Nathan Makin in the other.

'I'll come with you if you want,' Nathan had offered earlier. 'Not in my official capacity, but as an observer – a friend of the family. Then if you need to bring us in, I can use my influence with the city police.'

Joshua had been grateful. He and Nathan had never been close but they'd known each other since childhood. He'd seen the other rise to his present position and had noted that he was a man with the same ideas and ideals as himself – they thought alike on law and order and the rights of the common man.

Now they were all four heading for Mosley Street,

having decided that if the staff there had turned up and things were back to normal they would go on their way to Hickory and Putnam, where Lawyer Kenworthy was examining the documents that awaited Joshua's signature. If the Mosley Street premises were closed they would stop and go over the floors – every nook and cranny, every cupboard and box – aye, and the wardrobes in Charlie's rooms and the larder in his kitchen. Sam and James were humouring him in going there, he knew that, but he was determined on it. Ralph was settling old scores: against him, against his brothers and against Charlie Barnes. The ultimate in thumbing his nose at Charlie would be to keep his namesake captive in the very rooms that he himself had coveted all those years ago.

They pulled up at the pavement, James nodding when he saw the notice on the closed doors. 'Nothing's changed,' he said. 'It's as I left it. I told them all to have today off and that's what they've done by the looks of it. Come on – let's get in there in case Father's right.'

They told the cabbies to wait, and Joshua unlocked the main doors. Quietly the four of them inspected the front office and the rest of the ground floor, then the cellars, while the chief constable stationed himself by the stairs. 'Somebody could make their escape while we're searching,' he said in a low voice. 'I'll keep guard on the landings of every floor.'

They climbed the first flight with Sam recalling how on Christmas Eve he had missed Ralph by seconds and then found the note where the Madeira bottle had been. The place was silent except for the sound of their feet on the boards and his father's ragged breathing. Time and again Joshua had denied that climbing stairs robbed him of breath, but now it was evident that either exertion or tension was affecting his lungs.

Joshua looked in every corner, behind every bale. All was in order except that on the second floor the ink pad for the trademark stamp had been left with the lid off and seven rolls of cloth were in a heap instead of an orderly stack – evidence of the men's hurried departure. Silently he pointed upwards. They would be on the top floor if they were anywhere, he was certain of it. Ralph would get a thrill out of it.

They proceeded upwards and as they set foot on the last flight of stairs there came a sudden downdraught of air and the sound of oiled wheels in a runnel. 'The hoist doors!' hissed Sam. 'They're here! Stand back and let me go first.'

Joshua ignored him and forged ahead, gripped by fears for the safety of this impulsive son, this faithful son whose wedding was only seventy-two hours away. Why hadn't he made him stay at home? Why in God's name hadn't they brought weapons? He himself had only his stick – aye, and Jericho Mills. The mills were a weapon – a bargaining weapon, as were all his worldly goods, fruit of a lifetime's work.

Rage was rising in him again at the thought of what Ralph was demanding; it lent him a burst of speed so that he was the first to emerge from the gloom of the landing. They stopped as one man at what confronted them. It was very light, very bright. The hoist doors were wide apart and in the opening was a tall, silver-haired figure wearing high boots and a knee-length coat.

Joshua's breathing was audible, even to himself. This wasn't Ralph, he thought in bewilderment; he was too old. Horrified, he saw that the dishevelled little creature at the man's side was his grandson. With one hand the man was gripping him by the collar, balancing him on the wooden lip that edged the drop. In his other hand he held a long knife with the point against the boy's throat.

'Don't make a move,' Nathan warned them all.

'Watch your backs,' added Joshua hoarsely. 'There's others about somewhere.'

James, though, was watching his son. Bound at the wrists and ankles, a gag half choking him and with one eye closed and his cheek dark purple, Charles was shaking his head slightly, trying to tell them that there was nobody else there. Feeling the movement of the boy's head against his knuckles, Ralph jabbed the knife so that it cut into the skin. Charles uttered a cry of fear, muffled and despairing.

'Let him go,' cried Joshua. 'Let him go and you can have what you want!'

'Oh, yes, I'm sure I can! Do you think I'm an idiot?' Ralph took a tighter hold of Charles's collar and made him teeter over the drop. It was plain to see that he was tense as stretched wire, but there was a hint of pleasure, of gloating, in the way he looked down at his captive. Joshua groaned aloud. It was Ralph, right enough, but God *above*, he had aged; the golden hair was almost silver. He strained to see his features, but they were dark against the sunlit sky.

'Really, Papa,' said the voice that was hammered into his memory. 'Don't you recognise me? You have only yourself to blame if my looks have deteriorated, because I caught the smallpox as soon as I was put ashore at Botany Bay. The reason I didn't die of it was that I wanted my revenge – on you, you conceited old fool!'

Joshua stepped back at the venom in his tone. Charlie, he thought in anguish, he'll send him over the edge if we cross him. 'Put the lad to safety, Ralph, and then we'll talk,' he pleaded. 'I'll never sign if you harm him – surely you see that? Harm him, he thought, he was harmed already, both in mind and body. The lad was a wreck. He'd wet his britches, blood was oozing down his collar and his face looked as if it had been put through a mangle. It would be years before he got over this – if he survived the next five minutes. The other three were silent and immobile. Happen they felt like he did, that a hasty move or a wrong word would send the boy to his death.

'Where are your men, anyway?' he asked, trying for a touch of normality. Put him off his guard, he thought, get him to relax.

Ralph was a long way from relaxing. He bared his teeth, coldly furious. 'They took to their heels when Jericho's workforce came swarming over the moor,' he spat. 'That's something else to add to my list.'

Joshua opened his mouth to reply but swallowed the words. Dammit, it would kill him if he couldn't say what he pleased. He was short of breath again, practically wheezing, but from the labouring of his lungs an idea was born ... He shot a glance at the others. Sam was staring at Ralph as if he couldn't believe what he was seeing, but at the far side of him James seemed to know exactly what they were up against. His face was pale and set, his jaw tight. 'Let's talk, Ralph,' James urged. 'Put Charles to safety and we'll listen to your grievances.'

'Do you think I give a damn about his safety?' asked Ralph incredulously. 'He's a spoilt boy and son of a spoilt boy – one who could do no wrong in his family's eyes, in case you've forgotten.' He shook Charles as a dog might shake a rat. 'He's been serving a purpose – that's the only reason he's still alive. But you've all turned up here and put an end to my ransom plans. Therefore the boy is expendable. I don't care if he dies. Do you hear? I don't care.'

Nathan spoke up. 'It would be murder and we'd all witness it. I'm chief constable of Saltley. My word is my bond, and it would be accepted in any court in the land.'

Ralph turned to look at him and the sunlight caught the side of his face for an instant. Joshua gasped and felt a rush of compassion. It was appalling: the skin was scarred, pitted, *gouged*; he was unrecognisable as the beautiful youth he had banished to the other side of the world.

Ralph didn't bother to answer Nathan; he just held on to Charles and didn't take his eyes off the four of them for a moment. Joshua decided to follow his newborn plan. Always adept at a bit of drama, he produced a series of harsh, shaky breaths and for good measure rubbed his chest. The others dragged their eyes from the boy and he turned towards them as if in pain. He lowered an eyelid and then looked back at Ralph, 'I've got a proposition,' he wheezed. 'How would it suit you if ...?'

As he'd expected, Ralph paid attention. 'If I make over a – *Ah*!' He groaned and clutched at his chest, forcing a rasp to his breathing. James moved sideways as if to help him and at the same time edged nearer to his son, while Sam put an arm around his father's shoulders. Ralph was looking from one to the other warily; he held the boy more tightly but his knife hand was wavering.

James launched himself forward and clutched at his son. Astonished, Ralph let the boy go and howled with rage, lunging forward with the knife and grappling with his brother, who pushed Charles behind him, where he swayed on his bound feet, close to collapse. Sam leapt forward and pulled Charles out of danger, passing him back to Joshua, who gathered him in his arms while Nathan pulled off the gag.

In a frenzy of frustration, Sam was dancing on the balls of his feet, unable to intervene in the fight for fear of knocking both Ralph and James over the ledge. Ralph was toughened by years of rough living, he thought wildly, but Jimmy had never been a fighter ... He grabbed his father's stick.

With a strength he'd never known he possessed, James forced Ralph back until he was pinned against the winding gear of the hoist. Desperately Ralph whirled away from the winch and lunged with the knife, his arm upraised and the blade flashing. Joshua hugged his grandson and watched as if mesmerised, but Nathan edged closer to the opening, aiming to grab Ralph from behind.

Sam held the stick aloft, closing in to strike Ralph on the head or shoulder. Teeth bared, Ralph flung out an arm to knock the stick away but for an instant he staggered. Then he lunged again with the knife. James ducked and threw himself sideways, but Ralph followed through with the blow and lost his balance, whirling his arms like flywheels to avoid falling into the void. He clutched at the ropes of the hoist but they were too greasy to get a grip.

With a high-pitched scream, he fell out through the doors, his body black against the sunlit rooftops. An instant later there was a dull thud, as if a sack of grain had been dropped from the top of a barn. Down in the street a carter cried out and a horse neighed in fear.

The Schofields rushed to the opening and looked down. Ralph lay face upward on the cobbles, the knife still in his hand. James was gasping for breath but he swung Charles up into his arms as if he was two years old instead of eleven.

Sam was the first to reach the street, dreading that he would find Ralph still alive, with broken limbs or cuts and bruises. His brother's head lay at an impossible angle. The wrinkled, pockmarked eyelids were wide open, his sightless blue eyes open to the paler blue heavens.

Seconds later his father joined him. 'It's over,' said Sam. 'It's all over.'

CHAPTER SEVENTEEN

An End and a Beginning

Charles was sitting in the big swivel chair in the front office at Mosley Street, whirling round and round with his feet stuck out in front of him. He was feeling better. His uncle Sam had sent out for a meal and a waiter had delivered it in little silver dishes on a big tray. Then his father had brought a doctor, who'd examined him and said he was a fine young fellow and he'd be right as rain in no time.

His grandfather had gone out somewhere with Mr Makin and two policemen but before setting off had told him that his trumpet was safe at Meadowbank and that it was Rosanna who had followed the coach and watched where they took him. 'If we hadn't gone to the chapel and seen what had been done to the grave, I doubt if I'd have thought of you being here,' he'd said. 'Rosie set us on the right road. She's a good little lass and when we get home I'll ask her mother whether you can go across to say thanks.'

Men had taken Charles's uncle's body away. Mr Makin hadn't let anybody touch it until the Manchester police had seen it and written in their book that he was still holding the knife. Charles didn't think that you should be glad if your uncle died, even if he was wicked, but he *was* very glad. The funny thing was that even though he was glad, he had cried and cried when it was all over – he couldn't make himself stop. He'd been worried that they would think he was a baby, until his father had said that they all felt like crying, but it was easier not to when you were a grown-up.

A warm sort of feeling filled his chest when he thought about his father. He had always loved him; he was kind and gentle and clever, but sometimes he had wished he was more like his grandpa and his uncle Sam. Now, though, since he had rescued him and then wrestled like a prizefighter on the edge of the drop, he didn't want him to be different, not any more – not ever. He would be able to tell Rosanna all about what had happened. He might not say very much about his uncle Ralph, though, nor about being held over the drop or shut in the basket. He still felt a bit sick when he thought about that – it made the palms of his hands go all sweaty.

Nathan was quite definite about the inquest. 'There'll be no delay,' he said. 'They've suggested ten o'clock in the morning. Everything will be done according to the book but it'll be brief – little more than a formality – because there were witnesses.'

They were walking along Spring Gardens to the Reform Club, where Joshua intended to buy a splendid luncheon for the chief constable. He himself doubted whether he could face a meal, but he wanted to show his appreciation of the other man's support. He might not have affected the outcome of the fight between the brothers, but he couldn't be bettered as a witness. As for his own reaction to the death, he was too busy making arrangements and sending messages to think about it. That would come later, when he was on his own.

He had sent James and Sam home with Charles in a big hired carriage while he stayed in Manchester to 'see to things', as he'd put it. 'James and the boy need you more than I do,' he'd told Sam, 'so see them safely settled at home. I reckon there's one who'll be glad to see you back safe and sound. Give her a kiss from me.'

Sam was desperate to see if everything was all right

between him and Tizzie after their quarrel, but he'd also wanted to support his father, who might seem calm and collected but had just seen his youngest son fall to his death after threatening murder. Nevertheless, the vivid eyes were steady in the grey-white face and the breathlessness, both real and play-acted, had disappeared. 'You've missed your way in not taking to the stage,' Sam told him. 'You would have made a fortune treading the boards.'

'I made a fortune running a cotton mill instead,' his father answered, 'and I know which I'd rather do. Regarding Ralph, though. I've hoodwinked him twice over the years in matters of major importance, yet he's – he was really bright.'

'So is his father,' Sam said. 'Listen, you won't fix up anything about – about his funeral, will you, without telling James and me?'

'No, I'll discuss it with you in detail,' said Joshua and thought, Like hell I will, with your wedding only three days away.

Now, eating the Reform's excellent beef sirloin with little appetite, he stared down from the window into the bustle of Brown Street. 'Nathan,' he said thoughtfully, 'could I ask your advice on one more thing? It's about the funeral for my son.'

After their sleepless night Sam and James were nodding off and Charles was asleep by the time the hired carriage drew up at Meadowbank House. James lifted the boy out but he wakened as the servants met them at the door.

Hannah burst into tears when she saw him. 'Thank the Lord he's safe,' she sniffled, wiping her eyes on her apron. Ellie and one of the daily cleaning women hovered wide-eyed as the three of them entered the house.

'Go and tell the others he's safe, Ellie, especially the Raike family,' instructed Sam.

She hesitated. 'Mrs Schofield's in the sittin' room,' she whispered. 'She's been here over an hour.'

James exchanged a weary look with Sam, then took his

son by the hand and led him across the hall. 'Your mother's here,' he said gently. 'I expect she's been worried about you, so shall we put her mind at rest?'

One of Charles's eyes was closed but the other met his, unmoved and startlingly cynical in the battered young face. He made no reply, but held out his other hand to Sam, who clasped it firmly. James turned to Hannah. 'Will you prepare a hot bath for Master Charles, and afterwards see to his bruises?'

Esther was sitting by the fire with a tea tray at her side. She didn't rise to greet them, nor did she speak, but at the sight of Charles's face her lower lip quivered. 'So you've paid the ransom,' she said.

Typical, thought James. No tears of relief, no rushing to embrace her son. 'No we haven't,' he said shortly, 'my father hasn't signed anything.'

'What's happened, then?'

James pulled up an armchair and made Charles sit back in it. 'Ralph and his men had taken him to the empty chapel up at High Holdwell, but by the time we got there they'd left. Father had a feeling that they'd gone to Mosley Street and it turned out that he was right.'

'Papa rescued me,' said Charles proudly. 'Uncle Ralph was going to throw me out of the top floor hoist, but Papa saved me. He wrestled with Uncle Ralph.'

Esther eyed her husband in astonishment, then her eyes narrowed. 'So Charles's life *was* at risk? Is Ralph mad or something?'

'Not any more,' James said drily. 'He's dead. He fell out of the hoist and broke his neck.'

Esther dabbed at her nose with a tiny handkerchief. 'What a family,' she said with distaste.

'You were eager enough to take the name,' Sam broke in coldly. He knew he was wrong to say such things in front of the boy, but the dislike of years was too strong to be silenced.

'Maybe I was,' she retorted, 'but I've had cause to regret it.'

Charles stared at his mother with his one open eye. 'I'm glad I'm a Schofield,' he said clearly.

'Are you indeed?' She looked stunned rather than annoyed. 'But you're also half Buckley, don't forget.'

He squirmed against the leather of the chair. 'I'd rather be all Schofield,' he said flatly and got to his feet. He wanted to go and hold his trumpet, to see that it wasn't damaged. He wanted to talk to Rosanna ... 'May I be excused, Papa?'

'Yes. A good soak in the bath, like the doctor said, then Hannah will look at your cuts and bruises. I'll be up in a minute.'

Esther held up a hand. 'Just a moment, I have something to say. I'm – ah – I'm very pleased that you're safe and sound, Charles.'

He gave a polite little bow. 'Thank you, Mama. So am I.' He bent his head and limped quietly from the room.

James made to follow him but Esther stood up and barred his way. 'So you played the man at last?' she asked him with interest.

Sam answered for him. 'Aye, played the man and risked life and limb on the edge of a sixty-foot drop!' He was longing to get away to Tizzie but he couldn't leave old Jimmy battling with this cold little shrew.

She gave him a look of loathing. 'You all think you're so very clever, don't you? Hasn't it dawned on you yet that if Charles had been left with me this would never have happened?'

'What?' James was incredulous. 'When you sent him to the stables to practise on his trumpet and some days didn't even see him except at dinner? It would have happened, make no mistake. Ralph would have got to him wherever he was. Now, if you'll excuse us, Esther, we're all exhausted.'

She blinked uncertainly. 'So I'm to return home? Is Charles going to bed for the night?'

'I intend to see that he does. Thank you for your enquiries, but I expect your carriage is ready and waiting.' He rang the bell for Ellie.

Still oddly unsure of herself, Esther walked from the room and accepted her wrap. Sam wriggled his shoulders and told himself sharply that she had only herself to blame for her husband and son leaving her; there was no reason for him to feel the faintest spark of pity. Even so, he looked the other way as the small, erect figure went down the steps to her carriage.

Sam had arrived at Farthing Lane loaded with flowers, only to be told that Tizzie was 'out an' around in the town'.

'Where is she likely to be?' he asked.

'I don't know, Mr Schofield,' Rebecca answered with dignity. 'She were at the shop earlier on, then here for her dinner, then off out again. She said she weren't goin' to twiddle her thumbs like a ninkypoo – I *think* she said ninkypoo.'

'Nincompoop,' corrected Sam automatically. 'Well, Master Charles is safe and sound – tell her that when she comes in. And see to these, will you?' He bundled a great mass of creamy narcissi into her arms. He was so frustrated at Tizzie's absence that he was marching on the spot: left, right, left, right, like a soldier in the drill yard. There wasn't time to search the streets for her – he had to make sure that his father was all right. 'I'll leave Miss Tizzie a note,' he told Rebecca, heading for the desk. Such was his desire to talk to her, to apologise for what he had said on the moor, that he took several sheets of paper and wrote a message on each one:

'Sorry! sorry! sorry!'

'I love you, I adore you!'

'You're the most beautiful woman in the world!'

'I can't live without you.'

'Life will never be dull when we're married.'

'It was awful at Mosley Street – I was glad you weren't there.'

Rebecca stood by the door watching him in amazement. It took her an hour or more to fill a single piece of paper when she wrote a letter to Naomi, yet he had scribbled on seven or eight in less than a minute. On the last one he wrote, 'Tizzie, my love, my heart's delight – please, *please* don't change your mind!'

He jumped up and bundled all the sheets together. 'Put these where she'll see them as soon as she comes in. I have to go now.'

Sam raced to the carriage and headed for the station. Ever since setting off home with Charles and James he had regretted leaving his father. Nathan Makin was a rock, but no doubt he'd gone back to his work by now, and in any case he wasn't family – he wasn't even a close friend. It had been right to come back with the others, but his father had looked so ill when they'd left him at Mosley Street. His little act up at the hoist had been all too believable.

Deep in thought, Joshua was walking past Sinclair's Oyster Bar, having avoided the market stalls where traders were sweeping up and bellowing to each other. Nathan had gone back to Saltley an hour or more ago, brushing aside his thanks. 'There's more to my job than slapping folk in clink,' he'd said. 'If I've been of help to you I'm well pleased, so leave it at that. Now, I'll meet you at the coroner's first thing in the morning. Don't worry about it. Like I said, it's not a formal inquest.'

Since then Joshua had given instructions to a firm of undertakers, registered the death pending the enquiry and was now heading for a stonemason's yard beyond Smithy Door. One last task, he told himself grimly, then he could sit back for a bit.

The stonemason left his hammer and chisels and gave a hurried little bow when his lad ushered Joshua into the workshop, telling himself that here was a cotton master or he'd eat his hat. They were all cut from the same mould: well dressed, confident, keen on prices; but a bereavement affected them no different than folk in other walks of life. The man facing him looked drained as a slaughtered bull, except for the eyes, which were uncommonly sharp.

'Good afternoon to you,' said Joshua. 'I need a

headstone. Good quality, but plain and unadorned.'

The stonemason sighed. This one didn't throw it around. 'I have a catalogue of designs,' he tempted, 'angels, hands holdin' an open prayer book, happen a weepin' cherub. Look outside the door, sir, there's some examples of my work.'

In the yard were headstones, scrolled and elaborately carved, with various forms of lettering; there was a Madonna and Child in white marble and a cream-coloured angel with vast, soaring wings. Joshua eyed them soberly. 'I'm not doubting the quality of your work,' he assured him, 'but as I say, I require only a headstone. Very plain, very simple.'

'You'll know it'll be some while before it can be put in place? The ground has to settle, and they have strict regulations in the new cemeteries, though they're less fussy in the private burial grounds.'

'The grave will be in Philips Park Cemetery. There's no hurry to erect the stone, but I want to order it now. I'll let you know the plot number by post and you can send me your bill when the work's finished. Here's my card.'

The stonemason took it and sighed again. Joshua Schofield of Saltley ... Every businessman in Manchester knew that name – he was one of the top half-dozen cotton men in Lancashire. Top half-dozen or not, it didn't look as if he wanted to lay out an elaborate stone. And why Philips Park? It was miles away from his home town. He took out his order book. 'Stone, you say, Mr Schofield?'

'Yes. Good quality. About the size of that one over there.'

'And the inscription?'

Joshua rocked back and forth on his heels and toes. 'Ralph Joseph Schofield of Saltley.'

The man wrote it down and checked the spelling. No 'In Loving Memory' or 'Dear Husband of So-and-so' or 'Beloved Son' or whoever he might be, he noticed. 'And then, sir?' he prompted. 'Dates and so forth?'

'1848 to 1877.'

'Anything else, Mr Schofield?'

'Yes. The words, "As ye sow, so shall ye reap." In capitals, with quotation marks. That's all.'

The stonemason kept his eyes on his book. 'I'll see to that, Mr Schofield, and thank you for your order. I'll let you know when it's in place ready for inspection.'

'That won't be necessary,' said Joshua. 'I've been told I can trust you. Just do as I say and send me the bill. I bid you good day.'

The man stood up. 'Good day to you, Mr Schofield,' he said.

Sam was heading for the cab rank at Victoria when with relief he saw a familiar figure making for the trains. Apparently his father was all right but somewhat weary, because he was putting weight on his stick rather than swinging it. He frowned when he saw Sam. 'What's this? I thought you were with your brother?'

'I was,' placated Sam, 'but I've come back to see if you're – to see if I can be of help.'

Joshua swallowed his irritation. If there was one thing he couldn't abide it was being mollycoddled, even on a day like today. 'We'll talk on the train,' he said. 'Come on, it's due out in a minute.'

Once in their seats they discussed what might happen at the coroner's enquiry and then Joshua said, 'Kenworthy was all of a doodah when he reported back to me after cancelling the signing at Quay Street. I'm a bit disappointed in him – I'd have expected him to be more calm and collected.'

Sam eyed his father curiously. Why on earth should an elderly man of the law be calm and collected when he'd been told to safeguard a client's business against extortion by kidnapping? Poor old Kenworthy; he'd been out of his depth.

Disappointed or not, his father went on. 'I instructed him to use his own discretion about paying Hickory and Putnam for their work. For all we know they could be a genuine firm and if so I won't see them out of pocket because of a Schofield. And then another thing – you recall Charlie telling us what Ralph said about having taken rooms down near the Irwell?'

'Yes, of course I do.'

'Well, Nathan's put the Manchester police on to it. They're trying to find where he was staying, so we can claim his belongings and such.'

Sam's lips curled. 'Do we want to lay claim to them?'

'No, but we might come across something that'll clarify his actions – explain things a bit. We might even find details of a wife and family who'll have to be informed of his death. I have no option but to go through his things, Sam.'

'I suppose not, but what about his funeral? Do you want me to see to that?'

'God above, lad, let's get your wedding over, then we'll deal with the funeral; he won't run away from the mortuary. One thing we'll have to do is to make sure there's somebody at Mosley Street tomorrow. I had Bill Tetley round there before I left, wanting to know the top and bottom of Jones's backside. He says customers have been seeking him out at the docks and the Exchange because they can't get in at Mosley Street. What caused all this vomiting and diarrhoea, anyway? I've a mind to question James more closely about what happened. It could be Ralph's doing, like a lot of other things . . .'

They were still in discussion when the train pulled in at Saltley. 'I must call on Tizzie,' declared Sam. 'I missed her earlier on.'

Joshua shot him a look. 'I heard a gentle disagreement between you up on the moor,' he said drily. 'You're marrying a woman with a mind of her own, Sam, so it'll be no good you coming the lord and master all of a piece.'

'I'm well aware of that,' Sam said testily. 'But I wasn't going to let her put herself in danger.'

'Off you go and tell her so, then.'

'What are you going to do? Have a lie down for a bit?'

Joshua glared at him. 'No I am not. I want to look in on Lilah before I do anything else. I hired her to be a cook, not a punch bag for a maniac.'

Sam kept silent and hoped that nobody would cross his father in the next few hours. If they did, sparks would fly.

Black-plumed horses nodding, their harness gleaming in the sun, the hearse moved slowly through the cemetery. Behind it was a single carriage, occupied by a solitary mourner; Joshua was wearing his ordinary business clothes apart from a black silk swathe around his hat, added after he'd arrived at the undertaker's.

A Methodist minister was waiting to lead them to the grave, a stout, ruddy-faced man with a coat of ugly black tweed over his suit. He was as curious about this one mourner as he was about the occupant of the fine oak coffin that was without a single flower. Most of the funerals he conducted were traditional affairs with a tribe of mourners and wreaths by the dozen, but from time to time he was booked for one that was different. Sometimes it was a pauper funeral in a special section of a cemetery; twelve at once was the usual number, the bodies saved up until there were an even dozen for interment in a mass grave. At such times few mourners were present: maybe a scattering of workhouse inmates allowed out for an hour, or some ragged man or woman of the gutters.

Today's funeral was unusual on two counts: there was only one mourner and the grave was in unconsecrated ground. The mourner had explained why when he'd called at his little chapel in Blackley the previous day. 'I'm a believer,' he'd said briskly, introducing himself, 'and I need your help. I understand that you're a Methodist with an independent mind, but I've been refused twice already, so you'll oblige me by not wasting time. Now, I'm having a man buried at Philips Park tomorrow. I know it's Maundy Thursday but I want it done before Easter. It's a man who many years ago committed a crime for which he was never charged. If he'd been convicted he would have been hanged by the neck and buried in quicklime, so it seems to me only fair that he isn't laid in consecrated ground.'

The minister had hidden his surprise. 'Very fair,' he'd agreed, 'but there's unconsecrated ground at Philips Park, so what's your problem?'

'I want the burial service read for him by a minister of religion, that's my problem. The two I've approached so far wouldn't do it over a grave that's outside the Christian jurisdiction.'

'You say you're a believer. What about your own minister?'

'Nobody in my home town knows about this funeral. It's my responsibility because the man is my son. I want this done for him out of my – my deep feeling for his mother and also because of our family background. Can you help me?'

The minister was a tolerant man. His favourite text was 'Judge not, that ye be not judged.' In his time he had ignored orders and flouted rules, but only at the commands of his conscience. He'd looked at the gaunt old man facing him and nodded. 'Of course I'll do it,' he'd said firmly. 'I'll reckon it a privilege to ask God to have mercy on his soul.'

Joshua had held out his hand. He'd liked the man; his way of speech marked him as a native of Oldham, or maybe Rochdale, like his old friend Arthur Lawton. He'd booked him on the spot.

Now the bearers carried the coffin over the damp grass as the minister read from his book: '"I am the resurrection and the life, saith the Lord ..."' They were in an area that was almost untouched, but some distance away graves were set out in rows, and mourners were leaving one that was surrounded by wreaths, with eight or nine coaches waiting for them. To Joshua at that moment it seemed weeks rather than years since he'd stood at Rachel's grave and seen triumph on the face of his youngest son. Don't think of it, he told himself, or you'll make a mockery of the solemn words you've asked for ...

'"We brought nothing into this world, and it is certain

we can carry nothing out. The Lord giveth, and the Lord taketh away ..."' Ralph had been given plenty, that was a fact, but it had never been enough, had it? The ancient words came to Joshua, each sentence bearing a relevance to his son that seared him and yet somehow left him free. And then the bearers were lowering the coffin into the grave.

'"Man that is born of woman hath but a short time to live ..."' The minister had a deep, melodious voice and the words fell like balm on Joshua's aching heart. *Born of woman* ... Pictures presented themselves in his mind: Rachel, exhausted after a difficult labour and birth, holding Ralph – a baby so golden, so perfect that he seemed like a changeling when the other three had been red and crumpled after easy deliveries. He hadn't cried, he had merely looked up at his mother with a calm, almost adult self-possession that had set his father laughing. 'This one's no baby,' he had joked. 'In his mind he's a man full grown.' Then in time had come the precocious toddler, refusing to be cuddled; the scornful child at school, moved to a higher class because the work was too easy for him; the boy at home watching his brothers kicking a ball in the yard, then turning his back when they asked him to join them.

Why? Joshua asked silently. Why, why, why had he been like that? Why, now, did all this seem so dreadfully, wrenchingly final when he had always told himself that Ralph was dead from the moment he'd put him on board ship?

'"I heard a voice from heaven, saying unto me ..."' A clod of damp earth had fallen on the coffin – on the son he had tried to love. Aye, he'd tried, God only knew he'd tried and so had Rachel, but it had been like loving a stone wall. The times they'd talked it over in bed, baffled as to how they should handle him. In the end they'd given up trying to get close and made themselves accept that he was different from the others. Then in the years of the cotton famine they'd been so busy they'd let him keep his head in his books and go his own way. Had that been the start of it all? No. For years he had known that the seeds of Ralph's behaviour were inside him, rooted deep in the complex make-up of his being, planted maybe before he was born. Happen in some future century men would know more about such things – what could surface from generations long gone, what physical conditions could affect the mind ...

The minister paused before the final sentences, gesturing to remind Joshua that he could scatter earth on the coffin. He shook his head. He would put nothing on Ralph's coffin; not a wreath, not a flower, not a bobbin of yarn nor a shuttle from the mill he had coveted. A farewell token would appear to condone what he had done. If there was forgiveness for him it would have to come from someone other than his father.

The minister closed his book on the final amen. It was the end. Relief washed through Joshua like water. He had spared the others this bizarre blend of condemnation and Christian blessing, 'an eye for an eye' mixed with 'God have mercy on his soul'.

The minister waited, calm and compassionate. A fresh breeze was ruffling the grass, and Joshua felt the warmth of the sun on his bare head. There was an easing inside him and he felt very close to Rachel. He was well aware that she wouldn't want revenge, but he thought, he hoped, that she would approve of how he'd arranged things. He reached out to her in the deep communion of the spirit. *Rachel, my love, my darling, my life* ... The words tumbled forth unspoken. *Rachel, I love you, oh, how I love you* ... Then came his daily plea. *God, help me to live without her* ...

He straightened his shoulders and replaced his hat, then shook hands with the minister. 'Thank you,' he said simply, 'thank you.' He handed him an envelope. 'Use this as you see fit,' he said, and walked to his carriage.

He didn't turn round as they left the cemetery. The road in front was bright with April sun, and he looked straight ahead.

*

Sam burst into the office at Jericho, red faced, on edge and loaded with parcels. 'Oh, so you're here! I've been looking for you everywhere. You didn't leave word where you'd gone.'

'I've been seeing to things,' said Joshua mildly.

Sam plonked the parcels down. 'Wedding presents from the workers,' he said. 'I've had a request to go to the weaving shed next.' He sat on the edge of the desk and eyed his father closely. He wasn't as tense, he decided with relief. He still looked grey faced and weary, but the set of his head was easier, his shoulders more relaxed. Thank heavens for that – he'd been as awkward as hell since Ralph died. It had been the strangest Holy Week he'd ever known.

'Father,' he said carefully, 'Tizzie and I are in one mind about this, in fact it was her idea. We're going to postpone the honeymoon for a while. We want to be here with you and the others for the funeral and for a couple of weeks afterwards.'

Joshua blinked and swallowed. Careful, he warned himself. 'I appreciate that, Sam,' he said evenly, 'but there's no need for it.'

'We insist, Father. It's all arranged.'

'Then unarrange it. There's no need because the funeral's over. Done with. It was at two o'clock this afternoon.'

Sam gaped at him. 'But who was there?'

'The undertaker, the minister and me. It was a quiet affair, dignified and orderly. I think your mother would have approved.'

Sam was stunned but acknowledged the ultimate accolade. 'Do you want to talk about it?'

'No. I'll tell you later, along with your brother and sister. One thing I will say, he's been buried in unconsecrated ground. I thought that only right. Now, off you go and see the weavers. Happen they'll sing a doxology for you like they do for one of their own who's getting wed. They sang it for Sarah – twice over.'

Sam was aware of only one emotion: gratitude. He had dreaded having the wedding blighted by thoughts of Ralph, but now they wouldn't have to think about anything but each other. 'Thank you,' he said soberly. 'I daren't even imagine what it's taken out of you, but thank you.' He took his father in his arms and hugged him.

'Steady on,' said Joshua, clearing his throat. 'Tell Tizzie that your honeymoon goes ahead as planned. I'll always remember that you were ready to postpone it.'

'Tizz-wizz, you look lovely!' Mary, in her widow's black, was walking round her sister and viewing her from every side. 'It's going to be such a lovely day. I'm so happy for you and Sam!'

'No happier than I am,' Tizzie assured her. How could she be otherwise after that heart-stopping reconciliation amid the scent of two hundred narcissi? Sam had kissed her until, like some woman in a novelette, she'd almost swooned. 'We'll have to quarrel on a regular basis if this is making up,' she had told him. Passion had flared between them so fiercely that she knew they would have gone to bed if Rebecca and Naomi hadn't been in the house. Afterwards she could tell that Sam was glad they hadn't, and so was she.

Now she was so happy she felt as if her veins were filled with champagne rather than boring old blood. Happy that her dear Mary was with her on this, the most important day of her life; happy that the lodging house was already attracting top names from the world of the theatre and the music hall; happy that Ralph was no longer weighing on their minds; happy that Elizabeth was her bridesmaid because it would give her a bit of prestige at school. At that moment she was preening in front of the glass in a silver-green dress with a posy of rosebuds – the same flowers as those that were fully opened in her aunt's bouquet.

'You're so alike, you two.' Mary said that on average once a week, meaning it as a compliment to them both. Tizzie had to agree. Elizabeth wasn't pretty, just as she herself had never been conventionally pretty, but her bone structure and her colouring were dazzling and she was well proportioned. She had a certain air about her that Tizzie hardly even noticed because it echoed her own. She had clothed the child as near as possible to the conventions of mourning: her dress was subdued in colour and simply styled, her silver-green hair ribbons mingled with black – a touch insisted on by Mary. 'I've always been glad that you persuaded me to wear a twist of black ribbon in memory of Father on my wedding day,' she said. 'Elizabeth must do the same for William – it will make him seem nearer.'

Tizzie picked up her bouquet, and its ribbons trembled and shone gold against the creamy silk of her dress. 'Let's go down,' she said.

'Aunt Tizzie!' Elizabeth stood near the door, her silk-slippered feet planted apart like a boy's, her eyes shining like emeralds. 'Are you quite sure that I can call Lord Soar "Uncle Francis"?'

Tizzie could read her niece. 'Yes, I'm sure, but only when you address him. It wouldn't be correct to call him uncle when you speak of him to other people. Do you understand?'

'Yes.' Elizabeth wasn't too dismayed. Some of the girls at school would be watching them come out of chapel and she would be in the procession in front of Load Soar and Mr Schofield. That would make their eyes pop. Already Nellie Hopwood had changed from taunting her about living in a lodging house to asking what actors and actresses ate for their dinner and what time top-of-the-bill singers got out of bed in the morning . . .

Francis was waiting in the sitting room when they went down. 'Tizzie, my dear, you look lovely,' he said gently. 'Mrs Hartley, ma'am, I trust I find you well? And Elizabeth . . . my word, you look very elegant!'

Elizabeth composed her features into a mild, deferential expression and dropped him a perfect curtsey. 'Uncle Francis,' she murmured politely and managed to conceal a

delighted smile. She was taken out of the house and lifted
into a wedding carriage next to her mother, leaving Aunt
Tizzie and Lord Soar to follow them to Bethesda, where
she knew it was the first time in the chapel's history that
an earl had led a bride up the aisle.

The people of Saltley were turning out in force to watch
what they thought of as the wedding of the year. Word had
gone round that it was to be a quiet affair because of Mary
Hartley being in mourning, but never before had there been
a wedding surrounded by such events ... What about the
bridegroom's brother – the bad 'un – kidnapping his own
nephew just four days before the wedding and holding him
to ransom, and for his father's mill, at that? What about
him dying in an accident as soon as they found him with
the boy – a genuine accident, so it was said, witnessed by
the chief constable. Then there was the bridegroom's other
brother, the boy's father, taking his son and leaving his
wife to live alone in that great house with only a tribe of
servants – servants who were leaving as fast as they could
find other employers.

   As for the bride, the fact that she was marrying Sam
Schofield gave the lie once and for all to the nasty talk about
her and the dwarf. The Schofields might have a black sheep
in the family, but nobody had ever questioned their personal
morality. Those who had repeated the gossip were now
saying that they'd never believed it anyway – except for the
Boultons and the Waltons and a few of their friends.

   As two o'clock approached, people were crowding the
pavements outside Bethesda, watching the guests arrive
and eager to see what the town's best-known woman of
business looked like on her wedding day. In a stationary
carriage only yards away, Mrs Eleanor Boulton was
watching intently, her friend Bessie Walton nodding
vacantly at her side. 'Well, she's done it,' said Eleanor,
eyes narrowed. 'In spite of the stand we've taken about her
bringing down the morals of the town, she's managed to
get Sam Schofield to the altar. The way he was smiling

when he went in you'd think he was marrying the Virgin Mary instead of that carrot-headed trollop!'

'Trollop?' repeated Bessie, her vast pink face puckered with the effort of remembering. 'Trollop? Eli likes trollops. I told him that once and he took his belt to me.'

Eleanor lifted her eyes to the sunlit heavens. Here we go again, she told herself. The more Bessie lost her grip, the more she revealed about Eli, and none of it to his credit. Happen it was from choice that she retreated to her bumbling half-world . . . no doubt she found it preferable to the reality of living with an elderly lecher.

A few days ago Eli had announced that he intended to sit in his carriage opposite the chapel just to 'give Tizzie a look', as he put it, when she came out on her husband's arm. Clearly he was under the impression that a look from him would blight her day. But half an hour ago he had sent Bessie round on her own with a message that he wasn't well – again. Eleanor had asked Bessie what was wrong this time and the other woman had smiled above her chins, a cold little smile that for once held no confusion. 'Disease,' she'd said.

'Disease? What – his liver?' Everybody knew that Eli liked his port and his whisky.

Bessie shook her head and gave a quiet chuckle. 'It's not his liver that's troubling him. It's a wonder it didn't happen years back, but in those days he was more careful.' Eleanor stared at her, mystified. 'Disease,' repeated Bessie, as if to a child, 'picked up from women.'

It dawned. Eleanor sent up a brisk prayer of thanks that Ezra wasn't like that. He was an upright man, clean living; happen a bit lacking in – in warmth, in the ability to make her feel that he cared, but he was no lecher. She felt her usual impatience with Bessie. Why hadn't she given Eli what he wanted at home? If word got out what was wrong with him it would reflect on her and Ezra . . . 'I should keep this to yourself, Bessie,' she warned, but the fat pink face was vacant again, the head nodding. 'Oh, come on,' Eleanor said sharply, 'let's set off for Bethesda.'

Now they watched as Tizzie in her gleaming dress was
helped out of the wedding carriage by the young Lord Soar.
Eleanor sighed bitterly. Life wasn't fair. It wasn't fair at
all.

Inside the chapel Rosie thought that life was lovely. She
was sitting between her parents in a pew at the front – a
place of honour, Mr Schofield had called it – with her leg
in its wooden support resting on a stool. The pew faced
sideways so she could see all the messages on people's
faces. Everybody was happy, except for Mrs Hartley and
Mr Jellicoe. She would be sad because her husband had
died, but what was wrong with him? He was nodding
politely as people took their seats but she could tell that
something was hurting him even more than at the engagement party. Could it be that he didn't want Miss Tizzie to
marry Mr Sam? No. Everybody liked Mr Sam, and he
loved Miss Tizzie so much it shone out of him like the rays
of the sun whenever she was near. There could be another
reason why he didn't want them to marry . . . but she would
think about it later.

As for Charles, up in the choir next to the organ, she
could tell that he was very, very happy but a bit nervous
about playing, holding his trumpet in both hands and not
seeming to mind that everybody could see his black eye
and bruised cheek. When she walked in on her crutches he
had looked down at her and smiled . . . Oh, she did love
him. On Thursday he had come across to the cottage and
asked permission to speak to Miss Rosie, as if he knew that
her mam wouldn't like it if he called her Rosanna. He had
given her a bunch of daffodils and thanked her for
following the coach and then kissed her hand as if she was
a grand lady! Her mam had watched him and smiled, but
it was clear that she wasn't happy about him coming. As
for Charles, she could tell he was pleased to be in the house
for the very first time, though perhaps he felt a bit hemmed
in because it was so small . . .

All at once the organist played some crashing chords
and everybody stood up for the entrance of the bride.

Charles began to play the music by Mr Purcell, the piece he'd said was for her just as much as for his uncle and Miss Tizzie. Backed by the organ he played it fortissimo, just like he'd promised; very high and clear and piercing. It made little shivers go up and down between her shoulder blades – oh, it was lovely! Miss Tizzie was walking up the aisle with Lord Soar. She looked very, very beautiful and Mr Sam was staring at her so hard, Mr James had to nudge him to move forward.

Behind Miss Tizzie walked Elizabeth Hartley in a lovely dress, but instead of looking straight ahead her eyes were raised to Charles playing his trumpet, until they reached the front and he stopped playing. Oh! It was just like Elizabeth Hartley to give her a look that nobody else could see, a triumphant sort of look that said, 'You poor little nobody balancing on your crutches! See, I'm wearing a beautiful silk dress and I've walked in right behind Lord Soar ... and I shall be at the special room in the town hall for the reception.'

Matthew glanced down and saw his daughter blink and bite her lip. He took her hand and held it tight as the last notes of the trumpet shimmered on the air and everybody sat down. He observed the young bridesmaid curiously. She was full of herself, was that one, he decided.

Tizzie's roses with their gold ribbons registered at once with Sam. She'd remembered the bouquet he gave her all those years ago; proof, if he needed it, that she wasn't quite the practical, no-nonsense woman she made herself out to be. Those roses set the seal on his happiness; he could have leapt over the communion rail and kissed the minister on both cheeks. As he took Tizzie's hand in his, their minds met in one single, joyous declaration: the wasted years were at an end.

The ceremony was over and they were man and wife. Charles trembled a little as he raised his trumpet but played a perfect fanfare to introduce the Wedding March. Everybody rose to their feet for Sam and Tizzie, but Rosie stretched up tall on her crutches and thought only of Charles. She had known he was good on the trumpet, really good, but he sounded better than ever in a big building like this . . .

As they went up the aisle Tizzie knew at last what was meant by walking on air. Her feet didn't seem to be touching the floor; it was as if she was floating, conscious only of Sam's arm pressing hers against his ribs, of his eyes blazing with joy. Everyone was standing as they passed but their faces were a blur – until they came to Barney, when for an instant Tizzie halted. The dwarf's mouth was set in a wide, fixed smile, his eyes unrevealing as brown stones. She gave him a smile in return, just a little one, hoping that he knew it was specially for him, but she couldn't linger on her way out of chapel on Sam's arm. Seconds later they were through the door and standing in the sunlight, with everyone crowding behind them.

Eleanor Boulton was watching from across the road. If she'd been steadier on her feet and the labouring classes hadn't been cluttering the pavement, she would have gone to see the bride and groom at close quarters, just to show that there was one in Saltley who wasn't drooling and drivelling over them. She saw the Soars leave first in their carriage, no doubt to go and host the reception. Some quiet wedding, she thought acidly: a do at the town hall with an earl and countess shaking hands with all and sundry, crowds lining the streets as if royalty had descended on the town, and the bride looking like an illustration in a fashion magazine.

But the Schofield family were getting their comeuppance at last, with everything being out in the open about the shocking, disgraceful happenings in the family. What with one son a kidnapper and extortioner, another marrying a pawnbroker with a tainted reputation, a third who had deserted his wife, and a daughter whose first husband was a degenerate womaniser, they should all be hanging their heads in shame. But if indeed they felt shame why was Joshua smiling so proudly, so peaceably at the newlyweds?

Why was James laughing as he listened to the prattle of the youngest Hartley child? Why did Lord and Lady Soar look so blissfully content? Baffled, Eleanor stared from the carriage window. Then she saw Sam bend his head to whisper in Tizzie's ear. She leaned back and looked up at him, laughing wide mouthed and showing her splendid teeth. He took her hand and kissed the palm of it.

Though Eleanor sat quite still, something was moving inside the shored up flesh of her bosom, as if her heart was being picked up and given a good shaking. This was no marriage of convenience, she told herself reluctantly, no act of face-saving for Tizzie. There was deep feeling between them; more unusual still, there appeared to be friendship. Was this what the sentimental called love? She herself had no knowledge of such nonsense. Giving herself a mental shake, she sat up straighter, but the strange feeling lingered around her heart.

The wedding guests threw rice and paper flowers as Sam helped Tizzie into the open carriage, where ribbons fluttered along the reins and little gold bells tinkled on the harness. As Tizzie seated herself, she glanced across the road and met Eleanor's eyes. It didn't occur to her to snub her old enemy, she was much too happy for that. She just smiled and waved a hand and was surprised to see the older woman wave back; not a proper wave but a definite bending and stretching of her fingers. Sam held her hand as they drove away. 'I love you,' he said, laughing. 'Do you hear, Mrs Schofield? I love you!'

'Eleanor!' It was Bessie, jerked out of her mindless lethargy. 'Surely you aren't waving to that little madam after all we've said about her wicked behaviour? I thought you hated her?'

'I did,' agreed Eleanor, bewildered by thoughts and feelings that were beyond her comprehension. 'I did hate her – but happen I was wrong.'

The delicious meal was over, the speeches made. Joshua had been brief and to the point, welcoming Tizzie to the family and wishing them both well for the future.

One phrase he hadn't used – the customary 'I haven't lost a son, I've gained a daughter', because he *had* lost a son and only three days before, at that. Somehow, though, Ralph's burial had brought him a kind of peace. There was still self-searching to be done, still questions to be pondered, but there was nothing more that needed to be *done*. Even Ralph's personal belongings had been dealt with, not a letter among them, not a picture, just a small amount of cash and a few good clothes. The money had been used to pay his lawyers and his landlord, the clothes given away to the needy. End of Ralph, end of a life, end of a son.

But here, on this bright and beautiful April day, was a beginning. For another son and a new daughter. He saw their future stretching before them as a road climbing to sunlit uplands, a winding uphill road, for with temperaments like theirs life could never be flat or boring. It was a beginning also for Sarah and Francis, with the child she was carrying. Joshua's heart shifted with love. His little Sarah looked so radiant – almost as beautiful as her mother. Even James had made a new beginning of sorts – he had started a life without Esther, a life that obviously suited him. He was putting on weight and at this moment he seemed a new man, relaxed and good-humoured next to Mary Hartley and her brood and with his own son by his side. The lad was listening dutifully to young Elizabeth and happen wishing he was sitting next to little Rosie, but that hadn't been possible. Joshua might be a man who didn't stand on ceremony, but he had always known the disadvantages of getting overfamiliar with employees.

There was one employee, mind, who resisted familiarity far more vigorously than he did: Lilah, up and about again now and taking charge in the kitchen as they prepared for the do this evening. She had all but ordered him out of her bedroom on Thursday, even though Hannah and Ellie had been standing there like a couple of well-starched sentinels.

'I'll thank you not to come to me room again, Mr Schofield,' she'd said abruptly. Ellie had let out a nervous little snigger, but he, master of the house, master of Jericho Mills, hadn't known what to say in reply. He had stared at her in embarrassment and mumbled, 'Good God, woman, I'm here to see how you are. It was my son who attacked you, don't forget.'

'I'm not forgettin',' she'd said shortly. 'I'm not forgettin' anythin' about that evenin'.' The collar of her nightgown had peeped out above her woollen robe and she'd pushed it out of sight angrily. So that was it, he'd told himself. Plain as a pikestaff Lilah was embarrassed at having a man in her room. It would have been laughable if it hadn't also been appallingly sad, but surely a woman of such character knew that there was more to life than good looks?

Later that night he'd recalled the time he'd found her staring at a portrait of Rachel, the one on the wall next to his favourite chair. She'd brought him a pot of tea and some toasted teacakes one afternoon when he'd called in at Meadowbank after being in Manchester. He'd left the room to get some papers from his study and when he'd come back she'd been standing in front of the portrait holding the tea tray as if transfixed. She'd plonked the tray down and marched out of the room, lips pressed tight. At the time he'd merely thought she was busy, but that night it had come to him that she'd been comparing her looks with Rachel's. Poor Lilah. Poor anybody who did such a thing, because there wasn't a woman alive who could match his wife, not even Sarah. But Lilah was a woman of many qualities ... he'd have expected her to have more sense than be touchy about her looks.

And thinking of looks, here at his side Tizzie was glowing, looking more striking, more handsome than ever. 'You're happy, love.' He made it a statement rather than a question.

She turned her beautiful eyes on his. 'I'm very happy, Father,' she said.

He was highly delighted to hear that name on her lips, especially as it had come without prompting. He patted her hand. 'If you make him as happy as his mother made me, he'll be a lucky man,' he said and kissed her cheek.

At the other side of her Sam was watching them. Tizzie's regard for his father was what had come between them years ago, yet now it only served to bind them closer together. The final bond, the consummation of their marriage, would be in their own home. They had decided to spend the night there, just the two of them, after the family party at Meadowbank. Even now Rebecca would be seeing that everything was in order; the place aired, the fires lit, food for their breakfast. Then tomorrow off to Devon for their honeymoon. 'Devon?' James had said curiously, perhaps thinking of his own unhappy honeymoon in a foreign land. 'What made you pick Devon?'

'Tizzie knows somebody who owns a house on Exmoor. Far away from other habitation but very comfortable. It seemed to be what we were after, so we're renting it for a fortnight, complete with staff.' He tried not to look too pleased about it so as not to make old Jimmy feel bad, but now, observing this gathering together of those who mattered most to him and Tizzie, the phrase echoed in his mind like a promise: *Far away from other habitation ...*

He told himself that he wouldn't mind if it rained every single day while they were up in the wilds of Exmoor. She was his wife at last, and he loved her.

CHAPTER EIGHTEEN

A Son and Heir

It was time for Saltley Wakes, but no matter how often Martha told herself that everything was all right between her and Matthew, she still dreaded the arrival of the fair. Suppose he went looking for the girl? Suppose they took up where they left off?

She knew that he'd got rid of the lime-wood carving. After never so much as touching his cupboard for months, one day she'd opened the door and looked inside. Early that morning she'd reached out in her sleep to find him gone from her side. At once wide awake and alert, she opened her eyes and saw him standing naked by the bedroom window. He appeared to be deep in thought, the early sun edging his head and shoulders with gold. She wasn't surprised to see him without his nightshirt; he sometimes took it off if he was too warm.

Silently she studied the taut buttocks above his muscled thighs, the drift of dark hairs at the base of his spine, his body so pale, his neck and arms so very brown. What was he thinking, standing there? She longed to be close to him but hesitated to break in on his thoughts. In spite of herself she let out a little mew of protest – how could she not tell him she was awake when he was standing there stark naked, the only man she'd ever loved, the only man she'd ever wanted?

He turned at the sound and she saw that he was ready for the act of love, fully aroused. Instinctively she opened herself to him under the bed clothes, while he gave a rueful, awkward little laugh. 'I had to get out o' bed, Martha, or I'da been pouncin' on you in your sleep.' He looked down at himself as if at a naughty child.

She sat up and threw back the sheets, then lifted her nightie over her head and tossed it aside. 'Put the bolt on,' she commanded softly. He obeyed. They'd decided years ago that they mustn't risk Rosie walking in on something she wouldn't understand. He came towards her, black haired, his body painted amber by the sun. 'My liddle love,' he said, and buried his face between her small breasts.

It had been a time of strange, intense passion, leaving her dreamy and lethargic and fulfilled. When he and Rosie had left the house she went to his cupboard and in a burst of bravado flung open the door, ready to convince herself that the girl wasn't as young and lovely as she remembered. But the muslin-wrapped figure had gone, its place filled by a chunk of elm and a new chisel. Had he sold it? Had he sent it to the girl? Burnt it? Martha had no way of knowing, but surely, surely he couldn't have made such love to her, his wife, if he still had memories of the girl? She was singing to herself as she took the washing out of soak ready to go in the set boiler.

Weeks had passed since then, and now the wakes fair was coming. Mr Schofield was having his wakes tea party for family and friends, and Martha had been asked to help as usual. It had crossed her mind to refuse so that she could go to the wakes with Matthew, stay at his side, never let him out of her sight; but if she did that she would be acting like a guard, denying him free choice. No, there was nothing for it but to trust him.

'Agnes Irlam in our class is goin' to the seaside with her mam and dad,' Rosie announced as they sat down to their tea on Friday, 'for three days.' Her question hung in the air unspoken: Why can't we go to the seaside?

Matthew leaned forward and fixed her with his dark gaze, which was always specially gentle for her. 'One o' these days we'll all go to the seaside,' he told her. 'When I've the money to take you an' your mother in style, we're goin' away for a week – that's if I can get off my work for that long.'

Rosie stopped eating. 'A *week*? Where to?'

'To Devon,' he answered. 'Plymouth. I was born near there. We'll go an' see your aunties an' uncles an' your little cousins, but it'll be another year or two before I've saved enough money.'

Martha merely smiled. He'd had this dream for years, but it never came to anything. She was content for it to remain a dream. She was wary of him returning to his past because the past had caused his terrible nightmares. Sometimes she admitted to herself that she might even be jealous of his sisters and half-brothers; after all, they'd known him when he was a boy ... But if he wanted to go all that much, she would try to help him. Not just yet, though.

Rosie was already storing away the idea of going to Devon in favour of the here and now. 'They're settin' the wakes up,' she said. 'When are we goin', Dad?'

Matthew shook his head. 'Sorry, love, I can't go. I'll be busy at work. We've got such a lot on at present I'll be there all day tomorrow and maybe go back again in the evenin'. Mr Schofield's sent you a sixpence, though.' He laid it on the tablecloth next to the little blue jar of flowers.

Rosie kept looking at the coin as she ate her fried plaice. Why wasn't her dad telling the truth about not going to the fair? He hardly ever told a lie except to save somebody's feelings, but she could always tell when he did – it was written on his face as plain as plain. Her mother hadn't noticed; she was cutting more bread with her mouth slightly open, as if she was gasping with relief. Carefully Rosie looked under her lashes from one to the other. Grown-ups were funny, sometimes. 'Hannah Bennett's goin' with her big sister,' she told them. 'They'll let me go as well, if I ask 'em. Can I? Can I go, Mam?'

Martha exchanged a look with her husband. 'Aye, go on then, but you must be back here in time for the staff tea party. We'll be sittin' down about six o'clock, so don't be late.'

When they'd finished their meal Matthew went at once to his workbench, quite unable to stay chatting to Martha after announcing his decision. Nobody would ever know what it had cost him to relinquish the chance of seeing Jess, but he was trying to bury the thought of her just as he'd buried the carving. He felt sick with relief that his good little Martha knew nothing about her . . .

Take that morning some weeks back when she'd woken and seen him standing there thinking of Jess and ready to make love to her. She hadn't known that he'd made love to two women that morning – one flesh and blood, the other a memory. Oh, yes, 'twas better he kept away from the wakes. Billy and Jonas were having the day off, but he could find plenty to do round the bowling green. The institute was always busy at holiday times. The men of Jericho liked a game of bowls in their leisure, or to choose books from the library or to play dominoes or draughts. He'd be home in time for the special tea, but if he didn't return to work and Martha wanted to see the wakes he'd have to make some excuse to stay at home. He must see no confrontation between her and Jess; he wanted to make no comparisons.

Soberly he took out his gouges and chisels. He had been commissioned to make a cradle for Lord Soar's expected child and to carve the family crest at the head, though Lady Soar wanted a scene of baby animals – puppies and kittens and so forth – at the foot. If he made a good job of it there might be more orders from the aristocracy; that was how his name would get known, by doing work for grand houses. He closed his mind to thoughts of the best woodcarving he'd ever done.

Up at Moorview House Tizzie was having her Friday

evening business talk with Barney, an arrangement that had
recommenced at her request right after the honeymoon.
She still couldn't understand why Barney had been so
taken aback when she'd asked him. 'Mr Schofield won't
mind, then?' he'd asked edgily.

In high spirits after a blissful time on Exmoor, Tizzie
had laughed. 'Mind? Why should he mind? We're both
agreed that I'll continue with my business interests now
we're married. I talk business with you, pawnshop and
property and stocks and shares, so why should he mind?'

'Why indeed?' he'd retorted drily.

She'd shot him a look. Something had been putting him
on edge. Surely he didn't doubt that she and Sam were
happy? 'We had a lovely time on Exmoor,' she'd said
tentatively, 'but it's good to be back home.' She'd wanted
to reassure him that Sam was all she would ever want in a
man, yet she couldn't discuss him as if he'd been weighed
in the balance and by good fortune found to be satisfactory.

Since then she had seen a gradual change in Barney. She
thought it was because he'd become accustomed to the idea
of her being married, accepting that she was happy, that he
didn't have to worry about her wellbeing. If sometimes she
caught a look of resignation on his face, then it could only
be that he was getting used to her new status as a married
woman with her finger in countless business pies.

On the Friday before the wakes they were closeted
together in her study, which had resulted from one of her
few adjustments to the house: a wide, double-windowed
room overlooking the hills had been divided into two
studies, one for her and one for Sam. His was all dark-red
wallpaper and leather chairs and in a permanent muddle;
hers was carpeted in the same leaf green as the big oval
hall, with white walls and yellow curtains – a perfect foil
for her colouring. It was always very neat and orderly.

She'd had two of the special low chairs moved in so that
Barney could sit at ease as they talked, but afterwards they
always joined Sam for supper. He and Barney were on

first-name terms, though with a touch of contrariness Barney now addressed her as Mrs Schofield. 'You're a married woman,' he'd said flatly when they returned from Devon, 'so it's not fittin' to call you Miss Tizzie.'

He was right, of course, but the title irked her. It seemed to emphasise that their former closeness was disappearing, something she didn't relish at all. She would have liked to discuss it with Sam, after all they talked openly about anything and everything – except Barney. Sam was good with him, treating him with friendly respect, but she detected a reserve behind his good humour as if – almost as if he knew something that she didn't. It laid an awkwardness on any reference to Barney and she couldn't explain it, even to herself.

'Barney,' she said now, 'I want your opinion on something. I've talked to Sam about it and he thinks it's a good idea but it will affect you as well. I've been wondering whether to ask Naomi to be my secretary – to train her up as a sort of second in command. What do you think about that?'

He gave her a straight look. 'You're findin' that your business interests take up too much of your time?'

'No, not really, but when we have a family ...' She shook her head at his enquiring look. 'No, I'm not – not yet. You know as well as I do that what with the properties, the precious stones trade and the jeweller's shop, not to mention the pawnshop and the stocks and shares, there's quite a bit to keep an eye on. Naomi's bright, you know – too bright to work behind a draper's counter – but since she came back to Saltley she seems to have given up any ideas of being a governess. I think something happened when she was in Liverpool that put her off earning a living in that way.' She eyed him carefully. 'I shall still need your advice, Barney. Every property transaction you've advised me on has prospered – you know that. You and I can go on as usual, but Naomi will see to my correspondence, keep the books in order and take routine stuff off my hands, that's if you agree.'

He gave a thoughtful little smile. 'What about when she marries? She's a good-looking young woman.'

'I know she is, but there's no sign of her being interested in anybody, as far as I can see.'

'I think Albert likes her,' he said quietly.

'Albert?' Her voice rose. 'Albert *Lomas*?' Barney's second in command was a good man, but not exactly what she'd envisaged for Naomi. She'd seen a professional man for her, not a pawnshop assistant. She tried to smile. 'I've been matchmaking in my head,' she admitted, 'seeing somebody rather different for her, just as my mother did for me, years ago. It infuriated me then, and no doubt it would infuriate Naomi now if she knew. I must let things take their course between her and Albert, mustn't I?'

'Aye, Mrs Schofield, you must. As for her workin' for you – it's a good idea. Have you put it to her?'

'No, but now both you and Sam approve, I'll have a word with her. She could work in here – there's plenty of room for us both. I thought I'd book her in for a course of instruction on gemstones, the same as we both took years ago, so that in time she could take over the buying and selling of them. That's the sort of sideline she could keep on with after she's married. Later on I wondered if she could spend some time at the shop, getting to know the business.'

He nodded thoughtfully. 'It might be no bad thing if she sees a bit more of Albert. It might clarify his mind about her.'

'It might also clarify her mind about him,' she retorted. 'So we'll take the matter as settled and I'll see what she thinks.'

They joined Sam in the sitting room and the three of them chatted about the affairs of the town: the boom in cotton yarn and cloth; whose business was thriving, whose not doing so well. She and Sam stood side by side to see him off in his cab, then they went back indoors and straight to bed. Sometimes Tizzie looked back on the years when she'd slept alone unable to believe she'd existed without

Sam's big hot body sharing the bed. They always slept wrapped in each other's arms. He was a sensual man, direct and urgent in his lovemaking, yet so natural, so whole-some, so ready to laugh that joy always ran a close second to passion. Their wedding night had been a delight, banishing forever all thoughts of Edward Mayfield. He disappeared from her mind, from her memory, as if he had never existed.

They were so in tune that a glance, a smile, would have them going to their room to make love in the bed, on the hearth rug, and once, uncomfortably, in the bathtub. Sometimes she found herself hoping that she wouldn't start a baby for years, so as not to threaten such closeness, then she would look at Sam's face on the next pillow, feel his hand always touching her as he slept, and she would know that a baby, several babies, could never spoil what held them together. Life was good, she would tell herself thankfully, life was wonderful. It had been worth the long, empty years of waiting.

Things were just the same between her and Charles, Rosie assured herself. If anything, they were better since the kidnapping. Nobody actually encouraged them to be friends, but nobody stopped them, either. Even her mam said nothing when they met in the tunnel and he played his trumpet for her, or when they lingered in the shrubbery after school. It was just that he hadn't told her he'd decided not to be a musician ... Elizabeth Hartley had done that, bending over her as she was reading her book in a corner of the school yard. 'I think it's a good idea Charles deciding to be an engineer, don't you?' she'd asked briskly. 'My Aunt Tizzie says there's more money in cotton than there is in music. He can keep on with his music as well as being an engineer, can't he?'

Rosie hadn't known what to say. It had made her chest hurt to hear Elizabeth discussing him as if he was equal friends with them both. She'd examined the other girl's face. Yes, there were messages there ... They said, 'I like him. I like him a lot, so keep your distance, Rosie Raike, he's going to be my friend in future. Don't forget my Aunt Tizzie's married to his uncle!' But also on her face were uncertain little messages; they showed in the way her big green eyes were blinking, in the way she chewed her lower lip.

Rosie had managed a scornful little laugh. 'I dare say he'll change his mind lots of times before he decides what to do with his life,' she'd said, shrugging. 'I think his father and grandfather will want him to do a course on engineering whether he carries on with his music or not.' She'd closed her book and walked away, leaving Elizabeth staring after her.

On the morning of wakes Saturday Rosie wandered disconsolately past the end of the tunnel. Inside it was dark green, the hawthorns dense and the undergrowth matted with grass and twigs. She knew he wouldn't be there, not if he'd been telling Elizabeth Hartley things that he'd never even mentioned to her, his special friend ... And then she saw the golden gleam of his trumpet through the tangled branches. Beaming, she crawled inside. 'I didn't think you'd be here,' she said.

He stared at her in amazement. 'Why not? I'm always here on Saturdays after my lesson.'

She sat down next to him and polished the toes of her boots with her sleeve. They were the boots Mr Schofield had bought her and though they were the most beautiful boots in the world they were getting a bit tight. She wondered whether to ask Charles about what Elizabeth had said, but it would look as if she'd been talking about him behind his back. 'Has anything good happened?' she asked casually.

'I've been dying to tell you,' he said eagerly. 'My father's fixed up for me to have lessons in engineering after school on Wednesdays and Fridays.'

Ah ... She let out a little sigh of relief. 'Will it interfere with your music?'

'No, why should it? Father says I can do both. He says

by the time I'm fourteen or fifteen it will become apparent what I'm going to do in life. In the meantime I'll just learn as much as I can about everything.'

'What about your mam? Will she try and stop you?'

He shook his head. 'I only have to see her once a week, so she doesn't try to stop me doing anything. She doesn't like it in that little house with only a housekeeper and a maid, so she's cross all the time. Rosanna, she's horrible to the maid. The last time I was there she made her cry.'

Rosie patted his hand. 'I think it's because she grew up with your grandfather Buckley,' she comforted. 'I don't think he ever showed her how to be kind.'

'I never see him now,' said Charles in relief. 'I don't think Mother sees him either. He was furious when she had to leave High Lee Court.' He stared through the green tracery of leaves and fingered his trumpet. 'When we have children we'll show them how to be kind,' he said firmly. 'I'm determined on it.'

Rosie didn't answer. She just wrapped her arms round her chest and hugged herself tight. Why had she let Elizabeth Hartley upset her? She was just a bossy girl with three brothers, two of them nice and the other one, what? Smug? That was it – Abel Hartley was smug.

Later that day Rosie sat with her parents at the big trestle table for the servants' tea party. Mr Schofield and his guests had all eaten at five o'clock and now they were in the big sitting room with the glass doors open to the garden. Rosie had enjoyed going to the wakes with Hannah Bennett and her sister, but not as much as if she'd been with her dad. The tea was good, though; there were all her favourite foods, and the coachmen from Alsing and Moorview and Rochdale were telling jokes that made the grown-ups laugh. Even Lilah was laughing. She looked nice when she laughed because she showed her lovely teeth.

Her mam was laughing as well; her cheeks were pink and she'd put her hair up on top in a bunch of tight little ringlets. Her dad wasn't happy, though. He laughed when the others did, but it was plain to see he was thinking about something else . . .

When the meal was over Ellie and the hired maids were starting to clear the big table when from the sitting room came the sound of the piano being played by somebody who wasn't very good at making the notes sing but who didn't make mistakes. Unnoticed amid the bustle of clearing away, Rosie edged towards the shrubbery and looked into the room. There was Mr Schofield sitting with Mr Chadwick and the Lawtons from Rochdale, then came Mr and Mrs Sam. She could see Lady Soar; she looked all pink and happy and she was wearing a dress that hid her fat waist, because she was going to have a baby. Hannah Bennett had told her that ladies got fat before they had their babies. She said they carried the babies inside them, just like cats and dogs and sheep, which sounded uncomfortable, but Lady Soar looked as if she was enjoying it.

And there was Mr James, talking to Elizabeth's mother. Nobody ever seemed to notice that he liked her – he liked her a lot. She wondered why he couldn't divorce Charles's mam and marry Mrs Hartley. She was kind; she'd be kind to Charles if she was his stepmother, so it would even be worth Elizabeth being his stepsister. Getting divorced wasn't the sort of thing that ordinary people did, though, was it? Should she ask her mam and dad about it? Should she ask Charles?

Rosie edged sideways to see who else was there. The Hartley boys were sitting in a row next to their mother, straight as soldiers, but it was Elizabeth who was playing the piano. *Oh*! Next to her, turning the pages of her music, was Charles, nodding his head in time to the tune. When she finished playing everybody clapped and she curtseyed, a very deep curtsey, far too important looking for the end of a piano solo . . .

With a whirl of her skirts Rosie turned on her heel and headed for the stable loft. She wasn't going to stay and watch Elizabeth Hartley showing off.

*

It was two o'clock in the morning but the lights were lit in the private apartments at Alsing. Sarah was in labour; a long, slow, apparently straightforward labour, with an experienced midwife in charge and, at Francis's insistence, two doctors waiting in a nearby room in case they were needed.

The young earl stood by the window at the end of the long gallery that led to their rooms, wondering why he wasn't pacing back and forth like expectant fathers in books. It had been as much as he could do to force himself from his chair to his feet. Deep in his heart he knew that fear was rendering him immobile. Fear? More like terror – terror that something would happen to Sarah, because ever since that night – the night they'd really made love for the first time – he had known dread. It would catch him just when he was happiest, with Sarah in his arms or when he watched her stitching baby clothes. It wouldn't last, he would tell himself – it couldn't. Why should he, an ordinary individual thrust into an extraordinary life, have so much? Untold wealth, beautiful houses, countless acres of land, and Sarah, his wonderful, beautiful, adorable Sarah, the wife he loved more than all his celebrated possessions, more than life itself. He didn't deserve it and therefore he must expect it to be taken from him.

No matter how Sarah had tried to reassure him about the birth, his terror still simmered like a pan he had once seen on a tour of the kitchens. Set on the back of a fast-burning stove, it had been ready to come to the boil when a damper had been opened. In his case, he reflected, childbirth was a damper second to none.

There was no sound from the bed chamber; not a groan, not a whimper, not a – a scream. He stared emptily into the black autumn night. Who would imagine his little Sarah to be so brave, knowing what she did about the dangers of confinement? Wait! Was she conscious? Had the doctors been summoned without his knowledge? Were they even now fighting for her life, stemming haemorrhage and staving off collapse?

A footman edged towards him, offering a hot drink on a tray, but he flapped a hand at him. 'Tell nobody to approach until there's news,' he snapped. Wide-eyed, the man backed away. His Lordship never, ever, spoke to his staff like that. He was worked up, no doubt about it. Was there danger that they'd never suspected?

It was four o'clock before the door opened. Sarah's faithful maid Polly hurried out and dipped her knee. 'It won't be long now,' she whispered. 'M'lady says not to worry.'

'She can speak?' he asked incredulously.

Polly eyed him with well-concealed affection. 'She's all right,' she said, 'just gettin' a bit tired, like. P'raps if you could sit down for a bit, sir?'

'What do you mean, for a bit? Minutes? Hours? Days?'

'Not long,' she told him gently. 'Say fifteen minutes.'

It was nine minutes by his watch when a pink-cheeked little maid came out for him. He found the midwife standing calmly by the bed, hands clasped across her stomach. Polly was beaming and putting on a clean apron. Sarah, his Sarah, was sitting up against the pillows, damp haired and smiling, holding a bundle. 'Come and see your son,' she said. 'Sorry you've had such a long wait.'

He was staring at her as if at an apparition, ignoring the baby. 'My love,' he said simply. 'I was afraid you would die.'

'It was slow because he was the first,' she said. 'The others will be quicker. I'm a farmer's granddaughter, Francis – a healthy woman. I've told you that a thousand times. You have a *son*. Am I not to have a kiss for producing the new viscount?'

He kissed her cheek very gently, and only then did he look at the baby. He saw an ugly, red-faced creature with a swathe of silver-blond hair plastered across his skull. He wasn't ready to form any sort of attachment to it. 'The others?' he repeated hollowly.

'One every eighteen months, if we're lucky,' she said, yawning. 'We'll stop at six.'

For answer he pressed his lips to the palm of her hand. 'How soon may I send word to your father?' he asked.

She yawned again. 'Six thirty? They'll be up and about at Meadowbank by then.'

Francis didn't answer. Belatedly, he was watching his son and heir.

In the big bed at Moorview House Sam held Tizzie close. He had wakened suddenly, his mind on Sarah; for a moment he had actually writhed on the bed in a kind of dream agony. Then, just as suddenly, he was at peace. He smiled against Tizzie's springy hair, well aware of what must have happened. Such moments of closeness to his little Funny Face were now very rare, but there was no mistaking this one. He held Tizzie closer but didn't waken her. They would hear in the morning that Sarah had given birth and that all was well.

CHAPTER NINETEEN

Glad Tidings?

Tizzie was pregnant and she didn't know whether to be glad or sorry. She was certainly glad they'd had eighteen months of loving and laughing, of arguing and blissful making up before this ... this *presence* arrived inside her. Such a length of time to themselves was more than many a man and wife managed, rich or poor. Sam, of course, was delighted. She was glad about that, as well, though his reaction was hardly the surprise of the year. What she wasn't remotely glad about was her physical state.

Nobody had ever told her in so many words how gruelling it was to be sick not just in the mornings but at any old time of the day; actually vomiting – she who had never been ill in her life. She hadn't expected that her breasts, her familiar, high, firm breasts, would feel as if they belonged to somebody else, tight and sore and tingling. She was stunned at having to empty her bladder a dozen times a day, irritated to find herself craving meat at every meal, though to be sure she didn't keep it down for long.

Apart from all that, she was finding it a real temptation to sit around the house, dictating the occasional letter to Naomi or examining the stones that arrived by special messenger from Manchester or Bolton. She felt the need to take things easy because she was shockingly, staggeringly, constantly tired. Sarah had said, 'The sickness will pass,

Tizzie, and so will the tiredness. If you want to keep healthy go for long walks and breathe the good fresh air of the moors.' So that was what she did, reluctantly, it was true, but she did it, more than once actually being sick among the heather. It wasn't all sweetness and light being pregnant; there were times when she was quite sure she would have preferred to be barren.

And then she would remember the niggling doubts that had begun to plague her late in the summer ... *Would* she start a baby? Was she capable of conceiving? Sam had been marvellous, laughing away her fears and coming up with the latest theories about it sometimes being the husband's fault if there were no children. She had known at once what it must have cost him to even contemplate such a theory, let alone put it into words.

Then all at once it had happened, and she was running round to Mary's for advice and asking Sarah to tea after the infirmary meeting – a horrible meeting when she had had to excuse herself to go out to the WC to be sick. Mrs Boulton had been watching with steely, questioning eyes, so she'd made some lame excuse about having an upset stomach. She found such subterfuge craven, but Mary had advised her to wait until she was at least three months' pregnant before telling anybody outside the family.

Tizzie began to see her sister with a new respect. She'd had four children and throughout each pregnancy had helped William to build up his business, boiling hams and potting beef seemingly by the ton, not to mention baking her endless pork pies ... 'Didn't all that cooking at the shop turn your stomach when you were expecting?' she asked one day when she dropped in at Peter Street and found Mary rubbing in pastry in a big earthenware bowl.

Mary gave her sweet, reflective smile. 'It didn't seem to matter,' she said simply. 'I was sick when I was carrying Billy, but with the others it was just a bit of nausea now and again and it soon disappeared. You must try eating as soon as you've been sick, Tizz; that way you're less likely to bring it back again.'

Faced by such calm good sense from a widow with four children, Tizzie tried hard to look like a happy mother-to-be. There was a tranquillity about Mary these days, she thought; almost an air of fulfilment. The lodging house was thriving, booked up for months ahead. She herself still helped out with a regular fixed sum, but apart from that Mary supported her family by her own skills. She now employed a maid and a laundry woman as well as Annie, the latest addition to her staff being a once-a-week gardener booked for the spring of the coming year.

Tizzie watched her sister's busy hands thoughtfully. It would soon be Christmas, the second anniversary of William's death; but if Mary was dreading it she gave no sign. Ever since she'd taken up the responsibilities of her family again she had been gentle, patient, highly organised; the perfect mother and landlady.

With the pastry ready for the guests' evening meal and the little maid cleaning vegetables in the scullery, the sisters sat and chatted over a cup of tea. They could hear the sound of hammering from outside, where the old coach house was being converted into more bedrooms. There came a peal of laughter from young Johnny, causing Mary to let out a sigh. 'He's got a toy screwdriver out there so I suppose he'll be mithering the carpenter to death,' she said. 'He really loves it when there's a man around. So do the other two – you've seen what they're like when they're with Sam.'

Tizzie eyed her warily. 'It's only to be expected, I suppose, as there's no man in the family. Mary, would you ever think of marrying again?'

'Oh, of course,' said Mary derisively, 'men are queuing up to take on a widow with four children. Talk sense, Tizzie!'

Tizzie wasn't aware that she ever talked anything else. 'I didn't ask if anybody was making offers, I asked whether you'd think of marrying again. I meant if you ever met anybody you liked.'

Mary turned wide, reproachful brown eyes on her sister.

'Tizzie, how can you ask that? Surely you know that nobody could ever replace William?'

'I wasn't thinking of replacing him. I meant somebody who appealed to you in their own right.'

Mary looked round the big warm kitchen that doubled as a family dining room. 'I'm well set as I am,' she said quietly. 'I'm able to cope, and with your help I can manage for money. I can see how the boys need a father, but I'm not going to scour the streets for a husband in order to provide them with one. Billy's growing up fast. After Christmas he's going up to High Lee on Saturdays to help on the farm – it was good of James to arrange it for him. He says Billy has an aptitude for dealing with livestock, though if that's the case it can only have come from the Hartley side because they were farmers long before they were butchers, you know. They say at school that Abel's getting on really well with his figuring; he's so precise and proper I think he'll go into business of some sort. As for our Elizabeth, I don't know what to think about her, Tizzie. She's clever of course, like you, but oh, she's a handful. If she was seventeen instead of going on eleven I'd be convinced she was setting her cap at Charles. They were round here yesterday and when they'd gone I had to speak to her severely about being too familiar. It was – unsuitable.'

Tizzie nodded grimly. She'd seen and heard Elizabeth with Charles and unsuitable was a fair description. 'You said "they"? Charles wasn't on his own, then?'

'No, he came with his father. They brought some books on estate management that James thought might be of use to Billy. It does seem a shame that he can't live with his wife, Tizz, because he's such a nice man, but I do believe he doesn't mind being separated from her.'

'Why should he mind? *He* left *her*,' said Tizzie bluntly. 'I'll tell you this, if I'd lived with Esther for years, I wouldn't mind being separated from her either. Charles probably feels the same. Anybody can see he's happier and more confident now than he ever was.' She stood up. 'I'd better be going. I want to call in at the jeweller's, and if I don't get a move on Sam will be home before me.'

She didn't tell Mary that Sam liked her to be there when he arrived home. In the early days of their marriage he had said, 'I accept that you want to come and go as you please, Tizzie, but if you're going to be late home will you let me know in advance? It's such a dreadful disappointment when I walk in and you aren't here. The house is dead without you.' After that what could she do? It soon became second nature to arrange her day in order to be there when he came home.

Mary was eyeing her dubiously. 'Are you really going to walk all the way back to Moorview, Tizzie?'

'Yes. Sarah tells me that ideas are changing on women taking it easy in pregnancy. She says studies in London show that active women have easier labours than those who droop around on sofas all day long. They have healthier babies, as well. She walked at least two miles a day when she was expecting little Francis and he's healthy enough – he's firm on his feet already. She's keeping even more active with this one – she must be five months' or more by now and she's always on the go.'

Mary made a patting motion with her hand, as if to calm her. 'I just thought you were looking a bit peaky, that's all. Perhaps you should ease off on the exercise until you've stopped being so sick?'

Tizzie buttoned her coat and picked up her gloves. 'Up to now I don't like being pregnant,' she admitted. 'In fact, I detest it, but I can put up with it if in the end I produce a healthy child. I intend to do whatever's necessary to achieve that. Right?'

'Right,' said Mary. 'Just don't go at it like a woman possessed, that's all.'

Tizzie laughed for the first time that day. 'You sound like Sam. He's an absolute fusspot. I've told him that if I want to walk I'll walk, whether I'm tired, or heaving my heart up, or my bosom feels like cannonballs. And that's that!'

Mary gave her a hug. 'It will all be worth it when you've got your baby,' she said.

'It had better be,' answered Tizzie and set off for her jewellery shop. Once heading for Old Square, the thought of visiting the shop lost its attraction. Her manager was capable and very efficient, but he had never been able to conceal that he didn't like taking orders from a woman. Before her marriage it had amused her to exert her authority over him now and again, but living with Sam's easy acceptance of her business status made the manager seem old-fashioned and obstructive.

She was in no mood for winning another battle of words, so on impulse she changed direction and made for the pawnshop. It was a longer walk home from there, but if she was running late Gideon could get her a cab. She walked the crisscrossed streets, her mind on the shop. Business still thrived beneath the three gold balls; the town's prosperity had made little difference to trade – there would always be those who ran short of ready money.

From force of habit she eyed the shop front and found it clean and tidy, the brass nameplate over the door polished to perfection by Gideon. Ridings and Jellicoe . . . would it always be that? One of them would die first and if it was her she'd willed her half to Barney. She owed him that for his loyalty over the years. What she owed him for his personal regard, for caring what happened to her, was more than she could calculate.

It was good to hear the sound of the shop bell as she walked in. She wouldn't want to work behind that counter again but she liked coming back to the unique blend of smells, the cleanliness and order of the place. Albert was dealing with a customer, but smiled and dipped his head. 'Good afternoon, Mrs Schofield. Mr Jellicoe's just gone downstairs.'

'Good afternoon, Mr Lomas.' She always called him that in front of customers. In the last few months she'd been observing him closely, wanting to be sure what she thought of him. He was an attractive young man: tall and agile with smooth dark hair and honest brown eyes; not handsome, but with pleasant, rough-hewn features. She herself had always been more interested in his work than his looks. He was quick and accurate; he was keen, interested, willing, perhaps not clever in the way that Barney was clever; happen he wasn't even as bright as Naomi, but he certainly wasn't frightened of hard work.

She knew by now that Barney had been right; there was an attraction between him and Naomi and it wasn't all on his side. It was no use being disappointed that she wasn't making a better match if Albert was the man she really wanted. But she was still very young. There was time for her to change her mind.

Tizzie found Barney in charge of the dolly shop, taking in some table linen that looked good enough to have been pledged upstairs. His eyes widened when he saw her on the stairs, but he watched the customer leave before he spoke. 'Mrs Schofield,' he said quietly. 'This is a pleasant surprise.'

'Hello, Barney,' she said. 'How are you?'

'I'm all right. How are *you*?'

He was the only person outside the family who knew she was pregnant. She hadn't told him – he'd known. One day when she and Sam were only just certain of it themselves she had called in at the shop and without a second thought climbed on a stool to reach one of the boxes where valuables were kept, intending to check on a string of pearls.

Barney lurched forward on his short legs. 'Careful, Miss Tizzie,' he gasped, 'you mustn't—'

She took hold of the box and, climbing down, attempted a laugh. 'I mustn't what? And it's back to Miss Tizzie, is it?'

He wriggled his broad shoulders. 'A slip of the tongue, Mrs Schofield. I was frightened you'd lose your footing on that stool.' He waved a hand at the clean-swept floor. 'Or you might trip up – there's stuff all over the place.'

'Barney,' she said, 'you've guessed that I'm expecting, haven't you?'

The dark eyes met hers without evasion. 'Yes,' he admitted. 'I'm sorry if you see it as presumption on my part.' He raised his hands, palm upwards. 'It's just that I've known you since you were a girl, so now an' again I can read you, like. I'm – I'm pleased for you and Sam. You needn't worry, I won't mention it again.'

'I don't mind you knowing,' she protested, 'it's just that it's a bit early. We only told the family yesterday. How will it be if we tell you officially next month?'

'That'll be fine,' he agreed. 'You'll take care, then?'

She had gritted her teeth impatiently. 'Of course I will. I'm not ill, you know, just pregnant.'

Now, waiting for an answer to his question, he wore the same expression, concerned but guarded. It baffled her. 'I feel dreadful,' she said with her usual honesty. 'I'm very sick, Barney, almost all the time.'

He shifted his feet, scraping them on the stone floor. 'I'm sorry to hear it,' he said gently, 'but I've heard that it passes in time. 'You'll – you'll look after yourself, though?'

This time she wasn't impatient. There was concern coming from him; the deep, warm, abiding force that she could never put a name to. She nodded her head at him and smiled. 'Of course I will,' she said. 'Now, where's Gideon?'

'I've just sent him out to Dolly Redfern's for my tea,' he confessed. 'He'll be back in a minute. Mrs Siddall isn't in today, I'm afraid.' That was as good as saying that he couldn't, or wouldn't, ask her upstairs for a cup of tea. She gave a little shrug, accepting his unspoken ruling.

'You'll not be up to lookin' at property, I suppose?' he asked. 'I've heard of a group of dwellin's comin' on the market in a week or two, either for renovatin' or demolition in order to free the land. Either way might be a winner if the price is right.'

Tizzie unbuttoned her coat and perched on the edge of the table. 'A life-saver!' she declared. 'Something new to think about. Have you the time to discuss it?'

He gave that odd, tight little smile. 'I reckon I can spare five minutes,' he said drily. 'Here's Gideon, so we'll go and talk in the counting house, shall we?'

Later that week Tizzie was going through the books with Naomi. Always pleased with her assistant's neatness and accuracy, she said, 'Your work is really good, Naomi. Did you always hanker to do this sort of thing rather than teaching?'

Naomi blushed easily and now she turned bright pink at the praise. 'No, I never even imagined being your assistant, Mrs Schofield. It was always teaching that appealed to me in my younger days.'

She spoke as if her youth was long gone, thought Tizzie, who for once wasn't feeling sick, merely restless. 'I'm going to take a walk down to the shop,' she said. 'Do you want to come?'

Naomi's clear grey eyes brightened. 'Yes,' she said promptly.

Tizzie swallowed a sigh and risked one gentle question. 'How do you get on with Albert when you spend your half-days at the shop?'

At once the bright little face closed up. 'He's – very nice,' said Naomi primly, 'very helpful, and so is Mr Jellicoe.' She took a pencil from the wooden box on her desk, fiddled with it and then put it back.

Tizzie watched her carefully. 'Is anything troubling you, Naomi?'

To her consternation tears brimmed in Naomi's eyes until they looked like the skies above a rain-washed moor. Tizzie tried again. 'Is it something to do with Albert?'

At that Naomi twisted her handkerchief in both hands as if she was wringing a dishcloth. 'We like each other,' she confessed. 'I've liked him ever since I first saw him down in the dolly shop when my mother started working for you.'

She'd concealed her liking pretty thoroughly over the years, thought Tizzie. 'So what's the problem?' she asked lightly.

'Nothing can come of it,' said Naomi tightly. 'I can never marry a decent man.' She was still twisting the handkerchief. 'Promise you won't tell my mother?'

Tizzie didn't like the sound of that. 'What mustn't I tell her? Why can't you get married?'

'I'm not – untouched,' muttered Naomi. 'You know – by a man.'

Tizzie gaped. This was her sweet, good little Naomi, whose mother had guarded her like a tigress with a single cub. She herself had taught her to read and write, to speak properly; she'd always been protected . . . *Ah*! Except when she was in Liverpool! She'd been right in thinking that something had happened there. 'Did you fall in love when you were in Liverpool?' she asked. 'Is that it?'

Naomi burst into tears. 'I didn't love him,' she choked at last, 'I hated him. He – he forced me. That's why I came home. Don't tell my mother – she'll want to go and kill him!'

This couldn't be happening, Tizzie told herself. She couldn't be hearing right. 'Who forced you?' she asked hoarsely.

'Mr Morris,' said Naomi.

Tizzie gripped the seat of her chair in order to stay upright. She herself had arranged Naomi's position as governess, negotiated the terms of her employment. She had visited Mr and Mrs Morris in person; they were a solid, respectable couple with two little girls for whom they wanted private, full-time education. Mr Morris was a cotton broker on the Liverpool Exchange, a big, somewhat podgy man with shiny brown hair and close-cut side whiskers. This wasn't credible, but she could tell that it was true. It was clear that Naomi had never spoken of it before, never even hinted at it; doubtless she had only revealed it now because she was too ashamed to let Albert court her. 'Tell me about it,' Tizzie commanded. 'You'll feel better for it.'

'He came into my room when I was asleep,' whispered Naomi, echoes of old amazement in her tone. 'I wakened up when he got into the bed. It – I had my monthly, Miss Tizzie, but it didn't stop him. He just laughed and said, "very convenient," then ripped my cloth pad away and – I thought hell had opened and swallowed me up. Afterwards he said if I told anybody he would dismiss me without a reference, but it was clear he thought I should welcome it. I was crying so much I couldn't speak.'

Tizzie couldn't think of a single word that was worth saying. This had happened while she was preparing to marry Sam, her mind on him rather than her responsibilities. Guilt wrenched at her heart but was swept away by concern. 'It was just the once?' she asked, pleading.

Tears still wet on her cheeks, Naomi shook her head. 'No, it happened again the next night. It seems absolutely mad now, but it just never occurred to me that he'd come again, after I'd cried and everything. There was no lock on the door, but I hadn't even tried to barricade it. I was lying awake and he just – came in.

'I thought of you, Miss Tizzie – how strong you are. So I said if he didn't go I would tell his wife, and what would happen if I had a baby? You'd told me about babies, do you remember, Miss Tizzie? He – he just tied one of my stockings round my mouth and did it all over again. He's very strong, you see, very big. It was even worse that time, because I think he was really trying to hurt me. Afterwards he said if I made a fuss he would not only dismiss me, he'd deny it and tell everybody that I'd tempted him and offered to do it for money. He said the previous governess had never had a baby because they'd always done it at a safe time of the month. I had to wash the blood off the sheet when he'd gone. I stayed up for hours, drying it in front of the fire, then next day the maid complained to the housekeeper that I'd used up all my coal.'

Tizzie took Naomi's hands in hers. 'Why didn't you leave after the first time?' she asked.

'I was so worried that I'd let you down after you'd arranged the post for me, so ashamed. I – I thought you might start feeling responsible or something. I just didn't think he'd do it again, not with his family in the house. The girls were nice, you know, and so was Mrs Morris. I did wonder if she'd guessed after the first time because she asked me twice if I was all right, but I think it was just that she could tell I'd been crying ... I couldn't tell her, Miss Tizzie, I simply couldn't do it to her, and in any case I was so ashamed. After the second time I packed my bags and wrote a farewell note for the girls, then I left the house while they were having luncheon. I told you and my mother that I'd changed my mind about teaching so you wouldn't find out that I hadn't got a reference.'

Tizzie took the forlorn little figure in her arms, her mind racing. It came to her that Edward – dissolute, degenerate Edward had never been as brutal as Morris. He had liked to persuade, not to force ... All at once she realised that he was in her mind for the very first time since she'd married Sam, and fury boiled in her that she'd been made to think of him. She would deal with Morris later; Sam would help her. Right now she must do her best for Naomi. 'I'll have to think about all this,' she told her gently, 'but my immediate reaction is that if Albert loves you he'll marry you.'

'I couldn't deceive him!' protested Naomi, then more wistfully, 'Even if I did, he'd know, wouldn't he, that I'm not ... you know ... pure?'

'He might, but I'm not suggesting you deceive him, I'm suggesting you tell him! Listen, my mother was raped by a tramp – a vagabond, and she was frightened that he'd left her pregnant. My father had loved her for years, but he had no money. She told him about the rape and he married her at once. They started a baby right away and she thought it might be the vagabond's child, but it wasn't, because it grew up to look like the Ridings family. My parents were very happy, Naomi, and the baby was me. So think about that while you make your decision.

'Now, we won't go to the shop this afternoon, we'll stay up here and walk along the edge of the moor. If you want to talk, we'll talk; if you don't, we won't.'

*

Joshua was doing a walk through at Jericho. He strode the floors with eyes alert beneath the bushy white brows, asking questions, giving instructions and jotting down reminders. He'd stopped feeling self-conscious about the notebook; his memory was no longer faultless so he gave it a bit of help – it was simply a matter of prudence.

Word had been sent to Meadowbank first thing that Joe Whitehead had died during the night; a stroke, apparently, brought on by his constant bronchitis. The retired over-looker had been both friend and employee, so after dinner he was going to call on Joe's wife, Nellie, to pay his respects. He'd just been to the spinning room to tell the men, but they already knew.

The way news swept through Jericho could still surprise Joshua; it was as if invisible messengers paced the floors, relating to each and every worker what was happening in both town and mill. He'd come to the conclusion that it was because much of the work was repetitive – it demanded skill and concentration, but there was little variety for those at the machines. His mind pushed aside the word 'monoto-nous', because to him nothing in Jericho could ever be that, but he accepted that the same might not apply to his workers. It followed, therefore, that news, gossip, call it what you liked, could enliven the long working day. In a way it was good for production.

He slowed his stride to watch two of the heavy gang taking rolls of cloth from the weaving shed to the cut room and decided to spend ten minutes with the cut-looker next. Now and again he liked to comment on the work of individual weavers, both to their faces and to the over-lookers. Jericho produced some of the best yarn in Lancashire but it might as well be shorrocks if the finished cuts were full of floats.

Sam was crossing the yard towards the offices and paused to watch his father in the distance, knowing he'd been out on the floors for close on three hours. He was as upright as ever, still wearing his coat and tall hat despite the heat of the mill. Upright he might be, thought Sam, keen eyed and alert, but he wasn't the man he'd been before Ralph had shown his face again. It wasn't that he was losing weight, because flesh had been spare on his bones ever since Sam's mother had died, nor was it that he was becoming less nimble; it was as if whatever used to give him force and power had been switched off. There was no need to worry; old age was creeping up on him, that was all. He was past his three score years and ten.

'I've just been in the card room talking to Wain,' was his father's greeting. 'It struck me he wasn't up to the mark. There was a machine running rough but he didn't seem to have noticed, and one of his women –the tall one with ginger hair – looks too far gone in the family way to be on such work. I thought we made clear to him that he must move them from the machines when they're in that state?'

'We did,' Sam assured him. 'Didn't you have a word with him?' A couple of years ago he would have dealt with such minor matters on the spot.

Joshua sighed. Nobody could accuse his son of trying to usurp his authority. He himself was trying to back out a bit, to let Sam draw his own conclusions and make his own decisions, but it was more than he could do not to drop a hint when he saw something that gave him cause for concern. The lad was good with cotton, happen better than he himself had been at the same age, but he hadn't got a lifetime's experience behind him – yet.

'Wain likes his ale,' Sam told him. 'He has a name for drinking, but I've never known it affect his work – I'll have a word with his floor boss first, then take a stroll through the card room and sort things out.'

Satisfied, Joshua nodded. 'Seeing that lass in the family way put me in mind of Tizzie,' he said. ' She's looking a bit peaky, wouldn't you say? I was wondering if her sickness is a bit extreme. Has she seen the doctor?'

'No,' admitted Sam, 'but she's had talks with Sarah about it and she reads anything she can lay her hands on.

She says she's not having a doctor telling her to put her feet up and doling out nostrums.'

'That's what your mother used to say. Do you think you should have a word with the doctor yourself?'

'I already have, but don't tell Tizzie. He said that it affects a few women like it's affecting her. Some of them are sick right through the pregnancy, but that's quite rare. I asked if they give birth to sickly babies and he said no, the child will always take what it needs. So it's Tizzie who'll suffer, and I don't like the thought of that. I'm going up to Alsing in a couple of days to have a talk with Sarah myself. It's her who's put Tizzie up to all this exercise.'

Joshua shook his head in bafflement. He saw a lack of food as cause for the utmost concern. 'I don't know how she finds the energy without nourishment,' he said.

'Neither do I, but she has a will of iron, don't forget. She's off with Barney Jellicoe this afternoon, viewing a property that's coming up for sale.'

Knowing the town like the back of his hand, Joshua was all attention. 'Where?' he asked keenly.

'Out at Ryeworth, overlooking West Brook – that little courtyard of old cottages.'

'They're old, right enough,' agreed Joshua, 'and lovely with it. They were fine buildings in their day, but half of 'em are in ruins since they had a fire out there.'

'I know, but if the buildings are no good it's prime land for developing, being near the pits, and with a ready supply of water it's a good site for a new mill. Tizzie's thinking of shops, though, for the growing population over there. She needs no advice from me when it comes to property.'

'She takes it from Jellicoe, though?'

'Not always,' said Sam shortly. 'She makes her own decisions.'

His father shot him a curious look, then turned on his heel and headed for the cut room. 'See you later, then,' he said mildly.

Sam walked on towards the offices, deep in thought. What sort of man was he to be jealous of Barney Jellicoe?

He had only admitted it to himself in the last few months, and he was deeply ashamed of such an emotion, knowing as he did that Tizzie loved him with all her heart. It was just that she seemed to have this – this link with Barney. He didn't know whether it was mental or emotional; he couldn't put a name to it but it maddened him. As for the man's feelings for her, she must be blind . . . His wife, the cleverest and most beautiful woman in Saltley, if not all Lancashire, had been blind for years. Barney Jellicoe saw her not as a friend, not as a business partner, but as a desirable woman. He loved her.

Tizzie wasn't well, but she brushed aside Rebecca's doubts. 'I'm a bit dizzy now and again, that's all. Look, I've got to do something interesting or I'll go stark raving mad, so this little outing with Mr Jellicoe is just what I need. We're going by carriage, so stop looking like the knell of doom.'

'I shoulda thought you'd *hear* the knell of doom, not see it,' retorted Rebecca, causing Tizzie to roll her eyes in agreement. Sometimes she felt real regret that Rebecca had never been given an education; she often revealed flashes of ability that should have been encouraged in her youth. How many bright young minds had been neglected in past years, she wondered, stunted by lack of encouragement and poverty?

Opening the wardrobe, she announced, 'I'm wearing my brown coat and new velvet hat. 'I can't have the population of Ryeworth thinking a frump has arrived in their midst.'

'Ryeworth isn't exactly a place where folk crowd the streets,' Rebecca assured her, smiling. 'As for lookin' a frump, I've never yet known that, Mrs Schofield. But I do have the feelin' you should stay in after three dizzy do's in one mornin', an' – '

'That's enough!' There was a limit to what she wanted to hear. 'Mr Jellicoe will be with me, don't forget.'

'Aye, so he will.' The housekeeper calmed down. It would be a poor do if Barney Jellicoe couldn't be relied on to look after her, but Mr Schofield had been a bit sharp when he knew she was determined to go. That had been first thing, an' all, before she'd had her dizzy do's. 'Noah's out at the front with the carriage,' she said now, looking out.

Tizzie tipped the smart little hat forward and pinned it firmly to her hair. It was of brown velvet like her coat but with a flutter of bronze and amber feathers. She wasn't sure whether she liked it or not. She didn't seem to be sure about anything, any more, except that she was tired. 'Mr Jellicoe will probably come in for afternoon tea when we get back,' she said, 'so lay it in front of the fire in the study, will you, between the low chairs? We should be home by four o'clock at the latest. Noah will have to take the top road there and back so I can get out and heave my heart up in privacy if I feel the need.'

Rebecca's great dark eyes were anxious. 'I still think it woulda been better if you'd let Naomi go with you, Mrs Schofield.'

'Her being at the shop is why Mr Jellicoe is free for the afternoon,' Tizzie pointed out. 'I'll only be away for a couple of hours so stop worrying.'

Barney was ready and waiting, wearing his dark business coat and a new stylish black bowler with a high round crown. He swung himself up into the carriage with his odd sideways roll. 'Mrs Schofield,' he said, raising his hat. 'I hope I see you well?'

'I could be better,' she admitted. 'You look very smart, Barney. I like the hat.'

For once he looked almost light-hearted. 'I like yours, an' all,' he replied. He handed her a document. 'Here's the specification,' he said. 'I persuaded the agent to let me have it straight from the printers. Are you sure you feel up to goin'?'

'Don't try to stop me,' she said grimly. 'Noah, let's move.'

The hamlet of Ryeworth bordered Saltley Bog and was half rural, half industrial. The shaft of a new pit had been sunk there in the past year, but groups of old cottages still lined the deep gully cut by West Brook next to a stone cotton mill that was due for demolition, its water wheel a gaunt testimony to an earlier source of power. On higher ground was the group of dwellings they'd come to see, slumbering peacefully under the winter sun. Impressed, Tizzie eyed the gabled roofs and took out her notebook and pencil. 'Were they almshouses or what?' she asked.

'Just rented dwellin's, as far as I know. Datin' back a good while – 1750 or thereabouts. The agent thinks they were farm cottages but if that's right the farmer musta been a better master than most.'

'Let's go up, then,' said Tizzie. 'Noah, we might be a while. I want to have a good look round.'

The young coachman sat there stolidly. 'It's a bit cold for you bein' out o' doors for long, Mrs Schofield. Mrs Drury's sent a warm shawl. She says I'm to ask if you'll take it with you.'

Tizzie gritted her teeth. 'I'm warm enough, thanks. Come on, Barney.'

They climbed a rising path between winter-dead rose beds and stopped beneath an arch in the wall of the courtyard. 'You can see the layout of the place from here,' said Barney, pointing. 'You see them two fields over yonder? I'm told they've been sold to build pit cottages. Over to the right you can see five more terraces goin' up – they're to house operatives from young Fairbrother's mill. That long, low building over there is Bright's new laundry; you recall Fanny Bright buildin' up the business in the fifties an' sixties? Beyond that there's more new houses – little 'uns – for them who work the market gardens . . .'

'Quite a population, in fact,' said Tizzie, gazing at the scene. It was very quiet. There was only the sound of the water and the distant shouts of bricklayers at work on the new houses. Below them they could see an old man cutting winter cabbage in a garden plot and on the road from Saltley two shawl-swathed women trudging home with their shopping.

She felt the familiar onset of nausea and took in deep breaths, as Sarah had advised. She didn't want to spoil the afternoon because to her it was special – a bright little interlude to banish her low spirits. For this short time they were in this different world, set apart from the hurly-burly of the town. 'Thanks for coming, Barney,' she said impulsively, 'and for finding out all about this place.'

His dark eyes met hers, guarded as always. He merely nodded, then stood back and let her go on. 'Watch your step,' he warned, 'there's rotten timbers about. An' keep away from the house at that far corner – the door's all but fallin' off.'

Sick she might be, thought Tizzie, but this was what she needed. Notebook in hand, she tried to judge for herself whether these lovely old houses were 'ripe for renovation' as the agent said or 'ready for demolition' as she herself suspected. She eyed the expanse of the flagged courtyard. 'It's better than I expected, Barney, much better. This yard would lend itself to outdoor stalls, selling produce from the market gardens, say. As for this covered walkway, it's amazing – almost like cloisters. Look at the roof timbers and these old brick arches.'

Barney nodded. 'In summer there's roses an' honeysuckle climbin' all over 'em. I happened to call in for a look round five or six months back an' they were a picture.'

So he'd had his eye on the place for some time. She'd suspected as much, yet he'd laid it before her, not aiming to buy it himself. She wouldn't thank him again, though. He didn't like being thanked. She stopped at an open doorway. 'D'you think this room is special? It's pretty big.'

'The community hall, so the write-up says. Wait – ' he put out a warning hand as he read a rough notice on the door. 'It says here, "Caution – walls unsafe!"'

Tizzie wasn't paying attention. She peered inside. It was dim, the windows all covered and the only light coming through a hole in the roof and a broken shutter. From beneath a wave of sickness an idea was forming in her mind – a wonderful idea. Why hadn't she thought of it before? She would ask Barney's opinion … She took two steps inside the cavernous room and stopped. Spars of timber were reared against the walls on either side of her; more were crisscrossed on the floor, barring her way.

Barney leapt in front of her, arms outstretched. 'Go on out!' he said. 'Go back, I say!'

Knowing she'd been reckless, she turned to do as he said, but all at once her head whirled. Dizzy and confused, she tottered backwards, losing her balance and clutching at one of the propped up beams. It moved at her touch. Barney cried out and tried to grab her, but with a loud, theatrical creak the wood slid sideways and knocked her to the floor.

Tizzie's head was spinning, and a great wave of sickness was washing through her. She could see Barney's face. His teeth were bared in a silent howl; horror was in his upraised hands. She tried to get to her feet, but she couldn't move her arms. There was a weight across her chest. It was one of the beams!

'Keep still,' Barney was saying urgently. 'Listen to me, these lengths o' wood musta been proppin' the wall up. Don't move for a minute.'

She felt no pain, only the weight across her chest and neck. She stayed quite still, aware that she'd brought this on herself. It was strange, seeing Barney from this angle – he looked like a giant towering over her with his big head and those shoulders. His cheeks were all wet, though. Why was that? He bent down to her and she saw that his face was covered in sweat, enormous droplets standing all over it like glass beads. Was he sweating with fear?

Then he was feeling her arms, her legs, to see if they were broken, muttering, 'Excuse me, excuse me,' as he touched her. He grunted with relief at finding no evidence of damage and took her hand in his. 'You're between two big spars o' wood,' he told her, 'one on top, one under your back. I'll raise the top one an inch or two an' as soon as it moves, wriggle out. You'll have to be quick – go to your left, where it's clear. Then as soon as you're out, you make for the door – it's behind you as you lie here. Are you ready?' Carefully he gripped the beam and tried to raise it. It didn't move.

A shaft of sunlight pierced the gloom and she saw the sinews stand out on his neck as he strained. 'No good,' he gasped. 'Ah, I know!' With a squirm he lay face down, next to her but lower because she was raised up from the floor. Once his shoulders were under the beam he splayed his big hands and braced himself. 'When I raise it, get out,' he said. 'I'll follow you. Make for the door at *once*, Miss Tizzie.' He lifted his head and from only inches away his dark eyes looked into hers. 'Go right out an' stay there. Promise me!' It was a command rather than a plea.

'I promise, I promise,' she said, forcing back tears. 'I'm sorry, Barney!'

For an instant he stared at her and then smiled his beautiful smile. He nodded as if satisfied. 'You always did keep your promises,' he muttered.

He braced himself again and she recalled that he'd always been strong in the shoulders. Slowly he raised himself and she saw sweat dripping from his chin. Then the timber creaked and lifted on his back. She slid out and crawled on hands and knees to the door, her head still whirling. Go right out, he'd said.

She dragged herself through the doorway and, gaining her feet, turned to him, but he wasn't there. She cried out in horror and saw him flat on the floor with the beam still across his shoulders. She steeled herself to go back to him, but no – she'd promised to stay out. Well, she'd have to break the promise! 'I'm coming,' she shouted, but at that instant there came a groan of old timbers. She screamed as one by one all the beams slid heavily to the floor, obliterating all signs of Barney. Plaster fell in chunks from high on the wall and then there came a noise like the crack of a pistol. She leapt back as a single brick fell to the floor, followed at once by a deafening roar as the wall collapsed inwards, like the side of a house made of playing cards.

Dust filled her eyes, her nose, her mouth. She didn't know it but she was screaming as she scrabbled at timbers and bricks. She couldn't even see him, let alone get him out. She raced across the yard to the archway. 'Help!' she screamed. 'Noah! No – o – ah!'

The coachman came at a run, his boots striking sparks from the flagstones. 'Mrs Schofield!' he cried. 'What's wrong?'

'Barney's in there buried under rubble,' she gasped. 'Tons of it. The wall collapsed.'

Noah's fair young face stretched. He eyed her in alarm. 'You're hurt, Mrs Schofield,' he protested. 'Your neck's bleedin'!'

She grabbed his hand and dragged him along the walkway. 'Look at Barney, not me!' she snapped. 'Can you get him out?'

Noah stared into the room, aghast. Half the ceiling had fallen and wooden laths were spiked against the sky. Rubble was piled three feet high all over the floor, and somewhere under it was Barney. Even as they looked a brick fell from an untouched corner and broke as it hit a length of wood. Noah wet his lips. 'Don't touch anythin', Mrs Schofield,' he said harshly. 'Keep out! I'll go an' get the men from yon' buildin' site.' He turned to rush off and then realised that he couldn't trust her not to go back inside. 'Beg pardon, ma'am,' he said and, scooping her up in his arms, ran back with her to the carriage, where he put her on the seat. 'With help we'll have him out o' there in minutes,' he gasped. 'This way's best, you'll see! No, ma'am – stay *there*!'

Tizzie was wrenching at the door so he wrapped rope around the handle. She was screaming like a madwoman, but all at once she fell silent. She'd kept her promise after all. She clung to the seat as they careered along the road to the building site.

Six strong men couldn't keep Tizzie out of the room. There

was a foreman, three bricklayers, a hod carrier and Noah, grim faced now with the knowledge that if anything harmed her he must answer to his employer. The men worked with great caution, putting stays against the remaining walls and lifting each spar, each brick, with the utmost care. They would have worked for nothing with a man's life at stake, but Tizzie had simply said, 'Name your own price to get him out!'

'Hurry up!' she urged now, snatching bricks from their hands and casting them outside. 'We're coming, Barney!' she cried. 'It won't be long!' When there was no reply she clutched at the foreman's arm. 'He'll be suffocating,' she croaked. 'Hurry them up!'

'We'd do a sight better without you under our feet, missis,' he said bluntly. 'It'll do him no good if the rest of it comes down on top of him. Leave it to us.'

Faced with such confident logic, Tizzie forced herself outside. Why couldn't she just faint? she asked herself desperately. Other women lost consciousness when something awful happened; they achieved oblivion, if only for minutes. All that ever happened to her was that the floor seemed to tilt. She paced beneath the arches and found that she was wringing her hands. It was true, she thought; people did do that in times of anguish. Behind her the grunts and thuds and muffled curses continued.

It seemed an eternity before Noah came out, the whites of his eyes glinting in his dust-caked face. 'We've reached him, Mrs Schofield,' he sighed, 'but I think – '

Tizzie pushed past him, picking a way over discarded rubble. Barney lay where she had last seen him, still face down. His elbows were now forced out sideways but his hands remained splayed against the floor. She fell to her knees. His eyes were open and he was half smiling. In the sudden silence she could hear her own heart beating, fast and regular, but she knew that the heart inside that stunted body would never beat again.

Sickness was rising in her throat but she breathed deeply, willing it away. Gently she scraped away the plaster from beneath his face and brushed the dust from his curly grey hair. Above her the men were standing in a group, watching. 'Thank you,' she said quietly. 'I'll settle up with you as soon as I can.'

'Shouldn't we get him out o' here?' asked Noah, looking apprehensively at the remaining walls. Three of them laid him on the floor of the walkway, where once again Tizzie knelt at his side. 'Noah,' she said, 'go back to the town and get the undertaker – Mr Simmonds is the best. Tell him it's for me.'

One of the men shuffled his feet. 'I'll stay here with him if you want, missis. Till they get here, like.'

'No,' she said, 'that won't be necessary. You can all go back to your work now. I'll stay with him.' She flapped a weary hand. 'No arguing, Noah. Just do as I say.'

Reluctantly they left her. Noah ran to the carriage and leapt for the reins. The men walked down to the road, talking quietly among themselves, but Tizzie stayed where she was, at Barney's side.

She was to remember for ever how peaceful it had been, that time alone with Barney. Even when the tears came there was no noisy sobbing, no wild passion of grief – just a sadness so deep it was as if it came from a bottomless pit inside her. Tears rolled down her cheeks. She didn't wipe them away but let them run off her chin until they wet her coat. When her neck began to sting she recalled that Noah had said it was bleeding but knew she could look at it later, when she was back home.

As daylight faded and lights were lit in the cottages down the hill, she sat on the floor and held Barney's cold hand, observing the stunted limbs, the pelt of curly grey hair, the eyes that one of the men had closed. He was lying here dead and she didn't know what had killed him, whether it was suffocation, internal injury or strain on his heart. She didn't know what, but she certainly knew who. It had been her fault. If her mind hadn't been full of a new idea she would have listened to him; if she'd listened to him she wouldn't have entered the room and it would never have happened.

She'd told him she was sorry, though, and he'd smiled – even now his lips were curved. As surely as if he'd written it down in her notebook she knew he'd been happy to take the weight of that beam. He'd been aware of the risk, and content to take it – for her.

Somewhere inside her lurked the familiar sickness of her pregnancy, but it was being swept aside by a sense of loss that was the worst she'd ever known. Worse than when her father died: the shrunken, undemonstrative man who gained her respect only after his death; worse than her mother, who had left both home and pawnshop and for years treated her eldest daughter like a stranger; worse than her dear Mary's William . . . oh yes, much worse.

It must be getting colder, she thought hazily. She didn't feel cold, just sleepy, but she could see her breath like steam in the fading light. She wondered whether anybody had told Sam but saw no urgency. He was there at the back of her mind, in the centre of her heart, comforting and reassuring, like the prospect of a warm fire to a winter traveller. She was in no hurry to see him. This quiet time was for her and Barney . . .

CHAPTER TWENTY

'Out of the Mouths . . .'

Sam leapt from the carriage, grabbed the lantern from its hook next to Noah and ran up to the courtyard. After the bustle of Jericho and the town's lamp-lit streets the dark silence seemed full of foreboding. At the archway he turned to Noah. 'Where is she?' he demanded.

The coachman took the lantern and led the way across the yard. 'Over here, Mr Schofield. Watch how you go – there's rubble an' timbers an' such!'

Sam couldn't believe that she was here in this ice-cold heap of rubbish with only a dead man for company. Anger began to build in him. He'd asked her not to come, but would she listen? No – she'd go her own way if it killed her ... Killed her? 'Tizzie!' he cried, suddenly fearful. 'Tizzie!' The echo of his voice rolled emptily beneath the arches.

At his side Noah was taut as stretched wire, telling himself that he'd only done as he'd been told when he'd left her here with the corpse. He shouldn't have done it, he knew he shouldn't, but at least he'd gone to tell Mr Schofield rather than the undertaker. He caught at Sam's arm. 'Here they are,' he said, lifting up the lamp.

'Aah!' Sam gaped at the sight. Barney was face upwards on the flagstones, but lying across his chest was Tizzie, her hair in wild spirals about her shoulders, her hand holding

Barney's. Jealousy stabbed him like a knife thrust, followed at once by dread. For an instant he couldn't move. She'd miscarried; she was unconscious, perhaps dead, *both* of them were dead. He knelt down and turned her to him very gently while Noah crouched nearer with the lamp. She wasn't dead. Her hands were like ice but her pulse was there, very slow. 'Tizzie!' he said, weak with relief. 'Tizzie, sweetheart, it's Sam, come to take you home.' She was covered in dust, there was dried blood on her neck, her coat was ripped. He wasn't even sure if he should move her. He patted her cheeks and held her hands between his. 'My love,' he said, 'my darling love, I'm taking you home.'

She opened her eyes to see his face only inches away. 'Barney's dead,' she said wearily, then looked down at the squat body beneath her. 'I told Noah to bring the undertaker.'

'He'll be here in a minute. We sent for him from Jericho. He'll take care of Barney, never fear. Are you in pain, love?'

She shook her head. 'I'm sleepy,' she said, 'very sleepy.' He started to lift her up but she pushed his arms away. 'I'm not leaving Barney,' she said, as if amazed that he could think such a thing.

He ignored her. 'Noah,' he said, 'stay with him until the undertaker comes, will you? I'll drive Mrs Schofield home. I think she's suffering from the cold or shock – or both.'

With Tizzie protesting weakly against his shoulder he carried her past the bare flowerbeds and over the frost-rimed grass, then put her gently on the seat of the carriage. To his fury she struggled to open the door and get out. 'Stay *there*, woman!' he snapped. 'D'you want to lose the child?'

He couldn't see her face, but all at once she became still. Instinct told him then that she hadn't thought about the baby. Grimly he put her back on the seat, and leapt into the driver's box and headed the horse back home.

*

It was morning and pale sunlight slanted through the window. Tizzie was propped against pillows in her big bed, telling herself limply that she could hardly get up when that officious doctor had forbidden it in Sam's hearing. He'd been waiting to examine her when they'd arrived home, she could remember that much – that and Sam carrying her upstairs as if she was made of glass. She must have been in a bad way because she hadn't tried to stop him. She vaguely recalled the doctor prodding and poking and saying there was no sign of a miscarriage, then he had tut-tutted about her bruised chest and dressed the cuts on her neck, making pronouncements all the while.

As for her, in a bad way or not, she'd had to gather her wits and put on an act of being concerned about the baby. The truth was that ever since arriving at the courtyard with Barney she hadn't once given it a thought, not even when nausea had swept through her, not even when she had been under the beam. Sam, with his keen perception, must have sensed it and was upset. She could see it in the line of his mouth, the restraint of his endearments; in the odd, deliberate way he spoke of the pregnancy. He was loving and tender, kissing her cheek, fetching and carrying, sitting up all night in the armchair next to the bed, but she *knew*. Sam was never restrained; enthusiasm was his middle name. Once or twice she'd thought that something else was troubling him as well, but if he didn't want to talk, how could she find out what it was?

Rebecca came in with a drink of hot lemon, but she waved her away. 'Mrs Schofield, you must take plenty o' fluids,' said the housekeeper gently. 'You've got a bit of a fever, you know – a bad chill. Would you like me to sponge your hands an' face, to cool you down, like?'

'No, no. I'm a bit sleepy, Rebecca. If you leave me I might nod off for a while.'

Obediently the older woman left the room and Tizzie thumped the pillows in frustration. The staff were all acting as if she was at death's door, which was ironic when Barney wasn't only at the door, he'd gone through it. Her

whole being cried out to mourn him. Her friend of many
years, her true, faithful friend, had died because of her and
yet she must put on an act. After weeks of being sick
morning, noon and night she must pretend, for Sam's sake,
to be concerned about the baby. Bleakly she stared out at
the frost-laden moor. It wouldn't be easy, but she'd long
ago found out that anyone who expected life to be easy was
a fool. No doubt she would have to go through the whole
performance every time somebody asked her what had
happened.

Come to that, Sam himself didn't yet know the details.
At present he was out on Barney's affairs, doing what she
herself should have been doing. She hadn't had to ask him;
he'd taken it for granted that he would do whatever she
wanted. Barney was lying at peace in the little chapel at the
undertaker's. She couldn't for the life of her think of him
as 'the body', nor let herself admit that if she'd had her wits
about her he would be downstairs in the quiet little room
at the end of the hall ... There were no relations to be
informed because he had no family. She had never known
if he was an orphan or if he'd been abandoned at birth.
He'd never spoken of his past.

Sam had already been to Ryeworth and paid the
workmen for their help. Now he was at the pawnshop,
looking for Barney's instructions about the funeral. She'd
told him where they'd be – in the big desk up in his sitting
room ... Her mind raced through the arrangements. It
would be a small, dignified affair, with no expense spared.
No service in chapel, though; he'd never been one for
chapel. The shop would close for the day as a mark of
respect – there'd be time to warn all the customers.

Tizzie sat bolt upright and fumed. These were the last
things she could have done for him; arrange his funeral,
take charge at the shop, see to his affairs. Instead she was
lying here being coddled like a prize cow carrying a
pedigree calf.

Rosie was putting on her coat for school when Martha

came back from the laundry room with a pile of bolster cases for mending. She always repaired the fine linen because she was good with her needle. Mr Schofield paid her well and it was a bit extra to add to Matthew's savings for when they went to Devon. He was always telling her, 'When we go, we'll go in style, Martha. No penny pinchin' for the Raikes, eh?'

She suspected that he wanted to show off a bit in front of his sisters, to let them see he'd done well for himself. She saw nothing wrong with that; he'd left Devon an out of work under-gardener so why shouldn't he return well dressed and prosperous?

She looked critically at her daughter. 'Come here a minute,' she said. 'You look like Dolly Ragbag!' She retied Rosie's bonnet ribbons and fastened the top button of her coat. 'There, that's better. You've got your readin' book, now?'

'Yes, Mam.' Rosie was eager to be off. Sometimes she met Harry Butterworth on the way to school and he made her laugh. Not that she liked him as much as Charles, definitely not, but Harry was ever so funny . . .

'Just a minute, love.' Martha eyed her daughter thoughtfully. 'I suppose I'd better tell you before you hear it from somebody else. They're sayin' in the kitchen that Mr Jellicoe's dead.'

Rosie stared at her mother, her eyes dark and very serious. 'How did he die, Mam?'

'Well, they say he was crushed to death while he was out with Mrs Sam – an accident, like, in an old buildin' on the edge of the bog. Mrs Sam was hurt an' all but not serious.' Martha didn't mention the expected baby. Time enough for her to know about that when it arrived.

Rosie was stricken. She had to fish for her clean hankie because she thought she might cry. In her mind she could see the look on the dwarf's face that time at the party, and then again at the wedding. They had both taken place a long time ago, but she could remember how he'd looked as if it was yesterday.

Martha was eyeing her in bewilderment. 'Don't get all upset, love. You didn't know him all that well, now did you?'

'No,' sniffled Rosie, 'but he liked Mrs Sam, didn't he? It hurt him when she got married.'

Martha was intrigued. 'You what?'

'It hurt him when Mr Sam married her.'

'How do you know that, love?'

Rosie wriggled her shoulders. 'I could tell,' she said evasively. She'd stopped trying to explain to her mam and dad about the messages on people's faces. Now it struck her that her mam was looking dubious. Had she never seen for herself how Mr Jellicoe was feeling? 'He wanted to marry her himself,' she explained, as if she was the adult and her mother the child. 'He loved her, just like Mr James loves Mrs Hartley.'

Martha stared at her daughter open mouthed. 'Don't ever say that to anybody else!' she warned. 'Do you hear?'

'Yes, Mam.' Tears were edging down Rosie's pink cheeks. She couldn't help it when she thought of Mr Jellicoe's face at the wedding ... With a mumbled excuse she ran upstairs and found three pennies she'd been keeping in her top drawer. She hid them in her mitten and ran down again.

'Off you go,' said Martha, 'or you'll be on the last shove up.' Rosie ran off wiping her eyes, leaving her mother staring after her, bemused. 'Out of the mouths ...' she muttered.

After pretending to Rebecca, Tizzie found that she did indeed keep nodding off to sleep. She couldn't understand it. Nausea still plagued her and sometimes she was dizzy; she was used to that, but all this sleeping baffled her. Sam was in and out of the room, tempting her with drinks, plumping up the pillows, adding more coal to the fire; even now he was hovering restlessly by the window. 'Is there anything else I can do on Barney's affairs?' he asked. When she shook her head he backed towards the door.

'Then I'll get Rebecca to sit with you and just slip down to Jericho for an hour, if you don't mind.'

The door closed behind him and she leaned against the pillows. Mind? She was glad to have him out of the house so that she didn't have to watch for each change of expression, each tightening of his lips. She'd tried to show concern about the baby but it hadn't changed things; if anything the tension between them was worse. She was married to a gentle, considerate stranger; if she hadn't felt a bit light-headed she would have tackled him about it by now. She was nodding off again when Rebecca crept in. 'More flowers, Mrs Schofield,' she whispered, offering three yellow chrysanthemums wrapped in paper. 'The little girl brought them with a note.'

'Who? My niece?'

'No, ma'am. It was the gardener's daughter from Meadowbank. She must have walked up here after school.'

Tizzie fingered the flowers and laid them on the bed. They were a deep golden yellow, the colour of sunshine, the colour she'd always associated with the Schofields. It wouldn't suit the Schofield she was married to, she thought grimly, not at the moment. Thundercloud grey was more appropriate for him. She opened the note, which was written on lined paper like that in a child's exercise book. The writing was very neat, the grammar and spelling impeccable. It said:

Dear Mrs Schofield,
I am very, very sad about Mr Jellicoe. I liked him a lot. I hope he was happy before he died and I hope you will soon feel better.

Yours respectfully,
Rosanna Raike

Tizzie stared at it through sudden tears. She hardly knew the child yet she'd spent her coppers on flowers and said she was very, very sad about Barney. Nobody else had said that. Sam had said nothing at all; he had merely busied himself with arrangements. His father had called with an armful of flowers and said, 'What a terrible thing, Tizzie. What a way to breathe his last. You've lost a good friend in Barney Jellicoe, you haven't part.' Even he couldn't conceal that he was more concerned about her than about Barney. Sarah had sent hothouse flowers and a note that she would call next day, while Mary had given her a hug and whispered, 'Poor, poor Barney – you'll miss him, Tizz.' At the shop Albert was no doubt stunned, no doubt upset, but nobody, nobody had said they were sad – except a child who hardly knew him. And what had she meant by hoping he was happy before he died? One day she would tell her that he had been smiling ...

Sam was walking along a track on the edge of the moor. He hadn't been to the mill – that had been an excuse to get out of the house and think. He'd thought, right enough, and much good it had done him. Tizzie was ill – she didn't know it but she had a fever. He himself had a fever of sorts, but of the mind: a fever of resentment, of jealousy – aye, and of shame. He resented her not listening when he'd begged her to stay at home, resented her forgetting about the baby when she might well have miscarried in the midst of all that rubble. He was sick with jealousy that she'd been lying on top of Barney and holding his hand – that *was* a fever, to be jealous of a corpse, but worst of all was the shame. It shamed him to be glad that Barney was dead, but he couldn't help it. When Noah had told him the news he'd felt a great gush of gladness and relief that he need never again be jealous of the stunted little man who was in love with his wife. Never again? He'd been jealous within minutes when he'd seen Barney lying dead with Tizzie on top of him.

All his instincts urged him to talk to her about it. Once before he had neglected to do that and the omission had cost them long empty years. But now what could he do? What could he say? Tizzie was ill. He must swallow his feelings and look after her.

When he returned she was in a fresh nightgown with her hair in a thick, curly plait over one shoulder. Her skin was glistening and she had two patches of colour high on her cheekbones. She seemed calm enough but he would have had to be blind not to see that she was wary of him. God above, he thought wearily, they'd come to a pretty pass in twenty-four hours.

Three yellow chrysanthemums were in a vase on the bedside table. She stretched out a hand to stroke the curving petals and the green, woody scent of them came to him across the room. 'Look,' she said, 'these are from little Rosie Raike.'

He was touched. 'A kind thought,' he said quietly. 'She's a nice little lass.'

'She sent a note. She says she's very, very sad about Barney.' Tizzie was watching him with an intent, glittering gaze. 'Did Albert seem sad? And Gideon?'

'Of course they did,' he said stoutly. 'They were shocked, but very upset.'

'You're not upset, though, are you?' The words seemed to hang on the air above the bed.

He gazed intently at the flowers. 'Don't start imagining things, Tizzie. Try to relax a bit.'

'Relax? When my best friend is dead? If I don't mourn him it's clear nobody else will. I say again – you're not sad, are you? You haven't even asked how it happened.'

'Happen I don't want to know,' he retorted. 'You were determined to go with him even though I pleaded with you to stay at home. You let him take you inside a building that was unsafe. You risked your life and the life of our baby, and to cap it all you even forgot you were expecting. I'm sorry if all that overshadows Barney's death.'

Tizzie was pulling at the red-gold plait of her hair and now she tossed it back over her shoulder and glared at him. 'He tried to stop me going into the hall. He warned me but I wasn't listening.'

'That's no surprise. You only listen when it suits you.'

'I'd just had an idea,' she protested, 'about what I could

make of the place. I was thinking about that and I wasn't paying attention.'

Sam stared. There was an agonised ring to the words. 'An idea?' he repeated.

'It seemed so obvious. Before we set off I'd been thinking that Rebecca is quite bright, but she's never had any education. All at once, in that big room, I thought what a wonderful school could be made out of the place – for all the children in Ryeworth. A class in each of those lovely old houses; modern teaching in a traditional setting.' She stared emptily across the room. 'A catastrophic idea. Barney leapt in front of me and told me to get out. I turned to do as he said, but I went dizzy.'

'Oh dear, not dizzy?' Sarcasm dripped from the words. 'Rebecca told the doctor you'd had three dizzy spells before you even set out but it didn't stop you going, did it? What happened then?'

'To save myself from falling I grabbed at a great length of wood that was propped against the wall. It fell down on me and knocked me to the floor. It pinned me on top of another one that was lying there.'

Sam flinched and moistened his lips, but Tizzie was reliving Barney's last moments. 'He tried to get me out before anything else happened but he couldn't lift the beam. Then he slid under it next to me, to lift it with his shoulders so I could wriggle free. He made me promise to go right out of the room and stay there. He said he'd follow me. He lifted it and I did as he said, but when I turned round he wasn't behind me, he was still trapped under the beam. Even as I watched, the others all fell down on top of him, one by one. Seconds later the wall collapsed and buried him.' She looked him straight in the eye. 'Barney saved my life.'

Sam found he couldn't respond. Good God in heaven, the dwarf was winning on every count. He must credit him now with protecting Tizzie, with guarding her, with giving his life for her and their unborn child. He didn't want to hear any more. 'You'll have to excuse me,' he muttered.

'I'll have to go and think about this.'

'Think all you like,' she replied coldly, 'and when you've finished thinking, see if you can come up with a shred of gratitude. He's dead, Sam.'

She was caressing the chrysanthemums again. It infuriated him. 'What exactly did he mean to you?' he asked sharply.

'He cared,' she said simply. 'He cared about me when nobody else gave a damn whether I lived or died. Even Mary was wrapped up in her family. He cared!'

That stung him. 'Of course he cared! He was in love with you, woman! I can't believe you never saw it!'

A tide of colour rose from somewhere under her nightgown and stained her throat and then her face, obliterating the two red patches on her cheeks. 'He never so much as touched my hand if he could help it,' she whispered. 'He was my true friend.'

'A true friend who was in love with you,' he assured her.

'And you were jealous of him,' she said, comprehending at last.

'Yes,' he admitted. 'I was jealous as hell of the closeness between you. I'm not proud of it. I tried very hard to conceal it.'

'You succeeded,' she acknowledged wearily. 'Let's talk about it later – after the funeral.'

He took hold of her hand and kissed the hot palm. 'We'll talk when you feel better,' he said. 'For now, will you just remember that I love you with all my heart?'

'I'll remember,' she said, but gave no assurances that she loved him in return. 'Let's get the funeral over,' she repeated.

They got the funeral over without her. Delirious, she tossed in a fever so severe the doctor took Sam aside and warned him that he might lose her. 'Your wife has inflammation of the lungs,' he said, 'and she's weak with pregnancy sickness. Another woman would never survive, but with

Mrs Schofield there's hope because she has a strong constitution. She's to have round the clock nursing and the room kept warm but ventilated. She'll go in and out of consciousness but she must never be bothered with day-to-day matters. Tell her what you see fit about Mr Jellicoe's funeral as long as it gives her no mental strain. I'll be in each day – more often if I'm needed.'

Sam was beside himself. Remorse was his constant companion. He'd badgered her when she was falling into delirium; he'd burdened her with the knowledge that Barney had been in love with her. Whatever torment lay behind her fevered muttering, he must have made it worse. He hired nurses recommended by Sarah but was relieved when she herself came down from Alsing for hours at a time to supervise the sickroom. Tranquil, knowledgeable, well on in her pregnancy, she brought an air of normality with her and gave out reassurance with every breath.

Sam could do little for Tizzie except organise the funeral as she would have wished. A quiet funeral for a quiet man; orderly, expensive and very dignified. The frosty weather had given way to dense fog, so the hearse and carriages were half obscured. There were few to observe them; Christmas was fast approaching and the folk of Saltley were preparing for the break.

Barney was buried in a corner of the cemetery, close to the wall. Standing next to his father, Sam had to force himself to stop thinking about Tizzie, to listen and look at what was happening so that he would be able to relate every detail when she was well again. He closed his mind to the possibility that she might not recover.

They left the grave surrounded by flowers that glowed like jewels in the grey half-light: wreaths from the Schofields, from Mary, from Albert and Gideon and from half a dozen men of business who had dealt with Barney and Tizzie over the years. Joshua had offered to have the funeral tea at Meadowbank. 'With Tizzie so poorly you'll not want folk up at your place,' he'd said the day before. 'Lilah will see to it – she's a dab hand at catering. If there's folk coming from as far off as Bolton they'll want something inside 'em.'

He took Sam's arm as they walked to the carriages. 'Get back to Tizzie,' he advised. 'I'll look after the mourners. There'll be James there to chat to folk and Mary says she can stay for an hour.'

Sam rushed home to be greeted by Sarah at the foot of the stairs. 'Sammy!' she gasped, 'I saw you from the bedroom. I think – no, I'm sure she's turned the corner. She's going to be all right!'

She expected him to push past her and run up to the sickroom, but instead he flopped down on the bottom step, his face grey and his shoulders bowed. 'Thank God, thank God,' he muttered. For the first time in almost twenty-five years, Sarah saw her brother weep.

The convalescence was slow but steady. Tizzie got out of bed for longer each day. She walked to and from the bathroom and along the landing, but showed no inclination to be taken downstairs. Her sickness continued but she said quietly to Mary, 'You can get used to almost anything, given time.'

She took little interest in the pawnshop. Naomi spent more time there helping Albert, who was adjusting to being part owner. Barney had left him his share in the business, along with his furniture and household effects. The remainder of his estate had been willed to Tizzie, the solicitor keeping details until she was well enough to discuss it. She sat in her chair, ate tempting little meals, was sometimes sick and appeared to spend much time in thought. She was affectionate to Sam in the way a bright little girl is affectionate to her father when her mind is otherwise engaged.

Have patience, Sam warned himself, the real Tizzie will be back before long. He decided to take action on a couple of matters that might help her regain an interest in life. One day he returned home after a day out and was delighted to find Tizzie in the little sitting room at the end of the hall.

'It's wonderful to see you downstairs,' he said. 'How do you feel?'

'Not so bad,' she said limply. 'A bit tired.' She eyed him curiously. 'Has anything happened?'

'Yes,' he said, 'I've been to Liverpool to visit our friend Morris.'

That cut through her lethargy. 'Did you see him?'

'I did. While you were ill I put an enquiry agent on to him. He found out that it's Mrs Morris who has the money. He built up his brokering business with her income but apparently never got his hands on the capital. My man soon heard that there were rumours at the Exchange last autumn about him fathering a child on an eighteen-year-old, the daughter of a wealthy cotton shipper. She was a wayward girl, by all accounts, but up to then well guarded. The father refused to hush it up and thrashed Morris with a horsewhip on the dandy traps – you know, the flags in front of the Liverpool Exchange. Soon it was common talk that he was an unprincipled lecher with an eye for innocent young women. The child hasn't arrived yet, poor little soul, but I think we can take it that Mr Morris has had his comeuppance.

'I went to his business rooms but found another firm installed there, so I tracked him down to a seedy little office near the docks. I announced myself and Morris greeted me with open arms. "Mr Schofield, sir. Liverpool bows to the trumpet and the rose, sir," – all that stuff. I let him carry on and looked around me. He hadn't closed the door to the back room so I could see a shakedown bed and a bucket. He's been thrown out of the family home – I've confirmed it. His wife must have kept quiet about his adultery with maids and governesses but she could hardly ignore it when he seduced the daughter of a ship owner. They're legally separated and his business is more or less defunct.'

He saw that Tizzie was looking more lively than for many a long day. 'I'd like to tell all that to Naomi,' she said. 'Did you get the chance to mention her?'

'Of course I did. I told him that my wife employed a young lady who was once governess to his children, a Miss Naomi Drury. Would you credit he didn't even recognise the name? I soon enlightened him and finally said that as justice seemed to have been done I would bid him good day. Then I gave him something to remember us by.'

'What?' asked Tizzie blankly.

Sam rubbed his knuckles and gave a tight little smile. 'Oh, just a good punch or two on the jaw. You needn't look so dubious – I made sure he was coming round before I left.'

Quiet days followed as Tizzie gained strength, until by late February she was able to climb the stairs unaided. 'I'm not quite so sick today,' she told Sam in surprise as they took afternoon tea one Sunday.

By now a model of tact and patience, Sam kissed her gently on the cheek. 'Perhaps it's starting to fade at last, sweetheart. You're almost halfway, after all.' He had decided weeks ago that this would be an only child. It was sheer cruelty to make a woman of her temperament go through months of sickness and lethargy. She would have to ask Sarah's advice about ways and means of not having babies. The obvious way, the one sure means, didn't appeal to him in the least ...

Tizzie looked at him across the teacups and felt a rare tremor of energy pass through her. There was life ahead, she acknowledged carefully, life still to be lived. Barney was dead and nothing could ever bring him back; weeks of thought and soul-searching had made her accept that. Sam had been right about him being in love with her; she accepted that as well. It hurt almost as much as being the cause of his death. She could barely imagine what it had cost him over the years in concealment and self-control, but one fact kept her from wallowing in remorse – he had died smiling. She'd written to Rosie Raike and told her so. One day when she was really better she would have the child to tea ...

She picked up the teapot to pour a second cup for Sam and felt something move inside her, just below the waist of her loosened stays; a kind of fluttering, as if a butterfly was struggling to escape. Suddenly alert, she clapped a hand to her middle. Sarah had said, 'You'll be quickening soon, Tizzie . . .'

Sam was watching her. 'What's the matter?' he asked in alarm. 'Tizzie, what's wrong?'

She smiled – a real smile rather than the pallid curve of the lips that he'd grown used to. 'It moved!' she told him incredulously. 'It's alive – I felt it move!'

He was round the table in a flash, eyes alight. 'My clever, clever little love,' he said. 'Are you sure?'

She grabbed his hand and pressed it to her midriff. 'Here – can you feel it?'

He shook his head, hiding disappointment. 'Happen next time, but you'll have to get rid of the stays.'

Two days later he arrived home midafternoon to find her in shift and drawers having her rest on the bed. Sleepily she watched as he paced back and forth. 'What's on your mind?' she asked.

'I've been to the courtyard at Ryeworth,' he told her quietly. 'With a professional man – a surveyor.'

'It isn't sold, then? Kenworthy sent a note to say somebody had put a retainer on it.'

'That was me,' he said.

She sat up and stared at him. He noticed that her hair was glinting, something he hadn't seen for ages. Surely that was evidence of her feeling better? Happen it was a good omen for what he was about to suggest. 'Weeks ago I had the idea that when you were well again you might want to go ahead with your idea of turning the place into a school. All I did was make sure nobody else bought it until you'd had the chance to decide.'

'The school was a good idea,' she said regretfully, 'but I couldn't, not after what happened there. I never want to see the place again.'

He shrugged and sat on the bed. 'I thought you might

name it after him, as a sort of memorial. You could manage the place – you know you've always been interested in education.'

Eyes intent, she thought about it, then all at once lifted her shift and put his hand against her bare abdomen. 'There! Did you feel that one?'

He'd been expecting a positive jolt and couldn't feel a thing. It didn't matter – the touch of her skin was enough. He folded her in his arms and kissed her until they were both gasping, then he threw off every last stitch of his clothes and they made love at three o'clock in the afternoon, with pale March sunbeams slanting across the room. Sam warned himself to be gentle but in fact he was as urgent as on their wedding night; he simply couldn't help it.

Rebecca came up with a tea tray, but finding the door locked, took it back downstairs, nodding her head in understanding. Not before time, she thought.

Relief flowed through Tizzie like a calm sea over a rock-strewn beach. Life was liveable again. They'd made love at last and it was still wonderful. Already she felt as if Sam's boundless vitality had strengthened her innermost being. He was lying with his face against her neck, still slightly breathless. 'Tizzie, my Tizzie,' he murmured, struggling not to fall asleep in the aftermath of passion. 'I'm sorry, sweetheart, I'm sorry for being such a swine when Barney died.'

'I'm sorry too,' she said, remembering with amazement how she used to hate apologising. 'I'm sorry for resenting the baby and for forgetting about him when I was at Ryeworth. It was just that I couldn't bear to feel so ill.'

'Forgetting about *him*?' he repeated. 'It's going to be a boy, then? Tizzie, if it is a boy, do you want to call him Barnabas?'

That was something else she'd thought about during those long dark days, reaching the conclusion that they must have no echoes of old resentments, old jealousies, old remorse. The baby would be Sam's and hers – blood of the

Schofields and the Ridings – a new life and a new beginning, not a reminder of what was gone. 'No,' she said firmly, 'we'll remember Barney through the school. You're right about that, we'll go ahead with it, but we'll name the baby after our own families.'

At that Sam fell fast asleep with his lips against her throat and one hand cupping her breast, but she stayed awake in the silence, telling herself it was pure fancy that Barney's approval was like a presence in the room. No, it wasn't fancy; all at once she knew – she who was one for fact and certainty rather than instinct and intuition – she *knew* that wherever he might be, he was pleased by her decision about naming the baby. That was pure Barney.

Tizzie took Sam's hand from her breast and laid it on her stomach, ready for the next movement of their child.

It was half past five in the morning and Joshua was downstairs in his dressing gown. He'd been an early riser all his life – in his youth he'd had to be – but in the last few years he rarely slept after four o'clock and in summer would come downstairs before the house was astir, creeping about so as not to waken Lilah, because if she heard him she would be up and dressed in no time, checking whether he needed anything.

He suspected that she slept badly. Once, intent on trying to make himself a cup of tea, he'd gone down to the kitchen at 5 am and found her at the big scrubbed table, writing a list of some sort. 'Mornin', Mr Schofield,' she'd said, jumping to her feet and setting her apron crackling. She'd shown no surprise at him entering her kitchen at such an hour, but merely asked, 'Can I get you a pot o' tea? Or happen you'd like your breakfast?'

'What are you doing up at this hour?' he'd asked irritably. 'It's only five o'clock.'

She didn't say: 'I might ask the same of you.' Her expression said it for her. 'I'm just plannin' the meals an' the shoppin',' she said shortly. 'I'd rather do it when it's quiet, 'cos we get a bit busy later on.'

He pulled at his whiskers. 'Are you saying you've got too much to do? I've told you before, you have a free hand to hire extra help if you need it.'

'We've enough staff to run a bigger house than this, thank you, Mr Schofield. I just like to have an early start, that's all. Now, shall I get you a pot o' tea?'

'Aye, if you would.' Good humoured again, he chuckled in self-mockery. 'I came in here to make it for myself, as a matter of fact.'

She smiled back, highly amused. 'There's always a first time,' she said.

Now, weeks later, he paced the big room in silence as the summer sun climbed and struck gold from the chimneys of Saltley. He was thinking that he had as much company as a man of his age could wish for, but still he enjoyed an exchange of words with Lilah. She never grovelled; she showed him respect but no subservience, and he liked that. All but untutored, she could still come up with an opinion that many a time challenged his own. They were cut from one length of cloth, him and Lilah, and the same could be said of Tizzie. It was funny, that – his daughter-in-law and his cook being so much alike: honest, straight talking, capable females, both with an independent turn of mind. One was a woman of business, wealthy in her own right as well as from marrying a Schofield; the other cooked like an angel but had no home of her own, no capital, no man . . .

At the sound of a carriage outside he turned back to the window to see Noah from Moorview, come to put a letter through the door. Knowing what news it must contain, Joshua hurried to take it from him. 'Morning, Noah,' he said. 'Is everything all right up yonder?'

The coachman smiled. 'Aye, Mr Schofield. Mr Sam's sent you this letter so I won't spoil his news. He's walkin' on air, an' so are the rest of us. He said I hadn't to wake the house, but I can see you're up wi' the lark.'

'Happen I guessed what was afoot,' laughed Joshua, and hurried indoors to read Sam's note in private. It said:

Joshua Abel arrived at four thirty after a speedy, straightforward labour. A fine boy – 7½lbs in weight and perfectly formed. Tizzie amazingly well. Midwife excellent. Doctor not needed. I'll see you later.

Your ever-loving son,
Sam

Joshua read it twice, first with delight and then with relief. He'd harboured a dread that the child might have been harmed by the accident or the pneumonia. He sat down hurriedly and sent up a prayer of thanks. A granddaughter and now three grandsons – things were looking up – Sarah's baby girl called after Rachel and all three boys after him: Charles's second name was Joshua; the young viscount was Francis Alexander Joshua Dunmow Soar, and now Sam and Tizzie's baby was Joshua Abel. He must be the only man in Saltley to have three grandsons named after him. The last phrase of Sam's note revealed that he was in a state of some emotion: 'Your ever-loving son' ... It was no overstatement, though. That was what he was: ever loving ... aye, and ever loved.

Tizzie had done well, he told himself. After weeks of illness and low spirits she'd slowly got back to her old self, organising the renovations and rebuilding at Ryeworth ready for the school, preparing for the wedding of the little lass Naomi but – a surprise to everybody – taking a back seat at the pawnshop. Apparently she'd made over her share to Naomi so that the young couple would be partners in business as well as in marriage.

Business aside, Tizzie had been a model expectant mother, if somewhat obsessed by exercise. He could have laughed out loud a few months back as he'd watched her and Sarah stepping out across Alsing's lawns like a couple of soldiers on a route march. Still ... they'd both had good confinements and healthy babies. He jumped up to go and wake James with the news, but with a tap on the door Lilah came in. 'I thought I heard voices, Mr Schofield. Is everythin' all—'

Delighted to be able to tell somebody, Joshua grabbed hold of her hands. 'Be the first to know, Lilah,' he beamed. 'I have another grandson – a fine boy. Mother and baby both well.'

Lilah looked at their joined hands and gave an odd little baring of her teeth, more like a grimace of pain than a smile. 'Congratulations. I reckon that'll be a load off your mind.' She eased her hands from his grip but he didn't notice.

'I was a bit worried whether the baby would be all right,' he admitted, 'but he's perfect, according to Sam. I'll go and see them later on, when things have settled down a bit. You know, Lilah, I used to think that by the time I was turned seventy I'd have nine or ten grandchildren. It's funny how things work out, isn't it?'

'Aye,' she agreed, 'but there's plenty of time for more. Now, do you want your breakfast? I've got some best flitch in the pantry – you know you like that. What about a couple o' rashers with a sausage or two an' a fried egg?'

'That'll do nicely,' he said. 'I'll just go up to get washed and shaved.' At the door he turned. 'Is everything all right with your mother and sister?'

'Yes, thanks. That good dry house has done wonders for our Abbie's rheumatics. They do keep askin' whether they should pay you some rent, Mr Schofield.'

Joshua flapped his hand at her. 'If I can't afford to let your family live rent free it's time to give over! But in case they're worrying about when I'm gone, it's all laid down and legal: They have it rent free in perpetuity – that means for ever.' He made his exit at top speed, aware that his strong, no-nonsense cook was liable to burst into tears when it came to her mother and sister. He could do without that at half past five in the morning.

Behind him Lilah headed for the kitchen. He always remembered to ask about them. As for that mention of when he was gone ... If he died her own life would be over as well – empty, finished. She hoped the good Lord would have the sense to let her go first, she did that.

*

Rosie was walking home with Harry Butterworth, laughing as usual because he talked nonsense – clever nonsense. He himself was clever, that was why he was still at school when he was well turned twelve, the same as her. He had brothers and sisters, and his father made spectacles in a little room over Bennison's jewellers. Harry said his father had a special spyglass to look inside people's eyes, and he made them read letters from charts that were up on the wall, or if they weren't good at letters he showed them little pictures. Harry had asked his father if he could be a doctor when he grew up but had been told they didn't have enough money for the training ...

One day last week they'd been coming home and Charles had been far ahead of them, carrying his school satchel and with his golden hair all untidy under his cap. It had felt all wrong to be with Harry instead of him. It frightened her, the way she felt about Charles; sometimes she thought she loved him more than her mother and father, but whether she loved him or not, things were changing between them.

As if realising that she was deep in thought, Harry for once kept silent as they walked the sooty pavements. At his side Rosie's mind was on Charles. Things were changing between them because he himself was different. He was nearly thirteen and for weeks he hadn't been happy to meet her in the tunnel. She knew it without being told.

At last she had said, 'Charles, do you think we're getting a bit – a bit grown-up to meet here in the tunnel? My mother says I'm too old to get my clothes messed up.'

He hadn't been able to conceal his relief. 'Don't think I don't want to,' he'd said earnestly, 'but happen we are a bit too old. My father says we can still walk round the buttercup field and along the path.'

So his father had said something. But then so had her mam – her mother ... she was trying to stop saying 'mam'. 'He's gettin' a big lad, love,' she'd said the week before. 'It isn't fittin' you should both crawl under a hedge an' sit on an old rug where nobody can see you. You're a big girl now.'

So they'd stopped going inside the tunnel. From time to time they took a sedate little walk, side by side around the field. It was lovely to be with him, but it wasn't the same as being in the secret dark green of the tunnel. They didn't always have time for walks, anyway; Charles had extra work from his engineering course and she had to do English at home for the headmaster, because in September she was going into his special class for a year. Her parents already paid extra as she had turned twelve, and in the special class it would cost even more, but they didn't seem to mind. 'You have a brain, you must use it!' her dad said, but she thought her mother just wanted to keep her out of the mill.

It was exciting, learning new stuff all the time and doing good work, but sometimes she remembered what it had been like when she and Charles used to play hide-and-seek in the stables when they were younger. Life had been fun, then. Now it was all serious, concentrating on lessons and trying not to mind when Elizabeth was in the big house at family parties, playing the piano while Charles played his trumpet. She even hung around outside Mr Wild's school to try and walk home with Charles. He'd told her he thought Elizabeth was pushy. Even her Aunt Tizzie thought so, but she didn't say as much – it had just been written on her face when she'd mentioned her that day when Rosie had been invited to afternoon tea.

She'd worn her best dress and Mr Sam had sent the carriage for her. There was just her and Mrs Sam at a little table with china cups and saucers. They'd talked about Mr Jellicoe most of the time. Mrs Sam had told her that he was happy when he died. It was very clear that she'd liked him a lot, maybe even loved him, but not in the way he'd loved her . . . she saved that sort of love for Mr Sam.

Harry said, 'Ta-ra' as they reached Meadowbank, Rosie heading for the cottage and an hour's homework before she had her tea.

*

It was still very warm at eight o'clock that evening. Matthew was sitting by the open back door, working on a piece of lime wood with his smallest gouge, seeing what he could 'come up with' as he put it. Next to him Martha was mending his working socks and keeping an eye on Rosie, who was reluctantly hemming a handkerchief made from an offcut of Jericho's finest weave. 'Harry has three cousins,' Rosie announced suddenly. 'They live just this side of Holdwell. He goes to see them on Sundays.'

'That's nice, love,' said Martha absently.

'Charles has three cousins, too,' Rosie went on, 'though of course they're all babies.' Matthew was eyeing her in amusement. That tone meant that she had a point to make. 'Charles and Harry see their cousins, but I never do. I would *like* to see my cousins.'

'So would I,' Martha assured her, 'but you know your Auntie Bella's in Grimsby, an' in any case her girls are a lot older than you – too old to play. One of 'em's married.'

'I know,' agreed Rosie wistfully, 'but I've got other cousins, haven't I, Dad?'

So that was it. Another hint about Devon. Matthew smiled. 'There were nine the last I heard.'

Rosie put on her best smile. 'I *would* like to see them.'

'Perhaps next year at wakes time. I'm thinkin' I'll ask Mr Schofield for a week off work – maybe ten days.'

That silenced Rosie. Ten days! Agnes Irlam's family were going away on holiday but only for three days. Martha smiled and carried on mending. He was determined to return in style, was Matthew, but she'd never known anybody to take a week off work, never mind ten days.

Mention of the wakes always set her thinking, though. This year she was determined that she wouldn't mind in the least whether he went to the fair on his own or with her and Rosie. Three years had passed since he'd met the girl. It was over, finished. She accepted now that it had been over almost before it had begun. Martha looked at him sitting there content in the light of the evening sun. She was a fortunate woman, she was an' all.

CHAPTER TWENTY-ONE

The Return

Martha couldn't get over the difference between Devon and Lancashire. After a journey on five different trains it seemed as if they were setting foot on foreign soil when they arrived at Plymouth: the amazingly blue sea, the round hills patchworked in green and gold, the red earth and above all the soft, musical speech of the people, every one of them sounding like Matthew when he'd first arrived in Saltley.

They stayed overnight at an inn – not the Mizzen Mast where he'd lived in his youth, but a neat little place on a residential street. Next morning they bought flowers and Matthew took them to a churchyard near the docks to visit the grave of his little sister, Dorcas. They could hear the rattle of nearby winches on a cargo ship and above them seagulls wheeled and cried. He led them unerringly to the grave. It had a simple wooden cross that was weathered almost to silver, carved with only her name and her age.

Matthew gripped his hat between his hands, his heart wrenched by emotions he couldn't have named. With Martha and Rosie at his side dressed in their best, he stared down, thinking that their flowers looked far too grand for such a resting place and that he was ashamed to have Dorcas buried under so paltry a memorial. She deserved better of him, his clever little sister who had danced and smiled through life when there was little to dance and smile about.

Martha was remembering what he'd revealed on their wedding night, the words coming to her as clearly as if he was speaking them now: 'I saw her liddle body – insisted on it, I did. She looked like a side of lamb that had been overlong on the spit; charred an' sticky an' quite black . . .' Tears stung Martha's eyes and she touched his arm, reluctant to intrude on his memories but desperate to comfort him. At his other side Rosie felt for his hand and gave it a squeeze, while the gulls cried and the sea crashed endlessly against the shore. All at once he wriggled his shoulders. 'I'll be orderin' a proper stone within the hour,' he said, and led them away.

Later that morning he hired a carriage to take them to meet his family in a village outside Plymouth. His sisters wept tears of joy to see him at last and his half-brothers held him in clumsy embrace; evidence, if Martha needed it, of their love for the man who had devoted his youth to looking after them. Country people of modest means, they were clearly overawed that he had brought his family all the way from Lancashire on the train and could afford to stay in the village lodging house. It was like something out of a picture book, that house; a whitewashed cottage with a thatched roof, where they had the upstairs floor all to themselves and were waited on hand and foot by the landlady.

It had seemed like heaven to Martha at first, but before long she was restless and on edge at having time on her hands. 'Take it easy,' laughed Matthew. 'Didn't I always say you'd live like a lady one day – though to be sure I meant for ever rather than for a matter of days.'

His native air seemed to suit him, she thought, watching as he looked younger with each passing day. His tan deepened, his skin was smoother, his dark hair shone; in his good clothes and favourite wide-brimmed hat he made a striking figure as he showed them the places he'd known as a boy. She wondered if his sisters thought it strange that he had a plain, grey-haired wife who was no taller than her daughter, but if so, they gave no sign of it. She was Matthew's wife and that was enough for them; she was welcome in their homes, in their kitchens, at their tables.

Day succeeded golden day. Rosie developed a faint tan and a scattering of freckles across her nose. After the first few hours she had known the names of her aunties and uncles and all nine cousins, while her mother was still mixed up as to which child belonged to which parent. 'I do like them all, Mother,' she said earnestly, 'but they move so slow! It must be because they live in a rural community rather than an industrial one, like us.'

Martha didn't know whether to smile or frown at that, so she merely nodded in agreement. There were times when the child talked just like one of her books ...

Rosie herself wasn't sure that she liked being regarded as the cousin who was well off and who talked funny. She was the odd one out here in this warm, sunny, clean little place – oh, it was clean. Her mother had been stunned when she'd seen the women hanging out their beautiful washing. The sheets and tablecloths were dazzlingly white; it was as if they were lit from behind by powerful lamps. Rosie thought of the Saltley women with their set boilers and dolly tubs and possers, all toiling to produce white washing in the midst of soot and grime. Like her mother said, it was a different world here in Devon.

Each evening in their little sitting room they planned what they would do the next day. They visited Ryder Hall and stared through the gates at the elaborate grounds where Matthew had once worked as undergardener and slept in a potting shed, even in the depths of winter. They went back to Plymouth to the inn where he'd once lived with his family, finding that the stables where Dorcas had died were long gone, demolished to make space for more bedrooms now that the Mizzen Mast was prosperous again from being near the railway station. Always watchful, Martha detected a new ease in Matthew at the disappearance of the stables. The holiday was almost over before she made herself ask, 'What about your stepmother, Matthew? Don't you think we should visit her?'

He shot her a dark, defensive look. 'D'you think I'd take my child to see a woman who's rottin' away with the French pox an' shunned by decent folk? She's in a shack in the woods at the far side of Ryder and lives on what folk leave for her when they're passin'.'

'I know all that. I was there when Beth and Maggie were telling you. I just thought we could call with some food an' that. Whether you like it or not she bears the same name as us, Matthew.'

He narrowed his eyes at her. 'You always took her part, didn't you? I recall years back you told me she couldn't be all bad. Well, I'm tellin' you Fat Annie *was* bad. She leathered me every day of my life until I got too big for it!'

'She was wrong to do it,' Martha agreed quietly, 'but she didn't put you an' your sisters in the workhouse when your father died, like many a stepmother would have done. I'm thinkin' of you, Matthew. It's eased your memories to see the new headstone on Dorcas's grave, hasn't it? I thought it would ease you even more to see Fat Annie an' – an' make your peace with her.'

He shook his head dismissively. 'She's half-mad, so they say. She wouldn't know me.' Then he looked at his wife sitting by the window with her crocheting on her lap, her blue dress neatly pressed, her hair covered by her best lace cap. Concern for him was written all over her face; her pretty little mouth was tight with it. She'd been proved right many a time in their married life, he told himself, and 'twas true that resentment against Fat Annie did still fester in him. 'We won't take Rosie,' he said, weakening.

'No, course we won't. Happen we can leave her at your Maggie's, 'cos she likes to feed the hens an' do a bit in the dairy. Shall we go tomorrow, then?'

He shifted uneasily. 'It do shame me, Martha, for you to see a woman with my name who carries the pox.'

'I know,' she said gently, 'but she's not your flesh an' blood, love.'

He jumped up and gave her a swift kiss on the mouth. 'Don't blame me if you're sickened when you see her,' he said.

She was sickened, right enough. Fat Annie was housed in a stinking, half-rotten shed patched with rags and old boards to keep out the rain. The smell of decaying flesh was worse than Bushell's Yard in Saltley, much worse, because here it was the flesh of a living woman. When they went in she was sitting over a heap of dead ashes in a makeshift hearth, a shrunken little creature with one ear missing and no visible teeth. Martha tried not to show her revulsion, while Matthew stood silently in the doorway with his back to the light. 'Who is it?' wheezed the creature.

'Matthew,' he said abruptly. 'Matthew Raike. This is my wife, Martha.'

Red-rimmed eyes squinted at them. Martha noticed yellow pus lining the lower lids and she tried not to shudder.

'From Lancashire,' said the woman.

Matthew eyed her in surprise. Evidently she wasn't as mad as they made out. 'We've brought you a few things to eat, Mrs Raike,' said Martha, uncovering her basket.

'God, she sounds like a corncrake,' said the woman, 'but she's a priddy liddle soul, I'll grant her that. As for you, Matthew, you've growed a bit.'

Bereft of words, he nodded. This decaying bag of bones had called Martha pretty, which was more than he'd ever done, or ever believed, come to that. He could hardly credit that this woman had once been the great lump of flesh who had blighted his young life; that the spindly thighs beneath her rags used to open for any man with coppers to spare. Well, somebody had given her more than coppers . . . she was paying a thousandfold for what she'd done, but he crushed a stirring of compassion. He had a sudden mental image of her as she slung a baby against her shoulder and slapped a pot of half-cooked stew on the table for their dinner. In those days she'd had either a man in her arms or a child.

They stood there and looked down at her. Martha wished she could see a broom or better still a bucket and scrubbing brush. She had the urge to give the place a good swill out and then a good scouring . . .

'I've been awantin' to see you afore I die,' said Fat Annie.

'Well, I'm here,' replied Matthew. 'Have you somethin' to say?'

She scratched her matted head. 'I've had years to think about this. I want you to know I don't blame you any more for Dorcas dyin'.'

Matthew stared at her. *She* didn't blame *him*? What about him blaming her? She'd started him on the drink. If it hadn't been for her he would never have got a taste for the ale, never have needed to blot out real life; never, never had tried the gin that day and been in a drunken sleep when she'd tried to rouse him. That voice, shrieking in his ears, those great fat hands shaking him . . . They'd sunk through his stupor to surface in every nightmare.

All the same, he had the feeling that things were moving around inside his head, changing places. He tried to fill his mind with images of Fat Annie leathering him, of her lying drunk while they went hungry, but all he could see was her trying to rouse the only one who knew where Dorcas was hiding with her picture book.

'We didn't get on,' she said now.

'No,' he agreed, 'not at all.'

'I was wrong, there,' she said. 'I didn't want the responsibility of looking after you all – I couldn't face it. But I've said a prayer about it. I've said I'm sorry in a prayer.'

Bitterness filled him. 'That makes everythin' all right, then, don't it?'

But Martha was bending down, touching that dirty, claw-like hand; his clean little Martha, touching filth. 'I'm sure Matthew will think about what you've said,' she was telling her. 'We're going back to Lancashire tomorrow, but we'll leave some money so your sons can get you some food.'

The pus-filled eyes stared up at her. 'You might squawk like a fowl, but your heart's in the right place. Take Matthew away, will you? I could never do right for him, I could never match up to his mother – except in bed, o' course. I could give his pa what he wanted there, right enough.'

Matthew eyed her in disgust. The revolting old cow! He walked out and waited beneath the trees for Martha to join him. To his relief she made straight for a nearby stream and washed her hands. 'I warned you,' he said.

She didn't answer until they were back between the high, scented hedgerows. 'She's not all bad,' she said quietly.

What could he say to that, with a battle going on in his head? Maybe she was right. He took her hand in his and they began the long walk back to Maggie's. Neither of them turned to look at the wood.

They had collected Rosie, who was skipping ahead of them, a child again where minutes before she'd been a young woman helping in the dairy. Matthew slipped an arm round Martha's waist. 'I'm still thinkin', he said sheepishly. 'You were right, love, to make me go. We'll say no more about Fat Annie for now; let's be quiet on our last afternoon.'

But Rosie wasn't quiet. She ran back to them and asked urgently, 'Will everybody be there tonight, except for the babies?' Her dad had ordered a farewell supper for all the family and if it was still fine it was to be held on the village green. At first she'd hoped to wear her best dress, but it was so much better than anything her cousins owned that it would look as if she was showing off. Her spotted muslin would be more suitable, with the pink hair ribbons.

'They'll all be there, ready to say goodbye to Miss Rosie Raike,' said her dad. He was looking a bit like a gypsy again, walking along in his shirtsleeves; her mother was swinging the empty basket and holding hands with him. Then from somewhere up ahead they heard the squeak of a fiddle and the chatter of children. Rosie's eyes widened, while Matthew looked at the deserted landscape around them. 'Twill be a passing pedlar, I expect,' he said, smiling. 'You go on ahead, love, I want to be quiet.'

'I'll go with her,' said Martha, knowing he wanted to think about Fat Annie. 'We'll wait for you along the lane.'

He nodded. It was very warm. Faint wisps of cloud were stretched across the sky like fronds of bracken in front of a lake. It had been that kind of sky when they'd shown him Dorcas's body ...Deep in memories, he walked on, dragging his feet in the dust, his coat slung over one shoulder and his hat tipped over his eyes.

The chatter of young children came from beyond the next bend and he found five or six of them in a dip in the lane, playing intently with pebbles in plant pots. They were grubby, half-clad urchins, but healthy enough and kissed by the sun. He slowed to watch them and was startled by a rumbling and clattering from a grassy bank higher up the lane. 'Look out!' a man shouted wildly. 'Get out o' the way. Move! Take 'im with you!'

All in an instant a heavy waggon rolled towards them down the hill, gaining momentum with each turn of the wheels. The children squealed in terror and scattered, except for one little boy, who sat there and cried because they'd left him. The waggoner was running downhill like a madman, screaming and waving his arms, but the child didn't move, he just rubbed his eyes and whimpered.

Matthew leapt forward and scooped him up, throwing himself to the far side of the lane with the child against his chest. The waggon hurtled past them – a great six-wheeled affair in red and yellow. Even as he braced himself so as not to crush the child Matthew saw that the brake lever was broken, hanging useless by the driver's seat. The shafts were empty, pointing back up the hill.

The child felt warm and solid in his arms and was still crying as the man raced towards them, the whites of his eyes showing, his lips drawn back from his teeth. He was a broad, curly-haired individual and now he snatched at the boy. 'Here!' he gasped. 'Give 'im to me!'

Matthew held on for a moment. 'He coulda been killed,' he protested. 'He didn't move when you shouted.'

The man put out his arms and the little boy went to him, snuggling against his shoulder. 'He's my son,' said the man, with a kind of defiance. 'He didn't hear. He's deaf an' dumb.'

Matthew picked up his coat and hat, dusting them off against his thigh. Deaf and dumb? He looked normal enough – a fine little lad. Sturdy, he was; dark eyed and dark haired.

'I thank you, stranger,' said the man awkwardly. 'I was swingin' the waggon round an' I musta misjudged the slope o' the land. I grabbed at the brake handle but you can see what happened. I'll take the boy back and then bring the horses down here. 'Tis just as well his mother didn't see.' He set the boy on his feet and Matthew smiled down at him, feeling in his pocket for a coin.

But the mother *had* seen ... or heard. Beyond the man he could see a woman running towards them down a great curving field, alarm in every line of her body. She stopped suddenly, framed between two saplings with the sun shining through their leaves. It was Jess! Older, thinner, a woman rather than a girl, but it was her. He couldn't believe it. The wild dark hair was bundled on top of her head. She wore a patchwork skirt and a black bodice; her feet were in clumsy brown boots. It was her!

She didn't speak, but stood motionless, her lips slightly parted, while the boy clutched at her skirts. Matthew's heart was thudding, but there was a warning in her eyes. The man hadn't seen her; he was busying himself with the shafts, trying to ease the waggon off the lane. Jess shot him a glance and looked at Matthew with a finger to her lips, lips that were still very red, he saw, as if she'd been eating raspberries. Her warning was now so urgent he made himself tip his hat and say politely, 'Afternoon, ma'am. I reckon this be your boy?'

At his words the man whirled round, eyes glinting.

Deliberately Jess laid a hand on the boy's dark head and lifted her chin. 'Yes,' she said, 'his name is Benjamin.' At once the man went to her side but Matthew's eyes were on her hand. She wore a wedding ring. They were man and wife! He couldn't take his leave without talking to her – he couldn't. The child was smiling at last, his confidence restored by the presence of his mother.

'Twas powerful strange that he'd just been thinking of his little Dorcas and now here was a boy who reminded him of her. The same curve of the mouth, the same eyes. Jess still touched the boy's hair. There was an expression on her face as if she was saying: *See! Look at this child!*

All at once he knew. His very entrails knotted in protest and then untangled in joy. The boy was his! Her expression told him so. Deaf and dumb or not, this was his son! Jess lifted the small figure and kissed him on the cheek, then looked again at Matthew. At that moment, as if to confirm his new knowledge, a hurdy-gurdy began to play and the fiddle tuned up again, swelling the sound of a fair.

'Thanks again,' the man said, and with a proprietary flourish put his arm around Jess and the boy. Still she didn't speak; she merely bent her head and, still carrying her son, walked back up the lane with her husband.

One hand on the waggon, Matthew watched them go. He felt empty, desolate. The gaudy red and yellow paint beneath his hand seemed to mock the darkness of his thoughts. It was a fairground waggon, of course. The hurdy-gurdy belonged to a fair, so did Jess and the man, so did the boy. He could just make out the top of a tent as he followed them up the hill.

Then he saw Martha and Rosie on the fringe of a group surrounding a fiddler. Martha was watching Jess as she walked towards her. She looked small and very neat compared to the younger woman and the burly, fair-haired waggoner, who turned together into a field and headed for a huddle of caravans. This was no wakes fair, Matthew told himself; it was a poor little travelling fair, one that set up for the night in villages and small country towns. Perhaps it was about to move on? Perhaps that was why the man had been moving the waggon, why the hurdy-gurdy was playing a farewell tune?

Slowly he walked up the hill to join his wife and daughter.

For the first time the wakes tea party was at Sam and Tizzie's rather than Meadowbank House. The family were there in full force, except for Elizabeth.

Mary was unrepentant. 'I've let her go to watch the rehearsal at the Theatre Royal, Tizzie. For the last few weeks she's talked about nothing else but the stage, so when Mrs Bonardi – she's in this week's show and she's really nice – when she offered to take Elizabeth and keep an eye on her I said yes. I thought it would give Charles a bit of peace, and me as well, come to that.'

A wakes tea without her demanding niece had its attractions, thought Tizzie. 'She's a bit young to get stage-struck,' she said dubiously, half her attention on little Joshua, who was intent on getting through the door at the first opportunity.

Mary straightened her cap with a determined slap. 'I want her to know that it's not all silks and satins and applause on the stage,' she said firmly. 'I want her to find out that it's hard work, with constant travelling and long hours and getting hissed and booed. Unless you're top of the bill it's a pretty grim sort of life.'

Tizzie laughed. 'If Elizabeth went on the stage she'd make sure she was top of the bill!'

Mary shook her head. 'You've got to be good for that – really good. You know what she's like when she gets her mind set on something – there's no shifting her. I want her to see the seamy side of theatre life before she gets too keen.'

Tizzie thought that Elizabeth would only see what she wanted to see, but refrained from saying so. Mary found her daughter very trying and there was no point in making things worse.

'Hey, he's off again!' laughed James, as Joshua's small, determined figure crawled at lightning speed to the door. Tizzie ran to scoop him up for the twentieth time that afternoon. 'Mam*ma*!' he said clearly, and everybody laughed because he sounded cross.

Sam was watching from across the room: proud, amused, but just a little bit weary. What a child! He looked angelic, a golden-haired cherub, but he had the energy and staying power of a navvy. Happen that wasn't surprising when you looked at his parents, but he was certainly a handful. Sarah's lively offspring were docile by comparison.

Earlier in the afternoon Joshua had been put in the nursery for a rest with little Francis and Rachel. The other two had nodded off, but Joshua had screamed the place down until he was taken back to the grown-ups. Even now he was wriggling in Tizzie's arms, eager to be put down again.

When he was ten months old they'd hired a nursemaid for him so that Tizzie could spend more time on her business interests and in particular the school, which was nearing completion and would soon be needing staff. Within a fortnight the nursemaid had asked for a rise. Within a month she'd been dismissed – for smacking Joshua's bare bottom.

Tizzie had been furious. 'He isn't even one yet! I'm not having some jumped up little madam giving him a good hiding just because he has a mind of his own. He'll be disciplined, come what will, but not by beating him into submission. We'll go back to the old routine of Janey giving him his meals and keeping him clean because that bores me silly, but apart from that I'll look after him myself. He's going to be a well-behaved child with a lively, enquiring mind and I won't read a book to tell me how to accomplish it!'

Looking after him was what filled her days, with help from the staff when she needed to have an hour off on business. She played with him, made him do as he was told, put him to bed, showed him pictures, told him stories, got up with him in the night and loved him to death – they both did – but a day in his company left them worn out. Sam was glad to get to Jericho for a rest.

The child was off again, on his feet this time; firm on his feet at thirteen months, though too intent on speed to be safe. No wonder Tizzie had ordered the enclosure, thought Sam. Matthew Raike had made it to her specification: a set of hinged railings that formed a square, two feet high, which could be folded flat and moved from room to room. Set on a rug, Joshua could be put inside it with his building bricks and cotton bobbins and such, and he was safe. He liked it – until the previous week, when he'd piled his bricks in one corner, clambered on top of them and launched himself over the rails. He'd been half way down the hall before anybody had spotted him.

His grandfather watched the scene in amusement. The lad was no different than his father had been at the same age. Sam had been wilful, noisy, energetic, but by thirteen months he'd had a baby sister to compete with. Joshua had pulled Sam's leg about it some weeks back, but with little response. Sam loved the boy, there was no doubt of it, but he loved Tizzie more. He never said as much, but Joshua knew.

Now Joshua chatted to Joe Chadwick and John Fairbrother, who were always invited to family do's; between the three of them they had the ups and downs of the town's mills at their fingertips. But in spite of their talking, Joshua saw that young Charlie was at a loose end – in low spirits by the looks of it. Of course Rosie Raike was in Devon . . . happen he was missing her, or maybe he wanted to go off on his own. Fourteen was a funny age: no longer a child and not yet a man, with the body changing faster than the mind.

'Charles, Billy, you don't have to stay in with us,' he said. 'Go to the stables if you want, or out on the moor to get some fresh air in your lungs.'

Billy declined with his usual polite good humour. It seemed that James had lent him a book on the breeding of beef cattle and he was eager to start reading it. Charles, however, jumped up at once. 'I'll just go for a walk,' he said thankfully. His grandpa had the knack of seeing what he needed and, what was more, supplying it.

Outside it was cool and very quiet, except for the drone of bees in the heather and the song of a lark. Relieved to be away from adult conversation and the chatter of children, he walked the narrow path, thinking how odd it was that he, who disliked the country, was tramping the moor while Billy, who loved it, was indoors with his nose in a book. Billy was nice enough, but they had little in common; the other boy knew nothing about music and not much more about engineering. He was all for farming and livestock, ploughing and planting.

Charles wasn't enjoying the wakes tea party. He didn't think it was anything to do with Rosanna being in Devon; he'd been surprised and a bit guilty to find himself relieved that she was away. Somehow, Rosanna belonged to his childhood and he wasn't a child any longer. He knew he wasn't because his body seemed different and he'd started to think about – about things, especially at night. He had loved her for years, really loved her, but now it all seemed a bit silly. He must have loved her because she was pretty and kind and interested in whatever he told her.

He didn't think she'd be upset if they didn't see each other so much, because she liked Harry Butterworth. She was always laughing when she was with him, and they both had lots of friends at school ...

It seemed an eternity since they used to play hide-and-seek in the stable loft. He still liked Rosie's pink cheeks and her big brown eyes and her little hands with the very clean nails, but he did wish she wouldn't try to change the way she spoke ... It embarrassed him. Lots of things embarrassed him lately: the way he sometimes felt sorry for his mother, who he'd never even liked, let alone loved; the way his father made excuses to go and see Mrs Hartley when she'd oh so gently hinted that he should stay away. What embarrassed him most, though, was the talk among the boys at school . . . the remarks, the jokes about girls. He didn't even understand some of the things they laughed about, but they conjured up pictures that he couldn't help thinking about when he was on his own.

He walked on, gloomily whistling his latest piece for the trumpet – the difficult one that was very slow. His teacher had announced that he could do no more for him and had arranged for a top man in Manchester to hear him play to see if he was good enough to be taken on as a pupil. This man trained players in the brass section of the Halle Orchestra. Now Charles was practising nearly all the time – he could have been practising this afternoon, on his new trumpet. His grandpa had kept his promise and bought him a silver-plated one. Far more expensive than his old one, it had a better tone and was easier to play, but for some reason Rosanna had almost cried when she'd seen it; she hadn't been a bit pleased . . . But Elizabeth, bossy Elizabeth, had been thrilled to bits. Her eyes had glittered and she'd asked him to show her just how it was different from his old one. He couldn't be feeling fed up because she wasn't here this afternoon? No, of course he couldn't, she got on his nerves. But she did sort of liven things up. She – she was a bit like a woman, rather than a child. Rosanna, little Rosanna, was still a child, whereas Elizabeth was a child who talked like a woman – acted like one as well. She sort of flirted. He didn't know if he liked it – it frightened him a bit, but it gave him a taste of what it would be like to be grown up. Perhaps she wasn't so bad, after all . . .

Something was wrong – Rosie could tell. Her mother's face was sending messages so fast it was hard to read them. She thought that she was dismayed and unhappy but not surprised; as if something she'd expected for years had happened at last. Most of all, though, she was undecided about what to do next. Her dad was the same, somehow; intent on planning a course of action but determined to reveal nothing of what he was thinking. They weren't speaking to each other.

Outside on the village green the tables were set out for the family party and the cellar man from the inn was putting out the chairs. Rosie kept talking to fill the horrible silence; she was worried that the party would be spoiled if they didn't speak. 'I do wish that little fair had been coming here,' she said brightly. 'I know it wasn't anything like the wakes but p'raps they'd have hoopla and roll-pennies and we could all have danced to the hurdy-gurdy. Dad, do you think they'd have had hoopla?'

The look he turned on her was very strange. It was as if he was in a dream. 'Hoopla?' he said, as if he'd never heard of such a thing. 'Hoopla? Maybe so. Who can tell?'

'Rosie, it's nearly time for the party,' said her mother briskly. 'Let's have a look at you ... Aye, you've tied your ribbons nice. Now listen, I want you to go down an' get ready to welcome the family while me an' your dad have five minutes on our own.'

Matthew looked up warily but didn't speak, while Rosie stared at her mother, open mouthed. 'You're comin', aren't you?'

'Yes,' said Martha shortly. 'Go on, now. Do as you're told an' no more chatter. If anybody arrives just say we'll be a bit late. Say – say somethin's cropped up.'

With an effort Rosie kept silent and went down the stairs. They were behaving like they had once before when her dad had been working on that confidential undertaking. She was a lot older now, so if her mother wanted her to make folk welcome then she'd do it. She would tell them her mother and dad were delayed on a matter of – of business. It was still very hot so she'd make sure they all had something to drink; she'd tell the landlord that he mustn't bring food to the tables until her parents arrived.

Martha closed the door behind her and faced Matthew. Dressed ready for the party in his best shirt and waistcoat, he was by the window, watching her. She was looking old, was his little Martha, in spite of her pretty lace cap and blue dress. He could see her neat little shoes peeping out from under the hem, and he was filled with sudden resentment, recalling the heavy brown boots that Jess had been wearing. When he'd first seen her she hadn't been wearing boots, she'd been barefoot, then when he'd taken her to the birch grove she'd worn little slippers such as he'd never seen on Saltley women ... Danced along like a liddle sprite, she had. He sighed. What a fool he was to have believed he'd banished that night from his mind and his heart.

But Martha was standing to attention like a soldier, her hands down at her sides. Beneath the pinky gold of her suntanned cheeks she was very pale. She couldn't suspect? She hadn't seen anything, had she, except him walking up the hill behind Jess and her husband and the boy? Whether she had or not, he must go to Jess. He must hold his son again and feel that warm, solid little body; he must ask her if she was content in the marriage, if they had enough money, whether Benjamin was happy in spite of his affliction. He must tell her that he'd gone back to the wakes fair next morning to find her. 'Martha,' he said, 'Martha, I—' God in heaven, how could he put it?'

'Go an' see her,' she said quietly. 'I'll look after things here.'

She knew! 'See who?' he asked hoarsely.

'The girl.' She sounded weary and unutterably sad. 'Don't pretend, Matthew, not to me. I know you'd give your soul to talk to her.'

'My soul?' he repeated. He stared intently at her lips, as if to be sure it was Martha who was saying such things.

She flapped her hands as though she wanted to sweep him from the room. 'The girl,' she said, 'the little boy's mother – you met her on the wakes fair four years back. You – you had a feelin' for her, didn't you, Matthew?'

His jaw sagged. 'How do you know?'

'I just do. You didn't want to touch me after the fair, not for weeks – for months. You shut yourself away with your woodwork like a man possessed, yet you earned no money from it. When things were all right again between us I opened your cupboard and found the carvin'. I recognised her this afternoon. It was her, wasn't it?'

'Yes,' he said.

'That man who ran after the waggon – was it her husband?'

'Yes,' he said again. How much had she seen?

Martha's knees shook with relief on hearing that the girl was married. She had to set her feet well apart to keep standing. 'Was she married when you first met her?'

'No, o' course not. How could you think it?'

She looked him in the eye. 'Oh,' she said soberly, 'you'd be surprised what I can think when I put me mind to it.' She wouldn't ask about the child because she already knew the answer. He was three years old or more – a sturdy little lad ... She held up her hand. 'We'll say no more. If you want to see her, then go.'

It cut at her to see him picking up his hat even as she said the words. He didn't thank her. He could have no idea what it was costing her to send him to the girl. He didn't kiss her, he didn't say goodbye. He just turned his head away as if he couldn't bear to look at her. 'Matthew,' she said.

He was at the door. He was lifting the latch. 'Yes?'

'We'll be here at the party, me an' Rosie,' she said.

He ran down the stairs and out into the golden evening. From the upstairs window she saw him making for the lane and watched until he was lost to sight between the tall, flower-filled hedgerows.

The fair was still there, in the same field; he had harboured a fear that it would have moved on, the same as last time. There was a semicircle of caravans backing a scattering of stalls and sideshows, with a merry-go-round and a couple of swingboats in the centre. Country people were arriving, ready to spend hoarded coppers on an evening's enjoyment.

Hat low over his eyes, Matthew watched from behind a hedge. In his pocket he carried a scrap of paper taken from Rosie's exercise book with his home address pencilled on it. He couldn't bear to think that Jess and the boy might be in need when he was living in plenty. Ah, there was the man, turning the wheel of the children's merry-go-round: a circular platform set with crude wooden animals and a little green train. A cluster of parents and youngsters were waiting for the next ride, and a bell on the train rang continuously.

Matthew edged to where the caravans were set with their steps and rear ends facing towards the fair and the shafts pointing away from it. Which one was theirs? The sound of pebbles in a plant pot led him to the boy, Benjamin, who was sitting on the grass shaking his makeshift toy to a kind of rhythm. Something in the child's attitude told Matthew that though he might not be able to hear, he could feel the vibration of the pebbles as they rattled in the pot. A rope was fastened round his waist with the other end tied to a wheel, enabling him to move around without wandering off. Matthew nodded. As a toddler Rosie used to be tied to the leg of the table to keep her out of harm's way when Martha was busy. Maggie did the same with her youngest.

The boy was unaware of his presence until his shadow fell on the grass next to him. He looked up and recognising him, smiled, though Matthew fancied that the dark eyes were heavy, as if the child was weighed down with the knowledge of what he was and was not. Matthew wanted to pick him up, but even more he wanted to see his mother, so he went up the steps of the caravan and tapped on the door.

It opened at once and Jess was there, her hair escaping from its tie on top of her head, her eyes like the mists of Dartmoor and her lips moist and very red, as if she'd been biting them. Against her hip she held a rosy-cheeked toddler, boy or girl, he didn't know which but it had a look of the waggoner, bright eyed and with curly fair hair. Matthew felt as if he'd been kicked in the groin – it had never occurred to him that she would have another child. Jess grabbed his arm and dragged him inside, then jerked her head towards the fair. 'He mustn't see you,' she said.

She was meaning her husband, of course. 'Is he good to you?' asked Matthew urgently.

'Yes.' She looked at the toddler. 'This is Tansy – she's his daughter.'

'An' Benjamin?' He was desperate to know.

'He's yours,' she said, 'your son. Can you doubt it?'

He shook his head. 'I don't doubt it, for he's like my liddle sister. I'm sorry, Jess, I never thought to give you a child. I'm powerful sorry. How did you manage?'

'It was hard,' she said simply.

'What about your grandparents?'

'My grandpa died of a seizure when – he died before Benjamin was born.'

Knives were stabbing Matthew in the chest. He knew without her saying so that the old man had had his seizure when he'd learned that she was carrying a child. 'What about your grandmother?'

'She died soon after. It was a cold winter.' Grey eyes, dark fringed, surveyed him over the top of Tansy's curly head. 'Malachi – my husband – he married me when I was carryin' Benjamin. I didn't go hungry.'

Silently Matthew studied her face. It was still lovely, the skin fine textured and tanned to a deep, even gold. He reckoned she could be only – what – twenty-one? She looked older, years older. He had taken her youth, made her a woman almost before she was a girl. 'I went to find you next mornin' but you'd gone,' he said. 'I wanted to tell you I loved you, that I hadn't – hadn't just used you. Do you believe that?'

A small, pitying smile touched her mouth. 'Don't you love your wife, then?'

'Course I do, but 'tain't the same! I love my wife, I love my daughter, but 'tain't the same.'

He saw that she was listening to the noise of the fair, rather than to him. 'If the bell on the train stops ringing, Malachi might come in,' she said, 'so if it stops, go out by the drivin' seat and jump over the shafts.' Tansy wriggled and Jess set her down on the floor, where she stood on fat little legs and clutched at her mother's skirts.

'Money,' said Matthew doggedly. 'Can I give you money, to help with Benjamin?'

She shook her head. 'How could I explain it to Malachi? We manage. We're all right.'

He looked round the caravan. It was cramped, very cramped, but it was comfortable and clean. 'Benjamin,' he said, 'was he born deaf an' dumb?'

'Born deaf,' she said, 'though we didn't realise it at first. We took him to a doctor last summer. He said he's only dumb because he's deaf – stone deaf. Folk learn to talk because of what they hear, you see. We think he's clever, but he lives in a world of his own. You mustn't fret – Malachi watches over him.'

He mustn't fret? He would fret for the rest of his life. 'Can I hold him?' he asked. 'We had a baby boy once, but he died. Can I hold him, Jess?'

She nodded. 'He's your son, but look out for Malachi comin'.' She dipped her head, as if in apology. 'He loves me, you see.'

'An' do you love him?'

He shouldn't have asked. It was as if a barrier came between them: a heavy curtain or a high picket fence. They were separated where before they'd been close – close in the heart as much as in the cramped space around them. 'Course I love him,' she said coolly. 'He's a good man and he treats Benjamin as his own.' Then her eyes widened in alarm as the bell on the merry-go-round fell silent. 'Go,' she whispered.

He took her hand and pressed his lips to the palm, then reached in his pocket for the paper and laid it where his mouth had been. 'If you're in need write an' tell me,' he said, then leapt for the opening at the other end of the caravan. He turned for a last look at her and jumped to the ground.

As if feeling the thud when he landed, Benjamin turned to him at once. Matthew picked him up and crushed the small body against his chest. 'My liddle boy,' he muttered desperately, 'my liddle love.' The child's hair smelled of some woodland herb or other, just as Jess's hair had smelled on that enchanted night so long ago. The outcome of that enchantment was here in his arms – a son he would never know ... who would never hear him say he loved him.

Sensing anguish, Benjamin was tense against his chest, leaning back to look warily into his face. Matthew gazed at him, needing his image to store in his mind: plump golden cheeks, a firm little mouth with its corners turned down uncertainly, eyes long lashed and very dark brown. He yearned to see in their depths some sign of closeness, of affection, but there was just puzzlement. Life itself must be puzzling for a child with no hearing.

Matthew kissed him on the cheek, just once, and over the boy's head saw Jess watching them from the window, her face all eyes and mouth. He set him down on the grass again and looked up at her, laying his hand for an instant on Benjamin's head. Then he turned and walked away.

Malachi was pushing his way through the throng towards him. Matthew could have reached out and touched him but he passed by unaware, his eyes on the caravan and his family.

The party was going well. Everybody accepted without question that a man as prosperous as Matthew was bound to have business on hand when he came back to the place of his birth. The food was good and they were all related to each other, so there was talk and laughter enough despite the absence of the host.

Rosie was being really good, thought Martha thankfully. She was keeping her cousins occupied with games and singsongs, and one by one the village children were edging nearer and joining in. A fiddler had arrived, and Maggie and Beth kept saying it was the best party the village had seen in years.

As far as Martha was concerned it was the worst evening of her entire life, but of course she couldn't let anybody guess as much. She told herself she was putting on such an act she should by rights be treading the boards at the Theatre Royal in Saltley. She smiled and chatted and offered food, never once leaving the gathering to go and look down the lane to see if Matthew was coming.

She didn't know if he *would* come, though the husband of such a beautiful young woman would hardly give her back to the man who had fathered her child out of wedlock. Or happen the husband didn't want that sturdy little boy? Happen he'd be glad to see the back of him? What would she do if Matthew came back with the boy? She needed five minutes' peace to consider such a thing, but there was no chance of that. She smiled until she thought her mouth would set for ever in its idiotic grin; smiled until the fiddler played his last tune and the sun sank to its rest in a blaze of saffron and mauve. All at once it was dusk and too late for hard-working country folk to stay out making merry.

A hundred yards away Matthew was crouched on the grass beneath an elm tree. He would have to join them in a minute, he would have to! He must ignore the ache around his heart, put the thought of Benjamin to the back of his mind ... Reluctantly he walked towards the village green and watched from the shadows.

It wasn't until Rosie lined up the little ones for a farewell kiss that his absence caused open comment. 'Bain't we to see 'im again, Auntie Martha?' sniffled Beth's five-year-old boy, while Maggie's husband asked in exasperation, 'Where be 'ee *to*?' Martha made excuses and promised that he would be round to say goodbye in the morning, while from a thicket of hawthorns Matthew watched, and thought, and braced himself.

A minute later Rosie turned to her mother, eyes like stars, her hair ribbons fluttering. 'Mam, he's here! Me dad's here!'

He was approaching through the darkening shadows, the fading light catching his eyes and the gleam of his teeth as he smiled. Rosie hung on to his arm as if she would never let go, while he jokingly swept off his hat and bowed low to them all, apologising for missing the fun.

Martha saw at once that it was an act but stayed calm and pleasant as if she'd been expecting him to turn up at any minute. She stood at one side of him and Rosie at the other as they waved goodbye to everybody and the village sank back into the quiet of late evening.

Rosie observed them closely. She saw that her dad had stopped trying to decide what action to take – happen he'd taken it already – but her mother was looking as if she was about to collapse. They were staring at each other, here on the grass with only the light of a million stars to see each other's faces.

'It was a lovely party,' Rosie told Matthew earnestly. 'Me an' me mam looked after everybody so they wouldn't miss you.' She waited for him to tell her where he'd been, but he didn't say a word. She felt very tired. It was hard work pretending you were happy when underneath you were sad – no wonder her mother looked poorly. 'I think I'll go to bed now,' she said, all at once longing to be home in the garden cottage, in her own bed, knowing that Charles was across at the house.

'Aye, off you go, love,' said Martha. 'You've been a good girl, you have that. I'll be up in a minute.'

Matthew bent to kiss his daughter and she hugged him very tight, her arms around his neck. 'Home tomorrow, Miss Rosie Raike,' he said gently. Small for her age she was, his Rosie, but compared to Benjamin she seemed enormous. He watched her go indoors and knew that he could never, ever leave her. He felt as if part of his heart had been cut away and left in the keeping of a silent little boy and his young-old mother . . .

As for Martha, she looked pale in the dim light, pale and very plain, her grey hair silvered by the stars. He didn't know what to say to her, how to pay tribute to what she had done in sending him to Jess. What should he say? In the end he let words leave his tongue, simple words with only instinct to frame them. 'Martha, you're my wife an' I love you,' he said. 'There's things I must tell you so there'll be no more secrets, no more deceivin'. I've come back, ready to stay with you for ever, if you'll have me.'

She went into his arms and they stood there in the starlight, not speaking, not kissing, just holding each other.

From the upstairs window Rosie was straining to see what was happening, but she could only make out her dad's shirt and her mother's lace cap. Ah! His arms were round her. She sighed with relief and then smiled. Everything was all right again and tomorrow they would set off for home.

CHAPTER TWENTY-TWO

The Trumpet and the Rose

The Barnabas Jellicoe School was officially open. Speeches had been made, votes of thanks given and Barney's name spoken with more respect than Tizzie had ever heard in his lifetime.

She herself had given the guests of honour a conducted tour. The half-ruined buildings of eighteen months ago were now restored to their former beauty, with the interiors altered and modernised. Classrooms surrounded the big courtyard and a bright, high-ceilinged assembly hall had been made from the black chaos where Barney had met his death.

Once she had thought that she would never, ever return to Ryeworth, but in fact she had visited the place constantly since Joshua was born, consulting the architect, inspecting the rebuilding and finally supervising the decorating and furnishing. She had arranged for roses and honeysuckle to be planted beneath the arches so that the restored brick pillars would once again be covered in bloom as Barney had seen them when he had first inspected the place.

His legacy had paid for everything – his last gift to her had created the school that bore his name. There was a satisfaction in that; she saw it as right and fitting. Boys and girls would be educated in this lovely old place under a more enlightened system than Saltley had ever known. She wanted to see the children of the poor receive full-time schooling rather than spending half of each day at work.

The ceremony over at last, Sam handed her into the carriage and as soon as they were out of sight kissed her gently on the mouth. 'Well done, sweetheart,' he said, 'I'm proud of you. It's wonderful – a showpiece for all Lancashire.'

She laughed. 'I've got to make sure it delivers the goods, though, haven't I? And don't forget you made it all possible by preventing anybody else from buying it.'

As they gathered speed she turned for a last look at the school, nodding in satisfaction at the sight of its clean, mellow red brick glowing against the hill side. On the day Barney died she'd been driven away from there twice, once by Noah and once by Sam. Both times she'd tried to leap from the carriage.

Sam was watching her, well aware that she was remembering Barney. 'Do you think he'd be pleased by his memorial?' he asked, taking her hand.

'He'd be delighted,' she answered quietly. 'I'm sure of it.' There was a lightness inside her, a bubbling sense of freedom now that her final tribute to him was complete. The future lay ahead of them now like an untravelled road, well lit by the sunshine of their love. 'Sam,' she said, 'shall we try to have another baby?'

His bright blue eyes stared into hers. 'You'll have to persuade me very hard about that,' he said soberly. 'You might even have to seduce me!'

Laughing and kissing, they were driven back to Moorview, where Rebecca and the young maid, Janey, were hard at work looking after a noisy, high-spirited toddler.

Matthew felt that the bond between him and Martha was stronger than ever and he was thankful for it. He had told her that he'd made love to Jess only once. Then he'd told her about Benjamin, dreading that she'd be cut to the quick with having lost her own son. He'd been stunned when she'd taken it calmly, almost as if she'd already known.

She had even approved of him leaving their address with Jess – accepted it as the obvious, natural thing to do.

Last night, in bed, she'd asked what he'd done with the carved figure. He'd told her, adding, ''Twill be rotted away after all this time, though to be sure I did wrap it . . .' He sat up suddenly. 'I'm goin' to burn it!' he said.

Next morning, with Rosie out of the way at Sunday school, he put on his working boots and looked enquiringly at Martha. She was busy in the kitchen, dressed in her pink twill dress and her best Sunday pinafore. 'Go on then,' she said briskly. 'You don't need me there.'

What a wife, he thought in amazement – she knew that he needed to be on his own when he unearthed the carving. He lit a bonfire at the end of the vegetable plot and, taking his spade, began to dig beneath the lilac bush. The bundle was still there in the dark earth, the sacking half rotted, the oiled cotton sticky with soil and strands of hessian. He didn't relish seeing the figure eaten away by woodlice or rotting from the damp, but he couldn't resist having one last look.

He squatted down and slowly, reluctantly, unwrapped it. There, lit by the sun of a September morning, lay his carving of Jess: untouched, unmarked by her burial. He could hardly believe it. He studied her closely and found that she was different from the Jess he'd seen in Devon. This Jess was young and free of care, but oh, she was beautiful! Here and there the pale wood had darkened a little where the wrapping had pressed against it; her hair was darker, so were her fingertips and the hem of the ragged skirt. If anything, the long burial had improved his work. Had some deep instinct made him protect her more thoroughly than he'd intended?

Behind him the bonfire was crackling. He nerved himself to cast her on the flames, but from the kitchen door Martha shouted, 'Wait!' He guessed that she'd been watching from the window and seen him hesitating. She came down the path, wiping her hands on her pinafore. 'Has it rotted away?' she asked.

Silently he shook his head. Martha gazed at the figure and he saw her shoulders droop so that she seemed smaller than ever. 'You can't burn it,' she said at last. 'You can't – it's the best thing you've ever done.'

He pretended not to care. 'I have no use for it.'

She thought for a minute. 'I don't want it on show in the house,' she admitted, 'but how about puttin' it away in your cupboard to – to give to Benjamin when he's older? Or you could sell it an' put the money in a savings bank in case they ever have to pay for him learnin' sign talk an' lip-readin' an' such. Don't burn it, Matthew, and don't put it back in that hole!'

He laid the figure down and gathered Martha in his arms. 'I'll put it away,' he agreed, 'out o' sight. If ever they get in touch I'll send it – for the boy.'

She looked up at him and tried very hard to smile. All she achieved was a trembling of her pretty little mouth. What was a wooden image of a woman he'd made love to only once, she asked herself, compared to a flesh and blood wife who would love him till her dying day?

Rosie walked home from Sunday school determined to be sensible. It was no good deceiving herself any longer – Charles was avoiding her. They'd barely exchanged two words since she'd come back from Devon and then yesterday, when she was sitting reading at the top end of the buttercup field, he had walked along the path and given her a wave – just a brief wave – before going on his way.

She'd seen it coming for a long, long time. Weeks ago he had shown her his new silver trumpet. She'd cried, but he hadn't had the faintest idea why. The tears had come because such lovely things had happened with his gold trumpet. He used to hold it when they met in the tunnel; he would open the bedroom window so she could listen to him practising; he'd played 'The Last Rose of Summer' on it, specially for her.

Once upon a time they'd been so close he would have known why she was crying, but not any more. It hurt her

that he'd changed. It felt as if there was a stone lying where
her heart should be. She would have liked to blame the
change in him on Elizabeth Hartley, but she didn't think
he'd seen very much of her in the last few weeks. The truth
was he didn't love her, Rosie, any more. She would have
to forget all about them getting married.

She'd been wondering whether to write him a letter,
asking if he was tired of her. He was so polite he would feel
bound to answer it, but something kept telling her to wait.
Then, last week, he had said something unexpected and
very solemn. He'd said, 'Rosanna, I'll never forget that it
was you who saved me from my uncle Ralph.'

She could see now that he'd meant it to be a sort of
goodbye. If that was so, it wouldn't be dignified to write to
him, it wouldn't be – appropriate. In future she would be
there if ever he wanted to talk to her, she would listen when
he played his trumpet, but they would go their separate
ways. One day, if ever she stopped feeling sad, she might
look back on the time when they'd been so close and think
how lovely it had been . . .

When she reached Meadowbank she could smell a
bonfire as she crossed the yard, but indoors was the smell
of roast lamb. She would have to pretend she was hungry
or her mother would be worried. At that moment it seemed
to her that life was only half real – the other half was all
pretending.

After dinner they went for a walk in Soar Park, where
the population of Saltley was out in force, dressed in their
best. Her mother had asked her dad if he wanted to go for
one of his walks up in the hills, but he'd said no, he'd rather
go out with his wife and Miss Rosie Raike. Her mother had
gone all pink, like she did when she was pleased. Rosie
could tell that he'd made the choice as some kind of thank
you, but neither of them said what the thank you was for.

They walked on, exchanging greetings with people they
knew, when all at once her mother said curiously, 'You
don't seem to have seen much of Master Charles in the last
few weeks, love.'

Rosie took a deep breath. 'No,' she said clearly. 'I think we've outgrown each other. It was nice, though, having him for a special friend when I was younger.'

Martha allowed herself a small, relieved smile; the child wasn't going to be hurt, after all. Matthew strode on, outwardly unperturbed. He told himself that he'd dreamed dreams for his daughter but it wasn't the end of the world that they'd come to nothing. When she was a young woman with a good education behind her she'd be able to take her pick of the brightest young men in Lancashire.

Rosie walked between them and wondered how long it would be before she could think of Charles without it hurting.

Meadowbank House was silent. It was past midnight, with doors fastened and the lights turned off except in the staff sitting room, where Lilah was alone, wondering why Mr Schofield hadn't said goodnight.

Everything in the house was in order: Master Charles and his father were in their beds, the laundry woman would arrive at seven in the morning to start the ironing, Hannah and Ellie were asleep long since, but she herself never went to bed until he'd said goodnight. Usually he looked in to say something like, 'I'll be off to bed now – goodnight,' or 'I shan't need you again tonight, thanks,' but for once he'd forgotten. It wasn't like him at all.

Whether it was like him or not, she was a soft fool to be sitting here in front of a dead fire. The next day was a Tuesday when she was always up with the lark – it was his busy day at Mosley Street and she liked to give him his favourite breakfast. He had his dinner in Manchester, so she always baked a dozen of flour in the morning, in case he called in on his way from the station to Jericho. If he did he would have one of her oven-bottom muffins or the crust of a new loaf plastered with butter.

She went for a last check round the downstairs rooms and saw a ribbon of light beneath the door of the study. At once the darkness of the hall seemed bright as day. He hadn't forgotten to say goodnight, after all.

She tapped at the door and opened it, almost crying out in alarm to find him lying over the desk with his head on his hands. She edged nearer and found that he was fast asleep, his breath lifting the pages of a ledger in front of him. He was holding something ... She lifted the desk lamp and by its light saw that it was a picture of Mrs Schofield, a little painting in a round wooden frame. She was wearing a low-cut dress of some pale-blue fabric that had the sheen of silk. Across the picture, beneath the bosom, was written 'Happy birthday, my darling'. Lilah studied the lovely face, the cornflower-blue eyes, the wavy blonde hair that was drawn back to a thick coil behind her ears. She looked young and very beautiful – a happy woman in the prime of life.

Well, the days were gone when the sight of Mrs Schofield could blight her day. By all accounts she'd been a good woman – a farmer's daughter who wasn't frightened of hard work, able to run a house and cook a meal with the best of 'em. She'd earned the love and devotion of this man, so what more need be said of her?

It was very quiet. The fire had sunk to ashes, the gas jets were hissing and Joshua's breathing was still stirring the pages of the ledger. Lilah bent lower. She had never seen him so close, not even when she was serving his meals. What must he have been like as a young man if he was as striking as this at turned seventy?

She didn't mean to do it. Afterwards she was at a loss to explain to herself how it had come about, but she put a hand on his head and stroked his hair. It felt crisp and full of life – not how she'd have expected white hair to feel. She gave a sigh, a sigh of such pleasure he might as well have been kissing her hand.

As if he felt the breath of her sigh, Joshua opened his eyes and stared sleepily at the picture. For a dreadful moment she thought he was going to kiss it. 'Mr Schofield,' she said hurriedly, 'I'm sorry to wake you, Mr Schofield.'

He looked up at her, his eyes heavy. 'I nodded off,' he said wonderingly.

'I know. I thought you might want to go to your bed, like, bein' as it's Tuesday tomorrow . . .'

Joshua sat up. The lamp was doing her no favours, he told himself. Every line, every wrinkle was marked on her face as if with black ink, though for once she wasn't wearing that damned crackling apron. Gathering his wits he tried to push Rachel's picture out of sight under the ledger. There was no point in upsetting this good, plain woman by letting her see the likeness of his wife.

'You did right to wake me, Lilah,' he said, 'though I don't know what you're doing still up at this hour. I'll have my breakfast at the usual time in the morning, so goodnight to you.'

'Goodnight, Mr Schofield.' She left the room and closed the door.

Joshua shook his head and put the painting back in the drawer. He'd have to take himself in hand, he would that. For a minute he'd imagined that Rachel was stroking his hair. Thank the Lord he hadn't spoken to her out loud, like he sometimes did. Lilah would have thought he was a slate short.

It was said in Manchester that the trading floor of the Royal Exchange was the biggest commercial room in the world. Even so, it was packed tight on that particular Tuesday. Joshua, James and Sam were by their accustomed pillar, with one of Bill Tetley's bright young men elbowing back and forth at their bidding.

In recent weeks Joshua had been attempting to keep out of business transactions, but it wasn't easy. He was so well known that even after all these years men would approach him in preference to Sam. That wasn't what he wanted at all, because Sam would take over from him completely one day. James would back him up, of course, but his particular talents were of more use on the High Lee estate.

Deliberately Joshua let the press of bodies separate him

from his sons, and raised his eyes to the great dome with its familiar quotation inscribed in gold. 'A good name ...' he reflected. There'd been times when the good name of the Schofields had been under threat, but by God he'd done his best to protect it. Sharp practice, embezzlement, kidnapping, extortion, even murder hadn't succeeded in fouling the name that backed the trumpet and the rose.

Recalling the death of his old friend Charlie Barnes led him to thinking about the man's namesake, young Charlie, who had been given the afternoon off school in order to play his trumpet for an expert here in Manchester. His teacher from Saltley was going with him, and James intended to join them for the appointment.

Joshua didn't know what to think about it, and that was a fact. If the lad was good enough to be accepted as a pupil by a man with a national reputation it was likely he would choose music as his life's work, yet only yesterday he'd been in the engine house, listening to the sound of the two big engines as if it was the music of the spheres.

Still, he wouldn't interfere. The lad must make his own decisions after listening to his father's advice, because James was a new man since he'd got shut of Esther: calm, decisive, good-humoured. It was a pleasure to have him and Charlie living at Meadowbank.

'Father, are you all right? We wondered where you'd got to.' It was Sam, concern sharpening his tone to one of accusation. James was watching him as well, ignoring a potential customer at his elbow.

Joshua gritted his teeth. If they weren't trying to bundle him into a cab when he wanted to walk to Albert Square for a look at the town hall, they were warning him about climbing stairs or being on his feet too long. 'I wasn't a mile away,' he said shortly. 'Listen, as soon as I've had my dinner I'm going back to Jericho. I want to do a good walk through.'

'You're making a busy day for yourself,' Sam pointed out uneasily. 'Is there anything special you want to see at Jericho?'

'Nothing in particular,' replied Joshua, 'except have a look at my life's work. I've made a habit of keeping an eye on it over the years, in case you hadn't noticed.'

'Keep your hair on,' said Sam. 'You're no spring chicken, you know.'

Joshua snorted in disdain. 'Spring chicken or not, I'm off to the Reform Club for my dinner as soon as things slacken off here. If you and your brother want to join me I'll be more than pleased, but happen you'd prefer to eat with somebody nearer your own age?'

'Happen we would,' snapped Sam. Then he laughed and touched his forelock in mock humility. 'We'd consider it an honour to share your table, Mr Schofield, sir. Whatever you say, Mr Schofield.'

His good humour restored by the mockery, Joshua went back to the Schofield pillar. One of these days it would sink in with the pair of them – no mollycoddling.

Operatives in Jericho's two great mills were surprised to see their employer pacing the floors dressed in his fine business clothes: sharp eyes glinting, his notebook at the ready and swishing at the air with his stick.

They told each other it was unheard of for him to do a walk through on a Tuesday afternoon when he'd been busy doing his buying and selling in Manchester. Not that he'd find much wrong. He paid a good wage for a good day's work; it was rare for anybody to be found slacking.

Joshua walked on. Instinct had urged him to come and he was enjoying it. The smell of the place was perfume to his nostrils, the noise of machinery was music to his ears. Today he had a fancy to follow the process of his cotton from the newly opened bale right through to the woven cloth.

He poked with his foot at the latest delivery of coal, he marched through the dust of the card room; on, up, waving his stick in greeting as he went. As always he lingered in the spinning rooms. His first venture in cotton had been the spinning of it, with Charlie at his side and Joe Whitehead his first paid worker ...

Finally he was down at ground level again and heading for the weaving shed. He let out a chuckle as he neared the door; the weavers were singing, keeping together with the ease of a trained choir against the deafening clatter of the looms. He didn't know the tune – it was some popular song or other, but he went inside and stood listening to the women who could make or mar his finest yarn. He had a special place in his heart for his weavers.

Finally he made for the cut room, where the long benches were covered with cloth in the process of being examined. From force of habit he looked in the bad book on the desk and found no entries since the previous week. 'Carry on, carry on,' he said, going back to the yard.

He took out his watch and saw that it was after five. It was a wonder young Charlie wasn't somewhere around the place looking for him; the lad had promised to call in on his way home to tell them how he'd gone on. Happen he should knock off now and go back to the office to wait for him? Sam would be there, working on last week's production figures. No, he wouldn't do that – he'd go up on the tower for five minutes of pure indulgence, of balm to the spirit.

He headed for the stairs. He wasn't sure why he always felt close to Rachel up on the tower. In the first terrible months after she'd died, he'd wondered if it was because it was so high up that it seemed nearer to heaven – but that could only be the case if you took a child's view that heaven was up in the sky. He didn't see Rachel as being above the clouds, he saw her as a presence, anywhere and everywhere; a calm, sweet, abiding presence. He felt her closeness with each and every part of him: mental, emotional, physical – aye, and spiritual. There was a communion of the spirit between them.

He climbed slowly upwards until he reached the last steep flight that opened to the roof of the tower. There he stepped into the sunlight, out of breath but exhilarated. He could feel the thrumming of machinery up here, he could keep an eye open for young Charlie arriving, but best of all he could feel close to Rachel.

The air smelled fresh and very clean because it was blowing from the hills. Gasping a little but in reminiscent mood, he tried to see the old salt road where he had lived as a boy. There it was, broad and built up now, heading towards the Pennines and Yorkshire. It was the salt trade that had turned Saltley from a hamlet to a village and then to a town, long before cotton had caused it to expand to its present size.

Then he turned in the direction of High Lee, where he'd first seen Rachel. She'd been wearing a gingham bonnet and carrying milk from the dairy of her father's farm. He'd known he wanted to marry her before they'd even spoken. What a wife, what a marriage – she'd backed him every inch of the way in setting up his business. It was Rachel who had made his first flag, cutting out a trumpet from yellow cloth and stitching it to a grey-blue background. Hours and hours she'd spent on it so he could fly it from the roof of the first place he'd owned – a converted water mill on the banks of East Brook. 'Joshua of the golden trumpet,' she'd laughed, and that night they'd hardly slept for making love.

Smiling at the memory, he looked up at the great flag above his head and saw to his dismay that the bottom edge was frayed. He must have a look at that right away. He put down his stick and unfastened the thick ropes ready to pull on the one that would lower the flag. His arms were lifted as he saw Charles and his father coming into the mill yard far below.

James made straight for the offices, but as if knowing that his grandpa would be there, Charles looked up at the tower and took his trumpet from its case. Joshua could see it glittering in the sun; he could see the gleam of the boy's teeth as he smiled. It was clear that the lad had done well in Manchester ... But he must see to this rope; it was thicker than he remembered, heavier, wrenching at his arms, almost pulling them from their sockets ...

Charles was looking up at him. He lifted the trumpet to his lips and played a single note – a high, sweet clarion call

that held triumph...
Joshua hung o...
take off his hat ...
grandson saluted ...

But Joshua coul...
heavy to pull. All at...
chest and he cried out...
as if he was in a vice, a...
ribs, crushing his heart. ...
hand clamped to the rope, ...
then he understood. 'Rachel...
dear love!'

Half hanging from the rope,...
could see the flag above him. ...
thought in his agony; his family, his...

Seconds later, still grasping the ro...

Charles was staring up at the tower in ...
grandpa hauling down the flag or wh...
holding the rope? All at once he was fright...
into the office. 'Father!' he cried. 'Uncle...
quick! Grandpa's up on the tower. He's under...
and I think he's fallen down. The flag's at half-...

The Jericho Rose

Olive Etchells

1864: Keen to escape an unhappy past, Matthew Raike travels north from Devon to Lancashire. He soon sets his heart on employment at Jericho Mills.

The Schofields, a prominent local family, seem blessed with health, wealth and happiness - but misfortunes are waiting in the wings. Troubles are also on the way for Tizzie Ridings, the clever, flame-haired eldest daughter of a local pawnbroker. Her longing to escape her background will lead her into dangerous territory ...

Trying to survive as best he can on the little work there is to be found, Matthew meets Martha Spencer. Though he had never thought to find love, Martha breaches his defences - but deep in Matthew's past lies a secret he cannot bear to reveal ...

The Dominie's Lassie

Eileen Ramsay

As daughter of the local schoolmaster - the dominie's lassie - it was only natural for Kirsty Robertson to become a pupil teacher at her father's school near Arbroath. It was the first step on her road to qualification; the first step on a road that would lead her through both heart-rending difficulties and overwhelming joys - and not all of them academic ...

The year is 1908, with Kirsty in the full flush of her teen years and the Great War still a distant menace, far over the horizon. Before long, however, the trenches in France would claim the attentions of the two young men closest to her: Jamie Cameron, an old schoolfriend, and Hugh Granville-Baker, son of the local squire and object of her seemingly unrequited fantasy since their very first meeting.

As Kirsty endures her own problems in her struggle to qualify, little did she know how the fortunes of these two men and her relationships with them would come to shape a lifetime ...

☐	The Jericho Rose	Olive Etchells	£5.99
☐	Brighton Belle	Peggy Eaton	£4.99
☐	Daughter of the Downs	Peggy Eaton	£5.99
☐	Fancy Woman	Valerie Maskell	£4.50
☐	The Workbox	Valerie Maskell	£4.99
☐	Shopkeepers	Valerie Maskell	£5.99
☐	The Broken Gate	Eileen Ramsay	£4.99
☐	The Dominie's Lassie	Eileen Ramsay	£4.99

Warner Books now offers an exciting range of quality titles by both established and new authors which can be ordered from the following address:

> Little, Brown & Company (UK),
> P.O. Box 11,
> Falmouth,
> Cornwall TR10 9EN.

Alternatively you may fax your order to the above address.
Fax No. 01326 317444.

Payments can be made as follows: cheque, postal order (payable to Little, Brown and Company) or by credit cards, Visa/Access. Do not send cash or currency. UK customers and B.F.P.O. please allow £1.00 for postage and packing for the first book, plus 50p for the second book, plus 30p for each additional book up to a maximum charge of £3.00 (7 books plus). Overseas customers including Ireland, please allow £2.00 for the first book plus £1.00 for the second book, plus 50p for each additional book.

NAME (Block Letters) _____

ADDRESS _____

_____

☐ I enclose my remittance for £ _____
☐ I wish to pay by Access/Visa Card

Number   ☐☐☐☐☐☐☐☐☐☐☐☐☐☐☐☐

Card Expiry Date _____